I0545785

The Girl on the Rocks

THE GIRL ON THE ROCKS

A Doherty Mystery

Sam Kafrissen

International Digital Book Publishing Industries
Florida, USA

All rights reserved. Except for the inclusion of brief quotations in a review, no part of this book may be reproduced in any form without permission in writing from the author or publisher.

Copyright 2019 Sam Kafrissen
All rights reserved

First Printing
10 9 8 7 6 5 4 3 2 1

ISBN: 1-57550-087-6
ISBN 13: 978-1-57550-087-4

International Digital Book Publishing Incorporated,
Clearwater, Florida

Cover Photo:
The Greene Inn, Narragansett, Rhode Island
Printed in the United States of America

For
Jerry Rose
who died last year at 104

Chapter One

Winter. The worst time of year for Doherty and Associates Investigations Agency. Nobody's running off with someone who's not his or her spouse. Most commercial work was at a standstill with the shelves in stores devoid of goods after the Christmas season. Even embezzlers seemed to have taken a holiday until Spring. All of these thoughts were drifting through Doherty's head as he lumbered up Brookside through the recent snowfall to his office above Harry's Barbershop.

Agnes was holding the baby on her lap when Doherty came into the office. She was rubbing her index finger along its gums trying to get the infant to nibble on it. Doherty hadn't seen little Justin since the christening at the Sacred Heart Church down in Natick village.

"I'm sorry, I seemed to have misplaced his pacifier." That wasn't exactly an explanation as to why she'd brought her baby to work, but he let it go.

He walked around the desk and stood beside her. "Can I hold the little bugger?"

"Sure," she said as she handed the baby to Doherty so he could cuddle it. Holding the infant felt awkward, though there was no denying that the little guy was pretty cute. At this stage he was a spitting image of his father, Louie Benvenuti, Agnes' merchant marine husband.

"My mother had to go to the doctor's today so she couldn't take the baby. I'm sorry," she said, apologizing for a second time.

"Don't worry about it. It's not like we've got people breaking down our doors looking for help. Nothing serious with your mother, I hope?"

Agnes shrugged. "Who can tell with her? She never shares anythin' about her health with me or my sister. One time when we were kids she fell off a chair she was standin' on and broke her wrist. She didn't tell anybody. Just put an ace bandage around it and went back to work. Wasn't till it swelled up twice its natural size that she finally agreed to go to the doctor. He put a cast on it and told her not to do any heavy liftin' for a month. Two weeks later she cut the cast off sayin' it was too uncomfortable and that her arm itched. Her wrist hasn't been the same since."

"Well, you know how people their age are about being sick. They think they're just supposed to tough it out until the grim reaper comes calling. My mother was the same way." The baby began to squirm in his arms so Doherty was happy to return him to the bosom of his mother.

"Anything shaking here?" he asked, as if he didn't know there weren't any clients in the offing.

Agnes smiled. "No business since I came in. I've been here for about an hour," she added. Her voice was bright, obviously trying to make him feel better about not having any clients for the past three weeks.

"You might as well take the baby and go home then."

"Naw. I think I'll stick around for a while. With Louie on a cruise it's kind lonely at the house when it's just me and Justin. Bein' alone with him all day makes me a little stir crazy. You don't mind do you?"

"Suit yourself," Doherty said. He then wandered into his office to read the mail and maybe skim through the latest issue of the Sporting News. With snow on the ground and spring training still a month away, there wasn't much baseball news in the publication. Still it beat reading about all the political shenanigans in the morning *Journal*.

Doherty was beginning to dose off when Agnes appeared at his door holding the baby tight to her chest. "There's somebody here to see you; he seems mighty upset."

"Friend or foe?"

"Don't know. Nobody I've seen before."

2

Doherty removed his feet from the desktop and slid the knot on his tie up to his neck. "Well send him in. Could be a client."

A man rushed into the back office and looked around furtively. He was somewhere in his thirties and nice looking. His black hair was hanging over his forehead and he appeared to be very agitated. Although he was wearing respectable clothes, his shirt was badly wrinkled and he looked like he hadn't shaved in a couple of days. There was also something about this nervous visitor that seemed vaguely familiar.

"You Doherty?"

"Yes I'm him. Hugh M. Doherty, Private Investigator, at your service. Do I know you from somewhere?"

The man lowered his head, clearly not wanting to make eye contact. Doherty tried to get a fix on his potential client but couldn't recall where they'd met before. Then a light bulb went on in his head. The visitor was a guy named Richie Grimaldi, who spent a lot of his time hustling unhappily married women. They'd encountered each other about a year and a half ago while Doherty was on the trail of a woman named Marilyn Carney. She'd run out on her husband and Doherty found her shacking up with Grimaldi in a no-tell motel down by the beaches in South County. After agreeing to take the case on behalf of her husband Leo, he learned that she wasn't the first married woman Grimaldi had run his game on - and probably not the last. As for the Carney woman, Doherty convinced her to return home to her husband. For his part Grimaldi didn't need convincing of anything since he'd had what he wanted from her - a night of sex in a cheap motel.

Now this man who preyed on married women was in Doherty's office as a potential client. Under most circumstances he would've thrown the sleaze bag out on his ass. However, since Doherty and Associates hadn't had any paying clients in nearly a month, he wasn't about to show a potential customer the door no matter how unsavory he was.

"I don't suppose you've seen Marilyn Carney since the time we met down by the shore?" He hoped this revelation of their prior meeting might shake up his visitor.

"Carney? Was that Marilyn's last name?" Grimaldi asked, genuinely dumbfounded.

This guy was getting to be more unpleasant by the minute. "So what can I do for you, Grimaldi?" Doherty did not bother to address him as 'Mr.' or pretend he didn't know his name even though the man hadn't introduced himself.

"I understand you're pretty good at finding missing people."

Doherty didn't bite at the compliment. Instead he tamped out a Camel from a fresh pack and lit it. He didn't offer one to his potential client. He wouldn't do anything to give Grimaldi the feeling they were on equal terms.

"Who's missing?"

Grimaldi hesitated, already knowing how Doherty would judge the next thing out of his mouth. "A woman I spent last Saturday night with."

"Don't tell me it was at the same rundown motel down near Scarborough Beach." Grimaldi nodded, still not making eye contact.

"Room Six?" He nodded again, almost imperceptibly this time.

"Jesus, you are a piece of work."

"Look I know what you're thinking," the man said. "Do you want the job or not? There are a lot of other private dicks in the phone book who'd be happy to take my money."

Doherty sat gazing at the potential client while considering this last question. His impulse was to say 'no' and be done with him. But he needed the business, and maybe, just maybe, the job would end up with him rescuing another unhappy woman from the likes of Richie Grimaldi. He suggested that his visitor sit down so they could talk.

"I'll consider taking your case. But first you'll have to give me a few details before I ask you to sign an agreement. How does that sit with you?"

"Look, I didn't break any laws or nothing. Unless you think sleeping with some married dame is a federal offense. That's all I did."

Probably in a divorce action that would be enough, but Doherty wasn't interested in those kinds of legal matters. He'd tracked down enough men, and women, out having a good time with somebody they weren't married to to care much about what they were doing on moral grounds. Hell, if couples didn't cheat on their spouses he'd have been out of business a long time ago. It wasn't always a pleasant way to make a living, but it helped him pay the rent and put food on his table. Besides, it still beat being a local cop, which was what he he'd been. All the time he was on the force he was trying to avoid doing dirty work for the DeCenza political machine that ran things in West Warwick.

"Okay, calm down. Tell me what happened."

"Well I took this woman out to dinner at the Greene Inn down in Narragansett. Do you know the place?" Doherty shook his head. "Anyway, we had a couple drinks before dinner and another with the meal and then..."

"Look why don't we cut out the dating details for the moment and get back to this woman you say is missing. You ate dinner, you went to a motel to screw and then she left. So where does the missing person part come in?"

"That's just it. She didn't leave."

"What do you mean she didn't leave? Are you telling me she's still at the motel? If that's the case, then how is she missing?"

Grimaldi shook his head and nervously rubbed his two-day old beard. He still had the pencil-lined mustache, though what with his scraggly chin, it hardly made him look like Prince Charming.

"Maybe I'm not making myself clear. We went back to the motel after dinner, had a few more drinks and did whatever. And yes, it was in Room Six."

"Does that make you some kind of regular there?"

Grimaldi tried to brush off the question. "I guess. Anyway, I had a lot to drink, though I'm usually pretty good at holding my liquor. Mostly it's the dames who lose control. I try to keep track of their drinking 'cause I don't want them to pass out on me."

"No, you wouldn't want that to happen. Least not before you had your way with them." Once again Grimaldi ignored Doherty's snide comment. He knew what he was doing with these women and wasn't at all embarrassed about it.

"I musta slept through the night 'cause when I woke up in the morning she was gone."

"Maybe she came to her senses and went home to her husband."

"I don't think so. She didn't have a car. We drove down to the pier in mine."

"She could've called a cab. I hear they'll take anyone just about anywhere these days as long as they're willing to pay."

"That's just it. She didn't take her clothes, her bag or her coat. When we went to bed all she had on was a nightgown. I mean it was really cold that night. Nobody in their right mind would've gone out without a coat let alone clothes. And how was she gonna pay for a cab if her wallet was still in the room?"

"Where's her bag now?"

"In the trunk of my car. I took it along with her clothes and some cosmetic items she left in the bathroom. If anything bad's happened to her, I don't want it to be traced back to me or the motel."

"What's the girl's name?"

"Adrian."

"Adrian what?"

"I dunno."

"Well, maybe you should go down to your car and bring her purse up here so we can find out who she is."

"Does that mean you're gonna take me on as a client?"

Doherty waited to answer - just long enough to make Grimaldi uncomfortable. "You got money?"

"I got a hundred bucks on me and some change."

"Gimme the hundred to get started. You can keep the change."

Grimaldi returned a few minutes later holding a woman's fake alligator handbag and a brown tweed woolen coat. He handed Doherty the coat first and the PI checked through the pockets. All he found was a pair of thin leather gloves, a punched bus ticket and some loose change. Turning the coat inside out he searched through the inside pockets but came up with nothing but lint.

After Grimaldi set the purse down on the desk, Doherty turned it upside down and dumped out the content, quickly grabbing a metal lipstick tube before it rolled onto the floor. When he flipped open her wallet Grimaldi leaned in to get a good look at its contents. Her Rhode Island driver's license told them her name was Adrian Colardo and she lived at 215 Priscilla Avenue in Providence. It also said that she was five-foot three, weighed a hundred and fifteen pounds and her eyes were brown as was her hair. She was born on May 5, 1935, which put her age at 24. There was no other pertinent information on the license.

The wallet also contained a social security card, a dry cleaning ticket, a used movie stub to the Albee Theatre in Providence and forty-two dollars in three tens, a couple of fives and two ones, along with eight-six cents in coins. Stuffed into a secret compartment in the billfold was a small note folded in quarters that said Fortunato's with an address on Atwells Avenue in Providence and a phone number. This information was scratched in pencil by a delicate female script. Doherty handed the note to Grimaldi.

"Does this mean anything to you?"

Grimaldi smiled for the first time. "It should. It's a restaurant I own along with my cousin Anthony Fortunato. We've been in business for three years now."

"So I guess that makes you a regular entrepreneur as well as a gigolo." As with Doherty's earlier cutting remarks, Grimaldi chose to ignore this one as well. Together they picked through the rest of the contents from Adrian Colardo's purse. There were the usual items: the lipstick tube, a hand mirror, a small make-up case, a collection of keys on a chain with a St. Christopher's medal attached to it, a small embroidered tubular case containing a tampon, still in its paper wrapper. There was a pack of Parliament filtered cigarettes about half full, two books of matches, one with a pitch on it about getting into art school by drawing the women's pencil-line profile on the cover, the other advertising Fortunato's Italian Cuisine.

A small see-through plastic folder contained some black and white photos: two of a small boy in a cowboy getup, one of an elderly couple sitting on folding chairs in front of an opened garage door, one of a man in his late twenties or early thirties with greasy hair and an unhappy expression on his face, and one of the same sour puss guy standing next to a reasonably attractive woman, who looked like she wanted to escape from the photo. Doherty flashed this picture at Grimaldi.

"You recognize the woman in this photograph?"

"Yeah, that's her," he said. "That's Adrian."

He folded up the picture case and tossed it on the desk next to the other stuff from the missing girl's purse.

"How did you meet this one?"

The man began haltingly, "The first time was when she came into the restaurant with a friend. I was working the bar and they both sat down to have a drink. It was a slow night so me and her started talking. When her friend went to make a phone call I…"

"Charmed her and then asked her if she'd like to go out sometime. And she said 'yes'."

Grimaldi shook his head. "No, it didn't happen that way. Not that night anyway. It was getting late so I gave her a coffee, a double espresso, on account of her having to drive the two of them home over to Silver Lake. She was a looker and it didn't take long before I learned she was in an unhappy marriage."

"So you used her discontent with her marriage to run your game on her?"

"No, it wasn't like that. After she finished her coffee she paid for the other drinks, said goodbye and left. I gave her the espresso on the house."

"That was mighty white of you."

"Before she left she thanked me for the conversation and that was it. She'd never been in our place before, least not that I could remember. So after she was gone I figured I'd never see her again. I won't lie to you, she was nice to talk to and flirt up a little. You know how it is with attractive women when you're a single guy."

In fact Doherty did know how it was, though he never saw himself operating on the same low-rent level as a guy like Grimaldi. The only married woman he'd ever been involved with was a girl from town whose husband was up at the Howard Institution in the ward for brain-damaged veterans. Doherty had his standards and would never have dated her if her husband weren't already in a vegetative state.

"Then one afternoon outta the blue she came back into the restaurant," Grimaldi continued. "Only this time she didn't want anything to eat or drink. She asked me if we could go somewhere and talk. I told my cousin I needed to take some time. We weren't busy since it was between lunch and dinner so me and Adrian went to this little café down the street. I could leave the bar in the hands of Anthony's son, Tony.

"She told me she didn't have anybody she could talk to who wasn't always judging her. We must've jawed with each other for almost two hours. This Adrian and I talked about all kinds of stuff. You know about where we grew up, about our lives during the war and about how things are now for both of us. I felt sorry for the poor kid."

"I'll bet you did."

"Hey, it wasn't my fault her husband's a prick who knocks her around whenever he's in a bad mood. I was just being a shoulder for her to cry on."

"What else did she say about her husband?"

"I dunno. The usual. They were high school sweethearts. He promised her all kinds of good things after they were married, then never delivered on any of them. Guy couldn't hold a job for more than six months at a time. One of them I'm-okay- the-world's-wrong kinda men. When things got bad he'd take his frustration out on her. They had a two-year old kid by then. She told me she asked her parents if she and her son could come back home to live with them. They said no. Her mother told her she'd made her bed, now she had to sleep in it. Nice, huh?"

"And the boy in the picture, the one in the cowboy suit?"

"I guess that's the son. She thought if they had a kid, her husband would straighten up and fly right. But just the opposite happened. He didn't want anything to do with the boy. Every time the kid fussed or misbehaved he blamed it on her for being a bad mother. She said when he was a baby and cried at night waking them up, her husband would leave the house and not come back till morning. And he never told her where he went. When I met her she was what, twenty-four, going on forty."

"Sounds like she was ripe for the picking. So you told her you'd take her out and show her a good time. Am I right?"

"I could lie to you and say that's wasn't true. That I was just being a Good Samaritan. I meet a lot of women like Adrian. Married young and before they know it life is passing them by. Yeah, I do promise to show them a good time. And you know what, I usually come through. But that's about as far as I go. I'm not looking to take on any girl's miseries as a full-time job. Most of the time they just want to go out, have a few drinks, a good meal, a night on the town, and if I'm lucky, a healthy screw. And that's exactly what I give them. They don't really wanna leave home, they just wanna think they can if they need to. Or they need to think they're still attractive to other men. In this Adrian's case I'd say getting away from her husband permanently would be a good idea. But I wasn't interested in becoming any more involved with her than a night out."

"And now that you think she's disappeared you feel responsible?"

"No, Mr. Doherty, I never feel responsible for these dames. In this case I just don't want anything to come back on me if something has happened to her. I didn't do anything different with this Adrian than I've done with all the other girls I been with."

Chapter Two

Before Grimaldi left he signed an agreement to employ Doherty as a private investigator in the missing woman's case and forked over the hundred bucks for the service. Once he was gone Doherty hauled out a detailed street map of Providence and the adjacent cities and towns. He used the index on the backside to locate Priscilla Avenue. It was in neighborhood called Silver Lake, a section of Providence he was wholly unfamiliar with. It was wedged into a small part of the city south of Hartford Avenue and east of Neutaconkanut Park, close to the border of Cranston and Johnston. The map did not show any body of water nearby named Silver Lake.

He considered driving up to that neighborhood to check out where Adrian Colardo and her husband lived, then decided to wait until evening. Something told him that cruising by the house at midday when most likely no one was at home would be of little or no value. Right now he wasn't ready to confront the missing girl's husband until he gathered more facts and was certain she was indeed missing.

Two other pieces of business also had to be attended to in the meantime. First, he wanted to find out more about Richie Grimaldi. Although the guy had paid him a hundred bucks up front to find the missing girl, Doherty wasn't ready to rule him out as a potential suspect in her disappearance. He could've hired Doherty and coughed up the money in hopes of using a PI to

11

throw the cops off his trail if it came to that.

The second path Doherty wanted to explore was whether anyone, especially the girl's husband, had reported her as a missing person. On that score he'd have to wait a few days since the police didn't usually put much effort into finding a missing person until at least seventy-two hours had passed - unless the missing person was a kid. In a case like this their assumption would be that the missing woman had run off with someone who was not her husband, which was exactly what Adrian Colardo had done.

Late that afternoon Doherty tanked up his five-year old Chevy Bel Air and using the detailed map of the city found his way with only a couple of missed turns to the Silver Lake section of Providence. He took Dyer Avenue out of Cranston since it was a street he was familiar with thanks to a brief encounter he'd had with a girl named Maureen Donovan while working a case a few months ago. The girl ended up murdered, though not before giving him a brief tour of the Knightsville section of Cranston. They had also bedded down together a couple of times, circumstances he chose not to dwell on as he made his way to Silver Lake.

After crossing into Providence, Dyer became Pocasset Avenue. From what he could tell from the signs on the commercial establishments around Silver Lake, it was a predominantly Italian community. Before he reached the intersection with Hartford Ave, he turned down Webster and wended his way through a densely settled neighborhood to Priscilla Ave.

Fortunately most of the recently fallen snow had been cleared from the main streets. Snow-clogged streets brought back unpleasant memories of his father waking him around dawn on snowy days to help put chains on the rear tires of the family's Packard. He inherited that car after his father passed and drove the old clunker until it no longer could exceed fifty miles per hour even with the gas pedal pinned to the floor. He traded it in at Packy's garage in Warwick for the Bel Air, which he first rented and later bought outright. As far as he could tell the Packard was consigned to a scrap heap mere minutes after he left it at the garage.

Once he located Priscilla Ave he cruised slowly down that residential street carefully checking out the neighborhood. It was a partially rundown section of the city composed mostly of closely packed single and two-family houses built early in the century. Several on the street had seen better days. The Colardo residence was a small two-story job painted dark brown with white trim. Paint was peeling in several spots on the side that faced the street. The small yard between the house and the sidewalk was covered in gray slushy snow. The walkway from the house to the sidewalk had been shoveled only enough for a person to walk on if he put one foot in front of the other. The driveway beside the house was likewise only haphazardly cleared of the recent snowfall.

Doherty parked at the curb directly across from #215 and surveyed the scene. No one appeared to be home at the moment. There was nothing about the place that told him anything more about the Colardos than that their house was in the same state of disrepair as their marriage. That's assuming what the girl told Grimaldi about her husband was true. What was most pertinent to the case right now was how she'd described her husband to Richie as an angry young man with a violent streak. That alone made him a potential suspect in her disappearance.

Doherty killed some time cruising around the Silver Lake area before returning to Priscilla Avenue. This time there was a Dodge Cornet parked in the partially shoveled driveway. Some lights were on in the house as well. It was the end of the workday so there were more comings and goings on the street. As a result Doherty didn't look out of place parked by the curb staking out the Colardo residence. He smoked a couple of Camels and kept the motor running to keep himself warm. The radio was set to a station playing popular standards and swing music; they were interrupted every fifteen minutes by news flashes and the latest weather report. More snow was in the forecast.

A little after six an old Hudson sedan pulled up in front of 215 and an elderly couple emerged from the big car. He couldn't say for sure, but they looked like the two people who'd been sitting on lawn chairs in front of the garage in the photo from the missing girl's purse. They rang the bell and waited patiently on the front stoop. Doherty was kicking himself for not bringing his binoculars so he could get a better look at the two visitors.

In time the front door swung open. A skinny guy with black hair combed up into a pompadour was standing on the top step in a white T-shirt and black pants. He looked enough like the young guy in the photo with Adrian that Doherty could assume he was the husband. In time a fairly animated conversation ensued among the three on the doorstep. The young guy was gesticulating wildly with his hands. Doherty couldn't hear what was being said; it was obviously not a pleasant exchange. A small boy bunched up in a woolen winter coat and a cap with fur earflaps soon emerged from behind his father. Given how heavily the boy was dressed there was no way Doherty could tell for sure if he was the same kid in the cowboy outfit in Adrian's photos, though it made sense that he was.

More conversation passed between the greasy guy and the elderly couple before the boy was pushed in their direction. The kid was hustled by the old man and woman down the barely shoveled walkway to the Hudson. Meanwhile the husband stood in the doorway watching until the couple Doherty presumed was Adrian's parents drove off with the boy. The young guy then retreated back into the house, quickly closing the door behind him. Doherty lit another cigarette and waited.

Fifteen minutes later he came back out. This time he was wearing the same dark slacks along with a black leather jacket and a light colored muffler around his neck. He took quick steps through the uncleared snow, trying as best he could not to get any of it on his narrow toed shoes. He hopped into the Dodge and backed out of the driveway.

Doherty followed him through the neighborhood until he turned onto a bigger street that Doherty saw was Broadway. He continued to tail Colardo at a discreet distance. They headed in the direction of the city's center. Before reaching the downtown he cut a sharp left onto Atwells and headed up Federal Hill. A few blocks along he pulled over to the curb in the heart of the densely settled commercial section lined with restaurants, bars, grocery stores, packies and hair salons. Doherty drove by before sliding the Chevy into an empty space a half block further along. Through his rearview he watched Colardo get out of his Dodge and enter a taproom called The Four Aces.

Five minutes later Doherty passed through the door into the same place. As bars go it wasn't a particularly classy place but not a dive either. The husband was sitting at a booth along the far wall across from a girl with short, dark curly hair. Doherty took a detour by them as he walked to the bar. On his way he clocked their faces as surreptitiously as he could without drawing attention to himself. It didn't matter since the two of them were too busy making goo-goo eyes at each other.

Colardo had a hooked nose that marred his otherwise pretty boy face. The girl was dressed in a print dress that seemed more appropriate for a teenager than a woman guzzling a drink in a taproom. She looked like she was somewhere in her early twenties at best. Doherty assumed a seat at the bar where he could watch them in the mirror above the liquor bottles.

From the heavyset bartender he ordered a bottle of Gansett and a bag of peanuts since he hadn't had anything to eat since lunch. It wasn't long before Colardo reached out and took the girl's hand and drew it to his mouth and kissed it. She giggled when he did this. Her giggling drew a sour expression on his face. She tried to mollify him by reaching out to caress his cheek. He reacted by quickly grabbing her wrist and twisting it. The girl flinched when he did this. Then thinking better of it, he flashed her a smile as he let go of her arm. It took a few uncomfortable seconds before she returned the smile. This short scene gave Doherty a pretty good idea of the way Adrian's husband behaved with women. Doherty nursed his beer and exchanged some small talk with the barkeep about the predicted snowstorm. He never took his eyes off the couple in the booth, though he did his best not to be obvious about it.

When a waiter came by their booth Colardo asked to pay for their drinks. Not wanting to be caught off-guard Doherty quickly dropped a couple bucks on the bar for his beer and another bag of peanuts to take with him in the car. He exited the Four Aces and already had his motor running when he eyed the guy and the girl in his rearview getting into the Dodge. He pulled out after they drove past him, being sure to keep a car between them as they made their way further up Atwells. At the next street that was one way to the left they turned and he did likewise. A few turns later it was clear they were headed back to Silver Lake. When the Dodge pulled into the driveway on Priscilla Avenue, Doherty passed by and drove down the block. He turned around and slowly cruised by the house as the couple got out of the Cornet. At the end of the block Doherty took a couple of turns around the neighborhood before passing by 215 again. By this time Colardo and the girl were inside the house where a few lights were on.

He parked caddy corner to the building for about twenty minutes hoping no one would think he was up to no good and call the police. Only shadows of the couple inside were visible through the pulled down shades. It was too cold for Doherty to get out and go skulking around in the snow. In time the lights downstairs went off. A short while later a light came on upstairs in what he assumed was a bedroom. So much for Adrian's husband pining away for his missing wife. Doherty waited another ten minutes. When there was no more movement in the house, he turned the Chevy around and headed back to West Warwick.

Chapter Three

In the morning he put in a call to his old friend and former mentor Gus Timilty, who worked out of a large investigations agency in Providence called Briggs and Timilty. A few months back he and Gus had been involved in an unpleasant case involving the abduction of Gus' estranged daughter by some thugs from Boston. The story ended with he and Gus rescuing the girl, though not before Timilty shot and killed both of her abductors. His old pal disposed of the bodies in the trunk of the dead men's car, which he then abandoned in a remote section of the old shipyard by the bay in Providence.

Since both of the dead guys had long criminal records and were unaffiliated with any Boston crime organizations, after their bodies were discovered the deaths were written off as mob hits on two people no one was going to miss. So far there'd been no blowback from the shootings. Yet the killings put a dent in Doherty's friendship with Gus – one that had yet to be ironed out. They'd spoken a few times on the phone soliciting each other's advice on cases they were working, but that was the extent of their interactions over the past few months. The old conviviality they'd once shared had not been revived.

Gus wasn't in so Doherty left a callback message on his Dictaphone machine. Not sure if Agnes was going to come by today, he busied himself reading the morning *Journal*. Around ten-thirty the phone rang. He answered it by announcing "Doherty and Associates."

"Hey, pally, it's Gus. How's it hanging?"

"I'm doing okay. At the moment I'm working a case I need your help with," he responded without the slightest hint of friendliness. "You're not going to believe this: Do you remember the Carney case I worked last year? The one where I found that married woman shacked up with some gigolo in a motel down by the beaches in Narragansett."

"I think so. What's the problem? Has she gone on the lam again?"

Doherty had to laugh, recalling the uncomfortable conversation he had with the woman in the motel room while she was clad only in a sheer slip. "No, the guy who took her down there is now my client. Turns out another woman he was running his game on has disappeared."

"Maybe this new one just came to her senses and went home."

"That's what I thought at first. Turns out she left him at the motel some time during the night. She also left some vitals behind like her clothes, her purse, her cosmetics and her coat. My client thinks she might've been abducted. In any case I was wondering if you could hit up one of your contacts in the Providence PD to see if anybody has filed a missing persons report on the girl yet. Her name is Adrian Colardo."

"Married?"

"Yeah. Apparently to a guy who makes my client seem like a choir boy."

"Isn't that always the way. I'll see what I can scratch up for you. I gotta warn you when it comes to missing adults the city cops are usually pretty slow on the draw. They'll assume she just ran off with another guy. And it sounds like that's exactly what she did. If the husband's the shit bag you say he is, who can blame her? Anything else I should know about this lost girl?"

"Only that she went missing from the same motel where I discovered the Carney woman with my client last year."

"Guy's got a lot of imagination, huh?"

"Hey, who am I to criticize. Fellow probably has more sex than you and me put together."

"What about that girl from the bank you've been dating?"

18

"Who Nina? That's going fine, though she's tends to be a little light in the intimacy department. She was engaged last year to a guy who broke it off before they could make wedding plans. I think she's a little gun shy, or else she's holding out for another ring. And you know me."

Gus laughed heartily on the other end. "Yeah, I know. Mr. Lone Wolf. Doesn't want to get tied down with any woman for long."

"My record in the dating department hasn't been very good lately. Seems like my profession has a way of buggering up my relationships with women."

"I know what you mean. Same here. I guess we are who we are. I'll look into this missing persons thing for you. I'll even call a cop I know down in South County to see if anything's been reported to them. Be back to you in a day or two. In the meantime take care of yourself, pally."

"You too, Gus." That was about as personable as their conversations got these days.

Doherty decided he'd make another run at Colardo that afternoon, but first he had to put in a call to Richie Grimaldi. There was something about his new client and this girl's disappearance that just didn't sit right. He tried the home number Grimaldi had left on the agreement form but no one answered. Since the guy was a partner in the restaurant there was a good chance he'd be there, unless he was already working on some new unhappily married woman.

He got the phone number from the matchbook in Adrian's purse and rang up Fortunato's. The person that answered the phone was a young kid who didn't seem to know too many words. After a brief conversation he asked for Richie.

"Who's callin'?"

"Tell him it's Doherty."

The phone was slapped down on the counter and he could hear voices in the background. After some unintelligible back and forth between the kid and someone Doherty figured was Grimaldi, his client came on the line.

"You got something to tell me?" were the first words out of Richie's mouth.

19

"I got a couple of leads I'm working on. Right now I'm looking hard at Adrian's husband. All indications are that he hasn't yet filed a missing persons report on her. That's about all I can tell you at this point."

"That's what I get for a hundred clams?" The question came out like an accusation.

"Hey, asshole. It's only been two days. You'll get your money's worth. Right now I need to talk with you again to get some other things straightened out."

"Can't we do that over the phone. I got a business to run here."

"Yeah, I hear you. That kid who answered the phone could use a little work in the etiquette department."

Grimaldi chuckled. "You mean Tony. He wouldn't know what *etiquette* meant unless it was the name of a horse running in the fifth at Pimlico. Look, I can't get down to your place until tomorrow morning. How's about if I come there around nine?"

"That would be fine," Doherty said, although he usually didn't stroll into the office till ten most days. "And while you're at it, could you bring a picture of yourself I can have?"

There was silence on the other end of the phone. "Why do you need a picture of me?"

"Because I'm going to take a trip down to Narragansett and I need to trace your route the night Adrian went missing. The only picture I have of her is the one with her husband. I don't want to flash that around unless I have to. With a picture of you to show people, I can verify that someone saw the two of you at certain places at certain times. Otherwise all I got to go on is what you've told me. I need some corroboration from other people that you were where you said you were when you said you were. Right now your word alone and a nickel'll buy me a cup of coffee. If something's happened to Adrian Colardo and it gets traced back to you, you're going to need me in your corner with this info."

Doherty wasn't sure if this explanation made sense to Grimaldi. Nevertheless, his client agreed to bring a photo of himself to their meeting in the morning.

Agnes never showed that day so after taking a casual lunch at the Arctic News' downstairs counter, Doherty spent the bulk of the afternoon chalking down some notes on the trails he would pursue once he was done with Grimaldi. He didn't have much to go on except a husband who hadn't reported his wife missing because he was too busy cheating on her with a young replacement. That was all he had, along with a client who had some issues in the honesty department.

At four he dragged the Chevy out of Belanger's garage where it spent more time than it did on the road. Again he drove up to Silver Lake. The traffic was a little thicker today so it took longer to get to Priscilla Ave. Luckily the Dodge Cornet was parked in the driveway when he got to the Colardos. Most of the snow from the previous storm had melted so he could see actual pavement in the driveway and on the walkway in front of the house. He parked far enough away that Colardo wouldn't think anything of his Chevy among several other cars on the street.

Around five-thirty the cheating husband emerged from his house wearing the same leather jacket, but not the nice slacks or shoes from the day before. New snow had begun to fall, though so far only in light flurries. The traffic going toward downtown wasn't moving very quickly so it was a piece of cake tailing the two-toned Dodge in the slow moving stream. Once they'd bypassed downtown, Colardo headed up North Main Street in the direction of the Providence Arena. A few blocks before that landmark he pulled into the large parking lot adjacent to the big Sears Roebuck department store. Doherty parked the Chevy in such a way that he'd have a head-on view of the Dodge without being too conspicuous.

Colardo didn't get out of his car so Doherty waited patiently. The weather was causing his windshield to fog up, which gave him good cover. Periodically he used his handkerchief to clear a four-inch square to keep a close eye on the other car. A little after six he saw workers begin to file out of the Sears building. Colardo got out of his car and stood beside it until the girl he'd been with the night before came into view. She was wearing a heavy woolen coat that was unbuttoned. Doherty could see the orange salesgirl smock underneath. Obviously Sears Roebuck was her place of employment. She waved when she saw her married boyfriend. He didn't respond in kind. He just stood by his car trying to look cool smoking a cigarette as snowflakes gathered in his greasy hair.

They slipped into Colardo's Dodge and Doherty started his engine thinking they were about to exit the parking lot. Instead they sat in the front seat of his car and played kissy face in an unabashed fashion, oblivious to any passersby who might look in at them. It wasn't long before their car windows became completely fogged up. Doherty killed his engine and continued to watch them through the small square he kept wiping in his windshield. From the little he could see they were going at it pretty hot and heavy. He wondered if Colardo would have the gall to screw the girl on the front seat of his Cornet in the Sears Roebuck lot.

After fifteen minutes of passion the other car sprang into action. When Colardo's windshield wipers came on Doherty saw the girl rearranging her hair in the rearview mirror, trying to make herself look more presentable. They drove out of the lot and headed up North Main into another section of the city Doherty wasn't familiar with. Despite the inclement weather, Colardo was driving faster than he should have. Apparently the hot and heavy make-out session had added some adrenaline to his bloodstream. Doherty followed them at a discreet distance until they turned off the main drag. From there they took a couple of turns that led into a residential neighborhood. In a short time Colardo pulled up in front of a neatly appointed Cape-style house. An older man was standing in the driveway clearing the gathering snow off his car with a long handle broom.

With the Dodge idling Colardo and the girl engaged in few more seconds of making out before she got out of his car. Her boyfriend then quickly sped off, not bothering to wait until she entered the house. Parked a discreet distance away Doherty was able to observe the girl trying to smooth out her clothes as she approached the front door. The father, still holding the broom, cut her off before she got there. From the gestures he was making, Doherty could tell the man was not pleased with his daughter's behavior. Her mouth was also moving so it was obvious they were involved in a heated argument.

Pretty soon an older woman appeared at the front door in a housedress; she too joined the fray. Doherty was parked too far away to hear what they were saying, though it was a good bet the argument had to do with the girl's relationship with another woman's husband. The father then strode toward his daughter and slapped her across the face. Her hand immediately went up to her reddened cheek. Meanwhile the mother covered her mouth and stood frozen by the door. The girl quickly wheeled around and pushed past the woman into the house. Words were now being exchanged between the father and the mother. Doherty took this as his cue to depart.

Chapter Four

The next morning Grimaldi strolled into Doherty and Associates at ten minutes after nine. He was dressed casually, in clothes that were somewhere between his gigolo wear and a bartender's outfit. His hair was well oiled and his face was closely shaved save for his neatly trimmed pencil-line mustache. He looked much more relaxed than the unkempt fellow who'd burst into the office on Monday. His clean looks set Doherty to wondering if Grimaldi had another married woman on the line for the weekend.

He offered his new client a cup of coffee from the percolator behind Agnes' desk. Grimaldi accepted and asked for cream and two sugars to go with it. Doherty extracted a pint of cream from the small portable fridge recently installed in the office for just such occasions. He then escorted his client back into his private office.

"So, you said on the phone that you're looking at Adrian's husband for what happened to her down at the beach," Grimaldi said as an opener.

"No, what I said was I was taking a close look at the husband to see how he was carrying on in his wife's absence. For now, anything I dig up on him stays with me. Understand?"

"Hey, I thought I was the one paying the bills," Grimaldi protested.

"You are. But I've got to work this case my way. I don't want you sticking your nose in where it doesn't belong."

Grimaldi sipped his highly sweetened coffee. From the expression on his face it was obvious he was not happy with the way his PI was pursuing the investigation.

Doherty pulled a small pad out of his desk drawer and said, "Why don't we start at the beginning on the day you took this Adrian down to South County. Give me everything you can remember; try not to leave out any details."

The client screwed up his face into a thoughtful expression that seemed almost painful. "I told you about the time she came into my place and we went to Renaldo's Café to talk. I have to admit that was when I first started to work her like I did with the other women. I mean right then I could tell she was ripe for the picking."

"How did that ultimately lead to the night of lovemaking down in Narragansett?"

Grimaldi raised his hand. "I'm getting to that. You said you wanted all the details so lemme tell it my way. That Friday she came into the restaurant about an hour before the after work rush. Tony and Freddie were waiting tables and I was going back and forth between the bar and the kitchen. My cousin Anthony was the greeter at the door like he usually is. She sat down at the bar by herself. If I remember correctly she was the only one there having a drink.

"I could tell right away she was really upset. Said her husband called her folks and told them she wasn't able to take care of their son and they should take the boy to their place. Before long she started getting all teary eyed. What was I suppose to do? I couldn't exactly send her away. A half hour after he called her parents they came and took the kid. They didn't say anything to her. Just picked up the boy and drove off without asking any questions. After they were gone her husband smacked her a few times. She showed me the marks on her arms and face as proof. He told her she was a poor excuse for a mother. I suggested that she come back the next afternoon and bring an overnight bag 'cause we'd be going somewhere she'd be safe."

"Jeez, Richie, you're a regular humanitarian."

Grimaldi smiled but it wasn't a pleasant one. "To be honest with you, Doherty, a part of me was thinking maybe this girl was gonna be more trouble than she was worth. I couldn't very well send her back to her husband to get smacked around some more, could I? I mean she had nowhere else to go. So I did the only thing I know how to do: I told her I'd take her away for the weekend. Give her some time to figure out how she could get her kid back."

"Okay, go on."

"The next day she showed up at Fortunato's around three o'clock. I was still working so I told her she'd have to wait another hour or so. I gave her a few bucks and suggested she go buy something nice for herself for the weekend. I needed some time to make plans. While she was gone I called the motel and asked them to hold my room for the night. Then I cleaned up in the back and changed into some nice clothes. I always keep extra clothes here for *special* occasions."

"Like when you have to take a desperate housewife out for a night on the town?" Grimaldi ignored Doherty's remark.

"When she came back we got into my car and drove down to South County."

"How did she get to the restaurant?"

Grimaldi shrugged. "I dunno. She just kind of showed up. Could've taken the bus or a cab. I didn't ask."

"How was she dressed?"

The client wagged his head. "She looked good. All dressed up with some make-up on. Whatever doubts I had the day before quickly disappeared. I gotta tell you, Doherty, this Adrian was put together real good; not like some of the other girls I been with who look nice on the surface, but when they take their clothes off they're all loose flesh with stretch marks everywhere. And in the morning without their makeup on, I don't even wanna look at them. But this Adrian, she was a hot number. If I was her husband I wouldn'ta treated her like he did."

"Could be why you're not anybody's husband. Apparently you only know how to treat a girl well for one night."

Again Grimaldi ignored Doherty's comment and continued with his narrative. "First thing we did was drive to the motel to check in. The people there know me pretty good so getting a room this time of year wasn't a problem."

"I'll bet they do. Was it your usual room, number six?"

Grimaldi nodded. "When we got there I took a shower right away while Adrian freshened up a little. I didn't want to smell like tomato sauce all night. She looked so good I could've had her right then and there. But I knew I'd have to show her a good time first. So we drove back to the pier and went to the Greene Inn. It's a nice place - right on Ocean Road, not far from the Towers. The dates I take there always like the place 'cause it's classy."

"After you got to this inn did you drink, eat, what?"

Grimaldi smiled, savoring the memory of the first part of their night together. "First we sat in the lounge and had a couple of cocktails. I had two Cutty Sarks on the rocks and she had one of them whiskey sours with a cherry in it. I could tell she wasn't much of a drinker from the way she made a sick face whenever she tasted her cocktail. She didn't even finish it. She never had anything but a glass of wine at Fortunato's. I didn't care if she drank or not on account of how good she looked. Besides she was turning out to be a cheap date unlike some of the other broads I've been with. Sometimes a girl is so intent on having a wild time she tries to drink me under the table. I learned a long time ago if a woman gets too drunk she's not gonna be much good in bed."

Doherty was doing his best to keep a blanket on his disgust with Grimaldi's attitude toward women. The client wasn't making it easy. "All right, what happened next?"

"I decided it would be better to eat at the inn rather than go some place else since the weather wasn't too good. In fact it was freezing cold outside. They have a nice grillroom there so that's where we had dinner."

"What did you two eat?"

"I had some clam chowder and a steak for dinner. She ate some kind of fish; haddock I think it was. I was surprised when she ordered it 'cause most people I know only eat fish on Fridays."

This last remark caused Doherty to remember when he was dating Millie St. Jean, the married woman he'd seen for a while. They usually went out on Friday nights when she told her in-laws she was going out with her girlfriends. She and her two boys were living with them at the time. Being a good Catholic, Millie always ate fish on those dates. Doherty was raised

Catholic, but had given up the fish-on-Friday stricture as well as a lot of other things from his religion a long time ago.

"Did Adrian drink anything with her meal?"

The client raised his head as if lost in thought. "Oh, yeah. She ordered a glass of wine. I think it was that Mateus stuff. She only drank about half of it. I was starting to get worried that maybe she wouldn't have enough to drink to be up for doing what I hoped we'd be doing when we got back to the motel. The last thing I wanted after buying her drinks and an expensive meal was to spend the night listening to her sob story about how her prick of a husband treated her and her kid. The whole idea of me taking these married women down to South County is to help them forget their troubles – at least for one night."

"After the meal did you have dessert?"

"Yeah, we split some strawberry shortcake. That kinda perked her up. I could tell right away she had a sweet tooth. I ordered a coffee with it. From the way she acted during the meal I got the impression she'd never been to a restaurant that nice before. After we finished eating we sat and talked for a while about what we would do the next day. To be honest with you, I had no intention of doing anything with her on Sunday other than taking her back to Providence. I figured I'd tell her something came up at the restaurant and I had to get back right away."

Doherty gave Grimaldi as critical a stare as he could muster. It didn't appear to pierce his client's hardened surface. "After you paid the bill did you go right back to the motel?"

"More or less. First we took a little walk along the seawall. It was too freaking cold to stay out for long so we got into the car and went back to Room Six."

"Did you ever notice anyone following you or looking at you in a peculiar way either at the inn or the motel?"

Grimaldi shook his head. "Can't say that I did. Though it wasn't like I was checking either. I mean there was hardly anybody at the inn when we were in the lounge or the grillroom. Places down by the pier don't do much business this time of year, especially after Christmas."

"What happened after you got back to the room?"

"You know, the usual. I had another drink and then suggested she get into something more comfortable. I was hoping she'd brought some kind of sexy nightgown with her."

"Did she?"

Grimaldi shook his head in disappointment. "No. She put on this button-up thing that looked like what a kid would sleep in. To tell you the truth it kinda turned me off. Then she started yawning so I knew I had to work fast. Before we got too far along she told me she'd never slept with anyone besides her husband. The last thing I wanted was for her to start talking about him again and ruin my night. I'd brought a three pack of rubbers with me and figured I'd be lucky if I got to use one of them. Anyway, we did the deed even though I could tell the whole time she wasn't really into it.

"Some girls I been with haven't had a real screw from their husbands in so long they're like wildcats in bed. Not this one. She went through the motions, though all the while it felt like nothing more than her way of paying me back for the nice dinner. That was about it. Shortly after we were done she rolled over and went to sleep. It was a shame. She was young and nice looking. I mean she was tight all over. I was sorry she wasn't more enthusiastic about the sex."

"What did you do afterwards?"

"Me? I watched TV for a while. I must've fallen asleep 'cause the last thing I remember was getting up to turn off the set. When I did my legs felt a little rubbery. I'd had a lot to drink, but I'm used to it. I have what they call a high tolerance. Not that night though. Soon as I got back into bed I was out like a light."

"And the next thing you knew it was morning and she was gone?"

Grimaldi raised up his hands. "Yeah, that's about it. And like I told you before, the fact that she left her things in the room made me think she didn't leave willingly. That's why I came here to see you. I was hoping you'd be able to find her before any funny business happened."

"Did you call the office at the motel to see if they knew anything about her whereabouts?"

"Yeah, sure I did. I mean I know the husband and wife there pretty good. I went down and asked them if they'd seen the girl I was with. They both said 'no'. Then I asked if she'd called for someone to pick her up or called a cab. The husband said no calls were made from Room Six all night or that morning. The only other thing I could think of is that she slipped out and used a pay phone. The problem is there aren't any pay phones at or near the motel. There's one over at the beach pavilion, though I'm pretty sure it gets disconnected after the season's over. Far as I could tell she hadn't put on any clothes either, unless she'd brought some other stuff in her overnight bag I hadn't seen."

"She didn't leave a note or anything?"

"No. Just her clothes, her handbag and whatever beauty things were in the bathroom. That was it. At first I was kinda pissed off thinking she'd run out on me. Believe me, Doherty, that's never happened before. Occasionally some broad'll have second thoughts the next day and ask me to take her home. I don't mind 'cause I usually tell them something's come up and I got-ta get back to town anyway. But nobody's ever left me before I woke up in the morning like this one did."

"One final question: Do you think someone could've slipped something into your drinks at the lounge or in the restaurant? Something slow acting that might've caused the two of you to pass out at the motel?"

"Jesus. I never thought of that. I figured we were just tired 'cause it was the end of a long week and we'd been drinking and had sex. But this girl hardly drank anything all night. And me, like I said, I take pride in my ability to hold my liquor. Do you think somebody could've slipped us a mickey?"

"It's possible. I find it hard to believe you wouldn't have heard her if she got up and left during the night. Or better yet, heard somebody come in to take her. I'm thinking a guy in your business who beds down with a lot of married women must sleep with one eye open." The client smiled at this last remark as if it were intended to be a compliment.

"Before you go, Richie. I need to ask you something else: Why do you do what you do? Haven't you ever thought about getting married and settling down?"

"Haven't you?" he responded accusingly.

"I've tried, but my work keeps getting in the way. But you, you own part of a nice restaurant so you must have a fair amount of scratch. You're a

30

good-looking guy, who'd be a catch for some nice girl. This gigolo business is going to get you into bad trouble one of these days – if it hasn't already."

Grimaldi leaned back in his chair looking uncomfortable. "I was married once. I was only twenty-one at the time. Married a girl I'd been dating for about a year right before I got drafted. Everybody told us not to get married 'cause there was a good chance she'd end up a widow. We didn't listen to anybody. To be honest with you, one of the reasons I married her was that I wanted to get letters from a girl back home while I was in the service. Sometimes those letters were the only thing keeping me going. I was in the Pacific and I saw a lot of bad shit over there. Things a boy of twenty-one should never have to see." For a moment Doherty could relate to what Grimaldi was saying from his own war experience.

"I survived, but a lotta guys in my outfit didn't. After about six months those love letters that use to come from Marie every week started coming less and less. Our commanding officers told us not to take it personally; that the mail service was all screwed up over there. I wanted to believe them, though I knew they only said it to keep up morale. I 'specially wanted to believe that Marie was still yearning for me back home. Other guys would get those 'Dear John' letters, but they were mostly from girlfriends not wives. I thought me and Marie were different 'cause we were married. You know, I was young so I took all that *death do us part* shit seriously. I guess I believed she was being faithful to me because I needed to believe it.

"Don't get me wrong, I wasn't a choir boy when I was over there. After we liberated the Philippines I went to some of those whorehouses in Manila. Every guy did. We just wanted to get our nuts off after what we'd been through. For those twenty minutes with a Filipino hooker we could forget about all the blood and guts."

"What happened when you came home?"

"Well at first Marie tried to put on a good front. After all, guys like me were greeted as heroes. We had parades and all that other congratulations business and she seemed happy to be part of it. She liked everything about the celebrations except her soldier-boy husband. It didn't take long before I found out she'd been seeing some other guy the whole time I was away. And she was still seeing him on the sly while I was putting in sixty hours a week with my cousin trying to get our restaurant up and running. When I finally confronted her she told me about this Aldo fella she was dating. The worst part is the prick'd been a 4-F during the war while I was over there fighting and running the risk of getting killed.

"When I found out where he lived, I thought I'd go jack the bastard up and get my wife back. So I went to his place but when I got there the sonofabitch pulled a gun on me. Said if I ever came back he'd shoot me. Told me I'd lost Marie a long time ago, she was now his. That would've been funny, huh? Me going through all that rough combat over there only to get shot by some jerk-off here who was screwing my wife the whole time I was away."

"What happened after that?"

"What do you think happened? We got divorced. It wasn't long before I started hustling married women. Some headshrinker would probably say it was my way of getting back at Marie. And maybe he'd be right. After a while it just seemed like the right thing for me."

Doherty was flummoxed by Grimaldi's story. It didn't make him any more sympathetic even though it did put his behavior in a new light. "Haven't you ever met a woman, even a married one, you thought you could fall in love with?"

"Yeah, I been with some I coulda fallen for. But they were married and I'd be doing to their husbands the same thing that Aldo prick did to me. I found it easier just to show them a good time and send them packing when we were done. I know that sounds bad, but it's the way I choose to operate."

"Sounds kind of sad to me."

"Hey, asshole, don't be getting all sympathetic on me. I get more sex than any guy I know, and it's with a new piece of ass just about every week. I know a lot of married guys who climb into bed with the same old broad every night that wish they could trade places with me."

Having never been married Doherty didn't know about this nor was he about to speculate either. "You must strike out a lot. It's not like every married woman is anxious to jump into the sack with a strange man, no matter how charming you are. And no offense, Richie, but you're not exactly Cary Grant."

For the first time all morning Grimaldi laughed. "No, and none of these broads are Audrey Hepburn either. Let me ask you something, Doherty, are you a baseball fan?"

"Sure. Have been since I was a kid."

"What makes a baseball player a star?"

"I don't follow."

"It's a simple question: What makes a baseball player a star? I'll tell you what: if he hits .300 he's an all-star. You know what that means? That means every seven out of ten times he comes to bat he makes an out. Seven times outta ten! You do that in the restaurant business you're out on the street. You do that with women it still means you're getting laid three times - and for me, it's with three different broads every time. I'll take those odds any day. Sometimes these girls just wanna talk or have a shoulder to cry on. It doesn't take me long to figure out which ones I'm gonna make time with and which ones I won't.

"Girls are different from guys. They always wanna talk and most of them are married to men, who after a while don't give them the time of day. Me, I listen to them. I listen when they tell me their sad stories. Most of the time I don't have to listen all that hard. It's always the same story so I just smile and nod my head. It's not like they really want me to say anything that's gonna make them feel better. What they don't know is that all the time they're talking I'm trying to figure out if I'm gonna get this one into the sack or not. Then I just gotta figure out how to arrange it."

Doherty stood up realizing he'd had just about enough of Richie Grimaldi's philosophy on what it takes to be a successful gigolo. The discussion had been enlightening, though it hadn't done anything to advance his investigation into the missing girl. Despite Grimaldi's candor, Doherty wasn't ready to scratch him off his list of suspects. Before his client left he forked over the picture of himself Doherty had requested. It was a good mug shot that would help him trace Richie's moves down in Narragansett.

33

Chapter Five

D oherty knew he had to confront the missing girl's husband at some point. However, for the time being he decided to work around the outside of that circle before closing in on him. The husband wasn't the first person Doherty wanted to brace as a possible prime suspect. His inclination was to first talk to the elderly couple he saw at the house on Priscilla Avenue picking up their grandson. He was pretty sure they were the same couple in the photo from Adrian's purse. The problem was he didn't know their names or where they lived. He could go to the city hall in Providence and search for Adrian Colardo's wedding license in public records and work back from there. On the other hand it would be easier to ask Gus Timilty to dig up the info for him. He knew his old buddy had a contact at the city hall in Providence who could get background on the girl much faster than he could.

As if by divine intervention, while he was planning his strategy for the day, Gus rang him up on the horn. Agnes was in the outer office sans baby today, so she took the call in her usual efficient manner. When she discovered it was Timilty on the other end, their conversation took a decidedly personal tone, most of which was about her baby. Doherty waited patiently for almost five minutes before Agnes patched the call through to his office.

"Hey, pally, your secretary sounds like she's over the moon with her new son."

"I guess," Doherty said without enthusiasm. "She even brought the little bugger into work the other day when her mother wasn't available. Luckily we didn't have any clients," he said, for the moment forgetting that was the day Richie Grimaldi had come storming into the office. "I'm not sure how a prospective client would react if the first thing he saw was the company's secretary out front feeding a bottle to a baby."

Gus chuckled. "Oh yeah, I forgot. Doherty and Associates tries to promote itself as a hard-boiled operation."

"That might be funny except that most of my clients are married people whose spouses have run off with somebody else. I suspect any lawyer who does a lot of divorce work would feel the same way if the first thing that hit his clients when they came into his office was a secretary fondling a baby. I don't suppose any of the clerical staff at your place bring their kids to work."

"Touché, my friend. Anyway, the reason I'm calling is to tell you that as of eight p.m. last night no one has reported your Adrian Colardo missing to the Providence PD. I put in a call to my man down in North Kingston but haven't heard back from him yet. You might have better luck contacting your old friend Alex Klinoff down there. That is if he's still playing footsie with the local cops."

"I'm not surprised the girl's husband hasn't reported her missing. I've caught him on two occasions in the last few days making time with a young replacement for his wife. I'm planning to take a run at him, though I want to check out a few other angles first. As far as getting Klinoff involved in this, I'd rather not if I can avoid it. He's a good source, yet whenever I throw him a bone he tries to weasel his way into the middle of my cases. You know what they say, once a cop…"

"Always a cop," Gus finished. "If I get a call from down there I'll get back to you right away."

"I'd appreciate that. Now I have another favor to ask of you."

"You keep doing this you'll have to put me on a retainer. How about if you buy me dinner one of these nights instead? I haven't seen you since… since that business with my daughter. I'm starting to think you've been ducking me the last few months."

Gus was right about that. Doherty had been avoiding his old pal ever since the case involving his daughter and the shakedown operation her pimp was running ended in four murders. After that fiasco he was determined to put his business back on a simpler footing where his main responsibility was turning up lost people not dead ones. For the time being that meant keeping Gus at arm's length.

"I'd like you to find out what you can about the girl's parents. I don't know their names or where they live. All I know is that they drive an out-of-date Hudson and are currently taking care of the girl's son in her absence. I know I could dig them up by searching public records at Providence City Hall, but I have a hunch your guy over there can do the same thing in a fraction of the time."

"Indeed he can. One of the advantages of working for a big outfit like ours is we have connections all over the state in local governments. It'll cost you, though. I've got to periodically grease my man at city hall."

"No problem. I'll expense onto the client's bill."

"What're the names we should be looking at?"

"That's the problem. I don't know. I'm sure the parents and their address will be on the missing girl's marriage license. It shouldn't be any more than three to four years old, issued to a Colardo with the bride named Adrian whatever her last name was."

"Don't worry, pally, I'll get it for you. By the time my guy at city hall is done, you'll have this girl's school report card dating back to the first grade."

Doherty laughed. "He doesn't have to dig quite that deep. Just her maiden name and address prior to her marriage'll do."

"Yeah, I know, but my guy gets bored during the day if nobody comes in with a request. Whenever I call him to check on somebody in public records he sends me an Encyclopedia Britannica entry on that person."

"Okay, if that's what makes him happy. Anything you can find out will be much appreciated. And don't worry about the charge."

"I never was worried," Gus said before signing off.

It was already after eleven and Doherty wanted to get up to North Main Street as close to noon as possible. He thought it best if he cornered the husband's new girlfriend on her lunch break. That way they could talk without being conspicuous. The second promised snowstorm never materialized so the roads were drivable, only now covered in a grayish slush. He made good time, arriving at the Sears Roebuck store fifteen minutes early. This would give him an opportunity to search out the girl in the mammoth outlet.

He figured he'd skip the tool department, auto parts and lawn equipment, such as it was at this time of year. He would also bypass men's clothing and shoes. He first tried women's clothing and then home goods. Despite a thorough search of each of those departments he didn't see anyone resembling the young girl he'd eyed at the Four Aces or playing kissy face outside in the lot with Adrian's husband.

Having covered the entire first floor, he took the escalator up to the second floor. He arrived directly in front of the large appliance department and was immediately accosted by salesmen looking to sell him a washer, refrigerator, stove or more likely a new 21-inch TV. He knew from previous experiences at Sears that these guys were the only salesmen in the store who worked on commission, so he couldn't begrudge their aggressiveness.

Once he'd politely warded off their advances, he made his way to the toy department. When they were kids the Sears toy department only existed for Doherty and his sister Margaret in the four-inch thick Sears Roebuck catalog that arrived at their house every Christmas season. The toy collection alone spanned fifty pages and he and his sister would pore over the cornucopia of goods for hours from Thanksgiving until Christmas.

In the end his folks would opt to buy them cheaper versions of the toys in the Sears catalog from local stores in Arctic like Newberry and Grant's. He always thought it would've been thrilling to get a package each December for something ordered from the Sears Roebuck catalog. Seeing the toy department in person today, he found the inventory disappointing compared to the wealth of toys in those fifty pages.

It didn't take long for him to locate Colardo's new honey; she was working in the doll section. From its giant display, it was apparent that the new Barbie Dolls were the current rage. He'd read in the papers about the thousands of girls who got their first Barbie this past Christmas.

With the holiday rush over most of the toy shelves were only half full.

There were few customers in this section, so a forty-year-old man like him in a suit stuck out like a sore thumb. The girl he was looking for was standing on her tiptoes trying to slip some lesser dolls onto a shelf that was beyond her reach. Doherty dutifully stepped up and relieved her of the task. She gave him a shy smile while offering a thank you. The tag on her orange smock said her name was Denise. That was at least a start. With her short dark hair tied back from her face, she looked even younger than she had at the Four Aces. Still, she was cute in a healthy, teenage sort of way.

"My name is Doherty," he said, flashing the girl his PI license. "I was wondering if we could talk, Denise." He took the liberty of using her name.

She looked at his card, then at his face and then back at the card. She was obviously confused. "Are you with the police?" she asked nervously.

"No, I'm a private detective. I've been hired to find a girl who's missing. I thought you might be able to help me."

She shook her head. "I don't know anything about a missing girl." Her voice quivered with nervousness.

"Even if the missing girl is your new boyfriend's wife?"

"Nicky said she ran off with some other guy." Denise immediately put her hand to her mouth, realizing she had spoken too soon.

Doherty checked his watch. It was almost noon. "Do you get a lunch break soon?"

She looked around to see if anyone was listening to their conversation. Or maybe she was hoping one of her co-workers would rescue her. "I take a break in ten minutes," she said quickly. "I guess we could talk then."

"That's sounds good," he replied in a tone that was meant to make the girl feel less threatened.

"There's a small lunchroom down in the back. It's just for employees, but sometimes one of the girls will meet her husband or sister there for lunch. The bosses don't care as long as it's family. I'll tell them you're my uncle." That sounded reasonable since Doherty was too old to pass as her husband or brother, and bore no resemblance to the girl to be passed off as her father.

He breezed through the toy department for the next ten minutes, revisiting some of those precious childhood memories he'd seen only in the print catalog. At twelve fifteen he drifted back to the employee lunchroom. Denise was sitting by herself at a table for two. She was nervously chewing on her fingernails. An uneaten sandwich sat on a small plate in front of her. Without hesitation Doherty went to the cafeteria counter and ordered a bowl of chicken noodle soup. He scooped up a package of crackers and shelled out a whopping fifty cents for his lunch.

Taking the seat across from the girl he gave her his best avuncular smile. She continued to nibble on her nails.

"Aren't you going to eat your sandwich? I'm sure it's a lot more nutritious than your fingernails."

"You being here is making me nervous."

"I don't mean to," he said in a soothing voice. "Why don't we get acquainted? My name is Hugh Doherty and I live in West Warwick. What about you?"

She gave up a weak smile. "My name in Denise Petrucelli. I don't live too far from here – with my parents."

"How old are you, Denise?"

"Nineteen. No, I mean twenty-one," she said quickly.

Doherty knew this meant she used a fake ID when she and Nick were drinking at the Four Aces.

"Why don't we split the difference and say you're twenty." That brought a small smile to her face.

"What can you tell me about Nick?"

She shook her head. "I dunno. What's there to tell?"

Doherty spooned up some soup, giving the girl a chance to move on. "Let's start with how you two met."

"It was at a dance at the Italian-American Club in North Providence. He was there with some of his buddies. They liked to dance and so do I. They were older so me and my girlfriends thought it would be cool to hang out with them. Nicky's a terrific dancer so I noticed him right away. Just the way he held his cigarette. You couldn't blame a girl for falling for a guy like him," she said, adding a dreamy look to her face.

"Did you know he was married?"

She shook her head emphatically. "No, not then. Not that night anyways."

"When did you find out? When you went his house and saw the family pictures?" The girl blushed so strongly her face nearly turned scarlet.

"How did you know…?"

"I told you, Denise, I'm a private investigator. I saw you with Nick at the Four Aces. Then I saw him take you back to his house – and up to his bedroom."

At this point he was afraid Denise was going to break down in tears. She bravely held them back.

Her voice dropped a few octaves. "He told me his wife had hurt their son and he had to send Tommy to his in-laws for protection. He said she'd become *disturbed* after the baby was born. Nicky didn't think it was safe for little Tommy to be alone with his mother. He was afraid she was gonna do something to him or to herself. You know, like maybe commit suicide. He told me that was the only reason he stayed with her. Then she ran off with some other guy. What was I suppose to think?" All of this came out in a quick, nervous stream of words.

"I understand, Denise. It's not your fault. And if it'll make you feel any better, she did take off with someone else. But when I talked to the guy she went with, he told me she left Nick because he was abusing her. He has a temper, doesn't he?"

She shook her head emphatically. "He doesn't mean nothing by it. He was upset because of what happened with his wife and Tommy. Deep down inside I know he's a good man, and a good father."

"Apparently your parents don't think so." Once again Doherty caught the girl off-guard.

She squirmed in her seat and looked everywhere but at him. "They don't like Nicky because he's older and married."

"I bet they don't like it that you're sleeping with him either."

"Jesus," the girl said truly taken aback. "Is there anything you don't know?"

Doherty spooned up some of his now lukewarm soup. "Yeah, I don't know where Adrian Colardo is and neither does anyone else. I find it strange that she's been gone for three days and her husband hasn't reported her missing."

Denise Petrucelli picked up the uneaten half of her sandwich and stood. "You said it was true that she went off with some other guy. So why should Nicky report her missing to the police. She ran out on him and her son. What kind of a mother does that?" she said in a voice louder than she intended. This attracted the attention of several of her coworkers at neighboring table.

"Look Mr. whoever-you-are, I gotta get back to work. I'd say it was nice meeting you but it wasn't." His companion then swiftly left the little lunchroom, turning a few heads as she did. Doherty calmly finished his soup, which was now cold. At least he'd learned that Adrian's husband was named Nick.

Chapter Six

The drive that afternoon down to Narragansett wasn't nearly as pleasant as it was during the summer months. It was a trip Doherty'd made numerous times when he was younger and still worked at Quonset. In those days he and his buddies would spend Sunday afternoons swimming and sunbathing at Scarborough Beach. In the late afternoon they would wander over to Olivio's further along the beach where they'd sit at picnic tables drinking beer and eating clam cakes while trying to pick up girls. On days when he was successful in that pursuit, he'd stay later into the evening, often making out with some cute honey in the dunes. On Monday morning he'd wake up at home with a hangover, not being able to remember if the girl's name was Judy or Cathy.

He dropped off Route One and headed south toward the pier. His plan was to drive directly to the motel before backtracking to the Greene Inn. He chose to cruise down Ocean Road by the seawall at Narragansett before heading further south toward Scarborough. This way he could acclimate himself to the geography of the area. He passed by a large stone building just before the drive bent to the right and headed south. The tastefully mounted sign indicated this building was the Greene Inn. As Doherty suspected, it was a resort hotel. He gave it a careful going-over before continuing along Ocean Road.

A short distance further on were the famous Towers - two large stone buildings with an impressive stone arch that spanned the drive. He remembered hearing there had once been a casino in this building but wasn't sure if that was true. He knew there'd been a larger casino that burned down years ago somewhere north of the Narragansett Pier pavilion along the same drive.

Narragansett was quiet, as one would expect for this time of year. He passed by the breakfast place where he'd made Richie Grimaldi's acquaintance last year. He'd confronted the gigolo there on Marilyn Carney's behalf. At the time Grimaldi tried to act tough when Doherty suggested he return the woman to her husband. As it turned out Richie was already finished with Mrs. Carney and planned to bring her home anyway. The tough guy act was nothing more than a show he put on for Doherty's sake.

The road from Narragansett to Scarborough was a series of winding curves that passed by some stately homes that were miniature versions of the mansions that sat along the water across the bay in Newport. Those were the millionaire retreats that their owners once in all seriousness referred to as *summer cottages*. Doherty wasn't sure if the elegant homes along Ocean Road between Narragansett and Scarborough were year-round places or less elaborate summer cottages for the West Bay wealthy.

When Doherty had staked out the Anchor Inn on the Carney case he'd spent the night sleeping in his Chevy parked in the back lot of Scarborough Beach. It was the only way he could keep an eye out for Grimaldi and Marilyn Carney. Today both of the large lots behind the beach pavilion were empty save for a few stray cars parked here and there near the sea wall. Most likely they belonged to intrepid fishermen out surfcasting off the beach. He was tempted to take a walk along Scarborough for old times' sake. Instead he decided to get his business done at the motel first.

The place had that rundown look that so many resort establishments have during the winter months. Whatever off-season refurbishing needed to be done, with the weather being what it was today, most of the work would be confined to the indoors. Outdoor renovations would have to wait until the temperature was more cooperative. The motel itself was a one-story job that would have attracted little business if it were located anywhere else than by the seashore. With this locale the owners could charge exorbitant rates in the warmer months based solely on its proximity to the beach.

Only one car was parked in the motel lot and it was by the office. Doherty assumed it belonged to the proprietor. The door to the office stuck a little as he tried to wedge himself inside. There wasn't anyone at the counter or sitting at the desk behind it. Doherty hit the little service bell and waited. When no one showed after a few minutes, he wandered outside and began a room-to-room search. At Number Eight the door was ajar with a piece of wood propping it open a few inches. He knocked on it. Seconds later a man emerged from inside wearing a white painter's suit covered by a quilted hunting vest. The guy was probably in his fifties and looked kind of haggard. A paint hat sat atop his head and his hands were spotted with some light tan paint - the kind of non-descript color that covered motel room walls everywhere in America. A partially smoked cigarette was lodged in the corner of the painter's mouth.

He looked at Doherty curiously, which was understandable given that the Anchor Inn obviously didn't have many customers this time of year. In fact, Doherty wasn't sure if the place was even open for business.

"Can I help you?" the fellow mumbled, not bothering to remove the smoke from his lips.

Doherty looked into the room where he saw a stepladder, a paint tray, some rollers and a can with a couple of brushes resting on its edge.

"Are you the proprietor of this fine establishment?" he asked, not bothering to hide the sarcasm.

"Who wants to know?"

"Is that any way to treat a prospective customer?"

"Sorry, pal. We're not open. Didn't you see the sign? It says we're 'closed for the season'."

Doherty shrugged. "There wasn't any sign on the office door. Must've blown off in the storm."

The guy turned back to the room. "Look, buddy, I'm kinda busy right now so why don't you tell me your business or shove off."

"I'd like to talk to you about a fellow named Richie Grimaldi. I'm a private detective working on a case he's involved in." Doherty flashed him his license.

44

"I don't know nobody by that name." When the man tried to turn back to his paint job Doherty put a strong grip on the fellow's arm and said, "Oh, but I think you do. It'd be a smart move on your part to talk to me before the cops come around." That stopped the painter in his tracks.

"I'm in the middle of painting this room," he said, as if that explained his reluctance.

"It won't take long. Why don't you put a cover on that can and meet me back at the office. I'll make it worth your while."

After some hemming and hawing the owner of the Anchor Inn half-heartedly agreed. While he put things in order in Room Eight, Doherty walked back to the office. He stood outside in the cold smoking a cigarette while waiting. Once they were inside the guy excused himself to wash his hands. He returned to the counter and stripped off his vest and paint suit. Underneath he had on a flannel shirt and some well-worn dungarees. He tried to give Doherty a hard look, which was, as always, a waste of time. To facilitate things Doherty tented a sawbuck lengthwise and slid it across the counter in the proprietor's direction.

"What can you tell me about your relationship with Richie Grimaldi?"

"Damn, pal, how much do you think that ten spot is gonna buy you?"

"Let me put it this way: I know Richie uses your motel to bed down a never- ending series of women he's not married to. In fact, I rescued one of those women from Room Six just this past year. I also know he was here last Saturday night with a new girl. That girl has since gone missing and I've been hired to find her. Anything you can tell me about how Richie operates and what happened here this past weekend would help both of us. Understand this, once things get beyond me, it's possible the North Kingston police will become involved."

This last comment was a bluff, though Doherty was banking on the motel owner not seeing through it. He suspected certain things that went on at the Anchor Inn were already on the radar of the local cops. He was also willing to bet this guy had paid off a few of them to ignore certain improprieties that had occurred here.

"For more than a year now Richie's been renting a room from me at least one or two nights a month."

"Always Room Six?"

The man was taken aback by Doherty's knowledge. "Yeah, always the same room."

"Is there something special about that room?"

"Not really. I think Grimaldi likes it because it's not too close the office, but it's not too far away either. Who knows, maybe he's superstitious about the number six. You know how some people are; they do stuff for all kinds of crazy reasons."

"When does he come?"

"Either on a Friday or a Saturday. Always the weekend and never in season."

"Why not in season?"

"I dunno. Probably because that's when the rates go up and he doesn't think these girls are worth the extra cash. Either that or because I can't always guarantee him Room Six will be available. The way it works is he calls me a day or two ahead of time to reserve the room. If I have a lot of customers I put them in the other rooms before I give them six. I try to keep it open for him."

"Sounds like quite the special arrangement."

"Look, mister, there're a lot of weekends when Richie and his latest sweetheart are the only people in this place. We don't make much money here from November to March so when he calls and wants the room I don't argue. Sometimes the money I get from him for one night covers the motel's electric bill for the entire month. I gotta a right to make a living, don't I?"

"Sure you do. Look, I understand your situation. I just want some information, that's all. Ever have any trouble with Grimaldi or the women he brings down here?"

From the expression that creased the guy's face, he could tell there had been a few incidents. "Once in a while one of his girl'll have second thoughts after spending the night with him. When that happens she'll come down here to the office and ask me or my wife to call her a cab. Who knows, could be Richie's gotten a little weird with them. I don't ask. Maybe they thought their night with him was gonna be all fun and games until it wasn't."

"Have you ever had to call the police?"

46

The guy shook his head emphatically. "No, never. Not because of Richie anyway. Other customers, yeah. You know, things happen here like fights, property damage, people drinking too much and making too much noise. That mostly happens in the summertime. But we've never had any problems with Grimaldi. If some girl he's brought here wants to get a cab home, we call her a cab. Most times Richie takes them home himself without a fuss. He might be your idea of a cad, but from what I've seen he's always been on the up and up with the girls he brings here. They know what his intentions are before they go into that room. If they don't like it, that's their problem. The way I see it if they get upset they shouldn't've come down here with him in the first place."

"That's real neighborly of you."

"Hey, pal, this is a motel. People come here to spend the night and hopefully have sex. Even married couples like to have sex in motels. We don't run prostitutes out of here or let in any deadbeats. Things can get a little wild sometimes, especially in the summer. People like to throw loud parties in their rooms. But Richie Grimaldi isn't like that. Far as I can tell, he's a real gentleman with the girls he brings here. Why should I care if they're married to some other guy? Their husbands aren't paying for the room, Richie is."

"Ever have an irate husband come down here looking for his wife?"

He shook his head. "Not for anybody who's been with Richie. He's very discreet about bringing them here. I suppose when they get home some of these girls are too ashamed of what they did to tell their husbands where they did it."

"Okay, so what about last Saturday? How come you rented a room to Grimaldi if you're closed for the season?"

The Anchor Inn owner smiled. "We're not closed. I just said that to get you out of my hair. The motel's open all year round. That's one of our selling points."

"And last Saturday?"

"Typical visit from Grimaldi. He came by around five, paid his bill, in cash as always, got the key for number six and went to the room. Had a nice looking girl with him this time. Long black curly hair and a nice figure.

47

Made me a little jealous. Some of the girls he brings here I wouldn't touch with a ten-foot pole. This one was pretty attractive – and young." Doherty gave the proprietor a once over and decided most of Grimaldi's dates probably wouldn't touch him with a similar length pole.

"Then what happened?"

"Like I said, they checked in around five. Stayed in the room for, I don't know, forty-five minutes, maybe an hour. They were the only customers in the motel so I kept an eye on them. About six or so they drove off, heading back toward the pier. I figured he was taking this honey to the Greene Inn. I happen to know he always takes the good-looking ones there. The others he takes to some less fancy place."

"When did they get back?"

The guy screwed up his face in thought. "Maybe around ten, ten thirty. No later, 'cause I was up watching TV and there was still stuff on. Now that I think of it, I was watching *Gunsmoke*; it's my favorite show. The wife had already gone back to the room. Me, I like to stay up late."

"What time did you knock off?"

"I dunno, say around eleven, eleven-thirty."

"Did you sleep through the night or did something wake you up?"

"A few hours later the wife poked me, said she thought she saw lights out in the lot. That's not unusual. People drive down to Scarborough and turn around in our lot all the time. Teenagers like to use the back lot to make out in. But this was late. Around two in the morning."

"Did you get up?"

"Yeah, I looked out the window but it was hard to see 'cause it was all steamed up from the cold. Although I couldn't really see anything I was pretty sure I heard a car. I put on my robe and went outside to see what was up. By then all I saw of the car were its taillights. It was heading back down toward the beach."

"No idea what kind of car it was?"

"Not really. Like I said the only thing I saw were the taillights. They were the kind that had two round lights and a single vertical light above them. That's all I could see."

"What happened in the morning?"

48

"Grimaldi came into the office all upset. He always pays in advance so I only see him when he checks in. Otherwise he leaves the key and an extra buck in the room for housecleaning. On Sunday he came in here asking if my wife or I had seen the girl leave. Wanted to know if she came to the office to have us call her a cab. Then he asked if anybody came to pick her up. All I could tell him was about the car I seen leaving the lot in the middle of the night. Then he wanted to know if there was a pay phone nearby she might've used. I told him there was one over by the pavilion near the beach. I don't know if that one still works this time of year. It's a long walk over there from here, especially in the cold."

"How did Grimaldi seem when he came to the office?"

"He was really upset. Most of the time Richie's a cool operator. This time he was hot under the collar. I figured he was pissed off because this nice looking girl ran out on him. Truthfully, mister, I didn't feel all that sorry for him."

As Doherty turned to leave the guy asked, "Am I gonna have any trouble with the cops on account of this girl taking off?"

"I don't know yet. As of now no one's reported her missing. If someone does then I'm sure the North Kingston police won't have any trouble tracing her whereabouts that night back here. It sounds like this might be the last place she was seen."

"What should I tell them? Should I tell them you were here?"

"Sure. That's not a problem for me. You can tell them the same thing you told me. Although I'd leave out the ten bucks if I were you. They might want to confiscate it as evidence."

"What about Grimaldi? What should I do if he shows up here with another girl?"

"That's between you and him. I wouldn't worry too much about protecting Grimaldi. He's a big boy."

Doherty thanked the proprietor, whose name he'd never even inquired. He understood that aside from the taillights on the car pulling out of the motel lot, he didn't have anything new to go on. The only real knowledge he'd picked up at the Anchor Inn was about the kind of arrangement Richie Grimaldi had with the management.

Chapter Seven

Doherty did take that walk on Scarborough Beach despite the chilly temperature. Before heading out he took an old watch cap from the trunk of his car and pulled it down over his ears. Otherwise his woolen coat and gloves would have to suffice against the cold. Before hitting the sand he checked out the snack bar and bathhouse at the pavilion; both were locked up tighter than a drum. There was an open-air pay phone not far from the shuttered snack counter. The cord that connected the handset to the phone box had been snapped. No doubt the result of vandalism.

The water crashing onto the beach was pretty rough, which was not surprising given the latest storm that had tracked out to sea the day before. He hunched his shoulders and walked the distance from the main public beach down to the area where Olivio's operated in the summer. It was slow going as he was buffeted by a strong wind the whole time. The picnic tables at Olivio's that sat out on the sand during the summer months were all stacked up atop one another behind the restaurant, lashed down with ropes. Everything along Scarborough Beach looked stark, in contrast to the crowded merriment he remembered here during the summer. Nevertheless, walking on the beach brought back many fond memories of simpler times when his only concern was not to sleep too late on Monday morning after a late Sunday night down by the ocean. If he showed up late for his shift at Quonset they would dock his pay.

He'd hated the work there, though he enjoyed the camaraderie he had with the fellows in his department. When he first worked at the Point before going into the army it felt like a dead end job. After he was discharged and got rehired, he didn't mind the monotony of his tasks knowing that he, along with some of the other guys, were lucky to be alive given what they'd experienced in the war.

His time in combat had been terrifying as well as exciting at times. Working on the line at Quonset afterwards seemed like small potatoes by comparison. It wasn't long before he jumped at the opportunity to latch on with the police force in West Warwick. He thought being a cop would bring back some of the exhilaration he'd experienced in the army. The guys he worked with at Quonset said he was nuts to give up such a sweet deal working for the government. A lot of them had married since coming home and begun to raise families. He understood their desire for the security jobs at Quonset provided. Ironically, many of those jobs would disappear in time once the military no longer needed the products made there. The Cold War had changed America's plans for military preparedness. Now it was all about building atomic weapons and missiles.

In time working for the West Warwick police turned out to be just as unsatisfying as his job at Quonset. He might've blamed restlessness for leaving the police force after only three years on the job except that the cops were always in the hip pocket of the DeCenza political machine that ran everything in the little mill town. Being a gofer for Judge Martin DeCenza and his crew of flunkies was not what Doherty had in mind when he went onto the force. His unwillingness to do *extra duties* at the behest of the machine made him a persona non grata among many of his fellow cops. When Gus Timilty, his supervisor and friend, left the force it was a sure sign to Doherty it was time for him to move on as well. He knew his relationship with Gus along with his reluctance to play ball with the machine froze him out of future promotions. On such shifting ground Doherty and Associates Investigations Agency was born.

All of these thoughts were rolling around in his head as he slowly made his way back to the parking lot. For now he had to focus his attention on the

51

missing girl, Adrian Colardo, and what happened to her this past Saturday night. It was nearly five by the time Doherty pulled into Narragansett. He parked the Chevy along the seawall and walked across the road to the Greene Inn. The building stood four stories tall and was easily the largest on the coastal side of the town. It was a pretty impressive stone structure with a good sized lawn and an outdoor patio that faced the seawall and the ocean beyond it. Of course, the patio was now closed for the season like a lot of other places along the pier. The main entrance to the inn was on a side street away from the ocean winds.

Inside the first thing he noticed was the large check-in desk that faced the front door and spanned half the width of the lobby. To the left was a sign signaling the direction to the lounge. Beyond that was another indicating the way to the grillroom. He could see the dining area through a glass partition. Only a few of the large round tables and smaller square ones were set up for dinner. Beige tablecloths covered them along with matching napkins folded into small tents at each place setting. It looked like a pretty classy joint compared to most of the places where Doherty chowed down.

After perusing the dining room he ducked into the lounge. It was darkly lit, made darker by the wood framing that characterized the whole room. The decorations were intended to give it the look of an English pub, or at least what Doherty thought an English pub looked like from pictures he'd seen. There were a number of small tables scattered about with large glass ashtrays atop them. At the far end was an oak bar with only one couple sitting among its dozen empty stools. A bald man wearing a checkered vest, sleeve garters and a bow tie stood behind the bar wiping down a wine glass. Doherty took a seat within talking distance. The tender immediately set a cardboard drink coaster with the Greene Inn image on it in front of him.

"What can I get you?" he asked without ceremony.

"How about a Jameson straight up."

"You got it." The barkeep turned to the shelves of bottles, which held many more selections than Doherty was used to seeing in any of the taverns in West Warwick. The guy pulled down a bottle of Jameson with one of those metal pour spouts tucked into its mouth. After placing a cocktail glass in front of Doherty he filled it halfway with a healthy pour of the Irish whiskey.

"I suspect you'll need this. It must be pretty cold out there. I hear we might get another storm tonight or tomorrow." In Doherty's experience talking about the weather in Rhode Island often filled a lot of conversation space.

"I'll say. I just took a walk on the beach and nearly froze my keister off."

The barman laughed. "Not exactly beach weather is it? You should come back in the summer. This room and the outdoor patio are crammed to the gills with people. It's quite the happy scene here during those months, and good money for someone in my position. Are you from around here or just passing through?"

"I live up in West Warwick. I used to come down this way a lot when I was younger - mostly over to Scarborough. My friends and I would swing into Narragansett for food and drinks. I remember what it was like around here in the warm weather. Strange that I never came into this place."

The bartender smiled. "Not so strange. Your budget probably couldn't have afforded the inn back then. We don't get too many young people in here, unless it's some girl on the arm of her sugar daddy. The Greene Inn tends to attract an older crowd. People with enough money that they don't have to worry about the tab they run up."

Doherty sipped his drink and waited while the barman ambled down to the couple at the far end. Each of them ordered another round. The man was drinking some brown liquor on ice in a highball glass while the woman was working on something greenish in a large martini style glass.

When the bartender returned Doherty asked, "What's that green thing she's drinking down there?"

The barman smiled. "It's called a Grasshopper: Crème de Mint, Crème de Cocoa and light cream on crushed ice. Sounds pretty disgusting," he said in a lowered voice. "They're very popular among the ladies nowadays."

It was time for Doherty to make his pitch. "I was wondering if you could help me," he said as an opener. "I'm a private investigator and I've been hired to find a girl that's missing. I have good reason to believe she was in here last Saturday night with this guy," he added while sliding the photo of Grimaldi across the bar for the tender to see.

By the expression on the guy's face Doherty knew right away that he recognized Grimaldi. The man shook his head but without conviction. "I don't want any trouble," he said.

"I'm not here to make trouble. All I need to know is if this guy was in here last Saturday night with an attractive young woman – dark curly hair, nice figure," he said, repeating the description the guy at the Anchor Inn had given him. He could've also flashed the picture of Adrian with her husband, but didn't want to bring Nick Colardo into the conversation unless he had to.

The barman stood frozen, nervously wiping down another wine glass that was already sparkling to begin with. Doherty extracted a ten spot from his quickly diminishing roll of bills and placed it on the bar.

"Perhaps this'll jog your memory."

The man put down the newly polished glass and promptly disappeared the money into a pocket in his vest. He took a glance around the room as he did so, checking to see if anyone saw him cuff the bill.

Once the transaction was completed he leaned across the wood top and said quietly, "That guy comes in here all the time. He's easy enough to spot because he's only here in the off-season when we're not very busy. And he always has a different woman with him. Most of them are pretty nice looking too," he tacked on with a hint of resentment in his voice.

"What about last Saturday?"

"Yes, he was here with a woman like the one you just described. I could hear him working his charms on her. The whole time the girl seemed kind of uncomfortable, like maybe she hadn't spent much time in a cocktail lounge as nice as this one."

"What did they drink?"

The tender paused a few seconds trying to recall what his customers had consumed that night. "The guy had some kind of whiskey. It was either Bourbon or Scotch. I don't remember exactly. Those are his usual drinks. The girl didn't know what to have so he ordered a Whiskey Sour for her. He even asked me to be sure to put a maraschino cherry in her glass. I thought that was kind of strange; it was like he was ordering a drink for his daughter. This one did seem a little young compared to most of his other companions."

"Is that all that happened here in the lounge?"

"After a while he ordered another drink for himself. Now that I think of it, he wasn't drinking Bourbon that night; it was Scotch, Dewars or Cutty Sark, one of the good Scotches. The girl barely touched her Whiskey Sour. When she did she made a face that told me she probably wasn't used to drinking hard liquor. All she did was nibble on the maraschino cherry. He kept trying to encourage her to drink but she didn't. I thought he was being a little too insistent with her. I was tempted to tell him to leave her be, but you can't do that in this business, especially with a guy who comes in on a regular basis. There've been nights when he and his latest girlfriend were just about the only people in the lounge."

"What about on Saturday night. Were there any other customers in here around the time they were?"

"Yes, I think there were a few people here. There were a couple of businessmen talking about some real estate deal they were doing somewhere in South County. And those two were here," he said nodding in the direction of the couple at the end of the bar. "They're here almost every night. Big drinkers. Big tippers too so I can't complain. There might've been a few other people, but I can't remember if they were here at the same time as your couple. The guy in this picture paid their bill and they left around seven-thirty. I believe he and the girl went into the grillroom because shortly afterwards one of the waiters came in here asking for another Scotch and a glass of wine. I didn't see them after that so I don't know what time they left the inn."

"This is a tough question, but I got ask you: Is there anyway somebody could've slipped something into their drinks; you know, knockout drops or a Mickey Finn of some kind?"

The bartender took a minute to think of a response. "I don't see how. I was the only one who fixed their drinks and brought them to their table when they were in here or when they were in the grillroom. I wouldn't be surprised if that guy slipped something into his girlfriend's drink. He was awfully anxious to get her liquored up. Maybe he thought he wouldn't get to first base unless she let her guard down. Like I said, this guy's been in here fairly often with a lot of different women. Most of them drink a lot more than this latest one did. I have to believe he's looking for something more than having drinks and a nice dinner with them. What's his deal anyway?"

Doherty pondered how much he would share with a bartender who'd been so forthcoming with him. "His deal is that he preys upon unhappily married women. He takes them down to Narragansett for a nice dinner, some drinks and a quick screw in a motel not too far from here. He makes other promises that he never keeps. In the end he usually just delivers them back to their husbands and their tired little lives the next day."

"Sounds like a crooked character."

"I guess, but it's not like he's breaking any laws. These women are old enough to know what they're getting themselves into, even while he's doing his best to charm the pants off them."

"Should I do or say anything if he comes back with some other girl on his arm?"

"I wouldn't if I were you. Though it would help if you'd give me a call if he does. Here's my number," Doherty said as he fished one of his business cards out of his wallet. "By the way, how's the food in the grillroom?"

"Aside from being overpriced, it's pretty good. If it was summer I'd suggest the fish. Unfortunately, what they have this time of year is usually trucked in from Boston so it's not all that fresh. You can't go wrong with the meat dishes."

"Thanks, nice talking to you," Doherty paused as he extended his hand across the bar.

"Name's Roger Willis. I'm here most nights if you need any more help. And your generous tip is much appreciated," he said as he patted the vest pocket where the ten spot had disappeared.

Doherty settled his tab and left an extra couple of bucks for the man's time. He then took himself into the grillroom with one new thought dangling in his mind. What if Grimaldi had slipped the girl a mickey just so he could guarantee getting her into bed. Was he that much of a lowlife that he'd screw a girl while she was out cold? Maybe the cost of dinner would be a good indicator.

The grillroom was nearly as empty as the lounge. When Doherty checked the prices on the menu he could see why. After seating himself a waiter came by to ask if he'd like something to drink. He briefly considered having another Jameson then remembered he still had to drive back to West Warwick. He opted for a bottle of 'Gansett instead. A few minutes later his server returned and carefully poured the beer down the side of a tilted pilsner glass so as to not leave a head.

"Can I help you with anything on the menu?"

He took this opportunity to size up the waiter. He was heavyset but not fat. Looked like he was somewhere in his early thirties with dark hair that was swept across his scalp in an Ivy League style. He had a pleasant if servile smile plastered across his face.

"I was wondering if I could ask you a few questions?"

"If it's about the menu I should tell you right away that we don't have any specials tonight nor do we have the broiled scrod."

He looked up at the waiter and smiled. Pulling out his wallet he flashed the guy his license and said, "I'm a private investigator. I'm curious as to whether you were working here in the grillroom last Saturday night?"

Still smiling, the waiter answered. "Yes, I was. I worked the entire weekend, such as it was. After the snowstorm we hardly had any diners until Sunday night. Then it was mostly locals. There weren't too many travelers in town like yourself. It wasn't a very profitable weekend to say the least."

"Do you mind if I ask your name?"

Still smiling, he said, "I'm Dominic. Most everybody calls me Dom."

"You live down here?"

"I do now. I'm originally from Warwick. I lived in Florida for a few years then moved back up to Narragansett four years ago when I started working summers here at the inn. I bussed tables for a year then was promoted to the waitstaff. The manager said I had the right personality for this kind of work."

"I'm sure you do, Dom. That's why I'm hoping you can help me with this case I'm working on." It was Doherty's experience that appealing to people's vanity often got them to be more forthcoming than they should be. Nonetheless, it usually helped him figure things out with his cases.

"Why don't I first take your order, sir? Once I've put that in I'll have more time to talk. As you can see we're not exactly busy tonight."

"What do you recommend? That fellow Roger out in the lounge suggested that I stay away from the fish because it's not fresh this time of year."

"Who, Mr. Know-it-all behind the bar? He wouldn't know a fresh fish if someone hit him over the head with it. I can assure you the halibut is extremely fresh. Caught in these very waters just yesterday. However, if you're more inclined to have a meat dish there's always the steak. Personally I'd recommend the pork chops. Enrique does a terrific job with them."

Doherty assumed that Enrique was the chef. He also caught the drift that Dominic was not a big fan of the bartender. Knowing this might come in handy later on. According to the menu the chops would be accompanied by mashed potatoes and green beans julienne, whatever that meant. Doherty went along with the waiter's suggestion and ordered the pork chops.

"Your meal also comes with soup and salad."

"What kind of soup do you have?"

"You can choose between the lobster bisque or clam chowder." Doherty wasn't sure what bisque was so he opted for the chowder. The waiter quickly headed off to the kitchen to place his order. While he was gone Doherty extracted Grimaldi's photo from his coat pocket. When Dominic returned he informed Doherty that he could now talk for a few minutes.

Showing the fellow Grimaldi's mug shot Doherty asked, "Do you remember this guy being in here last Saturday night? He would've been with a good looking woman - somewhat younger than him."

Dominic nodded his head. "Oh, yes, I remember them well. He's been in here quite a few times since I started working the grillroom. Almost always with a different woman. Most of them are older than the one he was with the other night. She looked young enough to be his daughter." This was the second reference an employee at the inn had made to the disparity in ages between Grimaldi and Adrian Colardo.

"What else do you recall about them?"

"Well, he ordered the steak, rare like he always does. Most of the time he doesn't even look at the menu. This time he did because he ordered everything for his date. I believe she had either the flounder or the halibut."

"Did they order anything else?"

"They both brought drinks in from the bar. He was drinking Scotch and ordered another one to go with his meal. She was nursing some kind of light colored mixed drink that she barely touched. I'm sure Roger could tell you what it was. When the food came she asked for a glass of Mateus with her dinner. She didn't drink much of that either. Later she ordered a Coca Cola."

"The next thing I've got to ask you might be a little touchy. Is there any way someone could've slipped a drug of some kind into their food or drinks?"

This question caused the waiter to take a step backwards. "Well I certainly didn't. And I doubt very much Enrique would have. He's from France you know," he added as if this explained everything. "I'm sure he wouldn't want to get into any trouble that would cause him to have to return there."

Doherty'd been in France at the tail end of the war. People there were desperate and hungry at that time. He wondered if this was the reason the chef Enrique had emigrated to the U.S.

"What about the drinks?"

"Except for the coffee your man had with dessert, all the drinks would have come directly from the bar. I assume you've already spoken with Roger about the couple."

"Yeah, I have. What can you tell me about him?"

The waiter rolled his eyes. "We all refer to Roger as the 'captain', and believe you me it's not meant as a compliment. He's been here longer than any of the current staff - and acts like he practically owns the place."

Dominic leaned down so he could speak to Doherty in confidence. "If we don't give him some of our tip money, he has a way of being slow with our drink orders. And the diners don't like it if their drinks don't come when their food does, or beforehand. When their drinks are tardy, the customers blame the waiters even when the problem is with the bar. If we don't please Roger then it's us who end up having our tips shorted."

"I guess that means there's no love lost between the grillroom and the lounge?"

"That would be an understatement, to say the least."

Dominic turned toward the kitchen. "I should get you your soup and salad. I'm sure they're up by now."

"One final question before you go: Would all the drinks come from the bar, even the girl's Coca Cola?"

"Everything but the coffee the man ordered with their dessert. The coffee comes from an urn in the kitchen. They shared the strawberry shortcake for dessert. As I recall it was the only thing the girl ate with any enthusiasm."

"You've got an awfully good memory."

"Like I said, there weren't many customers in here this past weekend. They kind of stuck out."

For the most part the meal at the Greene Inn was excellent. In checking the menu listings Doherty saw even before ordering that everything was way above his usual price line. The chops were very tender, though they were covered in some kind of sweet brandy sauce that after one bite he scraped off before diving into the rest of the pork. Even the mash potatoes tasted exceptionally good. He discovered that julienne meant that the string beans were cut into long thin strips rather than served whole.

The check was steep but Doherty figured he would bill it off on Grimaldi as well as the sawbucks he'd slipped the guy at the motel and in the bar to pry information out of them. In the end he assumed his client would be grateful if his inquiries kept him out of jail.

Before leaving the grillroom Doherty asked for a cup of coffee to fortify him for the trip back to town. Dominic kept returning to his table, obviously intrigued with the idea of helping out a real live private detective work a case. Doherty did his best to maintain a level of amiability in the event that he'd have to get back to the waiter. He was inclined to trust him more than the bartender. Maybe it was because he didn't have to slip him a ten spot for information. Instead he left him a generous tip along with one of his business cards in case Dominic thought of something else that might be of use.

Chapter Eight

It had been nearly a week since Adrian Colardo had disappeared from the Anchor Inn and Doherty was no closer to finding the missing girl than he was when Grimaldi burst into his office last Monday. Rolling into work a little after ten he found Agnes sitting at her desk doodling with a pencil on a blank piece of paper.

"There's a message on your answerin' machine," she said by way of a greeting.

"Who's it from?"

"Gus Timilty."

"Did you listen to it?"

"Yeah, but it's kinda long. I think you better take some notes when you play it."

He slipped into the back office and propped his feet atop his desk in their usual spot. This particular section of the desk was getting well worn from the heels of his cordovans. He saw the red light blinking on the answering machine. Instead of playing the message he sparked up a Camel and took a half dozen puffs. There was something about continuing to do business with Gus that stuck in Doherty's craw, even if his old friend was only trying to help him with the case. The killings at the shipyard that fateful night had put a damper on his relationship with his old pal. Doherty wasn't sure it would ever be the same again.

He hit the play button and Gus' jocular voice came out of the squawk box.

"My guy down at city hall did a very thorough search for you on that Adrian Colardo girl. Like I promised, he got you more info on her than you're ever gonna need. Anyway here goes: She and Nicholas Colardo were married on June 16, 1956 at St. Bartholomew's Church on Laurel Avenue in the Silver Lake section of Providence. I can tell you who the best man and maid of honor were, though I got a hunch you won't care a whole lot about that. Adrian's maiden name was Nazzaro and prior to her marriage she lived with her parents, Gaetano and Nathalia. Father is Italian and commonly goes by the name of Gus, just like yours truly. He's 58 years old and works at Brown and Sharpe. Mother is Portuguese and is a housewife and always has been. Adrian, full name Adriana Cecilia Nazarro, was born at Lying-In Hospital on May 5, 1935. She's the youngest of three children born to Gus and Nathalia.

Family originally resided at 357 Ferris Avenue in East Providence when Adriana was born. Shortly afterwards the Nazzaros moved to 290 Merino Street, where they now live, in the Silver Lake section of Providence. By my calculation that's less than a mile from 215 Priscilla Avenue, where the daughter resides with her husband Nicholas and their son, Thomas. Boy was born on July 27, 1957; that makes him about two and a half. The Nazzaros have another daughter named Luiza, age 28, married and presently living with her husband and two kids in Bridgeport, Connecticut. She also has a brother, Gaetano Jr., generally known as Gussie, age 25. He's single and lives in New York City. Both Nick Colardo and Adrian Nazzaro graduated from Mt. Pleasant High School in Providence, he in '51, she in '53. There is no record of either attending any college, junior college, business, trade or secretarial schools afterwards.

"I told you my guy was thorough. I have a whole lot more that I can mail to you or you can pick it up here at the office. Give me a buzz to let me know what your preference is."

Gus rang off saying nothing more than, "I hope this helps you out, pally." Doherty played the recording over twice more, taking notes each time on the information he thought might be pertinent to the case. When he stepped through the door to the outer office Agnes gave him an expectant look.

"Did you get what you needed, boss?"

"I think so. Enough for now anyway. Can you do me a favor? Will you ring up Briggs and Timilty and request that Gus mail the rest of the material over to us."

His secretary gave him a wry look. "Don't you want to talk to him yourself?"

"No," was all he said before retreating back into his office.

A few minutes later he heard Agnes on the horn to Briggs and Timilty. He could tell she sensed that things weren't right between him and Gus. Under normal circumstances she would be his main confidant. But these weren't normal circumstances and he certainly didn't want to pass on to her any gory details about what happened that night at the shipyard or how it was affecting his relationship with Gus. Agnes had a high opinion of Timilty and he didn't want to spoil it by telling her how he'd murdered two men practically in cold blood. Although the events leading up to that confrontation may have made the shootings necessary, they were still killings.

Instead of spending more time chewing over that night, he took out his street map of the capital city and located Merino Street in Providence. It ran through the heart of Silver Lake from Hartford Avenue to Laurel Hill Avenue. As Gus had indicated it was a stone's throw from Priscilla Ave, where Doherty had staked out Adrian's husband Nick. It was time to have a serious conversation with the missing girl's parents; a conversation that no one was going feel good about when it was over.

That evening he drove up Hartford Avenue for the third time in less than a week. He'd purposely waited until the supper hour to be sure to catch both parents at home. Doherty was becoming all too familiar with the Italian grocery stores, restaurants, dress shops, social clubs and Catholic schools that dotted the Silver Lake neighborhood. Finding Merino Street was no problem. It was a left off Hartford. He parked the Chevy in front of the Nazzaro house, checking out the environs as he did. Through a narrow opening between theirs and the neighboring homes he could see that they backed up against a playground attached to what he presumed was an elementary school. Since it was dark and the dead of winter, there were no kids at play in the yard.

The street was a step up from the one that the Colardos lived on, but not by much. It was typical of many residential neighborhoods in Providence, where houses sat on plots of land not much bigger than the buildings themselves. The Nazarros' place was set back slightly from the street nestled close beside its neighbors on either side. The ancient Hudson was parked at the end of a short driveway beside the house. Perhaps Adrian's father had left it there on purpose anticipating the next snowstorm. That way an elderly man like Gaetano Nazzaro would have less to shovel when the expected storm hit the city.

The house itself was painted a light blue with white trim. It was simple and neatly appointed. A small screened-in porch separated the front door from the short path that ran up to it from the sidewalk. Doherty rang the outside bell and waited patiently. In time a sawed-off man with gray hair combed straight back over his head came out of the front door to the screen. He was wearing a brown shirt left open enough for his sleeveless undershirt to be seen underneath. The name 'Gus' was stitched across the shirt pocket. He was holding a copy of the evening *Bulletin* in his hands. He did not open the screen door. Instead he looked suspiciously at Doherty.

"Can I help you? If you selling something we no wanna buy," was the next thing out of his mouth. He spoke with a noticeable Italian accent. Doherty figured Gaetano, better known as Gus, was probably born over in the old country.

"Are you, Mr. Nazzaro?"

"Yah."

"My name is Doherty," he said holding his license up to the screen for the man to see. "I'm a private investigator. I wonder if I could come in and talk to you for a few minutes about your daughter Adrian?"

"Adriana? Is Adriana in some kinda trouble?"

"I don't know. Maybe. If I could come in..."

At that point a woman appeared from what Doherty assumed was the kitchen wiping her hands on an apron tied around her waist. She was even shorter than her husband and wide enough to qualify as squat. Her hair was in a neat perm colored black, no doubt to hide the gray.

"Quem e este humem, Gus?"

Doherty didn't understand what she was saying. He only got the Gus part that came out sounding like *Goose*. A not unpleasant smell of cooking fish wafted out from the kitchen.

"El quer falar sobre Adriana."

The man with the newspaper turned back to Doherty. "You'll have to excuse my wife. She don't speak English so good. She's more comfortable with Portuguese when she feeling suspicious. I will make her speak in English. The two men stared at each other for a few awkward moments until Gus Nazzaro unlatched the screen door and invited Doherty in.

He was offered a seat in a winged back chair in the small living room. "Natty, traga um pouco de café por favor," the man said to his wife. Then he turned his attention back to Doherty. "I don't speak so good Portuguese, only enough to make her understand. I speak very good Italian but my wife, she no good with my language. So we talk a mixture; sometimes Italian, sometimes Portuguese and most times English. It can be very confusing for our grandson."

"Is that the boy, Tommy, Adrian's son?"

The man gave Doherty a distrustful look. "Yah, he stay with us for a little time. What you want to say about our Adriana?"

"How about if we wait until your wife comes in?" As if on cue the stout woman appeared carrying a tray with small, espresso size cups of dark coffee. A bowl of sugar sat by the cups; both men took their coffee black. The wife sat uncomfortably on the edge of a print sofa without a drink of her own.

"I have reason to believe your daughter is missing. I've been hired to find her. As of now I have no cause to think she's in any kind of trouble."

"I don't understand," the father said shaking his head. "Nicholas say she go off with some man. Leave him and their boy alone. He say we should take Tomas because he is not safe with Adriana; that she is actin' like a crazy person."

"That one," the wife said making a dismissive gesture with her hand under her chin in reference to her son-in-law.

"I have reason to believe Adrian's husband Nick was abusing her. She may have run off because she was afraid of him. She told a friend that once she was gone Nick would call you to take the boy because he wouldn't want to take care of his son by himself. Is that what he did?"

"I say to her no marry that Nicholas," the wife chimed in. "I could tell he was no good first time he come here." She then added something in Portuguese that her husband didn't bother to translate.

"Why you think she missing?" the father asked.

"Because she left the man she ran off with. She thought he could keep her safe, but he wasn't able to." Doherty was trying to keep things simple. He wasn't sure how he could explain to these fine people Grimaldi's connection with their daughter without sullying her reputation.

The father said, "Adriana was always good girl, but sometimes she like the bad boys. We try to tell her but she no listen. When she tell us she wants to marry Nicholas Colardo, I say he no good for you. But she no listen to us. She asks us to make big wedding like Luiza's. We pay money for it from our savings. I no like wasting our money for her to marry that boy, but she is our daughter. What could we do?"

"Can you think of anyone Adrian would turn to if she was in trouble?"

"I dunno. Her sister Luiza maybe, but she now live in Connecticut. We don't know any of her friends since she moved to Priscilla Avenue with Nicholas." He appealed to his wife but she could offer little more than a shrug. "You talk wid him? Maybe he know where she is."

"No, I haven't had a chance to speak with her husband yet." Doherty paused here afraid of how the couple would take what he was about to say next. "I need to tell you something you're not going to like. I've recently been following your son-in-law and I've seen him with another woman - a girl really. She's only a teenager."

"I know that boy no good," the wife said again. "I curse the day she marry him."

"Now for the tough question: Do you know anyone who'd want to harm Adrian?" The wife looked confused so her husband explained to her in Portuguese. As soon as his words were out his mouth her hands flew up to her

66

face.

The father shook his head. "Everbody like Adriana - always. What about this man she run off with? Maybe he hurt her."

"I'm looking into him. Right now I'd advise you to contact the Providence police and report your daughter missing. They may give you a hard time because she went away with another man. But you must insist that they let you file a missing persons report no matter what they say. If you do eventually they will have to investigate Nick *and* the other man. That way if anything has happened to Adrian the police will be forced to act on it. I don't mean to scare you, but your daughter has been gone for almost a week and no one has seen her."

Both of the Nazarros looked like they were in a state of shock. Doherty handed the father one of his business cards and suggested he call him if they needed any further help. He left a thoroughly disheartened couple when he exited their home.

Chapter Nine

When Doherty came into the office the next morning he was surprised to find Agnes sitting at her desk working on her nails. She looked up and said, "You got a call this morning about a half hour ago. From some guy named Ferullo."

"Doesn't ring a bell. Did he leave a message?"

The secretary shook her head. "Said he needed to talk to you personally. I told him to call back sometime after ten."

Without exchanging any more words, Doherty poured a cup of coffee from the coffee machine on the shelf beside Agnes' desk and went into his back office. A few minutes later she came in and took the liberty of sitting in his client chair.

"I came in today 'cause I'm tired of you keepin' me in the dark. Are you gonna to tell me what's goin' on or am I suppose to sit out there twiddlin' my thumbs every day?'

"You could work on your nails some more."

"Very funny."

Doherty suggested that Agnes grab a cup of coffee for herself before they started to chat. When she returned he asked, "What do you want to know?"

"Well, first of all, what's this case you're workin' on that has you runnin' around so much? You've hardly been in the office and you haven't left me any notes to type up in over a week. The least you can do is tell me what you're up to."

Doherty sat back in his chair and took a moment to gather his thoughts. He trusted Agnes implicitly, but occasionally kept her in the dark on some of his investigations in case the police got involved. It was his way of protecting her since he didn't know if she'd be covered by client confidentiality as he was. Or at least as he always claimed he was when confronted by the cops.

"Do you remember the Carney case from last year?"

"Which one was that?"

"It wasn't much. I spent a night down in Narragansett trying to rescue a woman who'd run off with a guy who fancies himself as a *professional gigolo*. He was the one who preyed on unhappily married women."

"Oh, yeah. I remember. The husband came in here a couple of times. He wasn't much to write home about as I recall. A slob of a guy who'd been takin' his wife for granted." That certainly was an apt description of Leo Carney.

"Yeah, that's the one. Well, it turns out the harried guy who came in here Monday morning when you had Justin with you - he's the gigolo. He was looking to hire me. Seems as though another woman he was running around with disappeared last Saturday night from a motel they were shacking up in down near Scarborough Beach. The same motel I rescued the Carney woman at. This new girl's been gone a week and nobody's seen her. I didn't want to tell you I took him on as a client because I wasn't sure you'd approve."

"Let me get this straight. The gigolo the Carney woman ran off with is now your client. Well. I wouldn't approve of his actions, except..." Agnes hesitated here.

"Except what?'

"Business is business. And it's not like we've had a lot of action lately here at Doherty and Associates."

"So, it's okay with you that I'm now working for this guy?"

Agnes smirked. "It's okay by me if it means I get paid this week. It's not like you're helpin' him find a new woman he can take advantage of. How did he decide to come to us?"

"I don't know. All he told me was he asked around and found out I was good at locating missing people. He didn't put me together with Marilyn Carney until I reminded him we'd met before and what the circumstances were. That didn't seem to bother him. I docked him a hundred bucks right off the top for good measure."

"Well played, boss. I'm not surprised you took him on. You're a sucker for flattery. Does that mean you don't mind workin' for this creep?"

"Hey, Agnes, we've worked for worse people. As of now I feel like my real job is finding this missing girl. Hopefully I can do so before something bad happens to her. Unless it already has."

A look of genuine concern crossed Agnes' face. "Do you think maybe your client had somethin' to do with this girl disappearin'?"

"I don't know. I'm not ruling him out. Though I find it hard to believe he'd fork over a C-note to find a girl he disappeared himself. To my way of thinking the only reason he'd do something like that is if he planned to use me as cover. But that doesn't sound like his kind of game. He already admitted to me he doesn't always get to first base with the women he picks up. Yet, he is more than willing to play those odds."

"Sounds like a real sensitive guy."

Agnes was trying to put what he was telling her into some intelligible order. "Do you have any other leads?"

"Except for the guy who hired me, the only other person I'm looking at right now is the girl's husband. Since his wife's gone missing I've already caught him cheating on her with a younger replacement - a girl not even out of her teens. Aside from that I also visited with the missing girl's parents last night. They didn't know she was in the wind because the son-in-law told them she'd run off with some other guy, which she had. I strongly suggested they contact the Providence police and report her as a missing person. I don't know how seriously the cops'll take her case, but at least something will be on the record."

Agnes gave her boss a level stare. "There's somethin' else I gotta ask you about. What's goin' on between you and Gus? You don't seem very friendly toward him when he calls."

This was a tough one. He knew Agnes was aware of their longstanding friendship and had great respect for Gus Timilty. He didn't want to say anything that would diminish her regard for Gus, nor did he want her to know about what his old friend had done to get his kidnapped daughter back. As much as he disliked doing so, he felt compelled to keep Agnes in the dark about how that case was resolved.

"For the time being let's just say it's complicated. Maybe he and I can get back on an even keel sometime in the future. But not right now."

Agnes was perplexed by his weak explanation, yet wise enough not to pursue it with further questioning. A ringing phone alleviated the awkwardness in the room. Agnes picked up the headset from the phone on Doherty's desk and answered, "Doherty and Associates." A few seconds later she said, "Just a minute," and handed the phone to her boss.

"Doherty here."

"Hello, Mr. Doherty, this is Dominic Ferullo. I called earlier but you weren't in. I'm the waiter from the Greene Inn. We talked the other night."

"Oh yes, Dominic, I remember. To what do I owe this call?"

"Well, you were asking about a girl that was in here on Saturday night with Mr. Grimaldi. You said she was missing."

"Yes."

"I don't know if this is related, but a rumor is going around Narragansett that the police pulled a dead girl's body out of the water by the rocks between here and Scarborough. I don't know when this happened or if this is the girl you were looking for. Just in case it turns out to be her I thought I'd give you a call."

"Where did you get this news from?"

"Somebody was in the bar and they told Roger. He likes to be Mr. know-it-all so he made a big deal about spreading the news among the staff. That's about all I can tell you right now."

"Dominic, I appreciate you calling me. Let's hope this girl doesn't turn out to be the one I'm looking for. Give me a ring if you hear anything else."

After Doherty hung up he thought about how Roger the bartender hadn't called him even though he'd given him his card as well as ten bucks. He figured the barkeep wasn't interested in passing on any info unless more green was being offered in return.

Doherty waited a half-hour to consider what he'd just learned before putting through a call he didn't really want to make. Alex Klinoff was a former West Warwick cop who was on the force when Doherty first came on. He was bent like a lot of other local cops who did private work for the DeCenza machine for off-the-books payments. Klinoff had been working security for a private, high stakes poker game when two masked men with guns raided the action and took all the money. Klinoff ended up taking the fall for the robbery as Judge DeCenza had him summarily fired from the force for his failure to protect the game. Technically he was fired from the cops because he was wearing his uniform while doing private security work. No one mentioned that DeCenza's boy, Angel Tuohy, had insisted that Klinoff wear his blues while guarding the game. In the aftermath Alex lost his house, his family and his meaningful livelihood.

He later moved into the last piece of property he owned, a small cottage down in South County on Great Island. He winterized the place and now resided there alone year-round. To say he was living a humble existence would be an understatement. Last time Doherty spoke to him, Klinoff said he spent most of his nights listening to a police scanner and intervening where he wasn't wanted in preventing crime in and around North Kingston. By sucking up to the local cops he was able to continue *playing* at being a policeman.

Last fall he helped Doherty on a case involving two scam artists who were using sex films with prominent people in them to shake down those people for cash. One of the scammers was murdered in a heinous fashion near Bonnet Shores. In the aftermath Klinoff was able to use his connections with the local cops to help Doherty solve the case. However, he also tried to burrow his way into Doherty's business, which made him reluctant to keep in touch with the former cop.

The trouble was Alex Klinoff was the only connection Doherty had to law enforcement in South County. Before things went public he wanted to get some inside dope on the girl who'd been fished out of the water near Narragansett.

The phone rang six times before a groggy voice answered. Doherty identified himself right away.

"How're you doing, Alex?"

"How the hell you think I'm doin'. It's the middle of the damn winter and I haven't had no work in three months. I'm tryin' to live off the unemployment I collect, but it barely keeps me in booze."

Last summer Klinoff was making a living sandblasting and painting boats owned by rich people who kept them at a boatyard in Wickford. The job was only seasonal and a serious comedown from being a cop.

"I was wondering if you still had an in with the North Kingston police?"

"Not so much anymore."

"Why? What happened?"

"You know how I was always listenin' to the police scanner. This one night I heard about a scuffle over by the pier so I took a ride up there to see what was goin' on. There were a bunch of teenage kids havin' a rumble right outside this popular pizza shop. I waded in with my baton tryin' to break it up before the local cops got there. I guess I jacked up this one punk a little too hard. They say I broke a coupla of his ribs. Turns out the little bastard was the son of one of the Narragansett selectmen. Once the chief got wind of what I'd done he started askin' around about me and found out I was cozy with some of his cops. After that they started freezin' me out. Said I was bad news."

"What about your friend Joe? The one that helped me with the DeAngelo murder?"

"Who, Marengo? He left the force after he got accepted to the state police academy. Last I heard he was about to be sworn in as a statie. I think his relationship with me kinda put him on the chief's shit list. Besides, Marengo was too ambitious to let a guy like me drag him down. Look, Doherty, why don't you cut out all this friendship crap and tell me why you called?"

"Okay, okay. I heard the body of a girl was pulled out of the water near the rocks between Narragansett and Scarborough, maybe last night or this morning. Can you tell me anything about it?"

"Where'd you hear this from?"

"Just some guy I met at the Greene Inn the other night. I let on I was working a case concerning a missing girl down there and gave him my card.

He called me a little while ago with the news."

Klinoff laughed. "The Greene Inn, huh? You're gettin' up in the world, Doherty. You ain't gonna give me any more than that are you, dickwad?"

"You know how it is, I have to protect the confidentiality of my client."

"Yeah, yeah. You can throw as much of that happy horseshit at me as you want. Look, pal, this is one ex-cop talkin' to another. If you don't give me a little more to chew on I ain't tellin' you nothin'."

Doherty took a few moments to decide how much he would dangle in front of Klinoff to get what he needed. "The girl I'm looking for is in her mid-twenties, dark curly hair, good looking. She disappeared from a motel down there last Saturday night. Apparently she was shacking up with a guy who wasn't her husband."

"Who's the guy?"

"Sorry Alex, that's where I draw the line."

Klinoff let out a gravelly laugh. "Oh yeah, now I get it. The guy she was screwin' is your client, right?" Doherty remained silent, not wanting Klinoff to worm his way any deeper into the case.

Finally his former colleague opened up. "I don't know much yet. What I can tell you is that the girl they pulled out of the water sort of fits the description you just gave me. She was naked, beaten up and apparently strangled before bein' dumped in the ocean. I was told the cops suspect she didn't die from drownin' despite bein' in the water for some time. That's about all I know so far. There're rumors flyin' all over South County, but rumors can't give you what I can."

"I thought the local cops were freezing you out?"

"Officially they are. But you do what I been doin' for the past few years you pick up on who's crooked and who isn't. The crooked ones are the ones I can squeeze for info whenever I need it. I got enough stuff on them that they're ascared of me. Hell, I gotta do somethin' while I'm down here. I can't spend the rest of the winter sittin' in this shithole drinkin' myself to death."

"You got my number, Alex. Call me if anything else comes up you think I can use. I got a few bucks I can toss your way."

"Hey, I ain't no charity case."

"I'm not saying you are. Let's just say I'm hiring you as a paid inform-ant working for Doherty and Associates."

Chapter Ten

Immediately after getting off the phone with Klinoff, Doherty called Grimaldi at his home. As he expected, the phone rang a dozen times without anyone answering. He tried Fortunato's and Tony, the restaurant's Mr. Friendly, picked up. Before the kid could give him the third degree, Doherty identified himself and asked for Grimaldi. His client came on the phone a few seconds later.

"Richie, I need to talk with you. And I mean pronto."

"Why? What's up? Have you found Adrian?"

"I haven't but the North Kingston police might have. A girl's dead body was discovered washed up on the rocks between Scarborough and Narragansett sometime late yesterday or early this morning. That's why I need to talk with you right away in person."

"Jesus. We're kinda busy here. I don't think I can come down to your place for a coupla hours."

"Then I'll come to you. I think it would be best if we talked before the police got your name."

"The police! What would the police want with me? I haven't done anything wrong. I didn't kill anybody."

"Let's not jump the gun. We don't even know that the dead girl is Adrian. But if she is, I'm not the one you'll have to convince you're not responsible. You're my client and right now we need to plan a strategy before things go sideways. I'll drive up there and we'll talk."

Once again Doherty found himself driving the beaten path up to Federal Hill. Rather than going the long way through downtown Providence, he took another route to Atwells up the backside of the Federal Hill through Olneyville. The second predicted snowstorm hadn't materialized yet so the roads, for the most part, were completely cleared from the earlier storm. Still, the weather guys were predicting a severe northeaster for sometime in the next forty-eight hours. It set Doherty to wondering if the storm had arrived sooner would the dead girl's body have been washed out to sea and never found. Her discovery could turn out to be a very bad break for his client.

When he got to the restaurant it was closed, but Richie was standing by the door waiting for him. He was wearing a white cooking outfit and didn't look anything like the handsome gigolo who charmed the pants off so many married women. A brawny young guy he took to be young Tony from their phone conversation stood behind Richie. He gave Doherty the stink eye, which he deliberately ignored. Instead Doherty spent a moment taking in the ambience of Fortunato's Italian Cuisine. It was a relatively small place compared to the Old Canteen and some of the better-known eateries at the top of the hill. There was seating for about twenty people around a cluster of small tables topped with red and white-checkered tablecloths. Each had a basket encased Chianti bottle in its center with a candle stuck in the top. Across the room from the eating area was a small bar with eight stools abutting it. A half partition separated the bar area from where customers dined. Grimaldi seemed quite agitated, as well he should.

"Is there somewhere we can talk privately?" Doherty asked his client.

"Yeah, we can go into the storeroom. It's this way."

Grimaldi led him into a windowless space off the kitchen in the rear of the restaurant. It was lined with shelves containing large cans of tomatoes and tomato puree, as well as smaller containers of mushrooms, anchovies, roasted peppers and other condiments. Nearby stood a bench with a large pasta-making machine on it. A good-sized walk-in refrigerator that was emitting a loud groaning sound stood up against the far wall. In contrast to the chilly temperatures outside, the storeroom was hot and stuffy. The door to a small office attached to the storage area was open. He could see an old wooden desk inside covered with papers.

Grimaldi immediately knocked a cigarette out of a pack he took from his shirt pocket. His hands were shaking when he attempted to strike a match to it. It took a few attempts before he could ignite his smoke. Doherty joined him with one of his Camels.

"Okay, Richie, now listen carefully to what I've got to say. This morning the North Kingston police pulled a body out of the water near the rock flats between Narragansett and Scarborough. My source down there tells me it was a naked girl who'd been beaten up and strangled before she was tossed into the ocean. From what he passed on to me it sounds like she fits your description of Adrian Colardo. No positive identification has been made yet, at least not for public consumption. For the time being there's no reason for us to hit the panic button. Depending on her condition it could take the police a few days to identify the body. As far as I know nobody's reported your girl missing either up here or down there. To be honest with you, Richie, I'm not sure if it's a good or bad thing you didn't tell the cops last Sunday that Adrian had disappeared. But what's done is done.

"I will tell you I visited with Adrian's folks last night and strongly suggested that they file a missing persons report on her with the Providence police. I don't know if they have or not. Knowing the city cops, it could take some time before anything passes between them and the North Kingston PD, especially if they can't identify the body right away. If she was naked like I've been told, unless they find a fingerprint match it could be days before they're able to tag her. My thinking is that Adrian was probably never arrested so there's no reason her prints would be on file anywhere. That gives me time to do my own investigation - on the assumption the dead girl is indeed her."

"How can they tie her to me?" Grimaldi asked in a much weaker voice.

"Jesus, Richie, all I had to do was pass off a couple of ten spots here and there in Narragansett to get people to identify you as the guy who took Adrian to the Greene Inn and your favorite motel. You think those people are going to stonewall the cops on your behalf?"

Grimaldi pulled hard on his smoke, taking time to figure out another angle. "I'm telling you, Doherty. I didn't kill that girl. When I woke up in the morning she was gone. That's all I know."

"Right now I'm inclined to believe you. But we need to get a few things straight between us before I go any further with this case." Grimaldi nodded in agreement.

"Is there any chance *you* might've slipped something into one of her drinks either at the inn or the motel? Like maybe she was acting reluctant and you thought it would help get her into bed if her faculties weren't fully intact? You told me yourself you kept urging her to drink. The bartender at the inn has confirmed that. I mean you'd already doled out a lot of money on a good meal and the motel room. It makes sense you'd want to get rewarded for your expenses. Whatever you do, Richie, don't bullshit me on this. It's important that you tell it to me straight about that night."

Grimaldi gathered himself and looked Doherty in the eye. "I did not slip a mickey into that girl's drink, if that's what you're asking. Not at the lounge, the restaurant or the motel. I'll be honest with you, the sex wasn't all that great. But in my business you get used to that." This last remark came out as if to Richie screwing other men's wives was an occupation like running a restaurant.

"And as far as you could tell, you didn't see anyone following you to the inn or the motel?" Grimaldi shook his head.

"Did you notice anyone eyeballing the two of you in a suspicious way at either of those places?"

At this point Grimaldi looked uncertain. "I dunno, somebody might've. I mean Adrian was a looker, and she was a lot younger than me. Times when I'm out with a good-looking girl she tends to attract attention," he said proudly.

"Yeah. She certainly got the attention of the bartender and your waiter. Now I've got to ask something else: Have you ever dosed one of your women with something because you were afraid she wouldn't put out?"

Grimaldi's face betrayed a new level of discomfort. After some hesitation he said, "A coupla times I slipped something into a girl's drink back at the motel after we had sex 'cause she was getting all weepy. In those cases they were mostly feeling guilty about what they'd done with me. Personally, I wasn't interested in staying up all night listening to their sob stories again. I'd gotten what I wanted so I'd sprinkle a crushed up sleeping pill into their drinks to put them to sleep. I never did it before the sex, only afterwards."

"So you're saying you'd occasionally dose one of your dates after you screwed her just to shut her up?"

"Yeah, I guess you could put it that way," he said almost, but not quite, sounding contrite.

"What did you give them?"

"I don't know. Some kind of yellow pills I got from this doc who comes in here on a regular basis. I told him I was having trouble sleeping on account of things not going so good with the business and my ex-wife bugging me about alimony. He swapped them with me for a free dinner. Look, Mr. Doherty, I never gave those girls enough to cause them any harm. Just enough to put them out. What's this all about anyway? I thought you were eyeballing the husband as a possible suspect for Adrian being missing?"

"I still am, though right now he's acting a little too obvious to be her killer. Or maybe he's just stupid. I did learn that he has a temper. His in-laws as well as his new girlfriend have attested to that so I'm not ruling him out. Now I've got to ask you another question: Are there any girls you shacked up who were pissed off enough to want to get back at you? Either them or their husbands? Is it possible somebody could've killed Adrian to get revenge against you? Like maybe there's somebody out there who wants to frame you for murder."

"Are you kidding me?" Richie said, rubbing his chin as if the thought never occurred to him in all the time he'd been sleeping with other men's wives. "I don't know, there might be. I have no idea what goes on between these girls and their husbands once they get back home. That's not exactly my problem, is it?"

Doherty gave Grimaldi a sardonic smile. "Well, it sure as hell could be in this case. Come on Richie stop beating around the bush. Have you ever had any blowback from one of your trysts? You know like calls from the woman afterwards or a visit from her irate husband."

Grimaldi looked at Doherty but nothing was forthcoming. The stare down lasted nearly a minute. "A guy came in here once accusing me of defiling his wife. That was the exact word he used: *defiling*. He was a little pipsqueak so I didn't pay him any mind. I mean I could see why he was threatened by somebody like me banging his wife."

"What happened?"

"I had young Tony throw him out on his ear."

"That was it? Did he threaten you or anything?"

Grimaldi shook his head. "No, it was more like he was pleading with me. Kept asking me to leave his wife alone. I wasn't interested in her anymore, but he was talking like she was planning to leave him to run off with me. I think I might've insulted him when I said she wouldn't be worth it."

"Do you remember his name?"

"I think it was Desmond. The wife's name was Joyce."

"Is there anyone else you can think of that would kill Adrian Colardo to get back at you?"

"Who the fuck knows? Some of these broads are a little unhinged to begin with. I don't know what they say to their husbands after they've had a good screw from me. They probably go home and tell hubbie now they know what real sex is like."

"Richie, you better tone down the attitude, especially if the cops come by to question you. For the moment I'm going to operate on the assumption that the dead girl is Adrian Colardo and whoever killed her did so because he wanted *her* dead. Beyond that I'll have to check out some of the women you seduced as well as their husbands. If you can give me a list of women, as best you remember, who might've held a grudge after their overnight with you that would be helpful. You know, the ones who made a bigger deal about your night on the town than it deserved. It'll give me a chance to take a look in that direction."

"I don't know if I can remember them all."

"Do the best you can. It could be important."

"Is there anything else I should be doing right now?"

"Yeah, get yourself a good lawyer. You're going to need one if that body turns out to be Adrian. For the time being I suggest you refrain from seducing any more married women."

Chapter Eleven

One of the names Grimaldi gave Doherty was that of a woman named Doris who worked at the Cherry & Webb department store in downtown Providence. Not surprisingly, the gigolo wasn't exactly sure of her last name. What he did remember is that he picked her up at the store before taking her on their jaunt down to South County. He said she was still wearing a C&W nametag attached to her blouse when they checked into the motel. That was why he remembered her name and where she worked.

It was a long shot, but Doherty had the rest of the day free so he thought he'd stop by the department store to see if he could find someone working there named Doris who fit Grimaldi's description. He made some passes through various departments, none of which had any men around either as clerks or customers. After making a few subtle inquiries he located a Doris in the women's lingerie department. To say he felt like a fish out of water in this part of the store would be pretty accurate.

The Doris in question was a good-looking brunette well into her thirties. She was tall and a little bit large all over, though not in a displeasing way. She gave Doherty a teasing smile when he caught her eye.

"What can I do for you, handsome? You looking for something special for that little woman in your life?"

"Yeah, I guess you could say that," Doherty stammered.

Doris' look had a lot of 'I've seen-it-all' to it. "Wife or girlfriend?"

"Why? Does it matter?"

"Oh, yes, honey, a whole lot. With a girlfriend you're still on a mission, so you buy her something more on the suggestive side. With a wife, you've already reached your destination so you get her something she'll be comfortable in." This Doris was either the lingerie department's best salesgirl or a major league flirt.

"Actually, she's my fiancé," he lied.

That drew a smile. "Well, I guess that means you're still only halfway home. So, what's your pleasure?"

"I was thinking of a nightgown."

"Flannel button-up, or something a little more ...," she let the unspoken word hang in the air.

"Is *sexy* the word you were looking for?"

"Well aren't we the forward one?" she said flashing him a flirtatious smile. "Thinking about a weekend away before the marriage? Kind of like a test drive." With this last remark she'd just about put it all out there.

"When do you knock off for lunch?" he asked.

This last question drew a broad smile. Doris spun around to look at the big clock on the far wall. "In about ten minutes. How does that catch you?"

"Works fine for me. Where would you like to meet?"

"Is it snowing out yet?"

"Just a few flurries."

"There's a little Nedick's luncheonette around the corner. Why don't I meet you there in ten?"

"Sounds good."

"What about the nightgown?"

"Maybe another time." If Doris the salesgirl was disappointed at not making the sale, she didn't show it.

Doherty had no problem locating the Nedick's. It was less than a block from Cherry & Webb down a side street off Westminster. He quickly grabbed a booth as the place was beginning to fill up with the lunch crowd. A waitress dropped by his table and he ordered a black coffee. He told her he needed two menus as he was meeting someone. As promised Doris showed up only five minutes late. She was wearing a brown tweed coat with a fake fur collar and a man's style hat that she slipped off quickly before it messed up her hairdo.

After hanging up her coat and hat she slid into the booth across from him and teased out her waves with her fingers.

"So what's your game partner? And just so we're straight, I never did buy your story about the fiancé and the nightgown. You don't look like the marrying kind."

"Really, so what kind do I look like?"

Doris leaned in close enough that Doherty could smell her perfume. "You look more like the kind of guy who likes to mess around."

"And you?"

She gave him a knowing smile. "Maybe I'd be interested in playing after I knew my new playmate a little better."

"What about your husband?"

She held up her left hand. There was no ring on her third finger. "I don't have one."

"No, but you used to, didn't you?" Doris tried to recover her come-on smile but it was having trouble finding its former place. "How do you know that?"

Doherty pulled out his wallet and flashed his license. "I'm a private investigator, that's how."

Her look turned to one of disappointment. "Are you here on behalf of my crook of an ex-husband?"

Doherty shook his head. "No. In fact I have no idea who your former husband is. Nor for the moment do I care. I'm here to talk to you about a guy named Richie Grimaldi."

Their conversation was interrupted by the waitress wanting to take their lunch order. The salesgirl chose the Waldorf salad and a cup of tea. Doherty opted for a bowl of minestrone and a refill of his coffee.

"What do you want to know about Richie?"

He gave her a noncommittal look and said, "Whatever you want to tell me."

His lunch mate took the opportunity to light a cigarette, one of those new menthol kind. He would've joined her but he'd just finished a Camel before she arrived.

"I was having a hard time in my marriage. My ex wasn't working and he was taking money from me without asking. I would've given it to him, but I think his pride was hurt 'cause I was earning and he wasn't."

There was a pause in the conversation. Doherty looked at her calmly as an inducement for her to continue.

"It wasn't long before I found out he was playing cards with some guys and losing most of the time. All the while he was playing he told me he was out looking for work when he really wasn't. Eventually he confessed he was in trouble with the people he owed money to. Apparently they weren't the kind of men you want to be in debt to."

"So what happened?"

"I paid his debts and told him if he didn't stop gambling and found himself a job he could take a hike. We'd been married for eight years at that point, but we didn't have any kids. Not even pets."

"Is that when Richie Grimaldi came into your life?"

Doris hesitated here, clearly reluctant to volunteer anything about her encounter with the gigolo. In due time she continued, "Sometime around then, yeah. He was nice - and thoughtful. Would listen to my troubles and act sympathetic." This sounded like Grimaldi's act.

"He wandered into my department one day just like you did. He was also looking for a nightgown. Didn't make any bones about who it was for either. Said straight out it was for this girl he was dating. They were going down to the beach for the weekend and he wanted to buy her something *alluring*. I could tell from the way he talked that he was the kind of guy who played around."

"Did you call him handsome like you did with me?"

Doris gave him a sheepish grin. "I might've. Don't take it personally."

"No offense taken."

Their food arrived and they dug in, suspending their conversation for the time being.

"When did Richie show up to take you away for a weekend?"

"You don't miss a trick, do you?" Doherty didn't bother to respond.

"He came by about two weeks later. Told me things hadn't worked out with the girlfriend and he wanted to return the nightgown. Said she never wore it because it was too big for her. I didn't care if she had or not. It looked unused so I gave him his money back."

"Is that when he started to work his magic on you?"

"You're kind of a smart guy aren't you?"

"I like to think so," he said giving her one of his insincere smiles. "What about your husband? What was going on between you and him at the time?"

"By then I didn't care about Eddie or our marriage anymore."

"So you went with Richie, down to the Pier. And you spent a night at the Anchor Inn. Room Six. Am I right so far?"

Doris nodded her head. All flirtation had been squeezed out of her like the air from a balloon.

"What happened the morning after?"

"He was a perfect gentleman. He went out and brought back coffee and muffins for us. We spent the whole morning in the motel room eating and doing stuff. He acted like he was really sweet on me. Even promised to call the next day and maybe come by the store the following Monday. All the time I'm thinking this could be my shot at having a good relationship with a guy; not like the crappy one I was in with my husband."

"How did things play out with your husband?"

"I tossed him out the very next week. Told him I was through with him and his failures and that I wanted my freedom."

"Where did he go?"

She shook her head. "Last I heard he was living with his sister in Cumberland. Still not working. The cash I gave him to pay off his debts, money that he promised to pay me back, all down the drain."

"What happened with Richie Grimaldi?"

"I never saw or heard from him again. Until you showed up today."

"Any regrets?"

"About tossing my husband out? None at all. About what I did with Richie and what I expected afterwards? Yeah, a few. A girl doesn't like to be used no matter how sweet the user is."

"I hope I don't qualify in that department," Doherty said apologetically.

"Hey, you're just doing your job. You will have to pick up the lunch tab, though. That's the least you can do. You married or have a girlfriend?"

"I'm dating someone right now. I've never been married. I haven't had much luck with women in my life."

"Too bad for both of us. You're a pretty handsome fella even with that bump in your nose."

Doherty's hand reflexively went up and fingered the crook in his beak left over from a fight with Gerald Broyard, the schoolyard bully from his youth.

"I've got to ask you something difficult, Doris. Do you think your ex-husband knew about your weekend with Richie Grimaldi?"

Doris carefully considered her answer. "He obviously knew I went away with someone. He was there when I came home with my overnight bag. He asked me where I'd been and who I was with. I told him it was none of his damn business. That's when I let him know that we were through. I told him the sooner he moved out the better."

"Is your husband a violent man?"

"My ex-husband," she corrected. "No. If he was he wouldn't have gotten into trouble with people he played cards with. I think they took him for a patsy right from the start. He wasn't a bad guy; he just couldn't get his life together after he came home from the service. I hear that happened to a lot of GIs." Doherty could certainly attest to that.

The waitress came by and dropped the check onto the table. Doherty immediately cuffed it.

"One final question, Doris. What's your ex-husband's full name?

"Edward Donahue. Everyone calls him 'Eddie'."

Doris suddenly reached across the table and took Doherty's hand. "Any chance I'll see you again?"

"Could be. Maybe I'll come by and get that sexy nightgown for my girl-friend." Having never seen Nina in a nightgown, sexy or otherwise, he wasn't sure how she'd take such a gift.

Doris patted his hand. "Thanks for lunch, handsome. See you around

Cherry's sometime." She put on her coat and left quickly. He paid the check at the register and dropped nice tip on the table for the waitress.

Back at the office Doherty spent time scratching out some notes on the case so far. He couldn't tell from his conversation with Doris Donahue if her ex-husband was a legitimate suspect or not. She'd never told him who she went away with that weekend so it wasn't clear her husband knew about Richie Grimaldi. From her description of Eddie he didn't sound like the kind of person who was smart enough to work up an elaborate plan to get back at his ex-wife by killing Adrian Colardo in order to frame Grimaldi. Doherty wasn't ready to cross the Donahues off his list, though at this point they didn't deserved anything more than a question mark beside their names.

Another familiar person on the list Grimaldi supplied of his weekend girlfriends was the name Marilyn. Doherty assumed this was Marilyn Carney, even though it could belong to any number of other Marilyns. But since he knew from his earlier case that Mrs. Carney had gone away with Grimaldi, he thought it would be a good idea to have a chat with the Carneys if only to remove them as suspects.

He was also curious as to how their marriage was faring since the morning he'd rescued her at the Anchor Inn. After she returned home Doherty'd lectured her husband Leo on how to act so as to deter his wife from straying again. Why he thought he had the right to instruct any married man on how to be a better husband was beyond him. Nevertheless, after retrieving their number from his files he put in a call to the Carney residence. A woman answered on the fourth ring.

"Hello, Mrs. Carney. This is Hugh Doherty, the private investigator from West Warwick. I was wondering if you remember me?"

There was an awkward silence at the other end of the phone. While this transpired Doherty couldn't help but recall the image of Marilyn Carney in her sheer slip when he confronted her in Room Six at the motel.

"Yes, I remember you," she said in a voice that indicated she wished she didn't.

"Um, I'm calling to see how things are going between you and Leo."

Another awkward silence ensued. "What are you a social worker now?

If I remember correctly you're the private eye my husband hired to find me at that smelly motel. "

"Well, I am. I mean I was."

"Then why don't you cut to the chase by you telling me what you want? I have some errands to run and don't have any interest in chitchatting about my marriage with someone I hardly know. What's the problem? Does Leo still owe you some money for your services?" She spit out the last word as if it were a profanity.

"Something has come up relating to Richie Grimaldi. I assume you remember him. I'd like to talk with you and your husband about this matter – preferably in person."

Again the prolonged silence at the other end. "Has something awful happened to Richie?" she asked sounding hopeful.

"I can't really talk about it right now. When your husband gets home why don't you discuss this with him and get back to me. It's kind of important that I speak with the two of you." Doherty gave her his office number.

"Okay," was all she said before hanging up.

It was late afternoon when Doherty hopped into the Chevy and headed toward Providence. Snow was coming down harder now, but he wanted to confront Nick Colardo before the police got to him. Traffic was moving at a snail's pace all the way to Silver Lake. He kept the car running after he parked in front of Colardo's home on Priscilla Avenue. He needed to keep the windows clear so he could eyeball the husband when he emerged from the house. In spite of the bad weather he assumed Nick would still be picking up his new girlfriend at Sears Roebuck.

A few minutes past five Colardo exited the house. He was clearing the snow from his car when Doherty killed the engine on his Chevy and headed across the street. He was only about ten feet away when Colardo noticed him and stopped what he was doing.

"Are you Nick Colardo?" he asked knowing full well the guy was indeed him.

"Who wants to know?" Colardo asked; his lip turned up in a sneer when he spoke.

"My name is Doherty," he said while flashing his license. "I'm a private investigator. I've been hired to find your wife Adrian."

"Find my wife? Who the hell hired you to find my wife?"

"I can't tell you that."

Colardo turned to fully face Doherty. He set his legs apart and assumed a belligerent stance. "Why don't you get the fuck offa my property. I ain't seen Adrian in a while. She left me and our son and ran off with some other guy."

"Actually she's been gone for a week. Just enough time for you to get together with that little teenage twist Denise. I assume that's where you're heading right now. To pick her up at the Sears Roebuck store on North Main."

Colardo stepped up close to Doherty. Then out of nowhere he took a wild swing. It was a glancing blow, though it made enough contact to get Doherty's attention. Before his attacker could regain his balance Doherty crouched down and hit him with a hard right to his mid-section. Though he was a young guy, Colardo folded over like a sandwich sign. Unable to catch his breath, he fell onto his backside in the accumulating snow. Doherty grabbed Colardo by his greasy hair, immediately wishing he hadn't, and snapped his head back.

"Listen to me tough guy and listen good. Yesterday the police pulled a dead girl's body out of the ocean down in South County. There's a good possibility it belongs to your wife. While you've been running around with that young girl it looks like somebody may've murdered Adrian. If it turns out to be her you better start putting on your sad face."

Colardo glared up at Doherty, the sneer still on his lips. Because the look irritated him, Doherty hit Colardo with a quick jab to the mouth for good measure.

A small trickle of blood started dripping from his lip. "I told you I ain't seen Adrian since she left. Ran off with some guy leavin' me all alone with our kid," Nick whined.

"Yeah, the boy named Tommy, who you pawned off on your in-laws as soon as Adrian was out of sight. What I want to know is why you didn't report her missing to the police?"

Colardo took a moment to wipe the blood from his split lip onto the sleeve of his leather jacket. Snow was beginning to gather on his now mussed-up greasy hair.

"Why would I report her missin' after she ran off? She was actin' all crazy. When she left I was glad to see her go."

"Maybe she was acting crazy 'cause her husband was smacking her around on a regular basis."

"Hey, you got it all wrong. Yeah, I hit her a time or two. But she was gettin' hysterical at least once or twice a day. I couldn't take it no more."

"Is that why you found it necessary to jump into bed with Denise?"

Colardo kept shaking his head as if to clear out the cobwebs from Doherty's punch. "Do you think that dead girl is really Adrian?" Apparently the enormity of the situation was beginning to sink in.

"I'm sorry to say it looks like it might be. The police haven't positively identified the body yet, but from the way she was described to me, there's a good chance it's your wife. She'd been beaten, strangled and left floating naked in the ocean near Narragansett."

"Narragansett? What the fuck was she doing way down there?" Colardo lips began to tremble. It might've been from the cold though Doherty wanted it to be from sadness. He then brought his hand up to his face; Doherty thought he detected some moisture in his eyes. Though it too could've been from the weather.

"I hate to ruin your day any more than I already have, but if the body is identified as Adrian the cops will come looking for you."

"Me! Why me? I didn't kill Adrian. Why would I kill her?" It was the second time in the last twenty-four hours he'd heard a potential murder suspect use those same words.

"How about for the all the reasons you just told me. She was being a pain in your ass, she ran off with another man, and you wanted to clear the way for your new honey. Believe me, Nick, in situations like this the cops always suspect the husband first."

The expression on Colardo's face turned from sadness to fear. "I don't even know how to get to Narragansett. I couldn't've gone down there to kill her. I was just glad she wasn't here, that's all. I didn't want her dead or nothin'."

"Nick, the police are going to look at you and see a guy who isn't working and has all the time in the world to plan something like this. Whoever killed that girl dumped her in the ocean fully expecting she'd wash out to sea in the storm and never be found. If the body is Adrian's and she's been in the water for several days, there's no way they'll be able to determine when she was killed. That'll prevent you from using Denise as an alibi. In fact, you might want to stay away from her for the time being. Continuing to carry on with that young girl won't help your situation."

"Shit, man. That's gonna be a problem."

"Why?"

"She's been livin' here the last two days. Her parents threw her out of their house because she was goin' out with me. Jesus, what the hell am I gonna do?"

Doherty almost felt sorry for Nick Colardo, sitting in the snow with his world collapsing all around him. He reached down and helped the poor bastard to his feet. Handing him one of his business cards he said, "Call me if you need help or something else comes up. Right now I think you better get out of the snow. Go pick up your girlfriend and be sure to fill her in on what I've told you. You might want to drop the bad attitude too. Cops don't like punks who give them too much attitude. That split lip will be nothing compared to what they'll serve up."

Chapter Twelve

Using one of his many Rhode Island phonebooks it was easy for Doherty to locate an address for Edward Donahue in Cumberland. Getting up there the next morning was going to be more of a problem as the snow was still coming down pretty hard. He'd never been to Cumberland before. His state map told him it was just north of Pawtucket. With the map propped on his lap he drove through Providence then out Rt. 114, locally known as Diamond Hill Road, following the signs toward Cumberland.

Many of the cars on the road had their chains around the tires to provide them the traction in this weather. Doherty had no chains so the Chevy occasionally fishtailed through the snow as if it were sailing on a lake. Once in Cumberland he took a rural side road that had been barely plowed, though some sand had been tossed on it to make it somewhat drivable. Under most circumstances Doherty wouldn't have undertaken this journey in such weather, but he was battling against time. If, or when, the dead body was identified as Adrian Colardo, it wouldn't take the local cops long to trace her last night back to Richie Grimaldi.

After he entered the confines of Cumberland he stopped at the only open gas station he could find on a Sunday to ask for directions to the street where Donahue was supposedly living with his sister. He was told to take a couple of turns before finding the right house. It was a little Cape, probably built sometime between the wars, set off on a nice piece of land, a good distance from any neighboring homes. At the end of the driveway a mailbox had the names Garrett and Donahue on it. The Garrett was nicely stenciled whereas the Donahue was crudely painted on as an afterthought.

Smoke was billowing out of the chimney as he approached the house. There was no bell so he knocked firmly at the front door. Within seconds a woman answered. She was wearing a housedress with a gray cardigan sweater thrown over her shoulders and look like she was somewhere in her mid to late thirties. She had dirty blond hair that looked like it was in need of a brushing. Otherwise she was nice looking in a country girl sort of way.

"My husband's not here. He's at church," was the first thing out of her mouth.

"I'm looking for an Edward Donahue. Does he live here?"

The woman didn't answer right away. Instead she looked beyond Doherty to his Chevy parked at the end of their partially cleared driveway.

"What's this about?"

He flashed his license and said, "I'm a private investigator. I'd like to talk to Eddie about his ex-wife." He used Donahue's more familiar name to sound less threatening

A man slightly older than the woman came out from around a corner where he'd obviously been listening to their conversation. He had slumped shoulders and was balding. Overall his first impression was of a guy who'd been prematurely worn down by life.

"Is there something wrong with Doris? Is she sick or hurt?" he asked anxiously.

Doherty shook his head. "No she's fine. I'd like to talk with you about a few things that happened back when you and she were still married."

"You're not from O'Donnell's are you?" the woman asked accusingly.

"Sorry, ma'am. I don't know what O'Donnell's is."

"Why don't I and Mr. ...."

"Doherty."

"Mr. Doherty talk in private, Meg. We'll go into the den if that's all right with you."

94

The woman gave Doherty an unfriendly look before retreating toward the back of the house, leaving the two men alone. He followed Eddie Donahue into a small room paneled in dark knotty pine. There was a sofa and a reclining easy chair, both facing in the direction of a large, lightwood console television. On one wall were some wooden shelves resting on metal brackets attached directly to the wall. They were lined with books interspersed with small and midsized bowling trophies. Doherty stared at the various trophies. All of them had a bowler in mid-stride on top and a nameplate attached to their bases.

"Those are my brother-in-law Neil's. He's a professional duckpin bowler," Donahue explained. "Do you bowl, Mr. Doherty?"

"Not since I was a kid," he answered, thinking back to the tiny bowling alleys that occupied the basement of the Majestic Building in West Warwick. His uncle Patrick used to take him there periodically. Young teenage boys still set the pins by hand in those days. Nowadays, Doherty understood, the pins were automatically set by machines.

Donahue took a seat in the recliner and offered his guest the couch. Instead of reclining the chair his host sat uneasily on its edge.

"What's this visit all about? Is my ex-wife in some kind of trouble?"

Doherty shook his head. "I don't think so. But I'd like to ask you about the time back when you were still married that she took off for a weekend with some guy."

A sad look took over Donahue face. "Which time?" This response knocked Doherty off balance for a few beats.

"Are you saying she went away with other men on more than one occasion?"

Donahue laughed, but it was not one born of mirth. "Have you met my wife?"

Doherty nodded. "Yeah, I talked with her briefly at Cherry & Webb yesterday. She seemed nice enough," he added, purposely leaving out their lunch date.

"Did she flirt with you?"

"I wouldn't exactly call it flirting. She answered my questions and told me a little bit about how your marriage fell apart. Nothing in great detail."

"Fell apart?" he said in a voice that was now more angry than sad. "There was nothing to fall apart. I could tell Doris was disappointed in me right from the beginning. I think she married me only because she wanted to get out of her house. Later on she stayed because she felt sorry for me. How do you think that made me feel?"

"What about the gambling debts and the money she gave you to pay them off?"

At this reminder Donahue's shoulders sagged even more, if that was possible.

"She told you about that?"

"Yep." There was now an unpleasant pause in their conversation. Doherty was anxious to move things along before the snowfall built up, making it difficult getting back to West Warwick. "Now, what can you tell me about the weekend she took off right before she told you to move out. What did she say about that?"

"I won't lie to you, Mr. Doherty. Our marriage had been going downhill for a long time. I suppose a lot of it was my fault. I just couldn't seem to hold a job after I came home from overseas. I'd always get into some argument with my boss. You could say I'm the kinda guy who has trouble handling authority. That was the case even when I was in the army. Got thrown in the brig a couple times because of mouthing off to a superior. I'll be honest with you I was surprised Doris agreed to marry me in the first place. She was a real beauty back then. Probably still is, right?"

Doherty nodded but said nothing. He didn't want to break the rhythm of Donahue's narrative.

"I thought I could win back some of the money I borrowed from her by playing cards at O'Donnell's. That's the O'Donnell VFW Post in Providence. I was in a regular game with these three fellas. It took me a while to figure out they were tipping each other about their cards the whole time we were playing. By then they'd already taken me to the cleaners. It wasn't right, but once I figured out what was going on what could I do? There were three of them against me and I was already down a few hundred dollars.

"These fellas practically run the place. When I first got in deep I asked Doris to bail me out. You might say that was the beginning of the end of our marriage. She was working at Cherry's at the time and I didn't have a job. I promised I'd pay her back. I planned to as soon as I got ahead, but I never did. That's when she started running around with other men. Sometimes she'd make a date on the phone right in front of me."

"What about that weekend?"

"I dunno. Before then I thought she was just going out with these men to humiliate me. She always was a flirty girl. Hell, she flirted with me; that's why I fell for her in the first place. After that last weekend when she came home she was different. She told me she met a guy, a *real gentleman* she called him. She described him as the kinda man she could fall in love with. That's when she told me she wanted me out of the apartment and out of her life. I'll admit I took it hard. I could tell this time she was serious. So I took my stuff and moved out here with Meg and Neil. They never liked Doris; they took me in without asking a lot of questions."

"Are you working now?"

"Neil got me a few jobs removing snow. I shovel for people and sometimes at public buildings in town like the bank and the post office. Recently an old army buddy told me he might be able to get me on at American Screw come spring. I'd like to get my own place, but I don't have the cash right now. I feel bad mooching off my sister and her husband."

"What about O'Donnell's? Do you still go there?"

He gave Doherty a timid smile. "Sometimes."

"And the cards?"

Donahue looked away, not wanting to make eye contact with his inquisitor. "I play once in a while." Doherty tucked that piece of information away for the time being.

"Do you have any reason to believe your ex-wife might've wanted to do harm to the guy she went away with that last weekend? The one she thought she was in love with."

"Does that mean it didn't work out?" Donahue asked, sounding almost pleased.

"The way she told it the guy didn't last any longer than that weekend. Does that make you feel better?"

Donahue shook his head. "Actually it makes me feel worse. She never called me after I left. If nothing else, I could've been a shoulder for her to cry on." Doherty checked out Donahue's slumped shoulders and decided they wouldn't have provided much support.

"Did you ever learn who the guy was?"

"No. Never cared either. I knew if she didn't break up with me for him, sooner or later it would be for some other fella. Doris deserved to be with somebody who was good to her. I wasn't that guy."

"If it's any consolation, she's still single. Maybe after you get back on your feet you should give her a call."

Donahue shook his head and looked about as poorly as a man could. "I don't think so. That part of my life is over. But if you do see Doris again, tell her I was asking about her."

At this point Doherty felt like he'd hit a dead end, at least as far as the estranged Donahues were concerned. He'd cross Eddie Donahue off his list but keep Doris active. If she was so smitten with Grimaldi, who shook her off as easily as an old coat, he had no idea what she might do to get back at him. It reminded him of an old quote he'd heard one time in an English class: "Hell hath no fury like a woman scorned."

He shook hands with Eddie Donahue and thanked him for his time. He headed out into the snow, seeing that his car was already covered again with a thin layer. The sister was throwing shoveled snow from the driveway onto her lawn. Doherty gave her a goodbye wave, but she quickly moved in his direction.

"What was that all about?" she asked accusingly.

"Nothing really. I thought Eddie could help me with a missing persons case I'm working on. I'm afraid he couldn't."

"I'm sorry I was so rude when you first came to the door. I thought you were one of those men from O'Donnell's."

Meg Garrett's comment piqued Doherty's curiosity. "What can you tell me about them?"

"They cheated my brother out of a lot of money," she said firmly. "And when he couldn't pay, those bastards made him do bad things for them."

"What kind of bad things?"

"I don't know the whole story. I do know one time they made him move

98

some stolen merchandise. I also think they had him do something funny with a few of the bills at the post. You'd think as vets they'd look out for one another."

"Do you know who's behind all this?"

"I'm not sure. A couple of times I heard Eddie talking on the phone to somebody he addressed as Mr. Finnegan. Eddie acted like he was this guy's servant or something. It just broke my heart after all he'd been through." Doherty didn't know if she was referring to the war or Eddie's failed marriage, or both.

"Where is this VFW post?"

"In Providence on Charles Street, not too far outside of downtown. Do you think you can help Eddie get out of this jam? You're a detective aren't you?"

"Mrs. Garrett, I'm not a cop. I'm a private investigator. I only came here to talk to Eddie about his ex-wife and the case I'm currently working. I don't think I can help him. He's not my client. And since he doesn't have any money, he wouldn't be able to hire me anyway." It sounded harsh but Eddie Donahue's gambling issues weren't really Doherty's problem.

Meg Garrett abruptly turned away and went back to shoveling her driveway. Doherty walked over to where she was laboring and handed her one of his business cards. He told her if anything else bad happened in Eddie's life she should give him a call. He didn't know why he did this. Perhaps it was because Donahue was a vet who was not being treated well by other vets.

Doherty began the long drive back to West Warwick with some trepidation due to the increasingly inclement weather. Then, against his better judgment, he took a detour through downtown Providence and out Charles Street. Because the snow was now making visibility difficult, it took him two passes before he located the Sgt. Kevin O'Donnell VFW Post #365. There was a wet American flag hanging limply on its poll outside the small wooden building.

Inside the post was warm and nearly empty even though a VFW post was one of the few places somebody could buy a drink legally in Rhode Island on Sunday. Maybe the foul weather had kept its members away. Like most drinking establishments, this one had the familiar odor of peanuts and stale beer. Two men were playing what looked like pinochle at a table off to one side, while three others were sucking on beer bottles at a small bar against the wall. That was the whole of the crowd inside O'Donnell Post #365. The man behind the bar gave Doherty the high sign.

"Are you a veteran?" he asked as Doherty approached. He flashed his vet card, which the barman looked at carefully.

"Hundred and First Airborne, huh."

"That's right."

"What can I get you? First drink for guests is on the house."

"I'm looking for a man named Finnegan. They tell me he's a big wheel around here." The three guys nursing their beers turned and gave a Doherty a sidelong look.

"Whaddya want with Fats?"

"I hear this is a good place to play cards."

Nobody spoke for a good twenty seconds, though all eyes were now on Doherty. Even the pinochle players had stopped their game to glare at him.

"He's in the back through that door," the barkeep said, pointing with the beer glass he was holding at a closed door off to the right. As Doherty walked toward the door with the word 'Office' on a sign above it, the other men in the room went back to their lives.

He knocked and heard a muffled 'come in' from the other side. A very large man with several chins was sitting on the other side of a beat up wooden desk. A green shaded visor hooded his face and he was counting a substantial amount of cash laid out on his desk. His chins jiggled when he looked up at his visitor.

"Hello, friend. What can I do for you?"

"I understand you run a card game here. I was wondering what a fellow has to do to get dealt in?"

"Who told you that?" the big guy asked suspiciously.

"A fellow named Eddie Donahue."

"Donahue, huh." From his expression the man behind the desk obviously found this amusing.

"I say something wrong? I'm pretty sure that was his name."

"No, nothin' wrong. I'm just a little surprised Eddie would recommend our game to anyone, that's all. You see Eddie's a little in arrears with his dues." The two men stared at each other, neither acknowledging they knew exactly what Finnegan meant by *dues*.

"How's old Eddie doin'? I ain't seen him in here in a while."

"I just came from his sister's. He doesn't seem to be doing too good these days."

"Gee, that's a shame," the big guy said with false concern. "You should tell him to come back down here. Everybody misses him. And the interest on his dues is startin' to mount up."

"Is that right? How much do you guys play for in your little card game?"

Finnegan hemmed for a few seconds. "A smart player can walk out of here with a coupla hundred if he has a good night."

"And if he has a bad night?"

"Same thing. He could lose a hundred - maybe more if he's really unlucky."

"Like Eddie?"

All good humor had deserted the big man behind the desk. "What are you, Eddie's padre or somethin'?"

"How much is he into you for?"

"What?"

Doherty took the liberty of sitting on the edge of the big man's desk. "I asked how much he was into you for."

"Hey, pal, that's none of your business."

"Just answer the question," Doherty said. All friendliness had now left the room.

"Almost a grand. Maybe a little more with interest added on."

"Okay, here's the play, Mr. Finnegan. I'll get Eddie to pay off half of what he owes you - in installments. You and your buddies are going to forgive the other half 'cause I got reason to believe your game is rigged. If he comes in here to play again you tell him he's no longer welcome in your little card game. Not then and not ever. And one more thing, you can no longer use his debts to make him do outside jobs for you. Have I made myself clear?"

Finnegan gave Doherty his best smile. "Who the hell do you think you are comin' in here and tellin' me what I can and can't do in my own post?"

"It's not *your* post, it's a VFW post. That means it's for all the veterans who belong here, not just you and your cronies. This is what's going to happen if you don't do what I say. First, I'll put a call in to some cops I know here in Providence and tell them you're running a card game with stakes high enough to make it illegal. At best, they'll come by and temporarily close you down; maybe even charge you and your friends with a misdemeanor. At worst, they'll want a piece of your action, and they'll want it on a regular basis. If that doesn't work then I'll contact the headquarters of the Rhode Island VFW and inform them you're running a crooked card game at the O'Donnell post. That might cause them to close down your little clubhouse on a permanent basis."

"Why are you doin' this for a poor slob like Eddie Donahue?"

"Because Eddie Donahue is a veteran just like you and me. He fought and almost died for his country. We're supposed to stick by one another, over here just like we did over there. It's pricks like you that violate that code."

"Why you rotten bastard." Finnegan put his hand into his desk drawer for something, but the fat man wasn't quick enough as Doherty reached around and slammed the drawer hard on his fingers. The big man let out a loud wail that sounded like that of an animal caught in a trap. He drew his injured hand out of the drawer and held it tight hoping that would make the pain go away.

"Jesus H. Christ, I think you broke two of my fingers."

Doherty reached into the drawer and extracted a .22 pistol Finnegan had been reaching for. He was still holding it when the door flew open and the two pinochle players barged in. As soon as they saw Doherty had a gun they put their hands up in a peace gesture and slowly backed out of the room.

Meanwhile Finnegan was sitting behind his desk rubbing his injured hand and moaning.

Doherty leaned down in his direction. "Think about what I said. If you don't do what I suggested I'll be back. And next time it'll be with some friends."

Halfway home to West Warwick he emptied the slugs out of Finnegan's pistol and tossed it into an open garbage can.

Chapter Thirteen

The next morning the Carneys showed up at Doherty and Associates about twenty minutes after he did. Fortunately Agnes was there because he had a plan as to how he wished to question them and she was part of that plan. After a few minutes of uncomfortable small talk about the weather, Doherty asked Leo Carney if he could talk with him alone in his back office. Marilyn Carney responded to this request by flashing them a strange look. Agnes quickly intervened, offering her a cup of coffee. While she was distracted Doherty and Leo Carney withdrew into his office.

Once inside, with the door closed Doherty asked, "So, Leo, how are things going in your marriage?"

Leo bobbed his head several times. "Better. Yeah better. Me and Marilyn try to go out to dinner someplace nice at least once a month. And we both been doin' some volunteer work with kids at our church. She runs a little clothes design and sewin' group with the young girls and I coach a basketball team for eleven and twelve year-old boys. You know, not bein' able to have kids of our own always made us feel like we were missin' out on somethin'. This volunteer work helps us fill that part of our life."

"Not the same as having your own kids, though probably the next best thing."

"Yeah, you got that right, Mr. Doherty. Some of the kids I coach don't have such good homes, so I'm kinda like a substitute father for them. I think it's the same for Marilyn. I took your advice about dressin' up when I'm not at work."

Leo Carney stood up so Doherty could admire his chino pants and oxford shirt with a blue v-neck sweater over it. Except for his ample belly, he could've passed for one of those WASPy fellows you see walking around Newport.

"What about the other business?"

Leo gave him a blank look. Doherty was obviously being too subtle, or too polite.

"I mean about the sex stuff. No more of Marilyn running around with other men?"

Carney looked away as a sadness crept onto his face. He was silent for a couple of moments. "I thought everythin' was okay in that department. I mean we do it now and then and she never complains or nothin'."

"But?"

"A coupla times she told me she was goin' out with her girlfriends to the movies. When she came home I asked her about the show and she was kinda vague in describin' it to me. She'd say somethin' like it was one of them movies only girls would like. I didn't push it 'cause I guess I didn't wanna know what I suspected she'd been up to. At first I didn't have no proof. But the second time it happened I could smell some guy's cologne on her. She tried to tell me it was her new perfume. Said she'd changed it on a lark. That's how she described it: *on a lark*. Trouble was I knew that smell. A guy I work with always splashes it on his face at the end of the day when he's goin' out on a date."

"Did you confront her about it?"

Leo shook his head. "Not at first. I didn't wanna bring it up mostly 'cause I didn't want it to be true. After a while I couldn't hold back no more."

"What did she say?"

Leo had the most pitiful look on his face. "She tried to avoid the conversation but I kept after her. Finally she told me she'd been seein' that Grimaldi guy again. Said she ran into him at the movie theater and one thing led to another. 'Ran into him at the movies'. Like I was supposed to believe that.

105

You told me, Mr. Doherty, that you took care of him. You said he wouldn't bother Marilyn ever again." Carney had transferred his anger from his wife to Doherty.

"Are you sure it was Grimaldi she was with?"

"I dunno for sure. That's what she told me. Why shouldn't I believe her? It made sense since she doesn't know a lot of other men." Doherty wondered if what Leo was really saying is that he didn't think too many men would want to sleep with his wife.

Doherty got up from his desk and came over and patted Leo Carney on the shoulder. "Let me ask you something difficult, Leo. What did you do when she told you this?"

"What was I suppose to do? I told her she needed to stop or I'd leave her. I can't stay married to a woman who cheats on me. Not with somebody like how you described that Grimaldi fella. It would've been better if she slept with some guy I could respect, somebody who really cared about her. Not some fancypants who uses women and then tosses them aside like yesterday's newspaper."

"Did you do anything to get back at this Grimaldi?"

"Like what?"

"I don't know - maybe go after him? Try to hurt him or something? Anything to get him to stay away from your wife."

Leo shook his head as if lost in his own pain. "In lookin' back on it maybe I shoulda. But the way I saw it, it wasn't really his fault, was it? It was Marilyn's. She's the one who's married, not this other guy. I knew he was just usin' her but she couldn't see it."

"So where do you two stand now?"

"She promised me she wouldn't see him again and I believe her. I guess I believe her 'cause I wanna believe her. Far as I can tell, she hasn't been with him in a month or so. But hey, what do I know? They say the husband's always the last to know."

Doherty leaned back on his desk and tried to size up the situation. If what Leo was saying were true then he'd have to reassess his role working for Grimaldi. If his client wasn't being straightforward with him how could he continue to keep him on in good faith?

At this point he knew there was nothing he could say that would make Leo Carney feel any better. Besides he was a PI, not a marriage counselor and Grimaldi was his client. The best he could come up with was, "I'll take another look at this Grimaldi character. See what I can find out. There'll be no charge this time."

He motioned Leo toward the door. As they were leaving the office they could hear Marilyn Carney and Agnes laughing about something in the other room.

Mrs. Carney looked up at Leo and Doherty and said, "Can we go now? I've got a group of girls coming to the church after school today. It took us a long time to get here in this weather."

"In a minute," Doherty said. "I was wondering if I could talk with you in private, Mrs. Carney. It won't take long." Everyone, including Agnes, was unprepared for this request. Awkwardness filled the office.

Reluctantly the wife rose from her chair and preceded Doherty back into his office. She took the client's chair and immediately lit up a filtered cigarette. Doherty moved the glass ashtray on his desk close enough for her to reach it. Then he struck up a Camel of his own.

"So, how are things going, Marilyn?" He purposely used her first name, acting like they were close because he'd seen her in the motel room in her slip. She gave him a hard look and blew smoke in his direction.

"What did Leo tell you?"

"He told me a lot of things. Said you two were getting on better. That both of you were doing some volunteer work at your church. That he was dressing up more when he wasn't at work. That's about it."

"If that's about it, then what am I doing in here talking to you in private? I wasn't born yesterday, Mr. Doherty, so why don't you cut out the malarkey. Did Leo tell you I was seeing some guy on the sly?"

"Are you?"

"Is that any of your business?"

"It is if that guy is Richie Grimaldi. You might remember part of my task when I found you with him at the Anchor Inn was to insure he stayed out of your life. According to Leo he hasn't."

"Is that why we're here? To talk about Richie Grimaldi?"

"Why don't you tell me?"

Marilyn Carney was an attractive woman even if she was on the other side of forty. She'd cut her hair short, but that wouldn't deter other men from giving her the eye, especially a guy like Grimaldi. She crossed her legs and sat calmly smoking her cigarette, blowing smoke in Doherty's direction with each puff.

"I haven't seen Richie Grimaldi since that night at the motel."

"But Leo said you told him…"

"I know what I told him. I said that about Grimaldi for his own sake. It was convenient for me to use him to cover what was really going on. I was seeing someone, but it wasn't Grimaldi."

"I don't get it."

She gave him a smug look. "The guy I was seeing is named Barry. He's one of Leo's friends. We've known him and his wife for almost ten years. There was always this thing going on between him and me, but it was mostly just looks and funny remarks, nothing else. Nothing serious anyway."

"What happened to change that?"

"In a nutshell, Grimaldi happened. Once I'd been with Richie I saw how lonely I was being married to Leo. Don't get me wrong, Leo is a good man and he's been trying his best to be a good husband. It's just that he doesn't really float my boat anymore. I'm going to be forty-two next month and I don't have any kids. So what have I got to look forward to? Another thirty years or so being married to Leo. A girl only gets so many opportunities to be happy in this life. I feel like mine are just about used up."

"What happens next for you and this Barry fellow?"

Marilyn Carney shook her head. "Nothing really. He's got a nice wife and two kids. He says he loves me and that he always has. Personally I think he just wanted to sleep with someone who wasn't his wife. He's not going to leave Janine, and I don't really want him to anyway. He's a nice guy but not that much of an improvement over Leo. You see, Mr. Doherty, sometimes a woman just wants to be wanted."

Like his conversation with Leo, Doherty was at a loss for what he could say to make Marilyn Carney feel any better about her life. A lot of what she was feeling probably made sense to her. But as a guy who'd never been married it didn't mean much to Doherty.

"Then I guess I can assume you haven't seen or heard from Richie Grimaldi since that night at the Anchor Inn?"

She stubbed out her smoke and rose. "Yes, you can assume that. And I doubt I ever will again. I know his game and I don't have any interest in playing in it." When she got to the door she turned back and said, "I suppose I can count on you not to share what I just told you with my husband?"

Doherty agreed.

"And one other thing, Mr. Doherty. Please don't contact either of us again."

Doherty's interviews with the Donahues and the Carneys hadn't done much to advance his investigation. Although his client's brief involvement with each of these women had had a significant effect on their lives and marriages, neither of them provided any clues as to whether they or their husbands would be angry enough to kill Adrian Colardo in order to get back at Richie Grimaldi. All the conversations did was leave him with a jaundiced eye view of marriage, as if he didn't have one already.

Doherty'd never gotten close to the altar, though Dolores Bradley, who he dated a couple of years back, was pretty obvious in hinting that she thought it was time for him to put a ring on her finger. The fact that she still lived at home and they'd never advanced beyond making out in his old Packard left him pretty unenthusiastic about that prospect. In the end Dolores didn't seem all that disappointed when he broke it off.

After Dolores he dated Millie St. Jean, a sweet townie girl, who happened to be married at the time. Her husband was consigned to the ward for men with severe brain damage at the Howard Institution. It was his reward for serving his country in Korea. Although Gerard St. Jean was never going to leave Howard except in a pine box, it still meant that Millie was technically married. So that relationship had its own built-in limitations.

He and Millie split up as a result of some murders that crept into his line of work. Six months later she got her marriage annulled thanks to some intervention on the part of Judge DeCenza with the archdiocese. She subsequently married a guy she met at her church who was more suitable for her and to her in-laws.

Following his relationship with Millie he had a torrid one with Rachel Katz, a girl Doherty's thought about almost daily since they broke up. In her case his work had played a direct role in destroying whatever was meaningful between them. She was physically assaulted and raped by a despicable man Doherty was tracking in a case last year. Rachel never fully recovered and always secretly, and then not so secretly, blamed him for what happened. After Rachel he'd had a brief fling with a girl named Maureen Donovan, who was murdered – also in connection with a case he was working.

He was now dating Nina Vitale, a lovely young woman who worked at the Centreville Bank here in town. So far she had not dropped either the E word or the M word and he wasn't about to give her any reason to. Nina had been engaged to another guy when Doherty first met her, but it never advanced on to a wedding. She was reluctant to explain what had happened and he never pressed her on it. All in all, his record with women since he'd opened his practice in West Warwick had been uneven if not disastrous. Perhaps it was better that way now that murder investigations seemed to be dropping into his lap every few months.

He let these thoughts take flight by turning his attention back to the case at hand. Although Adrian Colardo's body hadn't been identified yet as the dead girl down in South County, for the time being he would proceed on the assumption it was. He made a mental note to call Alex Klinoff to see if the North Kingston police had gotten a positive ID on the dead girl yet. Up to this point he'd come up empty in pursuing the idea that she was murdered as a means for someone to get payback against Richie Grimaldi. The list of suspects who could've been involved in such a scenario was getting shorter by the day. Neither Doris Donahue's ex nor Marilyn Carney's husband appeared to be likely perpetrators of such an act. He wouldn't completely rule them out, though as of now it didn't seem plausible to count them in either.

His second line of investigation was to explore whether someone had killed Adrian Colardo simply because they wanted *her* dead. Who would qualify in this category? Obviously her husband Nick, and possibly Nick's current squeeze Denise. Doherty couldn't conceive of the nineteen-year old girl still living with her parents, at least until three days ago, being capable of such an act. Besides any woman involved in this murder would've had to have a strong man working with her in order to move the woman's strangled body a couple of hundred yards from the main road through the brush to the water beyond the rocks. In the dead of winter no less. Obviously the girl could have collaborated with Nick Colardo in his wife's murder. Or Colardo could've killed his wife entirely on his own – thereby leaving the field open for his new relationship with the teenage girl.

However, the most logical perpetrator of this crime was still his client, Richie Grimaldi. The search for the girl's killer was taking him in circles that ended with this same conclusion. His only other option at this point was to widen the circle of possible suspects, which meant other women Grimaldi had seduced and abandoned.

After a quick lunch at the Arctic News he returned to the office to pick Agnes' brain. She was on the phone with her sister when he came in, but quickly dropped the conversation when Doherty motioned for her to follow him into his office. He spent the next half hour laying out the different strands he'd been pursuing in the Grimaldi case. Agnes' first question was whether there'd been a positive identification of the body yet. She pointed out that if the dead girl was someone other than Adrian Colardo then he didn't really have a case at all. Or if he did, it was a simple missing persons case not a murder.

"I don't know, Agnes, you're married, what do you make of all these women running off with a guy like Grimaldi? Could you ever see yourself doing something like that?" This was not the kind of question he'd ever felt bold enough to ask his secretary before.

Agnes blushed and shot him a shy smile. "No, not with him. Especially now that I've seen Grimaldi and heard what kind of man he is. But you know we girls have our fantasies too just like you guys. With men I think it's usually about sex; sex with women they'd never be able to get in real life. For us it's more about romance. You know, wantin' to be in a relationship like you see in the movies. I mean look at me; I'm married to a merchant marine who's out at sea more than he's home. Don't get me wrong, Louie's a good guy and I'd never cheat on him. But that doesn't mean I don't fantasize about bein' with one of those actors I see in the movies or on TV."

"Hell, everybody does that. After Rachel took me to see Sophia Loren in that movie, *Two Women*, Sophia haunted my dreams for weeks afterwards. But I don't think I'd kill somebody on her account."

"What about that Donovan girl in Cranston? You went after the guys who killed her like it was a personal vendetta."

Her reference to Maureen Donovan's untimely death knocked Doherty off balance for the moment. "Yeah, but that was because I thought she was killed on account of me and my investigation. Besides, Agnes, talking about my love life isn't going to get us any closer to finding out who killed Adrian Colardo." This last remark was his way of changing the subject. "What do you think about the husband?"

"I dunno, boss. From the way you described him it doesn't sound like he's a strong enough guy to do such a thing. If the dead girl turns out to be his wife, the cops'll go after him anyway, won't they? That's how it always is on TV."

"And in real life too. Nine times out of ten when a married woman is murdered, it's the husband who did it. You know what they say, 'you always hurt the one you love'."

"Wasn't that a song?"

"Yeah, and a popular one too."

Agnes' laugh came out as a cynical cackle. "Well, I guess killin' somebody is about the meanest way to hurt them. I don't know about you, but I still get a feelin' that this has somethin' to do with Grimaldi. Except for the girl's husband, who else in her life would want her dead?"

"I don't know. The husband's new girlfriend maybe. According to Adrian Colardo's parents their daughter didn't have any enemies that they knew of. However, she was acting unstable lately. Both the husband, and to a lesser degree Grimaldi, have attested to that. Look, I've got to make some phone calls. Why don't you take the rest of the day off and we'll pick this up in the morning."

Agnes left the inner office and within ten minutes had packed up her gear and headed home. When she was gone Doherty put in a call to Alex

Klinoff. The phone rang ten times before the former West Warwick cop picked up.

"Yeah, who's this?" was his gravel road greeting.

"Klinoff this is Doherty. I didn't wake you did I?"

"It's two o'clock in the freakin' afternoon. Why would I be sleepin' at two o'clock?"

"Are you sober?"

"What business is it of yours?" he said slurring his words.

"If this isn't a good time I can call back later."

"Listen, dickwad, drunk or sober I can still talk with you. Let me guess, you're callin' to find out if the ME down here has identified the floater yet. Am I right?"

"Yeah, that's exactly why I'm calling."

"Then I guess it means you're not callin' to find out if I'm drunk at two in afternoon."

"I suppose not."

"Well for your information, I happen to be as drunk as a skunk. And I probably smell like one too. Anyways I can still give you what you want. The dead girl hasn't been ID'd yet mostly 'cause she was naked and in the water for too long. They've determined the official cause of death was asphyxiation by strangulation." Klinoff had a hard time getting his liquor soaked tongue around the word *asphyxiation*. "I was told she was found by some old guy out walkin' his dog. In a day or two they'll put out an APB to see if anybody has reported a girl missing who fits this one's description."

"Can they figure out how long she was dead before she went in the water?"

"Dunno. It'll depend on how long she was floatin'. Nothin's been released to the public yet. My source down here'll let me know as soon as they get a positive ID from someone or a photo they can use that don't make her look like a blowfish. If they get one they'll start circulatin' it around the area." Klinoff had a similar problem pronouncing the word *circulating*. "Does that bring your client into play?"

"I can't tell you that."

"Oh, man. You're no fun. Can't you give me a little somethin' to chew on? I gotta do somethin' with my brain 'sides picklin' it with booze."

Doherty carefully thought about what he could safely pass on to Klinoff that he would then slip to his friends on the North Kingston police force.

"You could check on missing persons in Providence. See if the parents of an Adrian Colardo have filed a report. She's the girl I'm looking for."

"What about the husband? She was married, wasn't she? Wouldn't he file one?"

"I don't think so. I can't tell you any more about him than that."

"Ah, you're no fun," Klinoff said again. "I thought I was one of your *paid informants*." Doherty heard a loud noise and figured Klinoff had dropped the receiver. When he came back on the line Doherty bid him good-bye and hung up.

The next call he made was one he wished he didn't have to. It was to Gus Timilty. He wasn't in his office so Doherty left a message on his answering machine at Briggs and Timilty for him to call back. He killed the rest of the afternoon scouring the list Grimaldi had given him of potentially disgruntled women. It was a list that required Doherty to do some heavy lifting. One name that jumped out at him was that of Joyce Desmond. She was the wife of the guy who'd come into Fortunato's to confront Grimaldi about *defiling* his spouse. He remembered Grimaldi describing the guy as a pipsqueak, who was summarily ushered out of the restaurant by the thuggish Tony.

He didn't know if this depiction of the husband eliminated him as a suspect - or was reason to believe he might be a real possibility. Perhaps he'd been so humiliated by what happened at Fortunato's he decided to get back at Grimaldi in a more serious way. He could've hustled up some larger friends to help him do the deed. Doherty wouldn't cross him or his wife off his list until he had a face to face with them. There were a few other names on Grimaldi's list, but they were only the first names of women he'd been with. In two cases Grimaldi'd put a question mark besides each to indicate he wasn't entirely sure if he remembered their names correctly.

Doherty was about to close up shop for the day when Gus returned his call. It was after five so he was surprised his old friend was still at his desk and not at some downtown lounge knocking back a few glasses of Bushmills.

"Hey, pally. What can I do you for?"

Doherty didn't know how much of his case he wanted to share with Gus, especially in light of how their friendship had soured over the past few months.

"I need to find a woman."

"Don't we all."

"No, not that kind of woman. One who is on my rather long list of suspects in that missing persons case I told you about last week."

"The girl from Silver Lake who's wedding stats you wanted my guy at the hall to track down?"

"Yeah, that's the one."

"Who's your client, her husband or some hustler?"

"Very funny. You know I can't tell you that."

Gus laughed. "I was just testing your integrity."

"Be careful, Gus. There are days when I don't have a whole lot of it left. In any case, I haven't been able to find this woman even though I've searched through all the phone books I have here. She's not listed under her own name and she has a common last name. I don't know her husband's name. There are a ton of people with the last name of Desmond in the Rhode Island phone books."

"What's her first name?"

"Joyce. I'm not sure where she's from either. Knowing the guy who sent me on this search she could be from anywhere in the state."

"Hmm. Let me write this down. Joyce, J-O-Y-C-E, right. D-E-S-M-O-N-D. Spelled as you would expect?"

"Yup."

"Okay, I'll get my guy on it first thing in the morning. But it'll cost you."

"How much?"

"Twenty bucks plus lunch."

"Lunch?"

"Yeah, pally, lunch. You been avoiding me like the plague for a while now. I'm not going to help you anymore until we talk things out over some food. Why don't you come into the city tomorrow? I'll treat you to lunch at some nice place."

"Not in Providence. I'll meet you somewhere in between."

"Halfway, huh?" Doherty could hear the disappointment in Gus' voice. "Neutral territory? Okay, how about if we meet at a little place I know in Cranston called the Miami Diner. It's at the intersection of Park and Warwick Avenue. I'll leave it up to your skills as an investigator to find it. I'll see you there around 12:30. Don't be late; I have a busy day tomorrow." Gus hung up before Doherty could reply.

Chapter Fourteen

The Miami Diner wasn't hard to find. It was wedged into a little triangle of land between the busy roadways of Park and Warwick Avenues in Cranston. It had a small lot that was already filled when Doherty got there so he parked on Park Ave. and walked through slushy snow to the eatery. He'd purposely slipped some rubbers on over to his cordovans for just these conditions. The front of the diner facing the intersection was classic, with a neon sign over the front door lighting up the place's name despite it being broad daylight. A large palm tree sign, also lit up, rested between the *Miami* and *Diner*. Another plastic palm tree leaned over one of the two Coca Cola signs flanking each side of the facade. The other had a sign above it advertising 'Charcoal Broiled Foods'.

Inside the place had a typical set-up with booths running along both sides and a counter across the back facing the grills and the kitchen. Gus Timilty was already settled into a booth sucking on a cigarette. Before plopping down in the space on the other side Doherty slid off his coat and looped it over the hook beside the booth. Gus' well-worn trench coat hung from a hook attached to the other side. As usual his old friend was nattily dressed in a jacket and tie.

They exchanged uncomfortable looks with neither of them saying anything for a while. In the bright light Doherty noticed that more gray hairs had crept up from Gus' temples toward the top of his scalp. Timilty was busy studying the greasy menu as if it were the Book of Kells.

117

"What are you having?" Doherty asked, breaking the awkward silence.

"I don't know. I'm thinking of maybe a hamburger. How about you?"

"I'm leaning toward the grilled cheese. With some tomato soup on the side," Doherty replied without even looking at the menu. He was sure the diner had one of his usual lunch bills of fare.

A waitress, who looked to be at least in her forties, wearing dark rimmed glasses with rhinestones in the corner of the frames approached their booth. Her hair was pulled back into a severe bun and the front of her pale yellow uniform was already stained with grease. She took a note pad out of the front pocket and a pencil from behind her ear.

"What'll it be, fellas?"

Doherty ordered first and chose the tomato soup, grilled cheese and a cup of black coffee. Gus had the burger with French fries and slaw. Instead of coffee he asked for some tea. The waitress dropped two water glasses on the table and swung back toward the kitchen. Once there she clipped their orders up above the window that opened into the cooking area and yelled something at the grill man.

"How've you been?" Gus asked tentatively.

"I've been okay. You know me, always living hand to mouth. It looks like that Colardo girl I asked you to track down may've been murdered. The North Kingston police found a body fitting her description floating near the rocks along the water between Narragansett and Scarborough. It should hit the papers sometime in the next day or two even though they haven't officially identified her yet. Apparently her naked body was discovered by some guy out walking his dog. My source down there tells me she'd been beaten up and strangled before being dumped in the ocean."

"And by your source are you referring to our old pal from West Warwick cop days, Alex Klinoff?"

Doherty remained noncommittal.

"You don't have to say. It doesn't really matter to me who you get your information from. What makes you think this body belongs to the girl you were hired to find?"

"I don't know exactly. I'm working on the premise that the girl my client was with at the Anchor Inn last Saturday was abducted during the night when both of them were dead asleep, possibly because somebody'd slipped knockout drops into their drinks earlier in the evening. It's got to be more than a coincidence that a girl who fits the description my client gave me washes up dead no more than two miles from the motel."

Gus took some time to consider what Doherty had just fed him. "Seems to me you're making an awful lot of assumptions, pally. What makes you so sure it wasn't your client himself who did this deed – if in fact the dead girl is the same one he was with?"

"Don't get me wrong, Gus, I'm not writing him off as a potential suspect. But it doesn't make sense that he'd come to me, tell me the whole story and then give me a hundred bucks to find a missing girl he'd already killed."

"Maybe he's using you to cover his ass."

"Then why wouldn't he just keep his mouth shut about the whole thing? If he'd dumped her in the ocean he would've had every reason to believe her body would wash out to sea and never be found – especially this time of year. Besides what's there to stop me from going to the cops and giving them everything he told me?"

"Nothing, except that confidentiality agreement you had him sign and the hundred dollar retainer. You give up your client to the cops right from the jump, you're not gonna get many more customers once word gets around. In any case, you still have to consider the possibility that he's using you to cover his tracks."

At this point their conversation was interrupted by the waitress delivering their food. She asked if they needed anything else. Doherty requested a coffee refill in a few minutes. In the meantime Gus stirred the teabag around in his cup. When she was gone they resumed their conversation in more hushed tones.

"I gotta tell you something, pally. I don't like you cozying up to Alex Klinoff. From my experience, once a bent cop, always a bent cop - even if he's no longer wearing a badge."

"Hey, I'm aware of that. Though you've got to remember he did help me locate Frankie DeAngelo, the very guy you went AWOL looking for. A case, I might remind you, which ended with you killing two people. So tell me, Gus, where do you draw the line between a crooked ex-cop and a murdering one?"

This last comment clearly changed the tenor of their talk. Gus gave him his most unfriendly glare. At least now Doherty had put his cards on the table.

In a much quieter voice Gus muttered, "Let me remind you that my smoking those two scumbags may very well have saved your life. They weren't about to give up Christina, and I'm sure they had every intention of disposing of you as a means of tying up loose ends. I don't have any regrets about what I did that night. If I were in your shoes, I wouldn't either."

That pretty much settled the question of any guilt Gus might be feeling about the shipyard shootings. As for Doherty he'd never know how that night would've played out. What he did know is that his best friend had murdered two men, more or less in cold blood. And apparently he had no regrets about it. Not then, and obviously not now.

"Do you want to talk about your current case some more, or would you prefer that this other thing stand between us?"

Doherty didn't know what to say so he concentrated on his soup and sandwich instead. The diner was filling up and there was a notable smell of cooking grease in the air. There was also a decided chill in their booth and it had nothing to do with the radiators not working.

Eventually he decided to change the subject. "One of the reasons I deal with Klinoff is that it takes a crooked cop to know other crooked cops. He's got some inside moves with the North Kingston police that I'd never be able to drum up on my own. So far he's helped me keep pace with the police investigation into the girl's death. That's given me time to look at other people before the cops come after my client. And despite what you're thinking and my own earlier qualms about him, I don't believe he killed anyone. He may have other moral issues but I don't see him as a murderer." He thought about following this last comment with another cheap shot at Gus, but held his tongue. He'd already said enough to ruin their lunch.

"Okay, so how have you been working this case so far?" Obviously Gus had decided to put the bad business between them aside for the time being.

"I've been looking at this murder from two perspectives: The first, and simplest one, is that somebody wanted the girl dead. That could include the husband, his new girlfriend, or some other parties I haven't identified yet. That's all assuming the dead girl is the same one that my client was shacking up with. The other path I'm following is that someone is trying to frame my guy for murder on account of previous things he's done."

"What kind of things?"

"Mostly sleeping with other men's wives. You see my client is what you might call a serial philanderer. Always with married women. Usually it's a one night, slam-bam-thank-you-ma'am kind of encounter. He takes them out, buys them drinks and a nice dinner and brings them back to a motel for a night of pleasure – his if not always theirs. He promises to take them on a nice trip, but then drums up some excuse as to why he has to take them home the next day. Often leaving them feeling used."

"Sounds like quite a character. You don't think a person like that is capable of murder?"

"No, I don't. It's a big leap from being a gigolo to being a killer. I know I'm not the greatest judge of character, yet from what I've seen and heard from him, I don't think he has it in him."

They took a break from their conversation and dove back into their food. By now Doherty's soup was tepid. Gus slathered his fries and burger with more ketchup.

"I thought you were on some kind of health diet?"

Timilty waved the question away and continued to gobble his hamburger, while the ketchup oozed from the sides of the roll.

Ignoring Doherty's comment Gus said, "By the way, I got what you wanted about that Desmond woman. She lives in Johnston with her husband Peter. I have an address here." Gus struggled to get inside his jacket pocket. He pulled out a slip of paper and passed it over to Doherty, who gave it a quick glance before stuffing it into his own pocket.

"Is this thing between us only about that night?" Gus asked motioning with his hand the distance across the table.

"Yeah, pretty much."

Gus leaned in and said in a quieter voice. "You don't think I should've disposed of those two bad boys that night? You think I should've shook hands with them and said 'thanks fellas for taking such good care of my daughter'."

"I don't know, Gus. Maybe what's been bothering me is that no matter how many times I replay it in my head I always see that look on your face. It wasn't something I'd ever seen before. Nor one I want to see again. Up to then I thought I knew who you were. Now I'm not so sure."

Gus finished his lunch and sat back calmly sipping his tea. He gave Doherty a level stare and said, "Hey, pally. What's done is done. I can't unmake what happened that night. Maybe I was a little out of control. But I don't have any doubt I did what I had to do. From what I read in the papers afterwards, it doesn't sound like anybody's gonna miss those two."

"I hear you, Gus. If Christina was my daughter maybe I'd feel different about it. I was hoping things could've been settled between us and Kevin O'Shaughnessy without bloodshed. I guess that's the difference between you and me. I saw too much killing over in Europe to want to go back to that if I can help it."

"It can be a mean world out there, especially for guys in our profession. Look at you. You thought you could make a nice little living searching for missing people. Guys or gals who'd run off with somebody they weren't married to. Now you find yourself getting involved with mob guys, pimps, crooked politicians and murderers. If you don't like the way your practice has turned out you could get a job stacking shelves at the A&P. Or better yet, go back to being an errand boy for the DeCenza machine."

Doherty was at a loss for words. Instead he laid two tens on the table and said, "That's for the info you dug up for me." Then he picked up the check and paid it at the register, leaving Gus sitting in their booth when he exited the Miami Diner. All the way back to West Warwick he wondered why a greasy spoon located at a major intersection in Cranston was named after a city in tropical Florida.

Chapter Fifteen

Doherty was sitting in his office smoking a Camel with his feet in their usual spot on the desk when Agnes checked in later that afternoon. She went immediately into his office and tossed the evening *Bulletin* in his direction.

"Front page, lower right-hand corner," she said.

Doherty unfolded the late edition of the Providence paper. His eye caught the headline: *"Woman's Body Pulled from Ocean."* He read on:

> Early yesterday morning the dead body of a yet unidentified young woman was discovered floating near the rocks along Ocean Road between Narragansett and Scarborough State Beach. The North Kingston Police estimate that the woman had been floating in the water for at least three days and perhaps longer. All they could report at this time was that the dead woman appeared to be somewhere in her twenties and had no clothing on when she was discovered.
>
> Arnold Manuel, a Narragansett resident, first discovered the body while walking his dog along the rocky shoreline. Manuel explained, "I had to get Barkley out of the house for his daily walk. I hadn't been able to walk him for a day and a half because of the

snowstorm. That's when I saw the body crashing up against the rocks."

Police believe they will be able to identify the deceased very soon as a number of feelers have been extended to other police departments around the state for reports on missing persons fitting the dead girl's description. They have issued a bulletin for information from anyone who may have seen a young woman entering the water along that part of the coast sometime between last Sunday and Tuesday. They are also asking that if anyone saw a person or persons in the act of carrying a body or disposing of one somewhere in the vicinity of where the girl was discovered they should immediately contact the North Kingston Police or the Rhode Island State Police.

No photos accompanied the story. From what Klinoff had said the body was too bloated for the police to publicly release any pictures. In addition it would have been in bad taste for a family newspaper like the *Journal-Bulletin* to print such pictures.

Doherty read the short piece through twice then looked up to see that Agnes was still standing in front of his desk.

"Interestin' that they didn't say anythin' about the girl bein' strangled."

"I'm not surprised," Doherty replied. "The cops probably want to give the killer a false sense that they're not immediately suspecting murder. I have no doubt the cause of her death will come out soon enough. What's bothering me is that they haven't identified the dead girl yet, at least not for public consumption."

"What're you thinkin'?"

"I'm not sure. I'm assuming Adrian Colardo's parents reported her missing after my visit to their place. If they didn't it could take some time for the dead girl's real identity to be discovered. In that case there may be only a few people who know who she is. You and me being two of them."

"It could be somebody else. Maybe this isn't the girl your client was with."

Doherty shook his head. "Based on the description Klinoff gave me, I've got to believe it's her. Everything points in that direction. The probability that she and Grimaldi had their drinks doctored at the Greene Inn, that she was abducted from the motel, and that the motel owner saw a car speeding away from his place in the middle of the night all add up to this body belonging to Adrian Colardo. Unless…"

"Unless what?"

Doherty was reluctant to put into words what had been sticking in the back of his mind all along. "Unless Richie Grimaldi has been trying to pull the wool over my eyes from the beginning."

"Pull the wool? What do you mean?"

"He could've murdered this Adrian himself and then decided to hire a PI to find her when he knew all along that she was already dead. It's possible he killed her for whatever reason and then dumped her body in the ocean. Maybe he figured she'd never be discovered, but just in case she was he'd have somebody like me to cover for him. Look at how it would appear to the police. Why would they believe he murdered the girl and then hired a private detective to find the very person he killed?"

"From what you've told me, boss, I don't think Grimaldi is that clever."

Doherty smiled at his secretary. "He's clever enough to get some reasonably intelligent women to swallow his pick-up lines and spend the night with him in a motel."

Agnes took a few seconds to think about what Doherty had just said. "That's different; in those cases he's takin' advantage of their desperation and unhappiness."

"Still, Agnes, that requires a certain amount of planning. How to get them to buy his pitch, how to get them to go down to the beach with him, how to get them into bed and then how to renege on his false promises. He's got to have planned out each of his conquests pretty carefully."

"That's all true but it still doesn't answer why he'd want to kill this particular girl. From what you've discovered so far, it sounds like he's been with some women who were a lot more difficult than this one."

Doherty was lost in thought for moment. "You're right. I don't believe he killed her," he said finally. "I was just thinking out loud. Besides it's not his style. If he wanted to hire a PI to give him cover he wouldn't have hired someone with such a sterling reputation as mine for finding lost people."

Agnes let out a soft chuckle. "Better be careful, boss. You don't want your head to get too swelled your hat won't fit anymore."

They both sat quietly for few minutes, pleased that the mood in the room had been lightened. "Where does this leave you now? What's next on your agenda?"

"I've got one more married couple to visit. Then I might have to back-track to some people I've already talked to. There are a few things that don't sit right with me. I have to figure out how to make them right."

The winter precipitation had turned from snow to rain leaving some roadways an obstacle course of slush and deep puddles. Cars were splashing large waves of water onto the sidewalks causing pedestrians to run for cover. Johnston was a town that sat just north of Cranston up Rt. 5 from West War-wick. It was nearly six when he reached the Desmond home. Joyce and Peter Desmond lived in a two story duplex in the growing center of town. Theirs was the right half of the side-by-side units. He figured he'd arrive at supper-time in hopes of catching both of them at home.

Joyce Desmond answered the door holding a young baby on her hip. She was a petite, attractive blond. The child had the two middle fingers of its right hand firmly stuffed into its mouth. Before Mrs. Desmond could say an-ything Doherty flashed his license and said in as friendly a voice as he could muster, "I'm an investigator and I was wondering if I could come in and talk with you for a few minutes. This won't take long."

The woman looked confused. Doherty could smell the odor of cooked food coming from somewhere in the house.

She turned around and shouted, "Pete, could you come to the front door please. There's a man here who wants to talk with us. He says he's an inves-tigator."

Once again Doherty saw the advantage of being confused with a po-liceman. While waiting for the husband he checked out what he could see of their apartment. Inside the doorway was a foyer that opened up into a small living room. Beyond it was a hallway that he figured led to a kitchen where the food smells were coming from.

A man appeared carrying a glass of some kind of bubbly soda, or maybe it was a mixed drink with soda in it. He was small like the wife, though not small enough to qualify as the pipsqueak Grimaldi described him as. He would only have looked unusually small next to Grimaldi's cousin's beefy son, Tony, who'd ushered him out of the restaurant. Desmond had brownish blond hair that was beginning to thin on top. He wore a cardigan sweater over a plaid shirt and looked to be about four inches and fifty pounds smaller than Doherty.

"What is this all about?" he asked. "We were sitting down having our supper." He was clearly irritated with the intrusion into their domestic life.

"My name is Doherty," he said showing his license to the husband. "I'm an investigator and I was hoping you and your wife could help me with a case I'm working on." Again he purposely left out the 'private' part of his job title.

The baby began to fuss in its mother's arms. "Why don't you come in and sit while we finish eating." The husband gave his wife a look of irritation that said, 'What do you think you're doing inviting a total stranger into our home?'

Doherty followed her down the short hallway into a small dining area. Only a low counter separated it from the kitchen. The whole first floor was tiny just like the couple who lived there. A young boy of about six was sitting at the table moving some peas around on his plate. Doherty gave the kid a quick wave. The boy looked up then immediately dropped his head back to his meal.

"Can I get you some coffee?" the wife asked from the kitchen.

"Joyce!" the husband blurted out.

Just to get under the guy's skin a little more, Doherty accepted the offer. While she was gone he glanced at the husband though neither of them spoke. The wife returned to the dining room with a cup of black coffee and the baby still on her hip. Pete Desmond had stopped eating and was now staring at their uninvited guest.

"What exactly do you want with us, Mr. Doherty?" he said through tight lips.

"I'm working on a missing persons case and a name popped up that I think you two are familiar with." Doherty's mention of a missing person got the young boy's attention.

Joyce and Pete Desmond exchanged looks of concern.

"Does the name Richie Grimaldi ring a bell with either of you?" This time the husband gave his wife a hard look. He couldn't be sure, but Doherty thought the real focus of Desmond's attention was on the baby. Grimaldi's name left everyone uncomfortably quiet. Doherty drank his coffee while dead eyeing the Desmond family over the rim of the cup.

Finally the husband asked, "Is Grimaldi the person who's missing?"

"I'm afraid I can't tell you that."

Desmond then turned to the young boy and said, "Jeffrey, are you finished with your supper?"

"All except for my peas," the kid said in a whiney voice that indicated he wasn't particularly fond of that vegetable.

"You can leave your peas this time. Why don't you go up to your room? Your mother and I have some serious business to discuss with Mr. Doherty."

Jeffrey rose but stood anchored by his place. "Are you a real detective, like on TV?" the boy asked.

"Jeffrey, go to your room!" the father barked at him.

"Peter," the wife pleaded, but he just gave her a cold look.

The boy slowly sauntered out of the eating area and up a flight of stairs. When they heard the door to his room shut, the man turned his attention back to Doherty.

"What is the meaning of this intrusion into our home?" Desmond asked. It came out more as a challenge than a question.

Doherty waited a few beats to increase his hosts' discomfort. "It's my understanding that some time ago Joyce here went off for an overnight with Richie Grimaldi. Is that correct?"

Joyce Desmond lowered her head but nodded briefly before she did.

"It was all a big mistake," Pete Desmond protested. "Isn't that right, honey?" His wife did not respond.

"A mistake, huh? What exactly was mistaken about your wife spending the night in a motel room with another man?"

"Why you sonofabitch. I oughta throw…"

"Peter, please, no more threats. I won't lie. I spent a night with that man.

128

I'm sorry now that I did. I never meant to hurt anyone. It was just…" she tailed off at the end and Doherty was not about to press her on what it *just* was.

Instead he turned his attention back to the husband. "It's my understanding that afterwards you went into Fortunato's restaurant in Providence where Grimaldi is part owner and threatened him?"

"Well, what's a man suppose to do when he learns that some nobody from nowhere has had his way with his wife?" Never having had a wife, Doherty was in no position to answer this question.

"Did you threaten Grimaldi?"

"I'd say it hardly amounted to a threat. I simply asked him to leave my wife alone."

"What did he say?"

Desmond bit his lip and looked away. "I'd rather not …"

"He told my husband he was done with me and I wasn't such a good lay to begin with. Those were his exact words, weren't they, Pete?" Desmond did not respond. He just sat there stewing in embarrassment.

"Then what happened?"

"Grimaldi had some big palooka who worked for him throw me out," Desmond mumbled.

"And that was the end of it?"

Desmond again looked directly at the baby now sitting on its mother's lap.

"Yes, more or less," he answered obliquely. Doherty did not want to contemplate what he was thinking. He took one last long look at the baby before standing to leave.

"Am I to understand that neither of you has had any contact with Richie Grimaldi since the incidents you just described?"

They both quickly answered, "Yes."

"Just for my records, how long ago did these two interactions take place?"

Pete and Joyce Desmond looked at one another. "Over a year at least. I don't remember exactly," she responded quietly. "Pete went to confront Richie just a few days after I returned. It was all over a long time ago, right honey?' she said turning to her husband. Desmond did not respond.

"I'm sorry I spoiled your supper. Thank you very much for the coffee, Mrs. Desmond."

Chapter Sixteen

Late the next morning Doherty drove up Atwells Avenue to pay his client another surprise visit. Grimaldi was alone behind the bar in Fortunato's. It was not yet lunchtime so the only other signs of human activity were the sounds coming from the kitchen. His client was busy setting up some wine glasses fresh from the dishwasher. When he saw Doherty he gave him a look that indicated he wasn't particularly happy to see his PI.

"Well, you're a sight for sore eyes. Have you found Adrian yet?"

Doherty took a seat on one of the stools and told Grimaldi to give him a fresh cup of coffee. He intentionally did not word it as a request.

Grimaldi brought over the coffee and stood leaning on the other side of the bar.

"Come around and take a seat, Richie," he said patting the adjacent stool. "We need to talk."

"Look I'm kinda busy getting things ready for the lunch crowd."

"I'm not asking. I said sit down."

Grimaldi cautiously lifted the flip plate on the bar and came over to the other side. He took a seat on the edge of the stool next to Doherty. "Have you found Adrian yet?" he asked again.

"I haven't, though I think the police have. Did you see yesterday's evening *Bulletin?*"

Grimaldi waved his hand. "I don't read the papers most days. They got nothing but bad news in them."

Doherty smiled. "Well, it looks like yesterday's bad news may be aimed right at you. The North Kingston police found the naked body of a dead girl in the ocean a little more than a stone's throw from the Anchor Inn. They haven't officially identified her yet, but my source down there described the deceased as bearing a striking resemblance to your Adrian."

Grimaldi covered his mouth with his hand. "Do you think it's really her? It could be somebody else, couldn't it?" His voice was weak with an edge of desperation in it.

"Yeah, it could be. However, if I were you I'd get myself a lawyer, and fast. Once they identify her it won't take long for the cops to find out she spent what may've been her last night alive with you."

"I didn't kill her!" Grimaldi protested. "Why would I spend a hundred bucks to hire somebody like you to find her if I already knew she was dead?"

"That's what I've been asking myself."

"Meaning what?" his client said challenging him.

"Meaning like maybe you hired me to cover your tracks. Maybe your plan was to kill the girl and then hire a PI to go on some futile search to find her. That would've been a pretty smart idea."

"Are you telling me you're sitting here in my place, taking my money and accusing me of setting up the whole thing?"

"I'm not accusing you of anything, Richie. I considered the notion that you might've hired me as an alibi. But the more I thought about it, the more I came to the conclusion you aren't clever enough to devise such a plan. Besides I couldn't come up with a good reason as to why you'd kill this particular girl among all the ones you've been with."

"What's that suppose to mean?" Grimaldi asked accusingly.

Determined to get to the point of his visit, Doherty ignored the question and said, "Let me ask you something kind of personal. Do you use protection when you sleep with these women?"

"You mean like rubbers?"

"Yeah, that exactly what I mean."

132

Grimaldi raised his head and stared at the ceiling, trying to recall the nature of his many sexual conquests. "Of course I do - most of the time."

"What do you mean *most of the time*?"

"Well, you know, some of these broads tell me they got some kinda device inside them. Like a diaphragm or something. I don't know too much about those things, so I just take their word for it."

"Jesus, Richie. You can be one stupid sonofabitch. Have you ever considered that maybe one of these women who told you she was using a device, might've been putting you on?"

Grimaldi looked confused. He shook his head and said, "Why would they do something like that?"

"Well, for one, maybe they were hoping you'd get them pregnant. Could be their husbands don't want kids. Or he might have something wrong with him so they can't have them. You know, things like that do happen. Some women'll do almost anything to have a baby. One of them might've thought you'd take her away from her sad marriage if you knew she was pregnant with your child."

"What kind of crazy broad would think that?"

Doherty had to shake his head at this last remark. "The same kind of crazy broad that would shack up in a motel with a guy she barely knew. There've been cases where women do that sort of thing and end up dead."

"Look, Doherty, you're making me nervous here. What're driving at?"

Doherty asked for a refill of his coffee and then laid things out for Grimaldi. "I've been looking at this case from two directions. The first is that perhaps somebody wanted Adrian Colardo dead for some reason I haven't been able to figure out. Once the body's identified, the cops will no doubt take a run at the husband. He's a likely choice especially since he has a bad temper and is already making time with a younger version of his wife. Problem is if he really wanted to get rid of his wife he could've just divorced her. Though since they're both Catholic that might've been a problem. Plus getting a divorce can take some time and a good chunk of cash. He's already committed adultery with his new girlfriend so there would be legitimate grounds for divorce."

"Yeah, the husband. I like that. He could've killed her 'cause she slept with me. Isn't that what they call a 'crime of passion'?"

Doherty ignored Grimaldi's grasping at straws. "The other way I've been approaching this case is by taking a close look at the women whose names you gave me on that list. Those women, or their husbands, could've had some leftover anger on account of what you did to them. One of them might've decided the best way to get back at you would be to abduct your latest conquest. And if she ended up dead all the better because that would make you a murder suspect."

"Why would some broad do that? Just 'cause I spent the night with her and then decided to drive her home the next day instead of taking her on a nice vacation like I promised. Hell, Doherty, you and I both know I'm only in it for the sex."

"That's the problem, Richie. You see a lot of women don't approach these things the way men do. They want to be loved not just screwed. Or at least be given the illusion that you really care about them."

"Hey, that's their problem, not mine," Grimaldi said dismissively.

"Oh, but it is your problem if one of them happens to get knocked up from one of your sexual escapades. And it can really go south if the husband gets involved."

Grimaldi was trying to wrap his thoughts around what Doherty had just presented to him.

"Are you trying to tell me that one of these broads and her husband could've killed Adrian to get back at me because I accidentally knocked her up?"

"Look, you've got to face facts, it is a possibility," he stated flatly, all the while keeping the slight resemblance of Joyce Desmond's baby to Richie Grimaldi in mind.

"What are you gonna do now, Mr. Private Eye?"

"I'm not sure. I've got a couple of people I want to check back on. In the meantime if I were you I'd prepare myself for a police interrogation. And whatever you do, be honest with them no matter how much of an asshole it makes you appear. You try to blur the truth while talking with them it'll only make you look like the dishonest, and possibly guilty, creep they're gonna assume you are."

134

Doherty floated through the late afternoon crowd at Cherry & Webb noting that except for the occasional store clerk, he was the only man in the store. It was a slow day due to the inclement weather, so there were no customers in the lingerie section when Doherty spotted Doris Donahue. She was leaning up against a counter where the cash register was talking to another salesgirl. They were laughing rather loudly at some ribald comment as he came within earshot. When Doris recognized him she drifted away from her friend and headed in his direction.

She gave him a come-on smile and said, "Did you come back to get that sexy nightgown for your girlfriend?"

Doherty shook his head and tried to put on a sad face. "Things didn't work out with her. At least I saved some money by not buying it when I was here last week."

"Does that mean you came back just to see me?"

"Maybe." He looked at his watch. It was twenty minutes to five. "What time do you get off work?" Doris Donahue upped the wattage on her smile.

"Five-thirty. But Ellen can punch me out if I want to leave a little early." He assumed Ellen was the woman she'd been gabbing with. He looked over to where the other girl was standing. She gave Doherty a knowing smile.

"Can I buy you a drink?"

"Sure. I can meet you somewhere at around five-fifteen if you don't feel like waiting around here in Cherry's."

"Sounds good. I don't know the city all that well so why don't you name the watering hole."

"We could meet in the Falstaff Room at the Sheraton Biltmore. It's a little pricey, but I'm worth it." They exchanged smiles and agreed to connect at a quarter past five in the lounge at Providence's most prestigious hotel. Doherty had a vague idea where it was; he thought he could find it in the half hour he had to work with.

The hotel was only a few slushy blocks walk from Cherry & Webb. On the way Doherty slipped into Shepard's to check out the men's shoe department where Stanislaw Krykowski, the ex-Nazi whose death he was responsible for, was working when they first encountered each other. A tall guy with a dark comb-over had taken the dead man's place in the department. Doherty didn't see the department supervisor, Barney O'Mara, either. He wondered if O'Mara still worked at the store. A lot can change in the retail trade in two years. He hoped O'Mara hadn't lost his job because he hired an ex-Nazi to sell shoes; a guy who also turned out to be a rapist and a murderer.

He strolled over to the Biltmore and entered the elaborate lobby of the city's most famous hotel. It was bigger than the ground floor of any hotel Doherty'd ever been in. He took particular notice of a notation way up on one of the columns in the lobby that explained this was the high water mark from the 1938 hurricane that had flooded the hotel as well as the rest of downtown Providence. Along one wall were historic pictures of the Biltmore during its early years including a few of it partially under water during various hurricanes. One was of Hurricane Carol, which Doherty remembered well from 1953.

The Falstaff Room was a well-appointed space with crystal chandeliers, wood paneling all around and an oak bar. He found a table far enough away from where a man was tickling some piano keys so that he would be able to talk quietly with Doris Donahue. There were a fair number of suits in the room drinking off a hard day's work handling other people's money. Doris arrived ten minutes late.

"Have trouble getting away from the store?" he asked.

"Not really. I'm just in the habit of making men wait." It was a comment that might've had other meaning if Doherty wanted to dwell on it.

"What's on your mind, handsome?" Doris was the kind of girl who liked to get right to the point, and then get business out of the way to make room for more pleasant things.

"I paid a visit to your husband at his sister's in Cumberland the other day."

"My ex-husband," she corrected. "How's poor Eddie doing these days? Is he working yet?"

"According to him he's doing some odd jobs. He did say an old army pal might be able to get him on at American Screw come spring."

Doris shook her head. "Eddie's got a lot of them - old army buddies

136

who are going to set him up in this or that. Never works out in the end. Seems to me there's a big difference from being a buddy in the army and being the same buddy out here in the real world."

Doherty couldn't argue with that assessment. He'd had a lot of pals when he was in uniform, but he hasn't seen any of them since he was discharged. Sometimes it's better to leave the bonds forged in combat back on the battlefields.

"A couple of things have been bothering me since we last talked. I'd like to get back to that conversation if we could."

Doris craned her neck and caught the attention of the waiter who was wending his way between the cocktail tables. "Let's get a drink first. Then we can talk."

The waiter approached their table with a small white towel draped over his arm. "Can I offer you a libation?" he asked obsequiously. The fellow was older and slightly stooped. He looked like he could've been working at the Biltmore when the place was flooded back in '38. He was wearing a starched white shirt, a black vest and a black bowtie. His hair was more of a memory than a current reality.

Doris ordered a dry martini with olives, Doherty a Jameson neat. He didn't know too many women who drank martinis, but he liked it that she was a serious drinker and not one of those girls who sipped fruity drinks with small plastic umbrellas in them. They talked about the weather and Doris' work at the Cherry & Webb while they waited for their drinks. Her martini was filled to the very brim, but the waiter did not spill a drop transferring it from his tray to the table. That showed experience in the trade. She took a good slug of her drink, following it with a sound that was somewhere between a sigh and a moan.

"Okay, Mr. PI, you can begin your interrogation now. Just make sure you keep the drinks coming."

"When we talked last time you said you tossed your husband out right after your weekend with Richie Grimaldi. According to Eddie you told him you'd found someone you thought you could fall in love with."

"Did I say that?" She shook her head. "I don't really remember what I said to Eddie at the end," she added trying to make light of the remark.

"Makes me sound like a louse, doesn't it?"

"Look, Doris. Let's stop beating around the bush. I've met Richie. You couldn't possibly feel like you could fall in love with a guy like him after only one night in some fleabag motel. I see you as someone who's a little more discriminating than that. Somebody who wouldn't be so easily swept off her feet."

"Discriminating, huh? I like that. You got some big words there for a small town detective. So what's your point?"

"Assuming what you said to Eddie about Grimaldi is true then I'm of two minds."

"Two minds, huh." She leaned forward and gave him a flirty look. "Does that mean both your heads are thinking about the same thing?"

He chose to ignore this remark, not sure how far he was willing to go in that direction with Doris Donahue. "One part of me is thinking you said that to Eddie purposely to hurt his feelings. Maybe you wanted him out of the apartment and the only way to accomplish that was to insult him in the worst possible way. No guy wants to hear that the person he loves is stuck on someone else - especially if the person saying it is his wife."

Doris licked her well-painted red lips. "Makes me sound awfully cruel, doesn't it."

"Yes it does. But I'm not buying it. I know you felt like your marriage had run its course and that your husband was something of a ne'er-do-well. But just from my short conversation with him I could tell that Eddie isn't such a bad guy. It's not like he was a drunk who beat you or ran around with other women behind your back. Some husbands can be real rats. He wasn't one of them, was he?"

Doris finished her martini and signaled the waiter for another one.

"What're you driving at? If you don't believe I said what I did to Eddie because I was fed up with him, then why else would I have thrown him out?"

Doherty sipped the last of his Jameson and decided to have another to keep Doris' martini company. When the waiter delivered her drink he asked for a refill.

"I think you really did think you were in love with Grimaldi. When you said what you did to Eddie, you thought it was true."

Doris let out a laugh that was loud enough to capture the attention of a few drinkers at nearby tables. "Me, in love with Grimaldi. Now that's a corker. Jesus, Doherty, what kind of a woman do you take me for? You think I'm the kind of gal who'd fall head over heels for a guy after one night in a cheap motel?"

"That's just the point, Doris. I don't think you were with him for only one night. I think you went out with Grimaldi a few times. At least enough times to fall under the spell of his limited charms. Yes, your marriage had hit a dead end. As a result you were more than willing to give yourself over to someone like Richie. I'm thinking you did so on more than one occasion. I can easily check this with him, but I'd rather hear it from you first. You're a smart girl. I can't imagine you falling for Grimaldi's game unless on this particular occasion he was playing for real. Or at least was able to convince you he was. So why don't you give me the whole story? Without the varnish."

A frown crept over Doris' face. She was still an attractive woman, even if her years were beginning to slide by. He reckoned she was still looking for more out of life than a job handling undergarments at Cherry & Webb, nights out with her girlfriends and an occasional roll in the hay with some guy who was only half interested in her.

"I first met Richie while he was tending bar at a restaurant he owns with his cousin up on Atwells Avenue. I was there with my girlfriend Angela. The two of us were sitting at the bar complaining about our husbands. Richie was down at the other end glancing at us the whole time. I could tell he was trying hard to act like he wasn't listening to our conversation, while all the while taking in everything we were saying. When we ordered the next round he told us it was on the house. We weren't about to turn him down since both of us were half stewed already."

"Which one of you did he come on to?" Doherty asked, anticipating Grimaldi's act.

She shot him a sheepish grin - or as sheepish as anything Doris Donahue could produce. "I think he was working both of us, trying to see who would crack first."

"And who did?"

"Why me, of course," she said proudly. "Angela's good looking and all

139

but she doesn't play around. Her husband is a mean bastard. And as big as a house too. I feel sorry for her having to get into bed with that hunk of lard every night."

"What happened next?"

"Nothing much. Angela left before she got too drunk to drive. She drinks those sissy type drinks that are more fruit juice than booze."

"What about you?"

"I stayed for a while. It was a Tuesday night so the place wasn't very crowded – either in the restaurant or at the bar. It wasn't long before Richie started coming on to me. You know, touching my hand every time he slid by my place. I was pretty drunk, though not too drunk to know what he was after. The next thing I knew it was almost closing time. I couldn't take him back to my place because Eddie was still living there. And Richie didn't offer to take me to his. When that didn't happen, I assumed he was just another one of those married guys looking for something different."

"And that was it?"

She gave Doherty a coy smile. "He closed up the restaurant and we went out to his car and made out for a while. I hadn't done that since high school. I let him feel me up but that was the extent of it. I was wearing a girdle and I wasn't about to squeeze myself out of it in the front seat of his Buick. After that I saw him a couple more times. One time I even shanghaied Angela away from fat boy to come with me. Richie brought along a friend for her. We had dinner on him at the restaurant and a few drinks afterwards. I remember we all had a real good time. But it was getting late for us working girls so we had to beg off. Angela caught hell from her fat husband when she got home, poor thing."

"What about Eddie? Did he have anything to say about your late nights out?"

"Oh, yeah, he had plenty to say. I was fed up with him by then. I told him he should keep his yap shut until he found somewhere else to live. You see I'd already been with Richie enough times to think we had something going on. All of this happened before the time he took me down to the beach. I've got to say he wined and dined me that weekend, including a fancy dinner at the Greene Inn. We spent the first night in a nice room there and the next

140

night at the motel. And if it doesn't embarrass you for me to say it, he was the best lay I ever had. There, I've said it and I'm not ashamed. That weekend reminded me of how making love with Eddie was like having a sandbag laid on my chest. Richie was different. He knew how to please a girl."

"How did things end between the two of you? Did he just stop coming by the store or calling you?"

"I wish it was that simple. I thought Richie was a real gentleman. I didn't realize that he was working his game on another woman the whole time he was squiring me around. And the worst part is she was somebody I knew."

"Really, who was it?"

"It was goddamn Angela, that's who! Can you believe that? I introduced them, helped fix her up with his friend, who treated her like a lady for a change on our double date - and then she goes and snakes Richie behind my back."

"What about Grimaldi's role in all this? Isn't he partially responsible?"

"What about him? The rotten bastard can burn in hell as far as I'm concerned." The booze was bringing out Doris' less attractive side.

She ordered a third martini and Doherty began to think the evening wasn't going to end well for either of them.

"One other question, Doris, before you get too tanked. How do you know this Angela? Is she a friend from work?"

"I met her and her husband at the VFW post. That was Eddie's idea of a good time: taking the wife down to the O'Donnell post for Las Vegas night or some other event like that. No matter how much they tried to toots up the place it still smelled of BO and stale beer. I'll always have bad feelings about the VFW because it's where Eddie lost all of our money playing cards, mostly with Angela's husband and some other crooks. She and I were the only wives who didn't think spending a Saturday night at the O'Donnell passed for a night on the town. I considered myself someone who was made for better things. That's when I decided I didn't want to spend the rest of my life with a small time loser like Eddie Donahue."

"Is this Angela married to a man named Mike Finnegan?"

"Yeah, that's her sweetheart. Everybody down there calls him Fats. She told me he wasn't so heavy when they first starting dating after he came home from the service. If you ask me I think he's put on those extra pounds by sitting on his ass at the post running scams on other vets like Eddie. The way I look at it now, Angela got what she deserved with fat boy. I thought she was my friend until she stole Richie right out from under me."

"If it's any consolation, Doris, I'd say not getting tricked into falling for Richie Grimaldi was probably one of the better things that happened to you this year."

She looked down at her drink. "I know. It's just that a girl my age can get lonely sometimes. I thought Richie was my ticket out of this hum-drum life I was living." She then put her head on Doherty's shoulder and he made no effort to remove it.

Chapter Seventeen

D oris raised the blanket and gave Doherty a good slap on his bare but-
tocks. "Time to rise and shine, handsome. You need to drive me to
Cherry's this morning. I don't want to be late for work."

He raised his head as best he could. Whatever was going on in his cra-
nium felt like thirty miles of bad road. He tried to swallow, but the inside of
his mouth had about as much moisture in it as the Gobi Desert. Doris was
standing at the foot of the bed clad only in a half slip and brassiere. She was
doing her best to brush her hair into some kind of order.

"Where am I?" he mumbled.

She let out a clownish laugh. "At my place in North Providence. You
better hop to it if you want to have some coffee before we leave. There's
some in the percolator on the kitchen counter. You'll also find a stale muffin
or two in the breadbox next to it."

After she left the bedroom he swung his legs over the side of the bed
and surveyed the damage. His clothes were strewn across the floor along
with some of the garments Doris had been wearing the night before. He gathered up what he could find of his duds and stumbled off in the direction of
the bathroom. Thankfully it was right off the bedroom. After splashing some
cold water on his face he found a bottle of mouthwash under the sink and
gargled with it for a full minute. There was a large container of aspirin in the
medicine chest so he took it down and swallowed three of them to ease the

143

pain in his head. Then slowly he began to wrestle his consciousness back toward reality.

After dressing in the bathroom he emerged to find Doris fully clad leaning on the kitchen counter. She had a cup of coffee in one hand and a cigarette in the other.

"Are you sure you're in good enough shape to drive?" she asked after scrutinizing her overnight guest.

"I'll be okay as soon as you pour me a cup of joe." She complied and handed it to him with a knowing smirk plastered across her face. After taking a big gulp he brought out his cigs and tamped the loose end of a Camel before lighting it. He felt his life starting to get back on track.

Doris looked at her watch. "We have to fly in about five minutes. I'm just going to touch up my face a little. Your coat and hat are hanging on a rack by the front door."

Before she could leave he grabbed her by the arm. "Tell me something, Doris, did we... you know?"

She gave him a wry smile and said, "I'm not the kind of girl who tends to kiss and tell. I'll leave it up to your imagination. My memory isn't so good this morning either. I was pretty far gone after those three martinis and the half a bottle of bourbon we drank after we got here. You did your best to kill the other half."

She sashayed off to the bathroom while Doherty took down his coat and fedora. When she returned he helped her into her woolen coat with the fake fur collar; she accompanied it with a wide brimmed hat. She then took his arm and led him down three flights of stairs out into the cold. He only vaguely remembered mounting the staircase the previous evening. His Chevy was parked at an awkward angle right in front of the apartment building.

"Where's your car?"

"Oh, brother, I had to leave it in the city last night. I was too snookered to drive. You weren't in much better shape, but I had a feeling you were more experienced at driving under the influence."

Doherty rubbed his eyes trying to bring the world back into focus. He wanted to rekindle the conversation about her ex-husband, Angela and the fat man at the O'Donnell Post, but he couldn't for the life of him remember where they'd left off.

The roads were more or less cleared of snow so it was an easy drive despite his diminished condition. He couldn't recall enough of the trip to Doris' place the night before for the return drive into the city center to be even vaguely familiar. She gave good directions and chatted about inconsequential things along the way. He mostly replied in grunts since nothing she was saying bore any relationship to his case.

"I hope I didn't get a parking ticket for leaving my car overnight. There must be a lot of people in Providence who leave their cars on the street at night, don't you think?"

"I wouldn't know," he stammered. "I still live in a town where most folks can leave their cars anywhere; even unlocked with the keys still in them."

Once inside the downtown area they could see a fair number of people bustling to and fro. The big city was coming to life for the new day. He wended his way up Westminster Street past Shepard's and pulled over in front of Cherry & Webb. It didn't look as if the store was open to the public yet.

"You can drop me here. The service entrance is just around the corner. Will I see you again, handsome?"

Doherty gave her his best smile, or at least the best he could muster under the circumstances. "I don't know. I'm not the kind of guy who tends to kiss and tell."

With that Doris slid across the seat and gave him the deepest French kiss she could work up that early in the morning. "Well, if you change your mind you can always find me in the lingerie department at Cherry's."

"Are you going to be all right?"

"I'll be fine. This isn't the first time I've come to work hungover. I doubt we'll have much foot traffic in this weather." She patted Doherty high up on his thigh. "Be seeing you, big boy."

After she got out he sat in the car and lit up another Camel. As much as he tried he was unable to piece together the various parts of his night with Doris. If they had gone to bed together he couldn't recall any of the details. What was important is that he remembered the gist of their conversation in the Falstaff Room about her ex-husband, the fat man and the fat man's wife. And of course Richie Grimaldi's role in the whole sordid affair. That at least gave him some leads for his next moves.

That night he'd been sitting in his car for nearly an hour watching the customers trickle out Fortunato's Italian Cuisine. Doherty was already sucking on his third Camel when the big kid Tony came out of the front door wearing a heavy plaid woolen jacket. He pulled on a knit cap and headed off into the night. Since he was walking up Federal Hill, Doherty assumed he either lived nearby or was meeting some friends in the neighborhood.

Doherty hadn't wanted to confront his client with other people around. He wanted Grimaldi's attention all to himself. Ten minutes later the lights were turned off inside the restaurant and Richie exited Fortunato's wearing only a light windbreaker over his white shirt and tie. Before he got too far Doherty hopped out of his car and cut him off.

"Well, well, if it isn't my private eye sneaking up on his own client."

"Shut up, asshole. Before you say anything more we need to get a few things straight between us if I'm going to continue working for you."

Grimaldi pulled his coat closed and turned up the collar against the cold wind. "Make it fast; it's as cold as a witch's tit out here."

"Have you had any visits from the police yet?"

"A coupla suits came by here earlier today. I ducked out back through the kitchen and let my cousin Anthony handle them," he said, as if dodging the cops was an everyday occurrence.

"That means they must've ID'd the dead girl as Adrian. I can assure you, Richie, they'll be back. You can't skip out on them forever."

"I know that. I just wanted to make sure I had a lawyer in my corner before I said anything to them. So what're you gonna do, Mr. Private Eye, to get me out of this jam? I thought I hired you to find the girl and prove me innocent if anything bad happened to her. You don't seem to be doing a very good job."

"No, you hired me to find Adrian. Unfortunately the police beat me to it. As far as proving you innocent of any wrongdoing, I could help you a lot better if you'd been on the level with me from the get-go."

"What're you talking about? I been square with you. I gave you a hundred bucks and that list of broads I'd slept with, didn't I. What more do you want?"

"Why don't we start with Doris Donahue?"

He could tell from the changed expression on his client's face that the mention of her name hit a sore spot. Trying his best to recover Grimaldi said, "Let's go someplace warm to talk this over. I'm freezing my gonads off out here."

"Sure, where to?"

"There's a tap room a block or so in that direction," he said pointing down toward the lower end of Atwells. "It stays open late. Anthony and I go there sometimes after work to unwind. It's a dump, but it has a good jukebox and it'll be warm. They know me there," he added as if that held some importance.

The two men walked rapidly through the bitterly cold night. The bar had a small sign outside that simply said *Louie's* on it. It was nice to be inside even if the place was the dump Grimaldi described it as. Dean Martin was belting out "That's Amore" on the jukebox when they walked in. Grimaldi exchanged greetings with a bartender named Sal then led Doherty to a plain Formica table near the back. Once they were settled he walked up to the bar to get a Jameson for Doherty and a Scotch for himself.

When he returned Grimaldi tried playing it casual. "What do you wanna know about that Doris broad?"

"Don't play slick with me, Richie. I know all about your affair with Mrs. Donahue. According to her she wasn't just a one-night stand like most of your other girlfriends. She made it sound like you were serious enough to spend some real time and money on her. I want to hear from you what happened between the two of you - and her friend Angela."

Grimaldi sipped his Scotch and tried to act nonchalant about the two women mentioned. "Hey, what can I say, Doris had the hots for me right from the first time we met. After that she wouldn't let go. The only way I could get rid of her was to two-time her with her friend. It was easy once that happened; she cut the cord herself."

Doherty wasn't buying. He leaned forward, his eyes steady on his client.

147

"I don't think that's how it happened at all. I think there's more to it. You're either going to tell me the whole story or I'm leaving this place and we're done," Doherty said not bothering to mince words. "The reason you're going to do it is because I think what happened between you and those two women might have something to do with Adrian's murder. I haven't figured it all out yet, though a picture is starting to come into focus. Now let's say we start from the beginning, and this time give me the story straight."

"Okay, smart guy," Grimaldi said reluctantly. "I met Doris one night when she and the other girl came into Fortunato's. I could tell right from the start that she was the kind of girl who liked to play around. It didn't take long for me to see I wouldn't have to put my usual hustle on her. She was already a few steps ahead of me.

"I went out with her a few times. I'll be honest with you, Doherty, I liked her right away. She was different from the other girls I been with. She could see right through all my bullshit, yet she took a shine to me anyway. It was as if she was a female version of me. I mean she was like the others in that she was in a dead-end marriage with some dull husband at home. On the other hand, she seemed more than ready to go off with me and never look back."

"How did her friend Angela come into the picture?"

"Hold your horses, I'm getting to that. According to Doris this other girl, Angela, could only get out of her house if she was going somewhere with one of her girlfriends. That's how I met the two of them that night they came into the restaurant. This Angela was nice looking and all, but she wasn't like Doris. Hell, most women aren't like her if you know what I mean."

Doherty had a pretty good idea of what he meant by this last comment based on his own experience from the night before.

"So what happened to queer the scene between you and her?"

"Like I said, me and Doris went out a few times. One time I brought along this friend of mine, George, 'cause Angela was gonna be with her. George is a real good guy and I knew from what Doris had told me Angela wasn't being treated all that swell by her fat husband. She really liked George though Doris said if Angela's husband found out about him she would be in for a beating."

"How about if we get back to you and Doris?"

"Yeah, sure. So anyway, I was kinda getting serious with this Doris. I mean I took her down to the beach and we stayed at the Greene Inn one night instead of the motel. Cost me a bundle but she was worth it. Let me tell you, Doherty, that woman knew her way around the bedroom."

In light of the events of the night before, Doherty didn't want to hear any more details about Grimaldi's sexual escapades with Doris Donahue.

"I'm following so far. What was it that blew things up between the two of you?"

At this point Grimaldi wouldn't make eye contact. His voice dropped a few notches, "Problem was I was starting to feel the same way about her. I mean I really liked her – and that wasn't supposed to happen. That wasn't the guy I wanted to be. I wanted to continue being the guy who had a different broad every other week. Not some weak-assed lover who was putting his heart out there to get it stomped on. All I could think about was that Doris was gonna do to me what my wife Marie had done. There was no way I was gonna let that happen again." As if on cue Sinatra came on the jukebox singing about Nancy with the laughing eyes.

"Was that why you put the hustle on Doris' friend Angela?"

"Yeah, you could say I felt sorry for the poor broad having to get into bed with her behemoth of a husband every night. It was like I was doing her a favor letting her be with a guy like me for a change." The Grimaldi who was full of himself was returning to the conversation.

"No, Richie, you didn't do it because you were feeling sorry for Angela. You didn't give a damn about her. The person you were feeling sorry for was yourself. You thought you'd cheat on Doris before she disappointed you. The real problem was that she was falling in love with you. She threw her husband out because she thought she could have something real with you. But instead you decided to screw everything up by seducing her best friend. You probably knew this Angela would be so guilt ridden afterwards she'd have to tell somebody what she'd done - and the first person she'd turn to would be Doris. She didn't know that you and Doris were stuck on each other, did she?"

Doherty didn't wait for Grimaldi to answer. "And when she told her, Doris figured you'd been playing her all along. The problem was you hadn't been playing her, had you? You wanted to drop her because you were afraid she'd end up breaking your heart."

Grimaldi looked like he was about to cry. Instead he got up and walked over to the bar for another round. He was using the time to get their drinks as an opportunity to regather himself. "How is it that you know so much about what happened between me and Doris?" he asked when he returned. "Are you screwing her now?"

The last thing Doherty wanted to do was tell Grimaldi about last night. That would only make the poor guy feel worse. Avoiding the accusation, Doherty instead said, "I needed to know how deep you were into things with Doris because I have an inkling her ex-husband and Angela's present one might have something to do with Adrian's death. Things are falling into place that lead me to think I have to take a harder look at those two."

"Do you happen to know if Doris is seeing anybody?" Grimaldi asked.

Doherty shook his head. "I couldn't tell you, Richie. But after what you did to her, I'd be surprised if she'd give you the time of day. I will tell you she's still working in the women's lingerie department at Cherry & Webb."

Chapter Eighteen

The next morning Doherty was knotting his tie in the bathroom mirror when he heard a loud knock at his door. He seldom had visitors to his apartment, certainly few before ten in the morning. As he finished the half Windsor, the pounding on his door grew louder. When he opened it two men in suits were standing on the threshold. One was Jerald Squillante of the Providence police department; the other was younger and unfamiliar. Squillante was wearing an expensive suit that did not fit him any better than the Robert Hall off-the-rack jobs he used to wear.

"Well if it isn't my old friend Sgt. Squillante. What brings you down here to West Warwick at this hour of the day?" The cop gave Doherty the squint eye then asked if he and his partner could come in.

"Sure. Step right up, sergeant, or have you made lieutenant since last we met?"

The Providence police detective and his cohort squeezed into Doherty's small living space.

"Nice place you got here," Squillante said sarcastically.

"I live alone so I'm not too particular. Who's your new boyfriend?"

"This is officer Damiani. Rollie say hi to Rhode Island's most crooked PI, Hugh Doherty."

The other cop just grunted. Neither man offered his hand for a shake.

Damiani was a good ten years younger than Squillante and had greasy hair combed back into a modified pompadour. Unlike most cops, the kid was dressed smartly in a suit that actually fit him. His tie was neatly knotted and understated. The only flaw in his otherwise classy appearance was the gum he was chewing.

"Can I offer you fellas some coffee? I just put up a fresh pot." The kid made a noise that sounded like a 'no'. Squillante, on the other hand, accepted without hesitation. Doherty stepped into his small kitchen and poured a cup for the cop and one for himself, both black. He then invited the two men to sit in his living room, though not before he tossed some copies of the Saturday Evening Post from the couch onto the floor to make room for them. The cops sat side by side on the couch while Doherty took the easy chair.

"You haven't answered my question, Squillante. Have you made lieutenant yet?"

The cop waggled his head as if searching for a satisfactory answer. "It's coming, just not right away." His partner gave him a look that had 'who are you kidding' written all over it.

"I'm sure crime fighting in the capital city will be much improved when you do. By the way how's my old friend Lieutenant Halloran? Last time we spoke you told me he was riding a desk on account of a bad back."

"He's gone."

"Gone like dead?"

"No, the nearest thing. He took a disability retirement; he and the wife moved to Florida." Brian Halloran had been the lead detective on the Spencer Wainwright homicide, Doherty's first investigation involving a murder. When he initially encountered Halloran Squillante was playing the role of the younger sidekick.

"What happened to your last partner, the one with the brush cut and the bad penmanship?"

"Who Donnelly? He's on a paid leave – suspension actually."

"Why, what did he do? Mess up your paper work?"

Squillante shook his head. "He beat up some nigger. Beat him kinda bad."

Doherty gave him a smart-ass smile. "I didn't know that was an offense

152

in Providence when the police did it."

"It is when it's the wrong nigger. By wrong I mean this boy was the son of the president of the state chapter of the NAACP. When the mayor heard about it he got his panties all in a twist on account of this bein' an election year. I guess he's countin' on the nigger vote to get reelected. You know what they say: shit rolls down hill. In this case it rolled all over Donnelly. Not that I miss him or nothin'. He was kind of a meathead. Damiani here has more smarts in his hip pocket than Donnelly would've been able to put together in a lifetime."

Doherty went to the kitchen to refresh his coffee. He offered Squillante a refill but the cop took a pass. Meanwhile Squillante's sidekick had gotten off the couch and was casually perusing Doherty's apartment, no doubt hoping to eyeball evidence of something illegal.

When he returned to the two cops he asked, "Okay, small talk aside, to what do I owe this early morning visit?"

Squillante looked at his watch. It was a quarter to ten. "Not so early by our standards."

Doherty shrugged, not wanting to say that he seldom checked into his office before ten. "I suppose real crime fighters never sleep."

Squillante ignored the remark. "I assume you read in the papers about that girl from Providence who was found floatin' in the ocean down by Scarborough Beach. The one they couldn't identify till yesterday." Doherty nodded.

"We been workin' with the North Kingston department as well as with the state police on the investigation." This information clued Doherty into why Squillante and his partner were sitting in his living room drinking coffee at 9:30 in the morning.

"I'd have thought that case would stay down in South County. I know how police departments can be when it comes to jurisdiction issues."

Squillante leaned forward and gave Doherty his best smile. His front teeth were yellowed and crooked, which along with his beak of a nose contributed to his generally unpleasant looks.

"Under normal circumstances they would. But you see, Doherty, while they were lookin' into this girl's death your name kept poppin' up. And since you and me have history together, I thought the least we could do in the name of criminal justice was pay you a visit. Don't worry about bein' too honest with us. I've already filled in Damiani here on our past dealin's."

Doherty sipped his coffee and volunteered nothing. He figured he would wait until Squillante offered up something in the form of a question. The prolonged silence was awkward for all of them.

"So, Doherty, why was it you were down in Narragansett askin' a lot of questions about this dead girl?"

"Who did you hear that from?"

"Well for starters, from a bartender who works at a place called the Greene Inn. I'm told it's kind of a classy joint. Right away that struck me as a little strange since it's not exactly the kinda place where you normally hang out." Doherty remained silent for the moment.

"The North Kingston police also told us you checked out a motel out by the beach. They say you left your card with the owner after askin' about the same girl and the guy she'd been shackin' up with. I could go on and mention the parents of the dead girl, who also had one of your cards. They told us you came to their house and suggested they file a missin' persons report on their daughter with our department. Anyhoo, all of this seemed like enough for us to pay you a visit."

"I've been working a case," was all Doherty said.

"A case, huh. Why is it every time you work a case somebody ends up dead?"

"That's not true," Doherty objected. "I work a lot of cases where I convince some lost soul to have a change of heart and go back home to his wife. In fact, I would say the bulk of my work is made up of cases like that. It's only when someone ends up dead that you come into my life. I guess that's understandable since you're a homicide detective."

Squillante's partner tried to give Doherty his tough guy look for cracking wise. He ignored him, having seen tougher ones in his time.

"I was hired by some guy to find this girl. I wasn't successful. The fact that she was dead and dumped in the ocean may've had something to do with it."

"How did you know she was *dumped* in the ocean?"

"I have my sources too. And don't get all excited thinking that either my client or I dumped her. That's not his style or mine."

"Why don't you make this easier on yourself by telling us who your client is?"

"I can't do that."

"Goddamnit, Doherty, this is a murder investigation! Not some game of cat and mouse. Is it the dead girl's greaseball husband who hired you?"

Doherty remained silent.

"Or maybe it's a guy named Richard Grimaldi that we have the dead girl spendin' the night with when she disappeared. Three separate people have already identified him as her companion that weekend. You know we could charge you with impedin' a police investigation."

"Look, Squillante, it sounds like you already got some bona fide suspects so what do you need from me? At this point I don't know any more about who caused her death than you do," he lied.

"Yeah, then why was it you were the one who went to the girl's family to suggest they file a missin' persons report days before she was found dead. How in hell did you know she was already missin'? Why weren't you satisfied that she'd just run off with that Grimaldi character? Unless, of course, Grimaldi's your client."

"Sounds like you got it all figured out, sergeant. Maybe after you leave here you should go interrogate Grimaldi if you think he's a suspect in the girl's murder."

Squillante stood and his sidekick immediately joined him on his feet. "You know, you really are a fuckhead, Doherty. One of these days you're gonna step in it and I'll be right there to make sure you lose your license - preferably for good. And if we get real lucky, maybe we'll be able to put your ass behind bars on some charge or another."

The two cops headed for the door.

"Sergeant, you forgot something."

"Yeah, what's that?"

"You didn't thank me for the coffee."

Squillante just snarled and left making sure to slam the door loudly on his way out.

Agnes was not at the agency when Doherty rolled in later than usual thanks to his visit from the Providence homicide detectives. He'd picked up a copy of the morning *Journal* at the Arctic News on his way to the office; the story of the Colardo murder was now prominently featured on page one. The reporter had done a good job of covering all the details of Adrian Colardo's last days with a yet-unidentified companion in the environs of Narragansett before her disappearance. Clearly the cops were being careful not to leak Grimaldi's name to the press until they'd done a more thorough investigation.

Yet no matter how Doherty read the tea leaves, it was apparent his client would be a key suspect in light of the circumstances surrounding the Colardo girl's last hours in the public eye. Whether the police in North Kingston would arrest and charge Grimaldi or wait until they had a more airtight case remained to be seen. He knew the cops would take a good hard look at Nick Colardo first since it was often the husband who was responsible for a spouse's untimely death. It was now more important than ever for Doherty to get in touch with Grimaldi before the proverbial shit hit the fan.

He still hadn't fully digested what the newsies were saying about the murder trail when Agnes showed up just before noon with little Justin in her arms. She heard her boss rustling the paper in his office and walked right in holding the little bugger. A pacifier protruded from the kid's mouth.

"Sorry, my mother had an appointment at the dentist that she forgot about. They called her and she had to pass off Justin for a few hours. Hope you don't mind."

He waved it off. "Not a problem. Have you read the morning *Journal*?" he asked. "Adrian Colardo's murder is now the biggest story in the news."

"I only had time to look at the headline and the first two paragraphs. Are they gonna charge Grimaldi with the girl's murder?"

Doherty shrugged. "Doesn't sound like it. Not yet anyway. I'm sure he's on their short list of suspects. How could he not be since he may've been one of the last people to see her alive? Except for her killer."

"Does that mean you don't think he did it?"

"To be honest with you, Agnes, I wouldn't be able to stay on this case if

I thought he was the murderer. I just don't see any motive for him to kill this girl."

Agnes shifted the baby to her hip and took a few moments to say what she was thinking. "Maybe she wouldn't come across with the goods and he lost his temper. She could've threatened Grimaldi by sayin' she'd tell her husband what he did to her. Who knows? All I know is that sometimes men don't like to be turned down. I hear they can get violent when girls do."

Doherty considered what his secretary was saying. He was familiar with the term men bandied about calling certain women 'cock teasers.' He'd heard it enough when he was in the service. It was usually directed at some dolly a guy thought was going to put out who then changed her mind at the last minute. Sometimes girls liked to flirt with guys, especially ones in uniform, never thinking that these men thought they were going to end up in the sack. Then there were other girls, girls like Doris Donahue, who would go all the way, but only after she made the guy earn it by buying her drinks and a nice dinner first. Neither world was all that familiar to Doherty. Prior to dating seriously as he had with Dolores Bradley, Millie St. Jean, Rachel Katz, and now Nina Vitale, most of Doherty's sexual encounters were with girls as inexperienced as him - or with hookers when he was in the army. Never with anyone who changed her mind at the last minute. Maybe they did the next day but not that night.

"Well according to my client his sexual advances have been rejected on a number of occasions. In fact, he likened his success rate to that of a ballplayer who bats .300 thus making him an all-star. On those occasions when he got them as far as the motel he got to home plate. Based on his past record, I don't see any circumstances where he would kill a girl simply because she wouldn't put out."

"Jeez, boss, men do it all the time. I read about it in magazines every week."

"Yeah, I know. And that's why those stories get into magazines. My guy isn't like that. Say what you will about Grimaldi, he's a professional at what he does. If a girl won't go to bed with him he just moves on to the next one. Richie is only in it for the action. The way he describes it he has no particular pride invested."

157

"And you believe him?"

Doherty had to smile at Agnes' accusation. "In his case, yes I do. I don't know if I would respond the same way, but hey, I'm not a gigolo. I like to think there should be something else besides sex in the relationships I have with women. Maybe that makes me old fashioned," he added, purposely pushing his night at Doris Donahue's apartment out of his head. That was not something he would share with Agnes since it was important to him that she not see him as a one-night stand kind of guy.

"Whatever you say, boss. But the police aren't goin' to see your client in the same light. Given that, what's your plan for gettin' him off?"

Doherty shook his head. "I don't know yet. I suppose what I've got to do if I'm any good at this job is find out who really killed that girl. I have a few leads but I'm going to need Grimaldi to help me out with them. If he's lawyered up already I don't know if I'll even be able to talk to him."

Things were pretty busy at Fortunato's when Doherty pulled up in front a little after noon. A few suits from downtown and the statehouse had drifted up to that part of the hill to join the locals who frequented the place for lunch. To bide his time Doherty took a seat at the bar hoping to catch a glimpse of Richie Grimaldi. The young guy Tony was working the taps while another fellow about the same age was clearing tables and scooping up tips. The other kid wasn't as burly as Tony and chatted more easily with the customers. A well-dressed older man with a bushy mustache and a substantial belly was out front seating customers in the eating section. Doherty assumed this was Grimaldi's cousin, Anthony, for whom Fortunato's was named.

Doherty ordered a Coca Cola and realized right away that Tony didn't recognize him from his previous visit. When Tony drifted back toward the kitchen, the guy who'd been clearing tables took his spot behind the bar. Doherty asked to have his cola replenished while looking around, still hoping to get the attention of his client. The kid responded to his request with a friendly smile. Doherty slipped him a dollar and asked if Richie was in. This unsettled him and he quickly excused himself retreating to the kitchen. A minute later Tony approached with his usual surly face.

"What do you want with Richie?"

Doherty flashed his license. "Richie's my client. I need to talk to him. It's important."

"Richie don't wanna talk to nobody."

"I understand that. But I'm pretty sure he'll talk to me if you tell him I'm asking for him. This could be a matter of life and death," Doherty added melodramatically. That brought the hint of something resembling a smile to the kid's mouth.

"I'll make a call. What's your name again?"

"Doherty."

"Yeah right. You're the private dick he hired." Doherty just nodded.

Tony headed toward the back room leaving the other guy he called Freddie to handle the bar traffic. Doherty waited patiently, nursing his second glass of soda. Five minutes later Tony returned and handed him a slip of paper. It had an address on it with some directions up to an area called Fruit Hill.

"He's at my fadder's place. That's the address. He said you should knock three times, wait a second then knock twice more. Otherwise he ain't openin' the door."

The directions were clear enough. The cousin's house was a sprawling Italianate style ranch with a good-sized yard out front. Some overly ornamented black wrought iron lined the steps and encased the front porch. The place was painted white with black shutters on all the windows. There was no car in the driveway and the shades were all drawn, giving the impression that no one was home. Doherty parked a half block away and took a good look around to see if there were any cops or news people staking out the premises. He would've been surprised if there were since Grimaldi's name hadn't been leaked to the press yet. Besides it was too damn cold for any sane person to be camped outside in this weather.

He knocked on the door in the rhythm he was instructed to use. No one answered right away though he did see a curtain move slightly in one of the neighboring windows. In time he heard the sound of several locks being unclasped before Richie Grimaldi opened the door a crack.

"What do you want?" Grimaldi asked. His eyes were bloodshot and his hair was a mess. He looked around furtively like a cornered rat.

"What do you think I want? To talk with you."

"Did anybody follow you here?"

"Richie, let me in before some neighbor gets suspicious. Nobody followed me and nobody but your cousin's son Tony knows I'm here."

Grimaldi opened the door and forcibly pulled Doherty inside before quickly fastening the locks again.

"Come in the kitchen. I just put up some coffee."

The Fortunato house was decorated as garishly inside as the wrought iron outside hinted it would be. The living room was mammoth with two big oversized sofas covered in colorful designs and a TV that was larger than any console Doherty'd ever seen. Heavy dark green drapes hung at the sides of every window. The kitchen was loaded with appliances, the centerpiece of which was a refrigerator that looked like a NASA rocket ship. The cooking quarters were about the size of Doherty's whole apartment.

The two men pulled up stools at a big island in the center of the room. Grimaldi handed the PI a heaping mug of black coffee. He asked if Doherty needed cream or sugar. He told his client he took his black.

"Nice place your cousin's got here."

Grimaldi looked a wreck. He craned his neck around. "Yeah, I guess. If you wanna live like Napoleon."

"So what's happening, Richie?"

"I suppose you read the papers. I did like you told me. I got a lawyer - some Jew lawyer my cousin recommended. Name's Saul Friedman. According to Anthony this Friedman has a few big shot clients up on Federal Hill as well as downtown. He agreed to take me on for a nominal fee. That fee being an arm and half of one of my legs."

"Is he a criminal lawyer?"

"Oh, yeah. Some of his clients are well-known wise guys. Anthony said that was a good thing 'cause this Friedman knows people all over the state: in city hall, in the statehouse and at the courts. He says all the known guys have Jew lawyers. I was desperate and didn't know where else to turn."

"What about the cops?"

"Yesterday morning some Providence guys came to my apartment and took me to a state police barracks down in North Kingston just outside of Wickford. They had me there all day for questioning. I haven't gotten much sleep since. I'm in a real bind here, Doherty."

"No shit, Richie. Well at least the papers haven't released your name yet. Did they formally charge you with anything?"

"No, not yet. Friedman said that's a good sign. I think he said that just so he can keep running up hours on my bill." Grimaldi seemed more concerned about his legal costs than the potential trouble he was in.

"Calm down and listen to me. First, you've got to stop thinking about your legal bills. If he gets you out of this jam, it'll be worth every penny you pay him. And if they convict you, you'll end up at the ACI where you won't have to worry about your lawyer's cost anymore. Richie, a girl is dead - strangled, naked, possibly sexually assaulted and dumped into the ocean like a piece of garbage. People all over Rhode Island will want to see somebody pay for that crime. Right now you're one of the prime suspects. What we've got to do is figure out how to clear your name. My hunch is they're not charging you with anything yet because they have no substantial evidence or a real motive. The best way to get you out of this mess is for us to figure out who did kill Adrian."

Grimaldi got up and went to a cabinet where he pulled down a bottle with some brown liquor in it. He poured a healthy shot into his coffee and held up the bottle to see if Doherty wanted a hit in his mug. He passed.

"Great. How the hell are *we* gonna to find out who killed that girl if the cops are too busy looking at me?"

"That's why you hired me, Richie. First the police will take a long hard look at Adrian's husband. So that means you're not their only suspect. In the meantime I've got a couple of ideas, but I'm going to need your cooperation and possible participation."

"You're not gonna want me to do something that'll make me look more guilty, are you?"

"I don't think so," Doherty said, not entirely certain that was true.

Chapter Nineteen

Back at the office Doherty was mulling over what he could do next to help get his client off the hook. He still had a few cards left to play. One was the motel owner, who had seen a car speeding away from his lot the night Adrian Colardo disappeared. Grimaldi was convinced someone slipped the two of them mickeys earlier in the evening to put them into a dead sleep. However, that could've been just a figment of Richie's imagination. As for the car in the motel parking lot, it very well could've just been some teens looking for a place to make out or drink some ill-gotten booze. The motel owner admitted that was a fairly common occurrence in his lot during the off-season.

If Doherty leaned on him again there was no guarantee the owner would offer up any more under his questioning. After all, for over a year he'd been providing Grimaldi with a place to bed down his different female conquests. Based on his experience Doherty expected if the Anchor Inn's proprietor was questioned by the police a second time he would shape his answers in a way to absolve himself and his wife of any responsibility for the girl's disappearance. If he were smart he'd just play dumb to the whole thing. Not only would that be true of the motel owner, it would probably be true of Roger Willis, the bartender, and Domenic Ferullo, the waiter, at the Greene Inn as well. Though the waiter seemed more forthcoming of the three about cooperating with an investigation.

Nonetheless, at this point Doherty couldn't rely on any of them providing enough information to help Richie Grimaldi get out of the jam he was in. Although his client might be innocent of killing Adrian Colardo, his overall behavior toward women made him a less than sympathetic character. In light of the circumstances around the girl's death, he was the perfect fall guy.

There would be a lot of pressure on the North Kingston and State Police to make an arrest as quickly as possible for this heinous murder. The killing of an innocent girl by a gigolo who preyed on unhappily married women made Grimaldi the ideal candidate. So far, though, all evidence of his guilt was circumstantial at best. The cops would be careful not to formally charge him if they'd have to release him later due to a lack of evidence. This gave Doherty some time to work with.

He was interrupted from his thoughts by a ringing phone. He heard Agnes pick up and then ask the caller to wait a minute. She poked her head into his office and said, "There's a woman on the line. Should I put her through? Sounds like a potential client."

Doherty hesitated for a few seconds, not sure he could take on another case while immersed in the Grimaldi affair.

"Yeah, put her through. The least I can do is see what she needs."

He picked up the buzzing phone and said, "Doherty here."

"Oh, Mr. Doherty. Thank you so much for taking my call." The female on the other end sounded pretty anxious. "This is Meg Garrett. I don't know if you remember me. I'm Eddie Donahue's sister. You gave me one of your cards when you were out at our house."

"Yeah sure, I remember. What can I do for you, Mrs. Garrett?"

There was some heavy breathing on the line. "It's Eddie. I'm worried sick about him. He got a call from that Finnegan fella down at the VFW post three days ago. Right after he put the phone down he left the house in an awful hurry and I haven't seen him since. I told him to stay away from that place. You know, Mr. Doherty, those men have not been kind to my brother. Eddie said he had some unfinished business to clear up with Fats Finnegan. That what he called him: Fats Finnegan."

"Did Eddie say what kind of business it was?"

"No, he just grabbed his coat and hat and ran off. That was three days ago. I had Neil call down to the VFW but nobody there had seen Eddie. Or at least that's what they told my husband on the phone. I wanted Neil to drive over there to see for himself but he wouldn't do it. He said he had no sympathy for Eddie. He's of the mind that whatever trouble my brother's in it's of his own doing."

"What do you want from me?" Doherty asked in a tone that was rougher than he intended.

"I guess I want to hire you to find my brother."

Doherty was about to say he was too busy with another case and wasn't available. But something about Donahue's disappearance clawed at Doherty's curiosity. For no discernible reason he had a funny feeling there might be a connection between the murder of Adrian Colardo and the disappearance of Eddie Donahue. Given his line of work Doherty was not the kind of person who believed in coincidences. He thought a return trip to the O'Donnell Post might shake a few things loose.

"You'll have to come down to my office and sign an official contract for my services. I usually charge fifty dollars plus expenses."

"I can't come to West Warwick today. Neil took the car to work and I don't have any transportation of my own since Eddie drove off with my station wagon. Maybe I can come tomorrow. I could send you a check in the mail."

He paused, thinking about Meg Garrett's situation.

"Why don't we assume you've officially hired me as of now. We'll take care of the paper work whenever you can get into West Warwick. In the meantime I'll make a run over to the O'Donnell Post to see what I can find out about your brother."

"Oh, Mr. Doherty. I can't thank you enough. I just hope nothing bad has happened to Eddie. He's led such a careless life." That certainly seemed to be the truth.

When he got off the phone Doherty began to hatch a plan that may've been a little farfetched. Yet it was one he hoped would bring him some satisfaction even if it didn't help locate Eddie Donahue.

164

Later that night he drove once more up to Fortunato's. The bruiser Tony and his pal Freddie were cleaning up the last scraps from the evening meal. Neither Grimaldi nor his cousin Anthony were anywhere in sight – only the two young kids. The front door was unlocked though the CLOSED sign was turned toward the street.

"We ain't open," Tony said over his shoulder, not bothering to look in Doherty's direction.

"I know. I saw the sign. I'm not here to eat. I need to talk to you." The kid stood up and looked at Doherty. He rubbed his dirty hands down the front of the apron he was wearing over his white shirt and tie. The other guy, Freddie, continued swabbing down tabletops, not bothering to pay attention to their conversation.

"I s'pose you wanna get in touch with my cousin Richie again?"

"Actually I wanted to talk with you first before we contact him. And maybe enlist your help in a little scheme I'm cooking up." Tony looked confused, but stopped what he was doing.

"Are you a veteran?" Doherty asked.

"I was in the reserves for six months down in Texas. I got an early discharge."

"An early discharge huh. What does that mean?"

"It means I got kicked out. They woulda given me a dishonorable but my fadder knew some people. So I got a general one instead. Did my basic and most of my combat trainin' before they sent me home."

"What did you do to get out so fast?"

"I punched out one of my superiors. Some little faggot from Georgia. Douche bag liked to make fun of Eyetalians so I broke his nose. They wanted to throw me in the brig, but my old man called somebody who knew somebody and they let me out instead. That's all I gotta say about my time in the army."

"Do you have a veterans card on you?"

"Yeah, I got one of them. Gets me discounts at a lotta places. Specially in the PX down at Quonset."

"Good, 'cause I thought you and me and Richie would take a little trip over to this VFW post on Charles Street. I'm hoping we can rattle up some people there."

"Sorry, pal, you lost me. What are we goin' to do?"

"I'm not sure yet. I don't know how this is going to play out. I'd feel a whole lot better if Richie and I took some muscle along with us - and you fit the bill. Your cousin Richie is going to be the bait. What about your buddy Freddie here?"

"No good. He ain't a vet. Are we talkin' about gettin' into a fight?" Tony asked, a broad smile cracking his face.

"Possibly."

Tony took off his apron and tossed it in a laundry bin. "I'll go call Richie."

Doherty and Tony drove to the cousin's house on Fruit Hill to pick up Grimaldi. His client was reluctant to accompany them until Doherty convinced him what they were about to do might help prove his innocence in the Colardo girl's murder. Anthony Fortunato was not at the house. When Doherty inquired as to his whereabouts, Richie let on that his cousin had a honey up on Federal Hill that he went to visit when his wife was at bingo. He whispered this in Doherty's ear, not wanting young Tony to know what his father was up to.

On the drive over to Charles Street the city was relatively quiet since it was late on a Thursday night. He parked as close to the post hall as he could in case they had to make a hasty exit. The plan was for Tony to go in first while Doherty and Grimaldi waited in the car for ten minutes.

When they entered the O'Donnell post the smell of peanuts and stale beer hit them as soon as they crossed the threshold. Tony was leaning on the bar engaged in some quiet conversation with the tender. Perhaps telling the guy about how he got his early discharge by punching out one of his instructors down in Texas. They made brief eye contact, though none of them acknowledged knowing each other. Doherty and Grimaldi flashed their vet cards at the bar and asked for two bottles of Gansett. The barkeep looked at Grimaldi's ID for an inordinate amount of time. The two of them took a table while Tony continued to lean on the bar sucking his beer directly from the bottle.

There were about a dozen guys in the place; some playing cards, others in loud conversations. A few of the regulars gave Doherty and Grimaldi a once over, but otherwise paid them little attention. When things grew quiet at the bar the tender slid into the back room where Doherty had smashed Fats Finnegan's hand in his desk drawer. Meanwhile Patti Page was crooning a song about Old Cape Cod on the jukebox. About five minutes after the barman had disappeared behind the door marked 'Office', Finnegan and three other men emerged from their lair and approached the table where Doherty and Grimaldi were sipping their beers. Finnegan recognized Doherty immediately and gave him his best sneer. It was almost enough to scare somebody's pet pussycat.

A large dark haired guy with his shirt unbuttoned enough to show the full front of his sleeveless undershirt said, "Which one of yous is Grimaldi?"

Finnegan answered for him. "He is," he said pointing at Richie. "This other bum is the guy who tried to jack me up about Eddie Donahue's debts." Turning his attention back to Grimaldi he said, "He's the sonofabitch who fucked my wife."

Richie quickly looked at Doherty as if to say, "What the hell have you gotten me into?"

"Stand up you rotten bastard," Finnegan said to Richie crowding his ample belly closer to the table. "I can't let what you done to my Angela go by the boards." Doherty noticed that Tony had moved a few steps away from the bar, but still gave no indication that he was with the two of them.

Grimaldi stood up and flashed Fats Finnegan his best smile. "Angela, huh. Now which one was she? Was she that little dark-haired girl who complained that her husband was too fat to screw her anymore?"

Finnegan pulled his fist back, but before he could hit Grimaldi Tony grabbed his arm and bent it behind his back. It was only then that Doherty noticed the splint on Fats Finnegan's other hand from the desk drawer crush. While this was going on the guy with the opened shirtfront stepped forward and slammed his fist against the side of Grimaldi's head. The gigolo bounced off the table but did not lose his footing. The other two moved in but not before Doherty was able to toss over the table to block their way. The beer bottles and glasses shattered when they hit the floor.

167

After Tony knocked Finnegan to the floor, he grabbed the other two guys around their necks and smashed their heads together. The fat man tried to get to his feet but not before Doherty stepped on his broken knuckles eliciting an ungodly scream. The one who'd punched Grimaldi now went after Doherty. Squealing from the floor Finnegan shouted, "Willis, get that sonofabitch. He's the guy who started this whole thing."

The Willis fellow grabbed Doherty from behind and held him around the chest in a tight bear hug. Doherty was having trouble breathing. He tried squirming away and soon was able to extend his hips far enough to slam his elbow into his attacker's solar plexus. He heard a loud *whoosh* come out of the guy before he dropped the bear hug and doubled over trying to catch his breath. For good measure Doherty hit him with an uppercut that sent him to the floor beside his fat friend. Meanwhile Finnegan hadn't moved. He was sitting on the floor whimpering, holding his twice-damaged hand.

While this was going on Tony and Grimaldi convinced the other two men to back off before any further damage was done. One of them was bleeding from a cut lip that dripped a fair amount of blood onto his shirt. The smile on Tony's face seemed to be enough to persuade these two that they didn't want any more to do with the young brute. The post's floor was littered with bodies, overturned furniture and broken glass. Out of the corner of his eye Doherty saw the bartender reaching under the counter. He quickly moved in that direction, picking up a broken beer bottle by its neck along the way.

He held the shard of cut glass up under the guy's chin and said, "I wouldn't if I were you."

The barman raised his hands in surrender. Doherty circled behind the bar and extracted a sawed-off shotgun from its rack underneath.

"I thought these things were illegal in Rhode Island."

The bartender looked embarrassed but said nothing. Doherty returned to the remains of the chaos, the shotgun firmly tucked under his arm. He pointed the weapon at Fats Finnegan.

"Where's Eddie Donahue?"

"I ain't seen Eddie in a coupla days," the big man protested.

Doherty racked a shell and moved closer to his prey. "I asked where

168

Eddie Donahue is. Now I want an answer." Finnegan swiveled his head around so that his chins flopped back and forth. He was looking for some back-up that was no longer there.

"Let's go into the backroom and talk, okay." Finnegan pleaded.

Doherty lowered the weapon and helped the fat man to his feet. "Tell your bartender pal to clean up this mess. It reflects badly on us veterans."

Once in the backroom Finnegan plopped his corpulent frame down into the chair behind his desk. He was massaging his damaged hand as he did so. Then with his healthy paw he reached into his desk. Doherty raised the scattergun as he did. Instead of a gun the fat man pulled out a fifth of Old Grand Dad and poured a glass for each of them. Not fully trusting his host, Doherty waited for Finnegan to take a healthy swig before he joined him.

"I think you busted somethin' in my hand," Finnegan said in a pathetic voice.

"It's only your left hand. You can still whack off with your other one. Now I'm going to ask you as politely as I can: Where is Eddie Donahue? And if you don't give me a straight answer I just might blow your other hand off."

Finnegan shook his head and his several chins with it. "I told you I ain't seen Eddie since last week. He came by wantin' to get into our card game and I done like you said. I told him he wasn't welcome to play here till he settled some of his debt. He tried to argue with us and it got kinda ugly. I had to have Willis escort him out to the hall. We told him he could drink here like the other vets, but he wasn't allowed in our poker game anymore. I even offered him the discount deal you suggested on what he owes us.

"He came by once after that just to have a beer. I think he was hopin' we'd let him back in the game. Look, I won't lie to you considerin' you're holdin' a shotgun in my face, Eddie was a good mark, but he don't have no more money. I found out his wife was coverin' his debts until she threw him out. Poor bastard never did know how to play cards."

"What about the off-the-books jobs you had him do for you?"

Finnegan took a big slug of his liquor and averted his eyes. "It wasn't nuthin'. Just some small stuff I'd throw his way to help him work off the

169

money he owed us."

"Small like how?"

Finnegan was reluctant to put into words the illegal jobs he'd had Donahue do for him. "I gave him some cash to put in his bank account and asked him to post-date some checks in his name for bills the O'Donnell owed. I couldn't very well cover those bills with money I won playin' cards. That's money I don't want to hafta account for."

"What else did you have him do?"

"Nuthin' really. A coupla times I had him drop off some hot goods to people I know. But hey, I don't hafta tell you that's how a lotta business is done here in Rhode Island. Everybody buys and sells hot goods. It's like our own special economy. Look, Mr. Private Eye, I know what you're thinkin' but I never had Eddie do nuthin' that would've gotten him in Dutch with the wise guys. Honest Injun."

Doherty was trying to suss out how things crossed between Donahue's ex-wife Doris and Finnegan's wife Angela. "What can you tell me about what happened between your wife and the guy out there that I came in with?"

Once again Finnegan shook his head and three chins followed suit. He pointed at Doherty and said, "That sonofabitch took my wife to some motel down south and screwed her. Then the bastard dropped her back at our house the very next day as if she was the mail. What kind of a man does somethin' like that? My Angela was in tears the whole weekend."

"Do you have any idea how they met?"

"She told me they met at a bar up on Federal Hill where she went to have a drink with her girlfriend Doris. It sounded like he sweet-talked her into goin' away with him. We was havin' trouble in the marriage at the time so I wasn't surprised. But he took advantage of her. I later found out he'd done the same thing with other girls, includin' Donahue's wife. What are you doin' hangin' out with a prick like that?"

Doherty didn't answer Finnegan's question, though he acknowledged that under the circumstances it was a legitimate question. "Did Angela say anything particular about Donahue's wife and her role in this whole thing?"

"Doris? What did she have to do with Angela and that Grimaldi bastard?"

He had to think for a few moments about what he was willing to share with the fat man. "Well, it seems that Donahue's ex-wife was dating Grimaldi right before he did what he did with your Angela. According to her she and Grimaldi were going at it pretty hot and heavy. In fact she used him as the reason she sent Eddie packing. That's when Donahue went to live with his sister out in Cumberland. It wasn't long afterwards that Donahue's wife found out Grimaldi was running his game with her good friend Angela. She was so angry she blamed your wife for snaking away the man she thought she was in love with."

"Jesus, what the hell kind of guy is your buddy anyway?"

"He's not my buddy, he's my client. Apparently the latest chippie he was knocking off ended up dead. For obvious reasons the cops are now looking at him as a possible suspect. Problem is I don't think he did it. Say what you will about him going around dicking other men's wives, that doesn't make him a killer. You might say he has too much skin in the game to want to ruin it by doing away with one of them."

Finnegan poured each of them another shot of whiskey and wrapped his swollen hand in his handkerchief.

"You better put some ice on that before it gets too blown up."

Finnegan examined his hand again and then looked back at Doherty. "So why did the two of you and that big goon come down here to cause trouble? What do you think was gonna happen by doin' that?"

"Hey, we didn't start the fight. You and your pal Willis did. I came here to find Eddie Donahue or at least learn something of his whereabouts. His sister hasn't seen him in three days and she's worried sick about him. She told me he got a call from you the other night and then rushed out of the house in a big hurry."

"I didn't call him. 'Cept for the money he owes us, I got no reason to see Donahue ever again. Anyway you slice it Eddie's nothin' but a loser."

"Could somebody else from here have called him? Like maybe that palooka out there you called Willis."

"Who, Brian? What would he want with Donahue?"

"I don't know. Maybe it has something to do with my client. He could've screwed Willis' wife."

Finnegan laughed at this last remark. "I don't think so. Brian's wife left him a long time ago. Ever since then Brian's sworn off broads. To hear him tell it women are the worse thing that ever happened to men. Now all he does is spend his time workin', drinkin' and playin' poker."

"You wouldn't happen to know if your friend Willis has a relative who works down in Narragansett, would you?"

"I know he has a brother named Roger. Came into the post a coupla times with Brian. Kind of a snooty bastard if you ask me. That's about all I can tell you about him 'cept that he's a pretty good poker player and can hold his liquor."

Doherty stood up to leave. He pulled a twenty out of his wallet and tossed it on the desk. "Here, this should cover the damage we caused."

"Finnegan tossed the double sawbuck back in his direction. "Keep your money, Mr. Private Eye. And do me a favor - stay the fuck out of O'Donnell's from now on."

Doherty handed the fat man one of his business cards. "If Eddie Donahue shows up could you give me a call? I promise I'll waylay him somewhere other than here."

When Doherty emerged from the back office most of the mess was cleaned up in the post hall. Grimaldi and his cousin Tony were sitting at a table drinking and joshing with the very guys they'd been fighting with earlier. The one with the split lip was holding a bag of ice up against his mouth. Doherty wanted to have a few words with Brian Willis, but the big guy was nowhere to be seen. He returned the sawed-off to the bartender and told Grimaldi and Tony it was time to leave. They made noises of disappointment yet followed him out anyway.

Doherty fully intended to drop Grimaldi and his young cousin off at their places, but Grimaldi insisted that they go back to the restaurant instead. They all agreed that the fight had made them hungry. Once at Fortunato's his client set about cooking up a batch of spaghetti with meat sauce. While the water was boiling Tony went out to the bar and snatched up a good bottle of red wine.

"I had enough beers. This Chianti'll go better with the spaghetti," he said as he expertly uncorked the bottle.

They drank the wine from long stemmed glasses while waiting for the leftover sauce to heat up. While they were reliving the events at O'Donnell's, young Tony told them that the fight at the VFW post was the most fun he'd had since snagging a Bluefin tuna off Block Island the previous summer.

When the spaghetti was ready Grimaldi set down three large plates in front of them at the kitchen counter. Between bites Grimaldi asked, "So, Mr. Private Eye, did you learn anything to help my situation from that punch-out at the post? Or was getting this sore jaw all for nothing."

"Well, I didn't find out anything about where Eddie Donahue is. That fat guy Finnegan said Donahue hadn't been there for a few days. Right now I'm inclined to believe him, though only as far as I could throw him. Which given his size wouldn't be very far."

This elicited a few good laughs among the three combatants.

"That doesn't sound like much. What does this Donahue mook have to do with Adrian's murder?"

While they were talking Tony went back into the kitchen and returned with another heaping plate of spaghetti for himself.

"It wasn't entirely a wasted visit. I did learn that the big, dark-haired guy - the one with his shirt open who sucker punched you, is the brother of the bartender down at the Greene Inn."

"Yeah, so what does that mean?"

"I'm not sure yet. It's possible the two of them acting together could've had something to do with Adrian's abduction. If they did then this Brian might've set it all up by getting his brother to dose your drinks at the inn like you thought."

They'd finished the first bottle of Chianti and Doherty was feeling fatigued from the night's events. Before he could beg off Tony uncorked another bottle and filled their glasses to the brim. Doherty was already lightheaded enough to worry about his drive back to West Warwick.

"Did I also screw the brother's wife somewhere in my travels?" Grimaldi asked with a smile.

Doherty shook his head. "I don't think so. According to the fat man this Willis brother doesn't have a wife anymore. Apparently she left him a while back and he's been off women ever since."

"Maybe he likes boys instead," Tony piped in. "I took him for a faggot when he hit you with that slap punch."

Grimaldi rubbed his swollen jaw again. The pain he was feeling told him Willis' punch had been a lot more than a slap. "How about if you just pay attention to your spaghet, Tony, while me and Doherty here discuss serious business."

"I don't get it. Why would this Willis guy care if I was screwing Adrian Colardo? I mean she wasn't his wife or Donahue's or the fat man's either. From what you're saying none of them even knew Adrian."

"Yeah, that's what has me puzzled. Why would they want to kill an innocent girl? I think if I can get in touch with Eddie Donahue he can help me get to the bottom of things. As of now I'm working on the assumption that Adrian was just a pawn in a scheme cooked up by some people who wanted to get you into serious trouble. Someone has a strong reason to put you in a frame. By making Adrian disappear they obviously accomplished that. When she ended up dead that frame now included murder. I'm still not counting out Finnegan. Something tells me his fat fingers are all over this."

They had just about finished the second bottle of red wine. Before his brain became completely addled Doherty was already formulating a plan on how he was going to move on Roger Willis, the bartender at the Greene Inn.

Chapter Twenty

Doherty and Nina Vitale had never spent a whole night together in the three months they'd been dating. When he stopped by her desk at the Centreville Bank on Friday morning to ask if she'd liked to go down to Narragansett with him overnight on Saturday she was taken completely by surprise. Their relationship undoubtedly had changed of late after two hot nights of sex at his apartment. One thing concerning him was what Nina would read into his proposal of an overnight in Narragansett. Would this be a gesture on his part of escalating their relationship to another level? After some thought she explained that the hard part would be coming up with a good excuse to throw at her parents as to why she was staying away over-night.

Doherty had met Nina's folks on two occasions and each time they told her afterwards they thought he was too old for her. They were probably right since there was a thirteen-year age gap between them. When Doherty first became acquainted with Nina at the Centreville Bank she'd been engaged to another guy for nearly a year. That relationship was later abruptly broken off before any wedding plans could be made. Nina was reluctant to share any details about this failed relationship with him and he wisely never pressed her on the matter. However, there were times when he thought perhaps he was nothing more than the guy who caught her on the rebound. On the other hand he did have one thing going for him: there weren't many eligible bache-lors in West Warwick who wore a suit to work everyday like he did. After the second meeting with her parents they made it clear to Nina that they didn't think Doherty was the *marrying type*. For the present he and Nina were content to enjoy each other's company without looking too far ahead.

He was honest with her, explaining that the trip to Narragansett was par-tially a business venture because he needed to talk to some people in relation to a case he was working. She didn't seem all that put out by this mostly be-cause she was too consumed with how she was going to run their getaway by her parents. She told him she needed a few hours to think about it.

Back at the office Doherty began sketching out what he hoped to ac-complish down in South County. He wanted to revisit the motel where he believed Adrian Colardo was abducted. Then he would confront the bartend-er at the Greene Inn about his connection to his brother and Fats Finnegan at the O'Donnell Post. He wasn't sure where things would go from there, but having Nina along would give him another good reason to return to Narra-gansett. Their time away together would let them see if their relationship had the potential for moving on to something more serious. For the first time in almost a year Doherty was ready to leave the ruins of his relationship with Rachel Katz behind him.

While he was mulling these things over there was a soft knock on the outer door to Doherty and Associates. Agnes wasn't in today so he hauled himself from behind the desk to answer it. Meg Garrett was standing on the threshold clutching a large purse to her chest. Her hair was a scraggly mess and she wore no make-up on her plain country girl face. When she slipped off her heavy woolen coat he saw that she was wearing a flannel shirt and dungarees tucked into rubber work boots. Not the standard outfit most wom-en wore around Arctic.

"Have you found my brother yet?" she asked by way of a hello. Doherty invited her into his office, offering her the client chair on the other side of his desk. He took her heavy coat and hung it on his antler rack.

"I was at the O'Donnell Post last night, but nobody there has seen Eddie since last weekend. Or so they said," he explained, not bothering to mention the melee he had precipitated there.

"And you believe them?"

Doherty shrugged. "I don't know what to believe about your brother. Right after I visited with Eddie at your house I stopped by the post to have a little talk with Fats Finnegan. With some persuading I got him to agree to ease up on Eddie's debts and permanently exclude him from their poker game. Last night Finnegan assured me that he's kept his part of the bargain despite your brother's protests."

Meg gave him a curious look. "Is that how you got those bruises on your face?"

"Well, it did take a little more persuasion than I bargained on for Finnegan and his pals to see things my way."

"What about the phone call Eddie got the other night? After that he left in such a hurry you'd've thought our house was on fire."

"Are you sure it was Finnegan who called him?"

Meg Garrett looked confused. "I can't say for certain. I try not to listen to Eddie's phone conversations. It hurts me so much whenever I hear him making another bad decision. All I know is that I heard the name Finnegan being used. Whenever I hear Eddie use that man's name I just know something bad is going to happen. He's been such a lost soul ever since that Doris threw him out." She uttered Donahue's ex-wife's name as if it were an expletive.

"So you don't really know if the call was from the post. Nor do you know for sure that's where Eddie was heading when he left the house."

Meg Garrett shook her head.

"It's okay, Mrs. Garrett. I'll continue to look for your brother. Right now I'm working this other missing person case. There's an outside chance they may be connected in some way," he added without further explanation.

"I have the money you requested. It's in a check signed by my husband Neil. I hope that's acceptable."

"Yes, checks are fine. I have to ask you to read and sign a consent form," he said while swiveling around and pulling one out of his filing cabinet. "All it says is that you have hired me to do investigative work for you. And that I can't be party to any illegal activities that the person I'm working for or searching for is engaged in. Do you understand?"

"What if Eddie is doing something crooked for that Finnegan fellow?"

"All I can do is find Eddie and convince him to go back home. If he's doing something illegal I can't protect him from the law. I won't turn him in, but if he gets caught then it's between him and the police. I can assure you *I* won't purposely do anything to get your brother in trouble. Nor will I turn him in if I can help it."

Meg Garrett carefully read the employment contract and signed it, making her his newest client. He wasn't certain it would get him any closer to locating Eddie Donahue. On the other hand if Eddie was the hapless character everyone described him as, he shouldn't be all that hard to find.

Nina looked at him cross-eyed when they pulled up in front of the Anchor Inn. The place still had a mid-winter weather-beaten look about it. She scrunched down in her heavy woolen jacket and stared straight ahead through the windshield, too polite to express her disappointment. She'd told her parents she would be spending the weekend in the White Mountains where her cousin was going to teach her how to ski. She hadn't anticipated this dismal place was their real destination. It wasn't exactly where she hoped to spend her first romantic night away with her new boyfriend.

He sat quietly beside her in the driver's seat doing his best to suppress a snicker. Finally he turned to Nina and said, "If it's any consolation we won't be spending the night at this fine establishment. I stopped here because I need to ask the owner some questions regarding the case I'm working on. Would you like to come in or would you rather stay here in the car?

Nina gave the motel another cursory glance. "I'll stay here if you don't mind. This doesn't look like my kind of place."

"Suit yourself. I'll leave the motor running and the heat on. Though I've got to say, being bundled up like Nanook of the North, I doubt you'll be cold."

"Who of the north?"

"Nanook. It's from an old movie."

"I'm only dressed like this because my parents thought I was going to the White Mountains to ski. Don't worry I've got some more suitable clothing in my overnight bag."

"Great. You can turn on the radio if you want. I shouldn't be long."

Doherty slid out of the car into the cold. The wind coming off the water was blowing hard across the empty Scarborough Beach parking lots. Although it was still mid-afternoon the sky was overcast enough that the light was on in the motel office. This time a little bell above the door rang when Doherty crossed the threshold. A frumpy, middle-aged woman was sitting at the desk behind the counter. A half smoked cigarette was stuck in the corner of her mouth. Must be a style she learned from her husband, or he from her.

"We're closed for the season," she said, not bothering to remove the butt or pay him much attention.

"I can see that. I was wondering if your husband's around."

Almost against her will she got up from the desk and shuffled over to the counter. She removed her cigarette and sent a plume of smoke in Doherty's direction

"Who wants to know?"

He took out one of his business cards and slid it across the counter in her direction. She lifted it up very close to her eyes and read it with her lips moving.

"What's this about? What're you investigating down here at this time of year?"

"It's about the girl they pulled out of the ocean the other day by the rocks. The one who'd been staying at your 'closed for the season' motel.

The woman gave Doherty a less than friendly look. "We told the police everything we knew about her, which wasn't much. It's not our fault that young thing got murdered. If you ask me she shouldn't been here with that fella in the first place."

"I understand your concern," he said, though he really meant her lack of it. "I'd still like to speak with your husband. And you too if you have the time."

The woman took the cigarette out of her mouth and smiled for the first time. A half-inch of ash clung to the end of it. "We're not exactly busy as you can see."

"Right, I forgot. You're closed for the season."

179

"Wait here, I'll go get Nathan. He's fixing a plumbing leak in one of the units."

The woman threw a sweater over her shoulder and hurried out of the office. Doherty used the wife's absence to check on Nina. When he looked out through the blinds he could see her wrapped in her heavy jacket moving her lips, apparently singing along with something on the radio.

A few minutes later the woman returned with her husband in tow. He was wearing dungaree overalls with a work shirt underneath. A greasy rag hung from one of his side pockets.

"Is that girl out in the car with you?" the woman asked.

"Yes, she is."

"She can come in and have some coffee if she'd like."

"I think it'd be better if she stayed where she is. I don't want her knowing too much about why I'm here. It could mess things up," he added, recalling how his work had already queered two of his previous relationships and gotten a third woman murdered.

"What can I do for you?" the husband asked, clearly irritated at being dragged away from his plumbing job.

"I just need a little more information about Richie Grimaldi and his comings and goings here."

"I told you not to let that fella bring all those girls down here. I knew he was going to get us into trouble," the wife said between tight lips.

The man gave her a stern look. "Brenda, please. What's done is done. Let's not go into all that again. At least we're still in business."

"Yeah, some business. Who's gonna want to stay here next summer after we've been smeared all over the papers?"

Doherty butted in, "My experience tells me you'll probably have more business than you can handle. People can be pretty ghoulish. Once they find out this was a possible murder scene, or at least the scene of an abduction that led to a murder, they'll be falling all over themselves to get a room."

The wife let out a disgusted harrumph.

"Okay, Nathan, what can you tell me about Grimaldi?"

"I already told the cops…"

"I'm not the police. And I'm sure you told them only what you needed

180

to in order to keep your operating license for the motel. I need to know more about him and that night."

"I don't understand," the wife piped in. "What's your interest in all this? Are you one of them ghouls you just mentioned?"

"Grimaldi's my client. I'm trying to prove he isn't responsible for that girl's death."

"Are you sure about that?" the wife asked skeptically.

"No. Not a hundred percent. But I wouldn't keep him on as a client if I thought he was a murderer. Besides, from everything I've learned about him, murdering women would be the last thing on his mind. By his own admission, he's only interested in them for sex. Grimaldi doesn't strike me as the sentimental sort."

Nathan took the greasy rag out of his pocket and wiped his hands on it. He then laid it carefully on the counter. "Like I told you last time, he comes down once, sometimes twice a month with a different woman each time. Always asks for the same room, pays cash up front and leaves before checkout the next day. There's never been any trouble with him, no loud noise or nothing."

"What about the women who left early?"

Nathan shook his head. "That only happened twice as best I remember. They came to the office the next morning and asked Brenda to call them a cab."

"Did they seem distressed?"

"Not really, just sad," the wife said. "Like maybe they thought coming here with him was a good idea until they realized it wasn't. Most of the girls he brings to the motel seem okay being with him. I don't know what his charm is," she said taking a quick look at her husband. "But I guess it works with them."

"Far as I can tell," Nathan added, "He's a real gentleman in the way he treats his dates."

"Okay, can we get back to the night he was here with the girl that got murdered? The two of them returned after dinner and went right to their room. Then what happened?"

"Like I told you last time, Brenda woke me up around two in the morn-

181

ing saying she heard a car out in the lot. At first I thought it was some teen-agers. They come around here late some nights. I put on my robe and went out to check the noise. By the time I got outside the car was already leaving. All I saw were the taillights. When Grimaldi came down here the next morning looking for his date, me and Brenda got suspicious. We still didn't think much about it till you showed up. Then I got to thinking maybe the missing girl went off with whoever was driving that car."

"She never came to the office to make a call or ask for help," Brenda put in.

"What happened in the morning when Grimaldi came round to see what you knew about his latest girlfriend?"

Nathan nodded his head emphatically. "All he wanted to know if we'd seen her. I told him we didn't know where she was. Far as we knew she was in the room with him all night. She never came down here to call anybody."

"Did you tell the police about the car - the one with the taillights you saw leaving the lot?"

The motel owners looked at each other. "No, I didn't," the husband said quietly. "I didn't want any more trouble than we already had. They were threatening to close us down just because the dead girl was staying here that night. They can't do that, can they? Our life savings are tied up in this place. The motel's all we have."

"Hell, Nathan, don't you think it's possible that whoever was in the car could've snatched the girl?"

"The police told us they believed Grimaldi was responsible for her being missing. We didn't want to interfere with their investigation."

"Interfere by withholding important evidence?"

The wife interrupted, "See here, Mr. Doherty, we've had just about enough of you. Why don't you get into your car and take yourself and your girlfriend off of our property?"

"Or what? You'll call the police?"

"Please, Mr. Doherty, we don't want any more trouble. We run a clean establishment here," the husband pleaded.

"Fine. I'll get out of your hair in a minute. Could you please describe again what you saw of the car that drove out of your lot that night?"

"Like I told you, I only saw its taillights."

"Tell me again as best you can what they looked like."

The man rubbed his chin trying hard to recall that night. "The car had big fins with two round taillights and a narrow vertical one running down under them on each side. I swear that's all I saw. I didn't see the license plate and I couldn't even tell you the color of the car or how many people were in it."

"One final question. Do you folks get good looks at the women Grimaldi brings to the motel?"

The couple stole glances at one another. Finally Brenda spoke, "Most of them, yeah. I try to check out who he's with. I want to make sure he's not bringing any underage girls or prostitutes into our place. That kind of trouble we don't need."

"I understand. Did Grimaldi ever come here with the same woman more than once?"

Brenda looked at her husband again before answering.

"Yeah, on three straight weekends last spring he came with this one woman. She was older than his usuals. A big woman, kind of busty, but attractive in her own way. From the way he acted with her I'd say they were already on intimate terms. I watched them and could see they were physical with each other even before they went into the room. Most times he ushers his latest from his car into Room Six as fast as he can. He was different with this one. It was like they knew each other well, if you know what I'm saying."

Doherty asked for a more detailed description of the woman. When the wife was finished he was pretty sure she'd just described Doris Donahue.

"You each have my cards. If you think of anything else could you give me a call. I also suggest if the police come back you tell them you forgot about the car when they were here before. If they hear about it from somebody else, keeping your motel open could be the least of your troubles."

Chapter Twenty-One

W hen Doherty parked the Chevy in a spot near the entrance to the Greene Inn Nina gave him one of her lovely smiles. "Now this is more of what I expected from a Casanova like you."

"Very funny."

Before they could gather their overnight bags from the trunk Doherty reached across to the glove compartment and retrieved a small box that he handed to Nina.

"What's this, an engagement ring?" she said with a wry smile.

"You wish. It's actually my mother's wedding band. Unlike the Anchor Inn, this place is quite respectable. They might look askance at an unmarried couple booking a room here."

"Aren't you the romantic," Nina said as she slipped the ring on her third finger. "It's kind of big," she added as she moved the gold band up and down her finger.

"Sorry. My mother had those Irish washerwoman hands. Not delicate digits like you, my dear."

"I'll just squeeze my fingers together and act like the dutiful wife."

Although the inn was one of the more desirable hotels in this part of the state, the place was like a ghost town in the dead of winter. Doherty saun-tered up to the front desk and asked for a room for him and his wife. The

184

clerk made a big point of checking his guest book as if there were only few rooms available. Finally he looked up and asked Doherty about his room preference.

Taken aback for a second he quickly recovered and requested a room a few floors up with a view of the water. After some unnecessary dithering the balding desk clerk gave him to the key to room 301. He then called for a bellhop to help them with their small overnight bags. Doherty didn't protest as he saw Nina out of the corner of her eye getting a big kick out of the formalities.

They followed the bellhop, a man who was a good twenty years older than Doherty, as he hauled their bags up the main staircase and then a narrower one to the third floor. Once inside the room the guy pulled back the curtains on the large French window that afforded them a wonderful view of the turbulent sea and the overcast sky. Before leaving he instructed them on the use of the in-room heater as well as the fireplace that came with three good-sized logs and some kindling wood. Doherty slipped the man a half dollar coin on his way out.

When he was gone Nina threw herself into Doherty's arms.

"This is magnificent. How does a guy in your line of work swing a place like this?"

"Only the best for you, my dear. And my client, onto whom I will bill part of our stay."

"Once again your sense of the romantic never ceases to amaze me."

Nina tossed her overnight bag onto the bed and began to empty its contents. She took out a very striking maroon dress and hung it in the closet, smoothing out some undetectable wrinkles as she did. She then held up something lacey and black.

"What is that?" he asked.

"It's called a peignoir. I shouldn't tell you this but I got it at my bridal shower. Needless to say this is the first opportunity I've had to take it out of mothballs. Don't worry, it wasn't really in mothballs so it doesn't smell. It's the least I can do for my husband," she said, holding up her hand with Doherty's mother's ring on it.

"Why don't we change and go down to the lounge and have a drink.

Technically it's a bar but here at the Greene Inn they prefer to call it a cocktail lounge." Nina took the maroon dress, some undergarments and a toiletry bag into the bathroom. While she was gone he swapped his khakis for a pair of gray woolen slacks, put on a clean white shirt and a black cardigan sweater. He used the mirror in the main room to straighten out his hair and splash on some cologne.

While Nina was tidying herself in the bathroom he picked up a local magazine that featured an article about all the wonderful activities one could engage in South County during the winter months. Since most of them involved doing outdoorsy things in snow or on ice, he quickly flipped through that section. The rest of the publication featured stories about local big shots with names that sounded like those of the men who signed the Declaration of Independence. He was checking out a few restaurant reviews when Nina finally emerged from the washroom. She looked like a million bucks.

'That dress suits you to a T," was all he could think to say.

"I thought of bringing something more demure, but since we'll be engaging in sin, I figured one this color was more appropriate. It's a good thing my mother didn't see me packing. This isn't exactly the kind of garment you take on a ski trip with your female cousin." She gave Doherty an open-mouth kiss before covering her lips with red lipstick.

Doherty motioned toward the door and they descended to the lobby. There was an enormous fireplace containing a roaring fire facing them when they hit the ground floor. Nina sauntered over to it and held her hands out to absorb some of its heat. He joined her and examined the stone carving above it. It had a weird inscription chiseled into it that read "Shall I not take mine ease in mine inn." He wasn't sure exactly what it was suppose to mean though he figured it went along with the English country inn ambience the place was trying to replicate. In the corner of the lobby was a fancy phone booth that looked like it had been snatched off the streets of London sometime shortly after the telephone was invented.

After doing their circuit of the lobby they made their way to the lounge that was just beyond the grillroom. The couple that had been leaning on the end of the bar the last time Doherty was here was occupying their usual places. So was Roger Willis, the bartender. He was wiping down some highball glasses when he spotted Doherty and Nina. His eyes first went to her, which elicited a leering smirk before he saw who she was with. His expression then changed dramatically.

Doherty seated Nina at a table far enough away from the bar that she wouldn't be able to hear anything that transpired between him and the barkeep.

"I'll order us some drinks. What would you like?"

Nina took a few seconds to consider her choice. "How about a gin and tonic with lime?"

"A gin and tonic it is. I'll be right back."

Doherty circled toward the bar purposely cutting off the exit at the end of it in case Willis had designs upon leaving the scene. He wasn't taking any chances, assuming Roger had spoken with his brother Brian after the fight at the O'Donnell Post.

"Why if it isn't the private eye?" Roger Willis said in a condescending tone as soon as Doherty got within earshot. "Working on another case?" he asked, looking over Doherty's shoulder at Nina, who had crossed her legs to reveal a fair amount of her lovely gams.

"No, I'm pretty much hoeing the same row. It's one that's related to the girl who was murdered down here last week. I'm sure you know all about it being the nosey-body that you are."

Willis decided to change the subject. "Would you and your ..."

"Girlfriend."

"Yes. Would you and your girlfriend like to order some drinks?"

"Yeah. She'll have a gin and tonic with lime and I'll have a Jameson neat. And, Roger, I would appreciate it if you didn't slip any knockout drops into either of our cocktails." That froze the bartender in mid-mix.

He turned and gave Doherty his meanest look. It wasn't even close to the ones Doherty had seen on the faces of adolescent boys around his neighborhood.

"I met your brother Brian the other night at the O'Donnell Post in Providence. I didn't know he did grunt work for Fats Finnegan. Did you?"

Roger Willis carefully placed two small napkins on the bar in front of Doherty. Before putting their drinks on them, he gave him a blank stare. "I don't know what you're talking about. And I don't know who this Fat whatever his name is."

"Really? Well he knows you. Said you played cards with him and his gang at the post a few times. Even complimented you on your poker skills and ability to hold your liquor. I suppose that comes with the territory," Doherty added, as his hand took in the bottles arrayed behind the bar.

Willis put down the drinks. "You'll have to excuse me. I don't have any more time for small talk." With the bar practically empty it was a curious thing to say. "If I were you I wouldn't leave that fine piece of pastry over there on her own for very long."

"I'll be sure to take your advice on that. And, Roger, if you refer to my companion as a piece of pastry again, I'll shove that bottle of Jameson you're holding right up your ass. Steel tip and all."

Doherty returned to their table with a fake smile plastered across his puss.

"A friend of yours from a prior engagement?"

He wasn't sure if Nina's question implied that he'd taken other women to the Greene Inn or if she was just ribbing him. Afraid if he followed that conversational train it would queer the whole evening, Doherty decided to let it go without comment.

He shook his head. "No, just another person like the people at the motel who might be able to help me with my case. I sense he knows more than he's letting on, but I'm not going to be able to get anything out of him tonight. Besides, I don't feel like ruining our time together by dwelling on what he knows or doesn't know." This last comment ended any further discussion about the bartender.

They drank and made small talk about such things as the ambience of the lounge, which was designed to look like an English pub. Or at least what Doherty thought English pubs looked like, having never set foot in that country. Somewhere in that time Doherty made a return trip to the bar to replenish their drinks. Roger Willis said nothing more than what was necessary to do his job. By the time they were finished with the second round Nina confessed she was hungry enough to eat a horse. When he pointed out that horse was not on the menu in the grillroom she expressed disappointment.

The dining room was about as sparsely populated as the lounge. There were two older couples at separate tables nursing martinis and similar drinks while quietly staring out the plate glass window that opened onto a terrace and the seawall beyond it. A maître d seated them at a table that likewise afforded them a view of the sea. The man was obsequious in the extreme while pulling out Nina's chair for her. This caused her to suppress a giggle.

"I guess neither of us is exactly used to this sort of service," Doherty said to ease any discomfort she might be feeling.

"Actually I kind of like it. It makes me feel special. I suspect in most of the hash houses you eat at they drop your plate in front of you with a crashing sound."

"Hey, that's not fair. I've dined at some of the finest greasy spoons in our fair state."

"I'm sure you have. You strike me as a real connoisseur of haute cuisine."

"What's with all the French you're slinging around? You better stop showing off, you're embarrassing me."

"I must've gotten it from my French-Canadian mother. You met Marie. I bet you didn't know she was a Canuck. It caused quite a scandal in her family when she married an Italian. When I was a kid she always mixed her version of French into our West Warwick version of English. My memere, which by the way is Canuck for grandma, lived with us until she died. She spoke nothing but French her whole life. Not really French French like they teach in school. More like the Quebec French they speak in Eastern Canada."

"I tried to pick up a little French when I was overseas during the war. I thought I knew some from living in West Warwick, but the Frenchies over there just looked down their noses at my feeble attempts. Only the kids would speak to me. I think that was because I gave them chocolate bars in return."

"What was it like being in France back then?"

Doherty tried as best he could to recall the few weeks he spent in Paris on leave before his outfit was mobilized for the final push into Germany. "It was kind of sad. The Frenchies didn't know what to make of us after all those years of being under the Nazi boot. They tried to act like we were lib-erators, especially the girls. It was hard for us too because we knew many of them had collaborated with the Germans after they were taken over. Still, we gave them food and cigarettes and they gave us wine and other stuff. In the end it seemed like a fair exchange. In any case we could tell there was al-ways some suspicion lurking behind their eyes."

"And what about you American GIs? How did you feel about them?"

"At that point most of us didn't trust any foreigners. I mean we'd just come from Italy where everybody had been all for Mussolini until they weren't. By the time we got up the coast north of Rome they made it sound like he was the worst thing that ever happened to them. Hey, I got a better idea. Let's not talk about the war. It was a long time ago and I don't want it to ruin our meal."

Just then the waiter named Dominic appeared at their table.

"Why, Mr. Doherty. So nice to see you again." Nina gave Doherty the same questioning look she'd tossed his way in the lounge.

"Dominic, I'd like you to meet Nina. Nina, this is Dominic Ferullo."

"Pleased to make your acquaintance," the waiter said with a small bow and a smile.

"Likewise," she replied with a broad grin of her own.

"Would you like cocktails?"

Before Doherty could order another Jameson Nina interrupted. "No, I think we're going to have some wine instead."

"Very good, I'll bring you the wine list."

Doherty gave her a quizzical look when the waiter withdrew from their table. "Wine makes me drowsy," he said.

"Better a drowsy lover than a drunken one." That more or less settled it.

When Dominic returned he presented the wine list to Doherty. Nina immediately snatched it out of his hand. After carefully perusing it she or-dered a bottle of something French.

"How did you know what to order? Did your memere also pass on wis-dom about French wines to you?"

Nina gave him a sly smile. "Not really. The only thing she knew about wine was the rotgut my grandfather used to make in our cellar. I ordered a bottle of something because I liked the name. Your friend the waiter seemed duly impressed."

"Well, that makes two of us."

When Dominic returned he presented the bottle of red wine to Nina. She took more time than was necessary to inspect the label before she nodded at him to pour her a taste. Once he'd done that she stuck her nose into the glass and smelled the wine. Next she swished it around in the glass before taking a sip. After a slightly prolonged pause she told the waiter the wine was acceptable. He poured a full glass for each of them while standing at attention with his other arm tucked behind his back.

Seeing they were satisfied with the wine Dominic took their meal order. Nina chose the lobster bisque as an appetizer and something called Duck a l'Orange for her entrée. Doherty had some tomato soup and a steak with baked potato and the green beans julienne for his main.

"That was quite the performance you just put on. How did you know what to do with the wine?"

She gave him one of her sly smiles. "I read about wine etiquette in a woman's magazine. I have a lot of time on my hands at the bank so I occupy myself reading magazines and paperback books. A lot of women's magazines have articles in them about how to act in restaurants so it looks like you know what you're doing. You ought to check them out sometime."

"No thanks. You certainly got Dominic's attention."

"She reached across the table and took Doherty's hand. "What about my husband? Was he impressed?"

"I think I'll reserve judgment until the night is over."

She lightly slapped his wrist. "You're such a bad boy."

"I suppose time will tell."

Doherty then excused himself, ostensibly to use the men's room. As he crossed the nearly empty dinning room he saw one of the dead-eyed older men at a table by the window giving Nina a good going over while his wife stared out at the sea.

Dominic was emerging from the kitchen with a tray carrying their appetizers and a basket of bread when Doherty intercepted him.

"I was wondering if you had anything more to tell me about the murder down here? Anything that might help my client?"

Dominic looked nervously around the room. "I can't talk now. Can we meet later when I get off my shift? Are you staying here at the inn?"

Doherty told him they were.

"Why don't you meet me down this side corridor around eleven?" he said pointing to a narrow hallway that led from the kitchen to the back of the building. "That's when I get off duty. This would be a good place because Roger won't see us here."

"That'll work for me. I'll meet you then."

"Your wife won't mind?" Dominic asked. It took Doherty a few seconds to realize that the waiter had seen the ring on Nina's finger and made the logical assumption.

"She'll be fine. She knows part of the reason we're here is because I'm working a case."

Doherty returned to the table and they dove into their soups. In time they swapped bowls and tasted each other's. He'd never had lobster bisque before and found it very tasty though somewhat heavy. Meanwhile Nina poured him a second glass of the French wine.

"Are you trying to get me drunk?"

"Only a little. I hear tell it takes a lot more than a few glasses of wine to get an Irishman drunk. Just don't get too drowsy on me."

"I promise I'll stay awake long enough to see you in your peignoir."

Their food arrived and everything about it was a class above what either of them was used to. Doherty was already trying to figure out how much of this costly meal he could expense onto Grimaldi. That would probably depend on how successful he was in helping his client avoid a murder rap.

Nina let out a small moan when she first bit into her glazed duck.

"What is that anyway?"

"It's a half of duck with an orange based sauce on it. I saw the recipe for it in Good Housekeeping recently."

"Good Housekeeping?"

"It's another woman's magazine. I doubt they have copies of it at Harry's Barbershop."

"You're right about that. Harry's library consists almost entirely of adventure magazines for manly men."

"Like my manly husband?"

Doherty was starting to get nervous about how often Nina, and now the waiter, were referring to them as a married couple.

Never having eaten a duck before Doherty was perfectly willing to try some of Nina's, especially after she mentioned half way through dinner that she was feeling full. The duck tasted like chicken only gamier. He didn't much like the orange glaze – he found it too sweet for his meat and potatoes palate.

Once they finished the bottle of wine they shared some baked Alaska for dessert. Doherty also ordered a cup of black coffee so as not to be too drowsy for any lovemaking he hoped would follow dinner. He also wanted to have his wits about him when he conferred later with Dominic the waiter.

After Doherty paid the bill they repaired to their room as quickly as they could after two cocktails, a bottle of wine and a dinner heavily laden with calories. Nina gladly kicked off her high heels as soon as they were inside the door and woozily fell into his arms. They'd made love twice before, but always at his apartment. Each time it felt furtive, as Nina was anxious about not staying out too late or arriving home too disheveled in case one of her parents was waiting up for her. But here at the Greene Inn, in the lap of luxury, they were more relaxed knowing they didn't have to be anywhere until morning.

When Nina emerged from the bathroom attired in her black peignoir outfit and her long dark hair combed out he knew this was going to be a night to remember. He was equally pleased to note that when she placed her jewelry on the bedside table she took off his mother's wedding band and placed it besides her necklace and earrings.

They made love slowly and gently with only some soft moonlight filtering into the room. Doherty'd never been with a woman who came to bed in such a sexy outfit. It clearly enhanced the experience. That, plus knowing they were far away from their humdrum lives, made their coupling that night better than either anticipated.

By ten to eleven Nina was fast asleep. He hadn't bothered to tell her about his planned clandestine meeting with Dominic Ferullo. Now he figured he would just slip out and return without her ever knowing he was gone. He put on his trousers and shirt and slid on his shoes without bothering with his socks. Nina had not stirred at all. Quietly leaving the room he was sure to lock the door from the outside so no one could intrude on her.

Dominic was standing where he said he would be pulling on a cigarette. Doherty sparked up a Camel when he joined him.

"So what have you got for me?"

The waiter craned his neck around to make sure no one was within earshot. "You know how I told you what a pompous ass Roger is; always the one who knows everything first. Anyway after that dead girl's body was identified he was all in a snit. I mean even more than usual. Most of the time he tries to be so cool, calm and collected, ruling the roost here at the inn like he's the cock of the walk."

"Yeah, yeah. I hear you. What was he like after he found out the girl had been identified?"

"Very nervous. Nervous in a way I've never seen him. And he was on the phone a lot. I mean Roger never gets phone calls in the lounge and hardly ever makes them. But every time I went in there to place an order he was on the horn with somebody. And each time he was holding his hand over the receiver talking in a low voice so no one could hear him. Just to get his goat I would purposely linger in the bar area trying to hear what he was saying. When he noticed me he'd get quite nasty. He'd tell me to mind my own business. On a couple of occasions he even said I should 'get lost'."

"That's it? He was having secret phone calls? Did you hear anything he was saying that would indicate who he was talking to?"

"No. I never could tell who was on the other end."

"Jesus, Dominic, that's not much to go on. Is that all you have for me?"

The waiter looked disappointed as he smoked his cigarette down to its butt end. "Well he did take some time off. Told our manager Vincent he had to go up to Providence to visit his sick mother. As long as I've been here Roger's never taken a day off unless he was scheduled to. Now he was running up to the city every other day."

"Maybe he was visiting his sick mother. That could be what all those calls were about."

Dominic smiled now for the first time. "Yes, except I happen to know that his mother lives in Florida. When I first came here I told Roger I'd lived in Miami for a while. He said his mother lived down there and he hated Florida. As a result, he said, it was why he never visited the old bag. Those were the exact words he used to describe her: 'the old bag'."

"So let me get this straight. Your bartender Roger sees himself as the head honcho around here. Never takes time off except when scheduled to, has few friends, seldom talks on the phone here at work and has a mother who lives in Florida. Then a girl he supposedly doesn't know anything about ends up dead close by here. And all of a sudden he's making personal phone calls on a regular basis and taking days off work to visit a non-existent sick mother in Providence."

"Yes. That's about the size of it," Dominic said vigorously nodding his head.

"Just one final question, Dom. It's obvious you don't like Roger. According to you, if the waitstaff in the grillroom doesn't kick him some of their tip money he dawdles in getting you your cocktails. On top of that he generally treats you and the other help here like his underlings. Is it possible you want to get Roger in trouble just because you don't like him?"

Dominic stood up to his full height for the first time. "No, I don't like him - I'll confess to that. None of us do. But you asked me to help you with your case and I'm trying to do that. I've worked here for four years, so when I describe Roger's behavior of late as being peculiar I mean just that."

Doherty patted the waiter on the shoulder. "It's okay, Dom. I was just testing you. Here, this is for your troubles," he said as he handed Dominic Ferullo a five spot.

Chapter Twenty-Two

A ray of sunlight peaked through the blinds, bathing their room in natural light. Nina was still sleeping, snuggled up against him with a smile on her face as if she'd just spent the night on cloud nine. Doherty'd been up for a while mulling over what Dominic had told him about Roger Willis' recent behavior. He was trying to figure out how he could now move on the bartender, or if he had any move at all.

Nina cozied up even closer and opened her eyes a slit. She moaned and shut them again. Her black peignoir set lay crumpled in a heap on the floor by the bed. He looked at her lying so peacefully next to him with her dark hair splayed across the pillow. He'd never seen her without her make-up on. She looked even lovelier minus the cosmetics. It had been quite some time since he'd awoken in the morning with a woman in bed beside him. For a few seconds he considered what it would be like to be married. This wouldn't be so bad he thought. He'd never felt this way before, mostly because his cases always seemed to have a way of interfering with his relationships. But now that he was forty he thought it might be time to settle down.

Living with a woman like Nina would have its plusses. She had her own job and friends so he wouldn't have to bear the burden of entertaining her all the time. And he wouldn't have to support her, which would be next to impossible given the threadbare nature of his investigations practice. It was all he could do to toss a few bucks at his secretary Agnes each week while still having enough walking around money for himself. The only drawback he saw to hitching up with Nina was that she was young enough to want kids. That could be a game changer. Add to that he had to consider that her parents didn't really approve of him; they already thought he was too old and irresponsible for their daughter. Thankfully Nina came fully awake to push the marriage topic out of his mind for the time being.

He tucked his right arm under her head, realizing with the peignoir outfit on the floor his bedmate was completely naked.

"Where did you go last night?" she mumbled in a tired voice.

"What do you mean?"

She lifted her head off the pillow. "You left me here all alone. Did you have another assignation?"

"I might've if I knew what an assignation was."

"I thought maybe you had a rendezvous with another woman while I was lying here dead asleep."

"Ah here you go with the French again. Apparently you weren't dead asleep since you knew I was gone. No, I did not have a meeting with another woman. I'm not that much of a sexual athlete to handle two girls in one night. How did you know I was gone? I tried to be as quiet as a mouse when I let myself out."

Nina gave him one of her more sincere smiles. "At some point I rolled over to embrace my lover, and low and behold, he wasn't here."

"I'm sorry. I had to slip downstairs for a short conversation with our waiter about the case I'm working on. I did lock the door to insure one of those old gents who was eyeing you in the grillroom didn't come up here to molest you."

"That was very thoughtful of you. But you're going to have to make up for the lost time."

He didn't know if that was an open invitation. Either way he took her in his arms and they were soon making love in the broad daylight for the first time. As with the night before, staying at a luxury resort like the Greene Inn put both of them at ease.

After they were done Nina got out of bed and stood beside him stark na-

197

ked. "So, what do you think?"

"Not bad for a bank clerk. Did you get that body from articles in your women's magazines?"

"I don't know. Did you get your he-man physique from the ones at Harry's Barbershop?"

Without waiting for an answer, she told him she was going to take a shower. While she was gone Doherty used the house phone by the bed to order a full room service breakfast for two.

Fortunately the food didn't arrived before Nina emerged from the bathroom. Her hair was wet and she was wearing a robe supplied courtesy of the inn so she wouldn't appear naked before the bellhop or whoever else brought up their breakfasts. When he informed her that he'd ordered up a morning meal she quickly slipped his mother's wedding band back on.

"Wouldn't want them to think anything sinful was going on in room 301."

"Wasn't there?"

"No," she said sternly. "I can't believe anything that feels this good could qualify as a sin. Now I think you better put on something besides your boxer shorts before our breakfasts arrive."

Doherty slipped on his Khakis and shirt, which he left hanging out untucked. He did his business in the bathroom and came out a minute before their food cart arrived. He didn't know how the inn got such a contrivance up to the third floor and didn't bother to ask. The deliverer was neither Dominic nor the older man who had carried their bags up the day before. He was a new face, falling somewhere in age between the waiter and yesterday's bellhop. Before he left Doherty gave him a generous tip.

The cart served as table so Doherty and Nina moved two chairs over to it and began to chow down. He wanted to say that a night of torrid sex had left him with a hardy appetite, then thought such a remark would be too crude in such a luxurious setting. The breakfast consisted of fresh squeezed orange juice, scrambled eggs, bacon, home fries and toast with butter and jam. A sprig of fresh parsley decorated each of their plates. The food was accompanied by a full pot of coffee and all the necessities to go along with it. Nina remained clothed only in the white bathrobe with the inn's dark green monogram on it.

"We should do this all the time," she said between bites.

"Yeah, sure. As soon as I get my first millionaire client."

"I could always embezzle some money from the bank. I do handle a substantial amount of cash every day. How about if I hijack a few thousand and we hightail it down to Mexico? I bet we could stay at a place like this down there for a good long time."

"And leave my lucrative investigations practice? I wouldn't think of it."

They talked little about the previous night while devouring the food in front of them. Finally Doherty broke the good humor by saying, "Listen, Nina, if we're going to go any further with this relationship I need to know something."

"Any further? How can we go any further than marriage," she said with a giggle, holding up her left hand with his mother's wedding band still on it.

"I'm trying to be serious here. I need to know what happened with your previous engagement. It's the one thing we haven't talked about since we started seeing each other."

Things had taken a turn with his inquiry. "I don't want to discuss it," she said firmly.

"I just want to make sure I don't screw things up like the last guy did."

"No chance that'll happen," she said evasively.

"At least tell me why you broke it off."

After a long pause she said, "I didn't. He did."

"I don't understand. Why would anyone in his right mind break up with a girl like you? Did he get cold feet about being married? I hear that happens to a lot of guys."

"Present company included?"

"We were talking about you, not me," he said, quickly turning the subject back to Nina.

"If you really want to know the truth, Doherty, I'll tell you why it ended. Turned out Darrell was queer."

"I don't understand."

"No, a he-man like you probably wouldn't. Before I met him Darrell was in the navy. He was too young for the big war; it was during the one in

199

Korea. He wasn't in action or anything; he was on a ship. He had this friend Chris that was one of his shipmates. Apparently they became good buddies as soon as they met. Chris was from somewhere out west; I think it was Washington State. Darrell never told me what happened between them. I think in his mind it was just one of those things that happens to some men when they're living so close together on a ship. I guess he thought when he got home he'd leave all that behind him."

"After you guys started dating nothing seemed out of the ordinary?"

"I don't know. I guess everything was kind of okay, mostly because I wanted it to be and didn't know any better. It wasn't like I was all that experienced myself. He was such a nice guy and my parents loved him. The only thing that was strange was he never wanted to have sex. I mean we kissed and all, but he kept saying he wanted to save our lovemaking for after we were married. I was pretty sure he thought I was a virgin. So I didn't say anything one way or the other. In case you're interested I wasn't. But that's another story I don't want to go into right now."

Doherty was still trying to digest what Nina was telling him about her fiancé to contemplate her previous sex life. "What happened to make him break off the engagement?"

"Chris showed up in Rhode Island for a visit. Darrell described him as an old navy buddy just passing through looking to share some memories about their time in the service. I didn't find out about the other business until later. Chris was a friendly enough guy so I didn't think anything at the time."

"What changed?"

"I don't know. Call it women's intuition. Whatever it was after a few days something didn't seem right to me. When the three of us were together, they were always talking about their time in the navy. I felt like the odd one out, which, I guess, was understandable. Then something else clicked in. I could tell things weren't the same between us after Chris left. Darrell seemed distant and withholding. Before that he was always talking about us and planning our life together once we were married. When I asked him what was wrong, he'd say 'nothing', but I could see the doubt in his eyes. Then just like that he broke it off. No explanation, no nothing. My parents were devastated. They thought he was a perfect gentleman. Just the kind of man I needed. They never said anything, but I could tell they thought I was responsible for Darrell's change of heart."

"How did you know he was… you know? Was it something you read in one of your women's magazines?"

"Oh, God no! They would never write about something like that. When it comes to men, the articles are all about how to please your man or how to support your man if he's having a hard time at work or finding a job. Not how to treat your man if he likes other men."

"How did you explain it to your folks?"

"I tried to keep it simple. I told them he got cold feet. That's what I've said to everyone. I think a lot of my friends believed it because I'd told Darrell all along I wanted to keep my job at the bank and wasn't interested in just being a happy homemaker. At least not until we had kids. I even convinced myself that was why we broke up. In the end I got pretty good at lying to myself."

"I think we should get dressed and go for a walk by the water."

Nina got up and came over to his side of the table. She leaned down and gave Doherty a big kiss. "That sounds like a great idea. I could use some air."

Although it was blustery walking along the seawall they didn't mind very much. They were glad to be out in the fresh air before heading back to West Warwick and their real lives. Nina held tightly to Doherty's arm as they fought their way against the wind. All the while two conflicting trains of thought crowded his mind. One was of Roger Willis and what role he may have played in Adrian Colardo's disappearance and subsequent death. The other was how good he was feeling about Nina while still being somewhat shaken by the story of her broken engagement.

Doherty had very little experience with homosexuals. The fact that she came so close to marrying one left him perplexed. He had nothing against people wanting to be with those of the same sex, he just wasn't familiar with that world. The brothers at St. James had preached so vehemently against it that the belief in its perversity was embedded somewhere deep inside him. On the other hand, the unmarried priests who lived so close together in their spartan abbey rooms seemed a little weird in its own right. There had always been rumors among the kids who were altar boys that this brother or that brother was sometimes a little too physical with them. Since Doherty'd never served as an altar boy he tried to keep his distance from the priests, some of whom doled out sadistic corporal punishment as if they enjoyed it. By the time he'd left the church he'd already come to believe that anything of a sexual nature the priests were opposed to couldn't be all bad.

There'd been rumors throughout high school about one boy or another being a *fairy*. Of course, nobody he knew had firsthand knowledge this was true; it was just something guys said about boys who liked art better than football or found themselves more comfortable in the company of girls rather than a bunch of boorish guys. He knew this underworld existed. He'd seen enough of it in the dark corners of Paris; it just wasn't something he was familiar with. And now he found himself dating a girl who almost married one.

These thoughts kept interfering with his plans on how to light a fire under Roger Willis. However he moved on the bartender, he had to assume Willis would've already phoned his brother and Finnegan after their conversation the previous night. In any case, he still had no idea how his suspicions would benefit Richie Grimaldi. He was rattling all these disparate thoughts around in his head as he and Nina headed back to the inn.

She squeezed his arm and said, "You're being awfully quiet. A penny for your thoughts?"

Doherty shook his head. "Sorry. I was trying to sort out all of what I learned yesterday that might help my client avoid a murder rap."

She looked relieved. "Oh, for a minute there I was worried you were thinking about Darrell and how your new girlfriend almost married a homo."

He laughed to ease the tension. "The thought has crossed my mind a few times since you told me about him. Right now I'd prefer to save that conversation for another time. This has been too nice of a getaway to ruin it by opening up that can of worms." He then swung Nina into his arms and gave her a big kiss for all the world to see. That is if there had been any world out in this nasty winter weather.

When they returned to the inn Nina made a quick path to the big fireplace where several large logs were cooking. She rubbed her hands together trying to get circulation back into them. Before checking out they repaired to the bar for a drink to warm themselves. Nina asked for something called a hot toddy while Doherty simply opted for a double shot of Jameson. Roger Willis did his best to avoid eye contact as he prepped their drinks. While Nina sat at a table by the window, Doherty gave Willis a stare that would have bored holes into a lesser man. As he did he could see a slight shakiness in the barkeep's hands. He was intent on rattling Willis' cage one last time before he left Narragansett.

"I'm going to be straightforward with you, Roger. I think you know more about that girl's death than you're letting on. If I sic the cops on you I wonder how long your I-don't-know-anything story will hold up. Right now I'm thinking somebody got you to dose her drink as well as Grimaldi's on the night she disappeared. I'll also bet dollars to donuts you had no idea the girl would end up dead. If I were you I wouldn't want to take the fall as an accessory to murder. That kind of rap will buy you quite a stretch at the ACI."

Willis gave him a quick sidelong glance and then went back to heating up Nina's toddy.

"I might be able to help you," Doherty continued, though not at all sure how. "The least I can do is assist you in putting together a strategy that'll keep you out of jail while those who committed the crime take the fall."

"I don't know what you're talking about," Roger said as precisely as he could. "I thought the police were after your client for that girl's murder." His voice sounded like that of man who had fallen into a ten-foot hole.

"Suit yourself, Roger. I'll tell you right now: I'm going to get my client out of this mess and when I do the police will be looking for the person or persons who did kill that girl. By then it'll be too late for you get out front of this by cutting a deal that'll keep you from going inside. I'm offering my help; if you don't want it that's your business."

"Your drinks are ready," Willis said in a shaky voice as he placed a glass half full of brown liquor and Nina's steaming mug on the bar.

It was a short ride up Route One back to West Warwick. They were both aware that their night in Narragansett had clearly changed the nature of their relationship. Or at least that's what they were feeling in the aftermath of their stay at the Greene Inn. Nina had borrowed her father's car to drive to New Hampshire and then covertly parked it in Doherty's space in Belanger's garage. That way no one who knew the car would have spotted it parked in town. She didn't think her father would be suspicious enough to check the odometer and see that it had been driven a little over a mile in two days.

Nina was talking hurriedly about the story she would concoct of her skiing adventure in New Hampshire. She thought her best plan should be to say that she fell too many times to see skiing as a hobby she'd be pursuing on a more regular basis. Doherty objected, suggesting she might want to reserve the ski trip for other getaways they could take. She thought it would be better to use her cousin in New Hampshire for trips in warmer weather, like to Lake Winnipesaukee in the summer.

They spent the balance of the afternoon at his apartment eating baloney sandwiches and reading the Sunday *Journal* until she thought it was late enough for her to return home from up north. To kill a little more time they made love in Doherty's unkempt bed. They both agreed that his bachelor pad fell far short of the accommodations at the Greene Inn. When she left he felt a loneliness he hadn't experienced in some time. To occupy his attention he watched the Ed Sullivan Show on the small TV Rachel Katz had bequeathed to him last fall on her way out of his life.

Chapter Twenty-Three

Despite the chilly weather Doherty decided to walk to the office on Monday morning. There was an extra bounce in his step thanks to his weekend sojourn with Nina Vitale. He was whistling as he walked, but that did not deter him from noticing an unfamiliar black sedan parked across Brookside Ave. from the entrance to Doherty and Associates. The motor was running and the windows were fogged up, though not so much he couldn't see the two heads in the front seat. One window was cracked enough that cigarette smoke was finding its way into the winter air.

He made it a point to walk close enough to the vehicle to be spotted by its occupants. Hastily climbing the stairs to the agency he informed Agnes she should join him in his inner office, as they were about to have some unexpected visitors. She'd barely gotten the words out to ask about his weekend when he unlocked his desk drawer and punched some slugs into his .38. The look on Agnes' face could've stopped a clock. When he heard the heavy tread on the stairs, he edged his door open enough to see into the outer office. The .38 hung by his side hidden behind the desk. Agnes cowered in the corner out of sight.

A loud knock was followed by two men moving into Agnes' space before being invited. Doherty relaxed once he recognized one of the visitors as Sgt. Squillante of the Providence PD. The other suit wore an unfamiliar face, one that was sorely in need of a shave. Doherty stealthily slid his gun back into the opened drawer.

"Who's your new sidekick, Officer Squillante?" he asked as the two men made their way into Doherty's office.

"Ever the smart guy, eh, Doherty. This here is Sgt. DeSimone of the East Providence police. I'm just taggin' along for the ride today given that me and you are like old friends."

Doherty stayed sitting behind his desk, not bothering to offer a hand to the East Providence cop. Instead he politely shooed Agnes out of the room. Wherever this conversation was going he didn't want her to be privy to it. Wisely she shut the door behind her.

"What can I do for you, Officer DeSimone?"

Without it being offered the East Providence cop dropped into the seat on the other side of the desk. Squillante remained standing while torching a smoke and giving Doherty one of his wiseass grins.

"When was the last time you were at Crescent Park?"

Doherty was taken aback by the cop's out-of-leftfield question. "I don't know. Maybe when I was twelve. I always liked riding the carousel there and snapping off the gold rings. Isn't the park closed this time of year?"

"You didn't happen to be there sometime over this past weekend, did you?"

Doherty smiled for the first time. "Not unless I took a time machine back to 1932. Why? What's this all about?"

"We need to know your whereabouts this weekend," Squillante butted in.

"I'm not sure that's any of your bus…"

"Just answer the question," the East Providence sergeant interrupted. His stern tone of voice right away made Doherty not want to cooperate with him.

"I was down in Narragansett with my girlfriend. We spent Saturday night there." This elicited a knowing leer from Squillante.

"What's the young lady's name?" DeSimone asked without changing his matter-of-fact tone.

"I'm afraid that really is none of your business."

"It is if we're investigatin' a recent death," Squillante threw in.

"Okay, okay. Why don't we start over with you telling me who's dead? Then maybe I can help you boys out."

"Look, Doherty, in case you haven't noticed, we're the ones carrying the badges," DeSimone said. "That means we get to ask the questions and you get to provide the answers. What do you know about a guy named Edward Donahue, formerly of North Providence, recently living with his sister and her husband in Cumberland?"

"Is Eddie Donahue the one who's dead?"

"I guess you didn't hear me the first time: we're the police so we ask the questions and you tell us what you know. Now, what can you tell us about this Donahue fella?"

Doherty decided it was probably in his and Richie Grimaldi's best interests to play ball with these two, at least up to a point. "I met him once at his sister's. He struck me as a bit of a sad sack. You know, one of those I'm-okay-the-world's-wrong kind of guys."

"We understand the sister hired you to find him when he disappeared. How's that going?"

"To be honest with you, I've been pretty busy with another case I'm working. I made a few gestures at looking for Donahue but nothing panned out."

"Well you can stop your search," Squillante broke in. "The East Providence PD found your lost boy sittin' in a car in the main parkin' lot at Crescent Park with his brains blown out. It was made to look like a suicide, but they're reservin' judgment on that."

"Why are they reserving judgment?"

DeSimone held up his index finger and said, "That's a question."

"For chrissake, Donahue's sister is my client. She paid me good money to find him and I didn't. If he didn't kill himself then I may have some hunches as to why he's dead and who did it."

Squillante pulled up the other chair in the room and sat with his elbows resting on Doherty's desk. "Okay. So then why don't you tell us what you know that might've caused this Donahue to buy a trip to the morgue?"

"I met him while I was working this other case. It didn't appear to have anything to do with Donahue even though it came to involve his ex-wife. When I questioned her she told me Eddie'd been spending a lot of time at the O'Donnell VFW post on Charles Street in the city."

"Yeah, I know the place," Squillante said.

"Anyway, she explained that Eddie had gotten into trouble there over some gambling debts. He continued to borrow money from her and lost it all playing cards. She eventually threw him out and that's when he went to live with his sister, Mrs. Garrett. She was also very concerned about Donahue's continued involvement with certain people at the post."

"Okay, go on," DeSimone prompted.

"Well, both women thought Eddie was being put up to doing some illegal jobs for a couple of the men at the post he owed money to. One is a guy named Fats Finnegan. I believe his real name is Mike, but everybody there refers to him as Fats on account of him being oversized. Apparently he runs the gambling action at the O'Donnell. The other fella is named Brian Willis. My impression is that Willis provides the muscle for Finnegan." He could've tossed Willis' brother Roger their way, but decided to keep the Greene Inn bartender to himself for the time being.

"Do you think these guys might've killed Donahue because he was gonna snitch on them about the illegal business they were involved in?" DeSimone asked.

"I don't know. I never got close enough to Donahue to figure out how much he was on the hook to them. It stands to reason they'd want to make it look like he took his own life since Eddie'd been on a downward spiral ever since he came home from the service. He certainly was a good candidate for suicide. At least that's the way his ex-wife *and* sister described him to me."

"Where would we find this wife?"

"Last I heard she was still living in the same apartment in North Providence she shared with Donahue when they were married. Her name is Doris. They're divorced but she's kept her husband's last name." He could have added that she worked at Cherry & Webb, but he didn't want the two cops to get the notion that Doherty was on familiar terms with Doris Donahue. Nor did he want them to barge into her place of employment and possibly get her fired by doing so.

"If Eddie Donahue was found with a gun pointed at his head and a bullet in his brain, why do you suspect this might be a murder rather than suicide? Sorry officer DeSimone, I know I put that in the form of a question."

"There was no residue on his hands," Squillante blurted out, much to the annoyance of the East Providence police sergeant. "Nobody holds a gun to his head and pulls the trigger without leavin' traces on his hand. And there was no back splatter of blood on his arm."

"Whoever tried to make this look like a suicide did a piss poor job," DeSimone added.

"I bet his sister wasn't too happy about Eddie's blood being blown all over the inside of her car."

"That's the thing. He wasn't killed in her car. Her station wagon is sitting in the driveway of her house."

"So whose car was it?"

"We're not releasing that information yet. And if you know what's good for you, neither will you."

The two men rose as if to leave. Doherty tried to hand one of his business cards to DeSimone.

"Don't worry. I'll know how to find you if we need to talk again."

Shortly after the cops left and before Agnes could ask him any questions about their visit, the phone in the outer office rang. She answered it after the second bell. Before transferring it to his phone she poked her head into his space and said, "There's an attorney named Saul Friedman on the line. Do you want to take the call?"

"Yeah, sure. By all means."

"Hello, Mr. Doherty, my name is Saul Friedman. I'm the attorney representing Richard Grimaldi in this unfortunate case involving the girl who was recently murdered in South County." The voice struck Doherty as one belonging to someone who grew up tough on the streets of Providence and was now trying extra hard to sound respectable.

"I know who you are. What can you tell me about Richie's situation? I've been away all weekend so I need to get caught up on things." Actually it was trying to sort out why Eddie Donahue was murdered that was distracting him from the Grimaldi case.

"Well, Richard was arrested, fingerprinted and charged by the North Kingston police on Friday. He is scheduled to be arraigned tomorrow so I will be driving down there with him in the morning."

"He's not in lockup?"

"No, he was bailed late Friday afternoon by his cousin Anthony Fortunato. Bail was set at $25,000 and apparently the cousin was able to borrow $2500 against the lease on their restaurant for the bond."

"What was he charged with?"

"Abduction and murder. They tried to throw in a few morals charges but they couldn't make them stick since all the evidence shows that the dead girl went down to Narragansett with Richard of her own free will."

"How did you get him bailed on a murder charge?"

"It wasn't easy. Turns out the presiding judge is an old golfing buddy of mine. I was able to convince him that Richard was not a flight risk and had significant roots in the community given that he was part owner of a well-established restaurant on Federal Hill," Friedman said in a self-satisfied voice. "The main reason I'm calling is to inquire how your investigation on Richard's behalf is going?"

"Well there are a few loose pieces floating around that I'm trying to put together. I know they add up to something though at this point I'm not exactly sure what."

"Hmm," the lawyer mused on the other end. "That doesn't sound too promising. Can you give me a few *for instances*?"

Doherty was considering how much to share with Grimaldi's lawyer, a man Richie mentioned had some mob clients as well as connections on the right side of the law. He was sure Friedman wished to see the meter on Richie Grimaldi run uninterrupted. There was also the possibility his lawyer wanted the case to go to trial for the publicity it would afford him.

"I don't know if you've heard about the fellow whose body was found in the parking lot at Crescent Park the other night."

"Yes, I have. Sounds like a suicide from what I've read in the papers. What does this have to do with Richard's situation?"

"Well the cops investigating it just left my office. And they not so subtly hinted they're looking at it as a murder rather than a suicide. They're keeping that under wraps for that time being, and I hope you will too."

"Fair enough. But what does this fellow's death have to do with our client?"

"I'm not sure yet what the connection is. But something tells me there is one and I mean to find it."

Resignation had entered into Friedman's tone when he said, "This sounds a little far-fetched to me. At Richard's request I'll leave the investigation up to you for the time being. I've heard good things about you, Mr. Doherty, so we'll stick with your original arrangement. Whatever you do, do not lose sight of the fact that a man's life is at stake here."

"Oh, you don't have to worry about that. Why don't you give me your contact info so we can stay in touch? I'll keep you up to date on my inquiries and you can keep me abreast of the legal maneuverings. By the way, how can I get in touch with Richie these days?"

"For the moment he's staying at Anthony Fortunato's house on Fruit Hill. The best way to contact him is through Anthony or his son Tony, who are now running the restaurant in Richard's absence. Do you know where his cousin's house is?"

"Yeah, I've already been there a couple of times," Doherty said before hanging up.

When he got off the phone with the attorney he was wondering if Friedman was angling to bring in his own investigator on Grimaldi's behalf. That would allow him to jack up his charges even more. Worse yet, it could leave Doherty out in the cold for the expenses he'd already run up out on his client's behalf, including his weekend at the Greene Inn.

Chapter Twenty-Four

After filling Agnes in on some of what transpired between him and the two cops as well as with Grimaldi's lawyer, Doherty grabbed a quick lunch at the counter downstairs at the Arctic News and headed for the big city. He hated driving into Providence but there were a few tidbits he needed to pry out of Jeru Squillante, the only cop he knew foolish enough to share them with a PI like him. Aside from being a less than honest cop, Squillante was the kind of detective who liked to show off by letting you know he knew more than you did, and then telling you what he knew. If he were a woman, he'd be the biggest gossip in town.

After dumping his Chevy in a parking lot, Doherty walked two blocks to Providence's main police headquarters. He had no love for cop shops, not just because everyone who worked in them looked at outsiders as potential criminals, especially the accused perpetrators who were temporarily housed there. Police stations also had that antiseptic smell that was a poor attempt to cover up the fact that these places were bastions of mostly grown men who had no women around to keep things tidy. As a result desks were often littered with too much paperwork, wastebaskets were seldom emptied, as were ashtrays. In addition, the bathrooms often lacked paper towels and at times even toilet paper.

The Providence central police station was much larger than the shack that had been the police headquarters in West Warwick when Doherty was on the force. That building had recently been torn down and the local cops now shared a modern municipal structure with the town's offices. The new space was cleaner, especially on the town side. The one time he'd been in the police section, Doherty could see that the cops were already turning their new digs it into a pigsty.

The first thing that hit him when he entered the Providence station was that the heat was turned up high enough to match the sauna bath at the YMCA. Granted it was cold outside, but this joint was so tropical that the cop manning the check-in desk was wearing a short-sleeved uniform shirt and was still sweating. He was overweight with a stubbly chin matched by a stubbly head of hair. It took him a full thirty seconds to raise his head from the sport pages to acknowledge Doherty's presence.

"What can I do for you, pal?" he muttered without making eye contact.

"I'd like to speak with Sgt. Squillante. Is he's in?"

The desk clerk made a sound that indicated he didn't think much of Jeru Squillante.

"Name?"

"Tell him Doherty is here. He'll know who I am."

The master of the front desk made it a point to turn the page on his newspaper before calling upstairs. Eventually he reached the detective bureau and asked for Squillante. When Jeru came on the phone the desk cop didn't even give him the courtesy of addressing him as 'sergeant'. He mumbled that a guy named Doherty was here to see him. He held the phone for a few seconds. Meanwhile Doherty shed his topcoat before breaking out into a heat sweat of his own.

"Second floor. There's an elevator down the hall, but if I was you I'd take the stairs. That lift's been here since the last century. It only works when it feels like it."

Doherty huffed his way up to the second floor. At the top of the stairs there were two signs pointing in opposite directions. One listed Vice Squad, Bail Office and Domestic Affairs. The other pointed to the Detective Bureau, Missing Persons and Arson. He followed those signs to a door whose upper half was frosted glass with the bureau's name stenciled on it in black lettering. He considered knocking, then decided to walk right in instead.

It was a large area with too many desks pushed too close together. Every one of them was stacked high with file folders. The air was thick with cigarette smoke. A bulletin board just inside the door had a couple of wanted posters tacked to it as well as some yellowed notices for events long past. One was for a Toys-for-Tots project the cops were being asked to participate in for Christmas. With that holiday two months past, he wondered why nobody'd torn the notice down. He saw another that outdid it, announcing a retirement get-together for a cop who had left in May of the previous year.

Doherty spotted Squillante sitting at a desk toward the far end of the room. His feet were propped up on it and he was jawing with two other plainclothes cops. They were all in shirtsleeves with their tie knots askew. Their conversation came to a halt when Doherty approached.

"Well lookee who's here," Squillante smiled his crooked tooth grin. "I'd introduce you to my colleagues, Doherty, but I don't want them to think me and you are bosom buddies or anythin'." He laughed and the other cops laughed along with him, though theirs were mostly fake.

"Doherty here is a private eye, down in little old West Warwick. What do you think of that fellas?"

None of the other cops responded but they didn't have to. Doherty knew that the police looked at PIs as one small step below actual criminals. And two steps below defense lawyers.

Squillante offered Doherty a chair on the other side of his mess of a desk. The two cops he'd been chatting with left the area and walked slowly to the other end of the large room.

"So, Mr. Private Eye. What can I do you for? I don't suppose you drove all the way up here to the big city to buy me a drink."

"I just wanted to ask you a few questions about the Donahue death. Stuff I couldn't ask about in front of your pal DeSimone. He didn't seem to like me asking any questions."

"Guy's kinda of a hard ass, ain't he? I don't know what I can tell you. Donahue's death isn't our case; it belongs to the East Prov division."

"I figured as much considering he met his demise in the lot at Crescent Park. It's my recollection the Riverside area is technically part of East Providence. Since it's not your case I thought you might be willing to fill me in on a few things. This'll be totally off the record, just between you and me."

"Oh, Doherty. I love it when you try to sweet talk me. Like I'm gonna fall for your happy horseshit."

"Whatever you say. Anyway since this is East Providence's case nothing you tell me is going queer any investigation you're working on here." He knew that Squillante was dying to blab some inside dope; Doherty just had to make it sound like what he was fishing for was incidental stuff.

"What can you tell me about the car that Donahue met his sad end in?"

"The car?"

"Yeah, you know, what kind of model was it, who was it registered to? Just a few details like that. Nothing that'll impact the East Providence investigation one way or the other."

Jeru Squillante put his feet back up on his desk and lit up a Lucky. He offered Doherty one, and although he generally preferred his Camels, he knew it was a good idea to take up the offer of a cig if he was going to get the Providence cop to spill what he knew.

"It was a Pontiac. 1958 Star Chief I believe. Two-toned, red and white. A little beat up but still a nice car. I don't know what they'll do with it now that it's got that Donahue guy's blood splattered all over it. It'll be pretty hard to sell somethin' like that at auction."

"Who was it registered to?"

"Nobody."

"What do you mean nobody?"

"Car's been off the road for over a year. Plates on it were stolen off a Buick in Westerly six months ago. Owner reported them stolen. He got new plates a week later. Stolen plates aren't exactly a high priority even in a burg as small as Westerly. If it happened up here in Providence we would've told the fella we were sorry and that would've been the end of it. We wouldn't've bothered to have him fill out a report."

"That's all you know about the car Donahue died in?"

"That's about it. Car's been impounded by the EP police and they're doin' a thorough examination of it as we speak. It's a possible murder scene so you can assume they'll be keepin' it for a while. What's your interest in

215

this anyway?"

"I shouldn't tell you this but I will," Doherty said greasing Squillante a little more. "The night the girl disappeared down in Narragansett, according to the proprietor of the motel where she'd been shacked up with my client, he heard a car in his lot about two in the morning. He didn't see anything but the taillights. I'm wondering if the lights on that car match up with those on the rear of a '58 Star Chief."

"Do the cops in North Kingston know about this car?"

"No. The motel owner never told them about it. When I first spoke with him he said he didn't think anything of it. The second time I asked him about the car he told me he didn't tell the police because he didn't want any more trouble than he already was in. He figured by withholding that info the first time they questioned him he'd be in even deeper shit if he spilled it to them later."

The cop stuffed out his butt and was quiet for a few moments. An unusual condition for a chatterbox like Jeru Squillante.

"I don't know, Doherty. Are you thinkin' the car Donahue met his sad end in could be the same one used to snatch that girl out of the motel? Seems kinda improbable to me."

"I don't know. I'm just thinking out loud. Could be I'm jumping to a conclusion that isn't there."

Squillante shrugged. "Neither case is in my jurisdiction so it don't make no never mind to me."

Those were Sgt. Gerald Squillante's final words of wisdom before Doherty left Providence Police headquarters.

The outside air felt significantly colder yet refreshing after leaving the hot box of the Providence station. Walking toward the lot where he'd left his car Doherty turned the collar of his coat up against the bracing wind coming off the Providence River. All he wanted to do was go home and work on some details of the case in the comfort of his apartment. However, there was one more stop he needed to make on his way back to West Warwick.

If his memory served him well, there was a Pontiac dealership on Reservoir Avenue in Cranston just over the line from Providence near the opulent Calart Artificial Flower building that dominated that part of the main drag. The structure where plastic flowers were designed and sold had an exotic facade and a large central tower. It was one of those landmarks just about everyone in Rhode Island had driven past at one time or another.

He was right; the car dealership was less than a block before Calart on the opposite side of the busy thoroughfare. He swung the Chevy into a space and took a few minutes to rehearse his routine in the event he was approached by somebody trying to sell him a car.

He'd walked only a few steps toward the new Pontiacs, all brightly polished sitting in the lot out front of the showroom, when a salesman came out and headed in his direction. Pontiac was featuring its classy new Bonneville model once again this year. The high horsepower car was named after the speedway and nearby salt flats out in Utah where many land speed records have been set over the years. Several of these cars came in two-toned models. One on the lot was a souped-up job with pin stripes and a number on the side to make it look like a real racing car. Although they were way out of Doherty's class, that didn't prevent him from admiring their futuristic styling.

A large man with black hair combed straight back from his forehead wearing a beige topcoat ambled in Doherty's direction. When he wasn't selling cars this guy looked like he could've moonlighted doing muscle work for the mob. As he sidled up to Doherty he pulled his coat closed across his chest and said, "It's colder than a polar bear's ass today."

"You can say that again," Doherty replied, hoping the fellow wouldn't.

The salesman gave Doherty a sidelong glance. "Pretty awesome vehicles, these Bonnies, huh. Are you interested in one?"

Doherty laughed to himself. "Maybe if I was ten years younger and had a little more cash to burn. I was looking for something used, maybe a year or two old. Do have anything in that category you can show me?"

The salesman looked disappointed. He obviously hadn't wanted to go out into the biting cold just to sell a used car. Since car salesmen worked on commission, Doherty figured this guy's would be much larger if he sold a new car rather than a used one. Still, it was February – a pretty slow month in the auto trade, so the salesman didn't have much choice.

"Yeah, I can show you some nice used cars around back. A few are a year or two old but they're still cherry. They don't have much mileage on them either. They were driven by people who liked to trade in their cars every year or two. Do you have any particular model in mind?"

They were now walking toward the back of the lot leaving the new models behind. It was getting near dusk so he was afraid he might not be able to get a good a look at the cars on the shady side of the showroom building.

"Maybe a Star Fire. Have you got any of them?"

"Yeah, sure, we got a couple I can show you. You know a new Pontiac won't cost you that much more than one a year or two old," the salesman said, still hoping to get Doherty to drive off in a 1960 Bonneville.

When they reached their destination the guy lit up a cigarette and pointed to two cars sitting side by side. "Both of these are Star Fires. This here one is a '59," he said pointing out a green one with a white scoop along the side that was wide at the back fenders then narrowed down to a point when it reached the front ones. "The red and white one is a '58. I can give you a good price on either car."

Doherty slowly circled the two cars, taking just enough time to ensure that his companion would become more uncomfortable in the cold. The 1959 model had a front that differed considerably from that of the '58. He preferred the more traditional styling on the front grill of the '58 model, though it didn't matter since he wasn't interested in buying either car. What he was focused on was the taillight arrangement on the '58 Star Fire. Two bullet lights with the vertical one underneath, clearly matching the description of the taillights on the car the motel owner had seen exiting his lot the night Adrian Colardo disappeared.

While he was carefully studying the rear end of the Star Fire Doherty noticed the disgruntled salesman blowing on his cold hands. Approaching him Doherty said, "I like the style lines on the 1958 model better. It's a little more classic."

"Would you like to take it for a test drive?" the chilled salesman asked expectantly.

"Naw, it's late and I need to get back home. Why don't you give me one of your cards and I'll get in touch with you if I'm still interested." The salesman forked over a business card along with a look of disappointment mingled with one of relief. At least now he'd be able to get in out of the cold. Doherty drove back to town convinced the description the motel owner had given him of the getaway car's taillights definitely matched those on the '58 Star Fire in the dealer's lot. Could it be just a coincidence that Eddie Donahue met his untimely death in a similar vehicle? One that had been purposely kept unregistered with dummy plates on it. Now Doherty saw a greater possibility that the two cases he'd been working were connected.

Chapter Twenty-Five

In the morning, after a quick breakfast of stale toast washed down with two cups of black coffee, Doherty headed north towards the capital city for what felt like the hundredth time in the past few weeks. He had a few important stops to make on this day, all of them in different parts of Providence. He parked his Chevy in a lot downtown and walked three blocks to the Cherry & Webb department store. The first thing he wanted to check on was how Doris Donahue was taking her late husband's death.

As far as he could tell the East Providence police were still selling Eddie Donahue's murder as a suicide, using that as a smokescreen while looking for his killer. Aside from himself and Jeru Squilante, and whichever Providence cops the sergeant had already blabbed to, few others knew that the East Providence police were secretly investigating Donahue's death as a murder. So far nothing had appeared in the newspapers to indicate it was being looked at otherwise.

He killed time scouring the big department store before he made his way to the women's lingerie department. Doris Donahue was nowhere in sight, though her friend, who's name Doherty'd already forgotten from his last visit, spotted him. She sidled up to ask if he needed some help.

"I was wondering if Doris was around."

"She's in the backroom doing some labeling. Are you sure I can't help you?" the girl said, not bothering to mask her own interest.

"No, I'm fine. I need to talk to Doris about a personal matter."

A sly grin attached itself to the girl's face before she made her way to the back of the store, doing her best to shake her rather ample hips as she did. Doherty assumed the routines the two women threw his way had something to do with the lingerie department not getting many male visitors.

Doris came from the rear of the store wearing a striped blouse tucked into a gray skirt. A small scarf twisted around her neck with colors matching those of her blouse completed her outfit. Her hair was nicely done and she was wearing more make-up than he remembered her fancying the night they spent together.

"Hello there, handsome. You're about the last person I expected to see in Cherry's again." The girlfriend hung around, hoping to get some vicarious thrill listening to Doris and her male visitor flirt with each other.

"I came to offer my condolences about Eddie."

Doris seemed disappointed, though she quickly replaced that look with one of sadness – or at least her best version of it.

"The poor guy. Things never went Eddie's way after he got out of the army. I guess I have to bear some responsibility for that. Not for his suicide, but for some of the other stuff that went wrong. His sister called me yesterday; wanted to know if I'd come to his funeral once the police released his body. I told her I would, but I wasn't going to stand in the front with the family. After our divorce I stopped thinking of myself as part of Eddie's family."

"Did the East Providence cops pay you a visit?"

"Yeah, they came by the apartment two days after his body was discovered. They offered their insincere condolences. They asked if I could think of any reason Eddie'd want to kill himself."

"What did you tell them?"

"I told them I could think of about a hundred reasons if they had the time. We talked for almost an hour. They asked about the trouble Eddie was in with those chiselers down at O'Donnell's. I let them know all about his gambling debts, especially the ones I covered for him. Personally I didn't think those debts were enough for Eddie to want to kill himself. But hey, what did I know? I hadn't seen him in almost a year so maybe he fell further down into himself than I thought."

"Did you toss them Fats Finnegan and Brian Willis?"

"I might've mentioned Finnegan. I didn't know Eddie'd had any dealings with Brian." Doherty made a mental note that she didn't refer to Willis by his last name as she had with Finnegan.

"What about the outside jobs they had Eddie do for them? You know, the illegal stuff?"

Doris shook her head. "I didn't know much about those either. I only knew about the gambling debts because he used a lot of my money to pay them off. Where did you hear about that other stuff?"

"From his sister Meg."

Doris shook her head in pity. "I wouldn't believe too much of what that one tells you. She never wanted to hold Eddie responsible for anything. When we broke up she said it was all my fault. As if Eddie hadn't squandered our household money gambling at O'Donnell's. She never gave me any credit for supporting us while Eddie was 'trying to get back on his feet'. She always made excuses for his failures."

That wasn't the picture Doherty had gotten from Meg Garrett about her brother. Nonetheless, it was evident there was no love lost between the dead guy's sister and his ex-wife.

"Look, I know you're going get busy up here in a little while and there's a lot more I'd like to ask you about Eddie. Do you think we could meet for a drink after you get off work?"

"And have it end like last time," Doris said with a sly grin.

"No I wasn't..." Doherty stammered.

"Save your breath, sweetheart. I've already got a date for this evening. Maybe I can give you a rain check."

"Sure, fine. I'll be in touch."

"I look forward to it, Mr. Private Eye."

There was something unsettling about the conversation with Doris Donahue. Whatever it was Doherty couldn't put his finger on it. Although she appeared less than sympathetic about her late husband's suicide, that wasn't surprising given that he may've been headed in that direction for a while. On top of that she made it sound like Eddie hadn't been part of her life since their divorce. Doris had clearly moved on to other men, including Richie Grimaldi - and briefly himself. Still, his curiosity was piqued as to who her date was for that night.

After retrieving his car from the lot he drove south down Charles Street toward the O'Donnell VFW post. It was still early in the day so he figured the veterans' watering hole would be relatively quiet. He was sure Fats Finnegan would be in residence even if he'd made it clear from their last encounter that Doherty was no longer welcomed at the post.

He parked out front and retrieved his .38 from the glove box. He hoped he wouldn't need it, but wasn't taking any chances after their recent brawl there. Especially since this time he didn't have Grimaldi and big Tony at his back.

There was an unfamiliar tender behind the bar so Doherty flashed him his veteran's card and asked for Finnegan. Two guys sat on stools nearby guzzling what appeared to be their third beers of the day. Neither paid much attention to Doherty's conversation with the barkeep.

"Who wants to know?" the bartender asked.

Doherty looked from side to side and then behind himself. "I guess I do since I don't see anyone else here. Is he in his office?"

"Maybe."

That was about as far as Doherty was willing to go with their ridiculous conversation. Instead he decided to just walk into the back office. That elicited a weak "Hey" from the barman.

Finnegan was sitting behind his beaten-up desk reading the morning *Journal*. The stub of a well-chewed cigar protruded from the corner of his mouth. He wore a metal splint on the fingers of his injured hand. When he saw Doherty he looked less than pleased.

"What the fuck are you doin' here? I thought I told you..."

"Skip the threats, fat man. I just came by to offer my condolences about Eddie Donahue's recent death."

He saw Finnegan trying to wedge open his desk drawer with his knee.

"I wouldn't do that if I were you. I'm packing today and I can get my piece out a whole lot faster than your fat hand can get into that drawer. So how about if I sit down over here and you and me have a nice conversation about your dearly departed friend, Eddie Donahue."

"Poor bastard, couldn't never do anythin' right," Finnegan said wagging his head so that all three of his chins jiggled. He slowly nudged the desk drawer closed.

"You mean like kill himself? He couldn't even do that right?"

Finnegan gave him a suspicious look. "What're you drivin' at?"

Doherty placed an elbow on the desktop and looked the fat man in the eye.

"Like maybe Eddie didn't kill himself after all."

"I don't follow."

"The police have reason to believe Eddie's suicide was not a suicide after all. It was only set up to look like one, and from what I've heard not set up very well. So let me ask you this, Fats, who would want Donahue dead and why?"

"How the hell should I know?" Finnegan was doing his best to sound offended. Doherty wasn't buying the act.

"I'm thinking maybe Eddie screwed up on one of those off-the-books jobs you and your buddy Brian Willis had him doing. Screwed it up enough that you had to get rid of him."

"What kind of a person do you think I am? Look Eddie was a loser. And yeah he did some work on the side for me and Brian. I'll admit that. But I ain't no killer. Besides, despite all his faults I liked Eddie. I felt sorry for him, but I woulda never wanted him dead. I ain't that kinda guy."

"What about Willis?"

"What about him?

"Is he that kind of guy? Is he somebody who'd kill Eddie if he screwed up on a job?"

Finnegan wagged his chins once again. "I dunno. You'll have to ask Brian about that. He's always had a private side to him."

"Does he still come into the post a lot?"

"I haven't seen him in over a week. I can't stop you from comin' back here to look for him but I wish you wouldn't. Like I said, Brian hasn't been around here for a while."

224

"Could he have blown town?"

"I dunno. Why would he?"

"Well, if you see him tell him I'm looking for him. And for your own safety I wouldn't let on to Willis that you heard Donahue's death might not've been a suicide. If he's responsible for what happened to Donahue he might decide he has to take care of you as well."

The lunchtime crowd at Fortunato's was thicker than usual when Doherty arrived just after noon. Apparently having one of the owners splashed all over the papers and on the TV as a murder suspect was good for business. There was something about possibly seeing a murderer in the flesh that brought out the worst in people. He was sure that many of the new faces at Fortunato's were only there hoping to catch a glimpse of Richie Grimaldi.

Tony and the kid named Freddie were busy waiting on tables while ignoring all questions about Grimaldi. The queries were obviously putting big Tony on edge. Still, business was business so he wasn't about to turn away any customers regardless of the morbid nature of their inquiries. Doherty hung by the bar until Tony caught his eye. Once he did, the big guy headed in his direction ignoring all requests from customers as he did.

"Well if it isn't the private eye. How you doin' Mr. Doherty? Been in any rumbles at the VFW lately?"

Doherty had to laugh. Big Tony admitted after the brawl at O'Donnell's that he hadn't had that much fun in a long time. "As a matter of fact I've just come from there. But there were no fists exchanged this time, only some words with the fat man."

"You want somethin' to eat? It'll be on the house."

Doherty looked over Tony's shoulder and saw the kid Freddie hustling his ass off as more customers pushed their way into Fortunato's.

"I haven't got time and you look awful busy right now. I need to talk to our mutual friend."

Tony nodded knowingly. "He's still up at my fadder's place. I'll give him a call and tell him you're comin'. Use the same knock as before." Tony then pushed his way through the crowd into the back room where he could call Richie in private. In the meantime Doherty headed out to his car. By now there was a line of customers waiting to be seated. People were like lemmings when something as grisly as murder was on the menu.

As before he used the three knocks followed by the two delayed ones on the door at Anthony Fortunato's Italianate home. Apparently none of the press boys had figured out that Grimaldi was holing up at his business partner's house. No doubt they'd encircled Grimaldi's place without knowing that the murder suspect was elsewhere.

He saw a blind split in one of the windows on the second floor that looked down on the front steps. Grimaldi was carefully checking out who his visitors were. A minute after Doherty's tapped out the coded knock a second time his client opened the door just enough to quickly usher Doherty inside. Before closing it Grimaldi took a quick gander up and down the street. With the door firmly triple locked they shook hands. His client's paw was damp with sweat. Richie looked troubled, as well he should be. He quickly led Doherty into the kitchen where he poured the PI a cup of black coffee without it being requested. He poured himself half a tumbler of Four Roses, no longer bothering to mix his booze with coffee.

"You don't look so good, Richie."

"What the hell do you expect? I was arraigned on a murder charge the other day and now my mug is plastered all over the papers and on every TV channel. I'm like the most famous guy in Rhode Island right now."

"Infamous would be more like it."

"Yeah, whatever."

"What's your lawyer saying?"

"To me or to the public?"

"I don't give a shit what he's saying in public. I want to know what he's advising you."

Grimaldi took a healthy slug of the whiskey and grimaced afterwards. "He thinks we should go to trial. Tells me all the evidence they've got so far is circumstantial. Nobody can put me anywhere else with Adrian besides at the Greene Inn and the motel."

"That sounds promising. How long did he say it would be before you'd go on trial if it came to that?"

"Six months. Maybe more. He's hoping the heat'll die down by then. He thinks the prosecutors will see their way to offering me a deal at some point."

"Richie, if they offer you a deal that means you'll have to cop a guilty plea to a lesser charge. If you do that you'll be admitting to a crime you didn't commit."

"I know. I know. But Friedman says it could be my best shot. Otherwise if I go to trial and they find me guilty I could spend the rest of my life at the ACI. I can't do that, Doherty. Guys up there find out how I used all those married women, I wouldn't last a year inside." All this talk of prison was getting Grimaldi very agitated.

"What else is your lawyer whispering in your ear?"

This question made Grimaldi nervous. "He thinks I should use one of his people for the investigations. I told him I was satisfied with your work, but he didn't agree." Doherty now understood that Friedman was only blowing smoke his way when they'd talked on the phone.

He took a seat beside Grimaldi on one of the stools that sat by the kitchen counter. He placed his hand on his client's arm and said, "Look, you can decide to do whatever you want. I mean it's your life that's on the line here. But if that shyster lawyer you hired is going to bring in his own investigator that guy's going to charge you a hell of a lot more than I am. If this case doesn't go to trial for six months, his meter'll be running the whole time. Before he's finished Friedman will own your percentage of Fortunato's and just about everything else you have of value. Because that's the only way you'll be able to cover his bills. I don't suppose your cousin Anthony would be too happy about that."

Grimaldi hung his head, absorbing just how bad his current circumstances were. "So what're you saying? I should take a plea agreement now and go to jail for a crime I didn't commit."

"No, I'm not suggesting that at all. For the present you should keep Friedman as your lawyer since he's been acting in your best interest so far. However, any new investigator he brings in will have to start from scratch. I've got some other ideas I want to run by you."

"Yeah, sure, whatever you say, Doherty."

"Okay. First of all did you hear about the guy who shot himself in the eah, it was in the papers; same ones my picture's been in. What about him?"

"I got it on good information that it wasn't a suicide at all. It was just made to look like one. The car the guy died in was a 1958 Pontiac Star Chief, unregistered, apparently stolen or taken off the road some time ago. It also had stolen plates on it."

"What does that mean for me?"

"I did a little checking around and found out the taillights on a '58 Pontiac match the ones the owner of the Anchor Inn saw motoring out of his lot the night Adrian was snatched."

Grimaldi shook his head. "I still don't get how this helps me. There must be a hundred Pontiacs like that in Rhode Island."

"I'm sure there are. But you see the guy found dead in this one was Eddie Donahue, the former husband of your old friend, Doris Donahue. I'm sure you remember Doris, right Richie?"

Grimaldi's expression was one of hopefulness mixed with embarrassment.

"Anyway, it turns out one of the goons you and me and your cousin Tony had that fight with at the VFW post is named Brian Willis. He's the guy who sucker punched you. It just so happens his brother is the bartender at the Greene Inn. The same person you suspected might've dosed your drinks the night you and Adrian went to dinner there."

"I'm not sure I follow. What're you driving at?"

"Please, Richie, bear with me for a minute. Turns out this dead Donahue guy was doing some illegal work for Willis and the fat man, Finnegan, at the post. Right now the Pontiac is in police impound in East Providence where hopefully they're going over it with a fine-toothed comb. If I can put a bug in their ear it's possible they might find traces of Adrian Colardo in that car. What I'm saying is the car Adrian was abducted in may be the same car Donahue was found dead in. I'm hoping the East Providence cops'll take my suggestion seriously, especially if it means they could solve the biggest murder in Rhode Island this year. Now you can go ahead and hire Friedman's investigator if you want, but I'll bet he wouldn't be able to put these pieces

28

together in ten years, let alone six months."

"I still don't see how this gets me off the hook."

"It doesn't yet, Richie. Right now you're the most unsympathetic guy in the state. You've spent a good part of your adult life preying on unhappily married women. Not only has one of them ended up dead, but I also visited another of your former dates who was holding a baby that looked remarkably like you. Hell, Richie, *I* don't even feel sorry for you. But you're my client and I don't think you killed that girl. My hunch is that whoever did it is likewise responsible for Donahue's murder at Crescent Park - a fellow who happened to be married to another one of your conquests. There are too many coincidences here, and I'm not a big believer in coincidences. It's not a pretty picture, Richie. I think the only way to get you out of this mess is for me to prove who the someone else is that killed Adrian Colardo."

Doherty spent the next half-hour with Grimaldi trying to convince him that what he'd uncovered could very well prove him innocent of Adrian murder. In any case it still felt awkward using the word *innocent* to describe Grimaldi's behavior. All the while his client kept hitting the bottle of Four Roses until he'd drunk himself into a stupor. Given his situation and the negative the press he was getting, Doherty couldn't blame him. When Grimaldi finally passed out on Anthony Fortunato's barcalounger, Doherty quietly exited the Fruit Hill house, again checking to make sure no newshounds were lurking in the bushes.

Chapter Twenty-Six

I t was dark by the time Doherty got back to the center of the city. He didn't need to leave the car in a lot; he parked it on the street instead and slid a dime into a meter, which would cover him until they went off at six o'clock. He walked down Westminster Street and turned up a side street and positioned himself in a dark doorway where he could observe the workers exiting Cherry & Webb through the service door. He lit a cigarette and waited not far from the second-story bridge that connected Cherry's to Gladding's and the Shepard Co.

Doherty was standing uncomfortably close to where he'd staked out Stanislaw Krykowski a year ago while working the Meir Poznansky case. On that day he followed Krykowski on two separate buses all the way into the center of Pawtucket to that city's Polish-American club. Today he had no idea what he would do once he spotted Doris Donahue leaving Cherry & Webb. All he knew was that it might be of interest to find out who her *date* was for that night.

It was bitterly cold and Doherty'd been wise enough to put on gloves for the surveillance. He turned his coat collar up and pulled his fedora down tight to his ears. Finally at five thirty the girls began to pile out of the service door on the side street by Cherry & Webb. He had to look closely for Doris, as they would soon be merging with the sales help leaving Gladding's and

Shepard's. He caught sight of her wearing her heavy woolen coat trimmed with the fake fur collar. Her large hat was pulled down on one side covering that ear. She was easy to recognize since she was almost a head taller than most of the other girls.

Doris walked quickly across town and Doherty followed at a discreet distance making sure she wouldn't spot him. The flow of workers out of the retail department stores into the city center helped him blend in with the crowd. She cut down the side street by the Albee Theatre and headed toward Weybosset Street, the largest thoroughfare through the city's center.

He slowed when he saw her cross Weybosset with the pedestrian light. Once on the other side she parked herself on the sidewalk in front of the big Loew's movie house. A movie called *The Apartment* was featured on the theatre's marquee. As Doris stood there she craned her head to the left and then to the right. Apparently she had no idea from which direction whoever she was meeting would be coming from. She stomped her feet to keep them warm since she was clad only in high heels. Doherty lingered on the other side of Weybosset. There was still enough pedestrian traffic at that hour that he wouldn't be noticed unless she was specifically looking for him.

About ten minutes later a large man approached Doris wearing a hat pulled low on his head, obscuring his face from Doherty's view. He had on a long gray topcoat and his hands were jammed into the side pockets. There was something familiar about his mannerisms, but Doherty couldn't place him. He didn't dare get any closer for fear Doris would see him tailing her. Her date reached out and took her arm, though it didn't appear to be a gesture of affection. After a few words they started moving briskly down Weybosset in the direction of the city's financial district, where Doherty's old acquaintance the accountant/mobster Frank Ganetti Jr. had his CPA office across from the Arcade. Two blocks along they turned onto a side street that had fewer pedestrians on it. Doherty hung back, though not so far that he couldn't see where they were headed. From her body language it looked as if Doris was not going with her date all that willingly.

The couple stopped beside a late model black and brown DeSoto with big fins rising above three bullet-like taillights in a vertical line. Doherty had lately become an expert on taillights. After opening the far door the fellow pushed Doris into the passenger seat. Doherty quickly crossed the street to get the plate number before they pulled out. He was just in time as the car sped off leaving tire burn marks on the pavement.

There was no way for him to follow them given that his own car was five blocks across town. Besides if Doris Donahue was in some kind of trouble it was probably of her own making. For a moment he considered cruising by her place in North Providence to make sure she was okay. Then he remembered he had no clear idea where her apartment was since the only time he'd driven there was in a highly inebriated state.

The next morning Doherty made two quick phone calls as soon as he got into the office. The first was to Gus Timilty to see if his guy in city records could get a quick lift on the plate of the two-toned DeSoto. Gus wasn't in but the secretary at Briggs and Timilty put him through to Gus' Dictaphone. The recording device saved Gus the trouble of having to admit to the secretary or anyone else at Briggs that he had a key connection inside the city hall records department. Although it was Gus' connections throughout the state that helped elevate Briggs and Timilty to the big time, he still liked to keep some of his informed sources strictly to himself. He once let on to Doherty that Johnny Briggs had too loose a tongue for someone in their line of work.

The second call was to the detective bureau inside East Providence police headquarters. He left a message for Officer DeSimone to contact him relative to the Donahue suicide. He knew that police departments often got dozens of calls on murders and suicides, usually from cranks, who had their own theories, or from people confessing to crimes they knew little or nothing about. It was why they commonly withheld important pieces of evidence from the public. It was their way of eliminating the freaks and weirdoes as possible suspects. He hoped his name would be bounced directly to DeSimone, who he was sure would recognize it from their previous interaction.

The third phone call Doherty made that morning was one he'd been putting off. It was to Meg Garrett, who he assumed was in deep mourning over her brother's untimely death. It took six rings before Mrs. Garrett picked up. Doherty identified himself and then offered his condolences. She accepted them in a sad and tired voice.

"I just don't know what to do with Eddie's things. It's not like he had a lot - just some clothes and his medals from the war. Do you think you could help me, Mr. Doherty? My husband doesn't want anything to do with Eddie's stuff. He told me he was too disgusted with how Eddie hurt me."

From what she was saying it was evident that the East Providence police hadn't told her yet that they were dealing with her brother's death as a homicide, not a suicide.

"Yeah, I'd be glad to help you out. I could drive out to Cumberland later this afternoon if you're going to be around."

"I'll be here. I've nowhere else to go right now. I don't really feel like seeing anyone. I can't even plan Eddie's funeral because the police haven't released his body yet. I don't know what's taking them so long." Doherty knew but wasn't about to spill anything to Donahue's sister until he heard from DeSimone.

"One other thing, Mrs. Garrett, I'd like to return the money you gave me to find Eddie. I never did find him so I don't feel like I fulfilled my role as your investigator."

"But you tried, Mr. Doherty. Except for me, that's more than anyone has done for Eddie in a long time. If you help me dispose of his things I'll consider the fifty dollars money well spent." Doherty wasn't sure about that but rang off telling Meg Garrett he would be there sometime after lunch.

No sooner had he put the phone down than it rang while his hand was still on the receiver. He picked it up on the first ring hoping it was DeSimone. Instead it was Gus.

"Heard your message. My guy got what you were looking for."

"That was fast."

"Hey, tracing plate numbers is small potatoes for him. He can do that in ten minutes."

"Okay, shoot."

"1959 DeSoto Adventurer. Registered to a Brian Willis, 1365 Orms Street, which I believe is somewhere in the Smith Hill section of Providence. Married a Diane Brousseau on June 12, 1948, divorced September 23, 1954. Willis is an army vet from the war; earned a Purple Heart for a wound he received on Okinawa. According to tax records, he has no dependents. Do you want to know where he went to high school?"

"Jesus, Gus, how does your guy get all this info so quickly?"

"Sorry, pally, that's a trade secret. Need anything else?"

"Employment?"

"Works for a beer and soft drink distributorship: Colonial Distributors in Olneyville. I think I heard a rumor at one time that Colonial may have a silent partner that operates a vending machine company on Federal Hill. But that might've been just a rumor."

"Is there anything those guys don't have their fingers in?"

"Briggs and Timilty for one. And I doubt they have any interest in Doherty and Associates. Okay, pally, now are you gonna tell me what your interest is in this Willis fella? Does it have to do with a job you're working on other than the Grimaldi case? Who, by the way, happens to be the most well-known person in Rhode Island right now."

"Don't I know it." He hesitated, not entirely sure how much he wanted to share with Gus. "Did you read about the fellow who blew his brains out the other night in the lot by Crescent Park?"

"Yeah, I saw that in the papers. What about him?"

"I've got it from a good source that it wasn't a suicide. It was a murder made to look like a suicide."

"Hmm. Go on. How did you happen to come by this inside information?"

"I'll get to that in a minute. Just a few days before this Donahue fellow bought the ranch, his sister hired me because he'd suddenly disappeared. Left her house in a big hurry after getting a phone call and nobody I talked to had seen him until he was found dead. So after informing the sister of his death, the very next day an East Providence police detective showed up at my door to see what I knew about this Donahue fella. Apparently the sister told the cop she had hired me to find her missing brother. And guess who this cop had with him as a ride along?"

"I couldn't even begin to fathom."

"Jeru Squillante of the PPD. I'm guessing he contacted the lead detective, a guy named DeSimone, when he heard about the case and my connection to the dead brother. I assume he told this DeSimone that he and I had a long term relationship as a way of nosing his way into the action."

"And when you got Squillante alone, Mr. Blabbermouth gave you more inside dope than he should have."

"Yeah, that's pretty much how things have played out so far. Now here's the kicker: The guy whose plate I asked you to run for me, well he's the brother of the bartender down at the Greene Inn in Narragansett where Grimaldi took the dead girl the night she disappeared. Grimaldi is convinced he dosed their drinks with something before she was later abducted from their room at the motel."

"Go on. This sounds like a pretty good movie."

"Anyway, yesterday I witnessed Donahue's ex-wife being manhandled into the DeSoto owned by the aforementioned Brian Willis. The very car I asked you to have your guy run the plate on."

"And that's it?"

"Not quite. Turns out this same woman, the dead guy's ex-wife, was another one of Grimaldi's conquests. Except in her case it was more than a one-night stand. Apparently she was sweet on him, and he on her, at least for a while. But then he double-timed her. And get this, he did it with her best friend, who it turns out is married to this corpulent fellow who runs a crooked card game at the VFW post where this dead Donahue guy owed a lot of money. Although you could say my client has commitment issues with women, everything about this murder is pointing me toward these characters that hang out at this VFW post."

"Do you think the ex-wife had something to do with her husband getting killed?"

"I don't know. There are just too many connections here to pass them off as mere coincidences. In addition, I have a hunch that the car Donahue died in may be the same one that was used to abduct the girl from the motel in Narragansett. When I spoke with the owner there he described a car pulling out of his parking lot late that night which sounds like a match for the one Donahue was supposed to have committed suicide in. I'm thinking it's a car used for illegal jobs by this crew of small timers operating out of the post on Charles Street. According to Squillante the car Donahue was found dead in was a '58 Pontiac Star Chief, no longer registered, with dummy plates on it."

"What do you need from me?"

"Some advice. I've been trying to get ahold of the lead detective in the Donahue murder-suicide. I'm thinking this East Providence sergeant isn't going to get my calls forwarded to him no matter how many times I contact the main switchboard at the East Providence station. They're going to dump me into the bin with all the other kooks who call with inside info on a recent murder. I need to get in touch with this DeSimone directly. If I do, I know he'll recognize my name. But time is of the essence here since it'll only be a matter of a day or two before they finish examining the car and send it off to a junkyard. If I can contact DeSimone, he could then order his forensic team to go through the car looking for traces of Adrian Colardo."

Gus breathed heavily on the other end of the phone. "I hate to tell you this, pally, but your best bet is probably through your buddy Squillante. You'll have to give him a bone to chew on to get him to connect you directly to DeSimone. I'm sure you can come up with something that'll make Jeru think he's in on solving the crime of the century."

Doherty thanked Gus for his sage advice. He rang off figuring he'd take another run at contacting DeSimone before calling Squillante. The rest of the afternoon was probably going to be consumed by his Good Samaritan mission out to Cumberland.

Chapter Twenty-Seven

He put in another call to the East Providence police station before he headed off to Cumberland. Gus was right, Squillante was probably the only way he could get connected directly to DeSimone while the Pontiac was still in the police impound. He didn't like having to rely on the Providence sergeant knowing that he would hold such a favor over Doherty's head forever. Plus he didn't fully trust the mouthy bastard.

It was an easier drive through Cumberland to the Garrett homestead now that the town workers had plowed the snow up against the sides of the road. The Garrett's driveway was cleared and an old Nash Rambler station wagon sat up close to the house. He eased his car in behind it. Meg Garrett came to the side door of the house as he was approaching the front.

"Please come in this way, Mr. Doherty. I was just making some muffins. They were always Eddie's favorites. I don't know why I'm making them now. I guess it gives me something to do." She continued to prattle on and Doherty let her talk without interruption. He figured it was what she needed to do to cope with her grief.

Once she'd relieved him of his topcoat and hat she offered him a seat at the small breakfast nook in the kitchen. She gave him a cup of black coffee, which he accepted without saying a word. Mrs. Garrett poured herself a cup of tea and took a seat across from him. He knew he was going to be in for a long afternoon of listening to her talk about the injustices the world had visited upon her brother. But he'd come voluntarily so what else could he do.

As expected she went on at some length in this vein. He did his best to look interested and sympathetic. At least the coffee, which she refilled twice, and the fresh muffins kept him awake enough to halfheartedly listen to her chronicle of Eddie Donahue's woes. Mrs. Garrett's face was drawn and she barely touched her tea or any of the delicious muffins she set out on the table.

When he could finally get a word in edgewise he asked if he could have a look at Eddie's room and his things. It was a small room, larger than a broom closet though not much bigger than a kid's room. She was right about Eddie not having much in the way of material goods. Three shirts, two pairs of pants, one work, one slightly dressier, and a faded sport coat made a weak statement in his closet. On the floor were two pairs of shoes, both badly worn, and a decrepit pair of bedroom slippers.

By the bed a book was propped open on a night table made out of an unfinished orange crate. A small lamp sat on the makeshift table. The book, a biography of General Eisenhower written by John Gunther, was wrapped in a frayed dust cover with the president's picture on it. He remembered Gunther as the guy who wrote a lot of books called Inside Africa, Inside Asia, and inside every other place on earth.

Across from the bed was a four-drawer dresser that contained some underwear, socks, a few T-shirts, two moth-eaten sweaters and a couple of pairs of pajamas. All of the clothing was badly worn with their colors faded. Two combat medals sat in their felt cases in the top drawer alongside the graying underpants and undershirts.

Doherty turned to say something to Donahue's sister but she was crying into the apron she'd been wearing while making the muffins.

"This is it," she said. "The sum total of my brother's life. He was my only sibling, Mr. Doherty. What am I going to do now?"

He knew she was looking for him to offer up some profound comment to help ease her pain. Instead all he could say was, "You can donate his clothes to the Salvation Army. What they can't use they'll dispose of or turn into rags. You should be able to get a decent suit pretty cheaply from them to wake and bury Eddie in once you've arranged with the police to have his

238

body sent to a funeral home. I would keep the medals if I were you. They probably represent the best years of his life."

Meg Garrett burst out crying again and fled from the room leaving Doherty to pick through the detritus of Eddie Donahue's sad life. While he waited for her to return he absentmindedly flipped through the pages of the Eisenhower biography. Written in pencil on the title page was a phone number. Doherty took out his pad and quickly wrote down the number. Before Mrs. Garrett returned he slipped his pad back into his inside jacket pocket and replaced the book on the nightstand. Then, on a premonition, he lifted the mattress from the bed and peaked underneath. He didn't know what he was looking for: girlie magazines perhaps or maybe a diary, though that was unlikely. What he discovered instead was a packet of letters with a rubber band wrapped around them. When he tried to remove the elastic it broke, indicating it'd been holding the letters together for a long time.

A quick perusal of them told Doherty they were the letters Eddie had received from Doris while he was in the army. His first thought was to alert the sister of their existence. Then he remembered how negatively she felt about Doris, holding her personally responsible for Eddie's failures. He was sure if he gave her the packet she would burn the letters without ever looking at them. In light of Doherty's suspicions about Doris and the two deaths that he was currently investigating, he decided to keep the letters for the time being. He stuffed them into his jacket pocket just seconds before Meg returned holding two large shopping bags.

"Could you help me put Eddie's things into these bags?"

"Sure," he said, as he proceeded to pile Eddie's clothes on the bed. Meanwhile Meg placed his medals on top of the dresser, carefully wiping dust off their cases before admiring them for a moment.

"Eddie was such a brave soldier. Sometimes I think he should've stayed in the army. At least there he knew who he was. I heard a lot of men did that after the war and made a career of it. They would've taken care of him, wouldn't they, Mr. Doherty?"

"Yeah, maybe. But he had a girlfriend back home - and like a lot of guys, I'm sure Eddie wanted to come home to get married and start a family."

"Some girlfriend she turned out to be!" For the next five minutes Meg went on about what a horrible wife Doris was to her brother. Meanwhile Doherty used the time to stuff what was left of Eddie Donahue's pathetic life into the two shopping bags. Before leaving he asked Meg if he could take the Eisenhower book, thinking there might be some other numbers inside. He didn't know if they were important, but it wouldn't hurt to find out.

"I don't know why he was reading that book. My husband and I aren't much for reading. Neil prefers to watch TV or go bowling. Eddie liked to read; he was always taking a book from the den in here to read at night. I guess reading and knowing stuff doesn't always make you a successful person. Isn't that right, Mr. Doherty?"

"I guess it depends on what you do with what you learn."

"Amen to that."

They dragged the two stuffed shopping bags back into the kitchen where Meg Garrett offered Doherty another cup of coffee. Even though he knew she was starved for company and wanted to talk more about her brother, he checked his watch and told her he needed to get back to West Warwick before dark. He then took two twenties and a ten out of his wallet and placed them on the table in the breakfast nook.

"I'd like you to take your fifty dollars back, Mrs. Garrett."

"You don't have to…"

"I know I don't, but you're going to need some money for the funeral and for a suit Eddie can get waked in. How about if you give me some of those delicious muffins in return and we'll call it even?" That elicited the first smile from Meg Garrett since he'd arrived.

She wrapped up six of the muffins in waxed paper and placed them in a brown paper bag.

"You can take these things to the Salvation Army," he said pointing at the filled bags. "Otherwise I'm sure if you call them and explain the situation they'll send somebody out here to pick them up." This was all the helpful advice Doherty could think of under the circumstances. "Let me know when the funeral is. I'd like to come."

They shook hands. Doherty took the muffins, the letters, and the Gunther book back to town with him.

Although it was after five by the time he returned to West Warwick, instead of going home he drove to the office. He needed to think some things through and Doherty and Associates provided a better atmosphere for that. At home he would get distracted by eating, reading a magazine or worse, watching something on TV. Everything was clear and simple at the office. If Agnes had come in that day she'd be long gone by now so he'd have the place to himself.

He tossed the packet of letters on his desk and then pulled out a bottle of Jameson and poured himself a couple of fingers. Before looking at Doris' correspondence to her soldier boy he put in a call to the Providence PD. He asked for the detective division and was surprised to get Squillante on the line right away.

"Well, if it isn't my old friend Doherty. What can a I do you for on this dark and dreary day?" He could all but see the smirk on the sergeant's face.

"I need to talk to your buddy DeSimone over in East Providence. Whenever I call the station house there I never get beyond the switchboard."

"DeSimone's probably had a half dozen losers callin' confessin' to bein' responsible for Donahue's suicide, or witnessin' it. Kind of funny since it really was a murder. Though so far only a select few of us know that. You haven't blabbed to anyone, have you Doherty?"

He thought about the people he'd mentioned Donahue's murder to but chose to keep that to himself. "No, I've kept my mouth zipped up. I was out to Donahue's sister's today and she still thinks it was a suicide, so I played along with her. She told me she's a little puzzled as to why they haven't released the body yet. She wants to make plans for his wake and funeral."

"Did you get anythin' of interest out of her?"

"Just a half dozen swell tasting muffins and a tale of woe about her brother's troubled life. Anything else she told me I'd prefer to share with DeSimone."

"Doherty, you disappoint me. I thought we was friends."

He didn't know how to respond to this last remark. Instead he asked, "Shouldn't you be out fighting crime somewhere? No murders in the capital city today?"

"We got one, just came in a little while ago. Some dinge shot another dinge down in the South End. We'll get around to it in a little while. Are you callin' to get me to set up a meetin' for you with Sgt. DeSimone?"

"That's about the size of it," he replied, knowing Squillante was now going to be part of any sit-down he'd have with the East Providence detective.

"I'll see what I can do for an old pal like you."

"You can call me here at the office - or at home," he added, giving Squillante both of his numbers, all the while regretting that the Providence cop would now have his phone numbers in his Rolodex.

Once finished with this business he turned his attention to Doris Donahue's letters to her overseas boyfriend. It was the kind of snooping into personal affairs that made Doherty uncomfortable. These were intimate exchanges between a girl and her guy in the military far away from home. Some of them were probably received when Eddie was in harm's way. The early missives were pretty unemotional, consisting of such matters as her job and her efforts at finding an apartment of her own, which her parents were totally against. Most of them ended with Doris urging Eddie to keep his head down while in combat.

Like a lot of friends and family on the homefront, she had no idea how random death was in war. Keeping your head down was one of the least likely ways of staying alive. Not being in places where the enemy was shooting at you or throwing a grenade or firing a mortar were about the only ways to stay safe in a war zone.

In time the letters became more intimate. Doris Donahue, as Doherty well knew, was a lusty woman. The longer Eddie was overseas the more she wrote about how she longed to be in bed with him – and other things. He wondered if somewhere in that time she found other men to fill her needs. Of course, none of that would find its way into her letters. Some of the passages were so graphic that Doherty was embarrassed reading them. After a while he began to purposely skip over those parts.

He wondered whether getting such mail boosted Eddie's morale or made him feel more vulnerable. When Doherty was overseas the only letters

242

he got were from his mother and his sister Margaret. Most of them were filled with mundane gossip about local people and things happening in West Warwick. They did nothing more than remind him of how homesick he was being half a world away. The occasional letters he got from school chums were mostly filled with reminiscences of crazy things they did together as kids.

He'd left no sweetheart at home so he didn't experience receiving letters like the ones Eddie got from Doris. He remembered men in his outfit getting similar letters. Although they raised their morale they often distracted them from their duties as soldiers. He also recalled guys getting *Dear John* letters from girlfriends breaking up with them while they were overseas. Sometimes these caused soldiers to take unnecessary risks, as if they didn't care anymore if they lived or died. Doherty had no such letters so most of the time he was able to keep his mind focused on his missions.

Doris' letters to Eddie sent closer to the war's end betrayed a certain amount of discomfort, as if she wasn't sure what it would be like to share her life with someone she hardly knew before he went off to war. Still she kept things positive, hoping no doubt that once her fella was home they could start a real life together. Thousands, perhaps even millions, of new babies were born during the first couple years after the war. Magazine articles said it was biggest bulge in the birth rate in American history. Given the intimacy of Doris' messages to Eddie he wondered why Doris hadn't hatched out a couple of kids after her guy came home and they were married. Maybe it had something to do with Eddie not being able to find permanent employment. A practical woman like Doris would be well aware of the cost of raising kids.

He'd just about exhausted Doris Donahue's wartime correspondence to her future husband when a couple of letters, notes really, slipped out from the bottom of the pile. He checked the date on the postmarks. These were sent more recently. One was dated barely three months ago.

Dear Eddie,

I got your letter and I almost threw it away as soon as it arrived. Whatever trouble you're in with Finnegan and Willis is your problem now. I tried to bail you out of your debts but then you only added more onto them. I told you a thousand times to get away from those bastards, that they were using you for no good end. Please don't write me anymore. As far as I'm concerned you're no longer part of my life.

Doris

No *love, Doris*, not even a *sincerely* or *yours truly*. She signed off as just Doris. Doherty couldn't blame her. She'd carried her ne'er do-well husband for years and had finally decided to break ties with him completely. However, the next letter postmarked more recently caused Doherty to straighten up and take notice.

Dear Eddie,

I have no idea how you got yourself into this mess or why you dragged me into it with you. I don't know how we're going to make things right. No amount of money is going to get either of us in the clear. Why I let you talk me into this scheme I'll never know. We need to get things fixed up and fast. Right now all I can say is that I'm scared.

Doris

The letter was postmarked a week before Eddie Donahue's body was found in the lot at Crescent Park with his brains blown out; two days after Adrian Colardo was abducted but before her body was discovered. He wondered what the hell Eddie had gotten himself involved in and why Doris had gone along with it.

While Doherty was musing about this strange turn of events his phone rang. At first he thought he'd let it go to the recording machine, then quickly changed his mind. He answered "Doherty and Associates."

"I'd ask for your associates but I know you don't have none." It was Squillante. "DeSimone will meet with us at his favorite sub shop around noon tomorrow over in Riverside. It's called Pasco's. You can't miss it; it's right next to a Del's Lemonade shop. You know how to get to Riverside?"

"Yeah, I'll find it. How come he doesn't want to meet at his office?"

"I'd like to think it's because he doesn't want be seen in front of his colleagues with someone like you. My other thought is that they're still promotin' Donahue's death as a suicide so maybe he doesn't want a Providence cop and a private dick wanderin' into his station queerin' their story. DeSimone's already strayed off the reservation by bringin' us in on this case."

Before Doherty headed home he rang up the phone number Eddie Donahue had written on the page in the Gunther book. It rang ten times but no one picked up. He made a mental note to try again in the morning. Failing that he'd ask Gus to have his contact at city hall trace down the person for whom the number was registered.

Chapter Twenty-Eight

First thing the next morning Doherty again tried the mysterious phone number Eddie had written in the John Gunther book. There was still no answer. He then rang up Gus only to get his answering machine. Before heading north toward Riverside, he left a short message asking Gus to track down the phone number written in Donahue's book.

As was his habit Doherty arrived at Pasco's ten minutes early. He liked to case out places before he entered them, even though on this occasion it was only for a lunch meeting. He sat in the car and smoked a cigarette while waiting for the other participants to arrive. DeSimone was there first, driving a two-tone black and white Chrysler that was at least as old as Doherty's Chevy. Because the sun was out and it was warmer than it had been in several days, DeSimone walked from his car to the sandwich shop wearing only a suit jacket. Squillante pulled up five minutes later driving an unmarked car that may as well have had police written all over it.

When Doherty entered the sandwich shop DeSimone was already sitting at a table nursing a bottle of Coca Cola; Squillante was at the counter ordering a sub. Doherty joined him and they exchanged a quiet greeting. He was hoping the Providence cop would low-ball his wisecracks in front of a straight arrow like DeSimone. Squillante ordered an Italian sub loaded; Doherty opted for a tuna with lettuce, tomato and mayo. In time one of the countermen brought all three subs to their table on paper plates. Doherty accompanied his with a cup of coffee while Squillante added 7-Up to his meal. Before any talk took place they each plunged into their oversized sandwiches.

"Pasco's has the best subs this side of the bay," was the first thing out of DeSimone's mouth, which was already filled with a large bite from his meatball sandwich. They all ate quietly for a few minutes, a circumstance that made the motormouth Squillante noticeably uncomfortable.

"I need to talk to you about the Donahue suicide," Doherty said, trying his best not to put any emphasis on the last word.

"Go on," DeSimone said before taking another big bite of his sub.

"I'm concerned about the car he was found in. It was a '58 Pontiac Star Fire I've been told." DeSimone turned his head quickly in Squillante's direction.

"Maybe it kinda slipped out that the car was a Star Fire," the Providence cop said, not at all apologetic about passing this detail on to Doherty.

"For God's sake, Jerald, we're trying to keep a lid on this case until we get a bead on who wanted this Donahue fella dead."

"I could give you a list," Doherty put in. "But let's wait on that for the time being while we discuss the car."

"Why is the car so important to you?"

"Well you should know that my current client is Richie Grimaldi, the guy the state and local police are taking a hard look at for the murder of that girl down at Narragansett. I'm sure you've read about him in the papers. In any case I have reason to believe that the dead girl was abducted from a motel near Scarborough Beach by somebody driving a 1958 Pontiac."

Squillante snorted as if to say that's all you got. Thankfully he didn't add anything else.

"And where did you get this information?" DeSimone asked in a voice indicating he was taking what Doherty was saying seriously.

"From the guy who owns the motel where my client and the girl were shacked up the night she disappeared. He told me he was woken up late that night by a car leaving his parking lot. All he saw were the taillights. After he described them to me I did some checking around and found out they matched those on a 1958 Pontiac. Just to be sure, I stopped by a Pontiac dealership the other day to get a first hand view."

"Doherty, do you know how many Pontiacs there are in the state of Rhode Island? A '58 Star Fire isn't exactly a rare car," Squillante butted in.

"The sergeant is correct. You're gonna have to give me something more substantial."

"I will, but first I need you to make sure the car Donahue met his sad end in stays in police custody for the time being and is not towed off to some wrecking yard to be squashed into a box of metal. I doubt anybody will want to buy it at auction with blood splattered all over it."

"Are you kiddin' me. Some freak'll want it just 'cause it is the car a guy had his brains blown out in," Squillante said with a chuckle.

"All I'm asking right now, Sgt. DeSimone, is that your guys go through the car to see if they can lift any other prints besides Donahue's, and maybe, just maybe, find some evidence that it was used to kidnap a young girl."

"It will please you to know that my people are closely examining the car as we sit here eating our lunches. Whose prints exactly should we be looking for?"

"Those of a guy named Finnegan. His first name is Mike; he's a vet so his prints'll be on record somewhere. If not with the police then with the military. The others would belong to a guy named Brian Willis, also a vet and somebody, I'd hazard to guess, the Providence police are already familiar with."

DeSimone glanced at Squillante. "I'll look into it," the Providence cop said without much enthusiasm.

"Why do you think these two murders are connected?" DeSimone asked, lowering his voice so no one else in the sub shop could hear his question. They all looked around. It appeared that everyone in the place was more interested in devouring his lunch than listening to other people's conversations.

"It's a little complicated so I'll spell it out as best I can. In case you didn't pick this up from the papers, my client has a habit of bedding down with women who are wives of other men. Often ones who are unhappily married. It's what he does in his spare time when he's not running a restaurant called Fortunato's he owns with his cousin, Anthony Fortunato, on the back-side of Federal Hill. He often meets these women at the restaurant. One of the women he seduced is married to the Finnegan fella I just mentioned. Another one was married to the late Edward Donahue."

"Sheesh," was all DeSimone had to say. Meanwhile Squillante was thoroughly amused by Doherty's tale of depravity.

"In any case, these two guys are regulars at the VFW post on Charles Street, the Kevin O'Donnell #365. The Willis fellow has a brother who tends bar at a place down in Narragansett called the Greene Inn. It's a pretty classy joint where my client would take only his special girlfriends. On the night Adrian Colardo went missing she and my client had drinks and dinner there. According to him they both conked out later at the motel. He's convinced someone slipped a mickey into each of their cocktails. My best guess is that someone is likely the bartender, Roger Willis, brother of Brian."

"Maybe it was the sex that knocked them out," Squillante suggested with a sly grin on his face.

"Is that all you have?" DeSimone asked sounding skeptical.

"Not entirely. According to Donahue's sister as well as his ex-wife, this Finnegan and his sidekick Willis often had Donahue doing dirty work for them to help pay off some gambling debts he owed. Some of it involved illegal activities."

"I'm still not getting it. How does that relate to the dead girl?"

"I haven't put it all together yet, but I'm getting close. Let's suppose this Finnegan guy decided he wanted to get back at Grimaldi for the way he treated his wife. You know, by using her for sex and then sending her home to her fat husband with tears in her eyes. I'm thinking there's a chance he and Willis thought they'd throw a scare into Grimaldi by having one of his dates disappear."

"There's a big jump from playing what essentially sounds like a prank, albeit one involving kidnapping, to committing murder."

"I understand your skepticism. Let's suppose for a minute you find some traces of this girl in the same car that Donahue died in. What would that tell you?"

"It might tell us Donahue killed the girl because of what your guy did with his wife. Pure revenge, mon ami," Squillante said, self-satisfied with his explanation.

"Or he could've done it at the behest of the two guys you just mentioned he owed money to," DeSimone suggested.

"That would make sense if Donahue's suicide was really a suicide. Hypothetically speaking, let's say he loses control and unintentionally kills the girl he's abducted to get back at some guy who screwed his wife. After which he feels remorse and takes his own life. Could be that's what it was suppose to look like. And if Donahue was the real killer and is now dead, there's no way to prove that my client didn't kill the girl.

"The police could argue my guy got upset because she wouldn't do something in bed he wanted her to do, lost his temper and killed her. Then drives her body a few miles away, drags her through a hundred yards of brush in a blinding snowstorm in the middle of the night, dumps her in the ocean and returns to the motel. The next morning he goes down to the office acting like the girl has disappeared and he doesn't know what happened to her. Plausible but highly unlikely. No matter what, it still leaves the question of who killed Eddie Donahue and why."

"So what's your explanation, smart guy?" Squillante asked.

"I don't know yet. Right now I'm thinking whoever killed Donahue did so because Donahue was the weak link in their plan. He couldn't object to doing dirty work for these guys at the post on account of the money he owed them. But kidnapping somebody, and then being an accessory to a murder, maybe that was too much for him. When the other men involved saw that Donahue couldn't be trusted to keep his mouth shut, they had to take care of him."

"Maybe his pals bumped him off because he couldn't pay his gamblin' debts," Squillante suggested. "I seen that happen before."

"I know, but I don't buy it," Doherty countered. "With Donahue dead he'd never be able to pay them anything. These people aren't organized loan sharks. They don't strike me as the kind of guys who would kill somebody because he couldn't pay off his debts. Finnegan and his pal Willis seem too small time for that."

DeSimone had just about finished his sandwich and was draining the last of his cola. "I'll tell you what I'll do, Doherty. I'll make sure my people go through that Pontiac with a fine-tooth comb. I'll ask them to look for any traces of a young girl having been in the car, even in the trunk. If we find anything that remotely connects to the girl killed down in South County, I'll contact the state police as well as my colleagues on the North Kingston force. What you're suggesting may be a long shot. But if your client didn't kill that girl then somebody else did - and it's our duty to find out who."

DeSimone stood to leave. "I've got to get back to the station. Here's my card," he said handing one to Doherty. "This will get you through to my office without having to deal with the switchboard. My home number is on the back."

DeSimone left the sub shop. When Doherty tried to follow him, Squillante grabbed his arm. "What aren't you tellin' us?"

Doherty knew full well that for the time being he had to keep Doris Donahue and her letters to Eddie Donahue, especially her last urgent messages, to himself. If she was part of the kidnapping scheme he hoped it would eventually come out without his assistance.

"Nothing, Sergeant. I wouldn't keep you in the dark after all you've done for me."

Squillante gave him his best crooked-tooth grin. "Fuck you, Doherty, and the horse you rode in on."

Chapter Twenty-Nine

There was a considerable amount of foot traffic in the lingerie department at Cherry & Webb when Doherty wandered into the area. He was immediately spotted by Doris Donahue, who left a customer to greet him.

"Back to cash in that rain check?"

"What's with all the women up here today?'

Doris laughed. "Everything's on sale on account of it being George Washington's birthday."

"I didn't know Washington sold lingerie. I thought he only sold slaves."

"Whatever his business was, it's not for nothing that his mug's on the one-dollar bill. Listen I gotta get back to work. Are you here to invite me out for a drink?"

"Sure, why not. Can we meet in the Falstaff Room at the Biltmore again? That is if you don't have another hot date on the line."

Doris considered Doherty offer for a few beats. "I suppose I can meet you. I'll certainly need a drink after this day is over."

"What time can you get there by?"

Doris looked at the clock on the far wall behind the cash register.

"I get off at 5:30. I'll try to be there by six. A girl needs some time to freshen up before stepping out with a gentleman. Do you think you can entertain yourself till then?"

"Does that mean the store's not extending your hours in honor of General Washington?"

She shook her head. "No, we'll have sold enough merchandise by then for everyone to be happy. I'll meet you in the Falstaff Room at six. And don't be late." Doherty gave her his best smile before she turned to get back to her customers. He headed out of the women's lingerie department thereby removing the only man in that part of the store.

To kill the next two hours Doherty walked up to Providence's big public library that sat on a little rise across the street from the Majestic Theatre, one of the four large downtown movie houses. While working a case last fall he became familiar with the library and the various means of researching material there. After passing through the main entrance he took the large open staircase up to the circulation desk on the second floor. A short, elderly woman in a frumpy dress had replaced the young girl with the headband and glasses that helped him when he was there last year.

He asked her about searching out people through copies of the *Providence Journal* and *Evening Bulletin*. The woman directed him to a card catalog where everything in those papers was compiled in alphabetical order. The papers themselves could be retrieved from another set of shelves in the next room unless they were more than five years old. Then someone would have to bring them up from a storage room in the basement. Apparently all of the Providence papers were available in their original copies, unlike the out-of-town ones like the *Boston Globe* and the *New York Times*, which were on microfilm if they were more than five years old.

His first line of attack was to look up the Kevin O'Donnell Post #365. Most of the entries he found were about Staff Sgt. Kevin O'Donnell, a Providence resident killed at the Battle of the Argonne Woods in the First World War. It was for him that the post was named. Doherty skipped all of these along with a story about the dedication ceremony at the post. He was, however, intrigued by an entry from two years ago in which the police were called in to put down a brawl at the O'Donnell. Without much effort Doherty was able to locate the issue of the *Journal* that ran a small story about the fight that required the intervention of the Providence police. Several people were arrested and charged with "making a public disturbance," a journalistic euphemism for a party that got out of hand. Among those arrested was one Brian Willis. There was no mention of Fats Finnegan. When it came to actual fighting Doherty suspected Finnegan was too fat to be of much help.

Returning to the card catalog he worked backwards but found no other mention of the O'Donnell Post. Turning his attention now to Brian Willis, he found half dozen entries under that name, though at least four of them were in reference to other Brian Willises. One was an obituary for a man from Foster, and three others were for a Brian Willis who owned a Ford dealership in Woonsocket. Doherty decided to check those three anyway. They turned out to be exactly as advertised; pieces on a car dealer unrelated to the Brian Willis at the O'Donnell. The other two entries caught his attention because each of them referred to a Brian Willis being arrested by the Providence police.

The first story was the same one he'd found while researching the O'Donnell Post. The second had to do with an incident in which the Providence cops were called to the scene of a domestic disturbance. In this case Willis was arrested for assaulting his estranged wife who already had a restraining order against him.

According to the *Journal,* Willis had attacked his wife and a male companion outside a restaurant on the East Side of Providence. Those at the scene described how Willis had thrown the man to the ground and was kicking him mercilessly while his wife tried to intervene. When police arrived they found the man on the ground, a William Meade, in serious condition. The victim was taken by ambulance to Rhode Island Hospital. As for Mrs. Willis, she was attended to by medical personnel at the scene for minor injuries before being escorted to the hospital where Meade had been taken. The article reported Mrs. Willis had multiple abrasions around her face and neck.

The police reported that those who witnessed the attack described how Willis had viciously attacked the pair in an unprovoked manner. Doherty checked the date on the story. The events had occurred nearly five years ago. There was no follow-up story in the card catalog as to whether Willis had been charged with any crime related to the assault.

Doherty made a note to contact Gus Timilty in the morning to see what his friend at public records could dig up as to what resulted from this obvious assault and battery. It was already a quarter to six by the time he extricated himself from the sordid tales of Brian Willis' past. He hurried down Washington Street and turned the corner into the lobby of Providence's most famous hotel. The Falstaff Room was to the right off the lobby, a discreet distance from the main entrance. Despite today being some sort of holiday in honor of the first president's birthday, only a few tables were occupied in the large wood paneled lounge. Someone was fingering a piano in the corner near the bar, playing what sounded to Doherty like a soft version of Duke Ellington's "Sentimental Journey." Doris was already seated at a table nursing a martini.

Doherty handed his coat and hat to a girl cloistered in a small closet just inside the entrance and moved to join Doris.

"I started without you," she said. "It's been such a hectic day I couldn't wait to have a drink." A waiter immediately appeared at their table and Doherty ordered a Jameson neat.

Doris took a pack of Winstons from her handbag. Doherty joined her with a Camel and torched both of their cigarettes with his engraved Zippo.

"How was your date last night?" The reminder appeared to make Doris nervous.

"Oh, you know. So-so. Nothing to write home about," she stammered. "I'm hoping maybe this one will turn out a little better." He waited patiently before responding, though he noticed a slight tremor in her hand as the cigarette made its way up to her mouth.

"You know the car they found Eddie's body in? The cops now think it might be the same one the girl Grimaldi was with down at the shore was abducted in."

Doris was clearly taken aback by this comment that seemed to come out of nowhere. "What do you mean abducted? The papers said Grimaldi was being charged with murdering that girl. Would serve the bastard right. I knew all his tomcatting around would catch up to him one of these days."

"It won't if I have anything to do with it. I don't think he killed that girl. And now the cops aren't so sure either."

255

Doris drained her martini faster than she should have and signaled to the waiter for another. Her hands were now visibly shaking and her complexion had turned pale.

"What are you doing hanging around with somebody like Brian Willis?" he asked out of the blue to catch her off-guard.

Doris Donahue looked shocked, or as shocked as someone of her nature could be. "Have you been spying on me?"

"I'm a private eye, remember. It's what I do. You haven't answered my question. What were you doing with Brian Willis?"

Doris' second martini arrived just in time. She was going to need it given where their conversation was headed.

"Brian's a friend of mine," she said without much conviction.

"You didn't exactly look like friends when he shoved you into his DeSoto last night. You know he has a history of beating up women, don't you? Including his ex-wife."

"That bitch cheated on him the whole time they were married."

"Is that what he told you?"

Doris nodded her head, though all conviction was draining away along with her second martini.

"Was he the one who got you to buy into their plan to kidnap Grimaldi's latest conquest?"

"No!" she said too quickly. "I don't know what you're talking about."

"What I'm talking about is the scheme that ended up getting your poor husband Eddie killed."

"Ex-husband, let's not forget. I was told by the police that he killed himself."

"Yeah, but he didn't. It was just made to look like a suicide. However, the cops saw right through that poorly executed part of their plan. Whatever Eddie'd gotten himself into ended up costing him his life. Now why don't you tell me what you know about the scheme Willis and Fats Finnegan cooked up? Especially the part where they got your ex-husband to play a role in it?"

Doris took her time with this martini, all the while trying to determine what she would be willing to share with Doherty. She spoke slowly, trying hard to be careful with her words. "They were just suppose to do something that was gonna get Richie into trouble. Finnegan said he wanted to teach the no-good sonofabitch a lesson once and for all. It was a two-man job so they needed Eddie's help. Fats can't do any heavy lifting because he's got a bum heart." Doris paused here and Doherty waited patiently for her to continue. He sensed that she was about to tell him the whole sordid tale.

"The plan was to kidnap the girl and then have somebody acting as her husband call the police to report her missing. They assumed Grimaldi would be arrested as the most obvious suspect in her disappearance. They wanted him to spend a few nights in jail before they released the girl."

"What exactly was your role in all this?"

Doris sipped her drink. She was hoping to drag out her story as slowly as possible. Perhaps figuring Doherty would drink along with her and that would cloud his train of thought. "It wasn't clear at first. I was just supposed to call Eddie and convince him to help them out. I went along with it because I wanted to see Richie suffer for what he'd done to me. And to Fats' wife Angela, which soured our friendship."

"Were you the one who called Eddie that night when he ran out of his sister's house in an all-fired hurry?"

"Yeah, that was me. I told him Grimaldi was bothering me again. I said he came by the apartment and molested me. I needed to get Eddie on board with the others. They were devising a plan to teach Richie a lesson and wanted his help. They knew if I told Eddie my story it would be a surefire way of getting him to go along with them. After all I'd done to him the poor guy was still in love with me. He wrote me a letter almost every week after we split up telling me how much he missed me. Even though I never wrote back to him I knew Eddie would do anything for me if I asked him to."

"I bet you never figured on him ending up dead."

Doris began to tear up. She dabbed at her eyes with her cocktail napkin. Doherty handed her his handkerchief. She quickly surveyed the room to see if anyone was looking at her.

"You don't know how guilty I felt when I heard Eddie had killed himself. I assumed he did it because he was racked with guilt about what happened to that girl. I couldn't help but feel I was partly responsible."

257

"Spare me the remorse. Let's go back to what happened after he and Willis took the girl."

With dry eyes now Doris continued with her story. "Well first they had to knock her out. Willis' brother, the bartender at the Greene Inn, took care of that by slipping something into their drinks. It was supposed to be some slow acting drug that wouldn't put them out for at least an hour or so. Personally I was hoping they would pass out before Richie got to screw her. According to Brian once they both passed out taking her was easy. They snatched her from the room at the motel later that night and stuffed her in the trunk of the car before driving to Roger's house in Narragansett. He said Richie never stirred the entire time they were in the room."

"How did they get in? Wasn't the door to Room 6 locked?"

"Brian is good at that kind of thing. He said getting into the motel room was a piece of cake."

"What happened once they had the girl that sent things down Queer Street?"

Doris finished her second martini and signaled for a third. Doherty couldn't blame her; she was going to need all the liquor she could handle to complete her confession.

"They locked her in a room at Roger's. The plan was to hold her for a couple of days while the one pretending to be her husband told the cops she'd been taken against her will by some sleaze bag named Richie Grimaldi. He'd then be picked up as the likely suspect in her disappearance; maybe even be charged with kidnapping. While they had the girl at Roger's house they would wear masks whenever they went in to feed her or take her to the bathroom. That way they figured she'd never be able to identify them once they let her go."

"How was Eddie handling all this?"

"Not very well. He kept calling me saying he was afraid Brian was going to do something bad to the girl. Whining all the while about how he never thought his gambling debts would end up getting him involved in something like this."

"What was he afraid Willis was going to do?"

"Like what he did. Brian raped the girl. According to Eddie, Willis

258

couldn't keep his hands off her. I mean she was a cute little thing and only wearing a thin nightgown when they took her. Once they had her at the house Brian decided to take advantage of her. After that Eddie said things got out of hand. I guess Brian has a history of beating up women. Eddie told me that while Brian was having sex with her he smacked her around just for fun. When she wouldn't stop screaming he lost his temper and choked her. After he killed her they had to devise a new plan for getting rid of the body. To dispose of her Brian got my fool of a husband to help him carry the girl down to the rocks and dump her into the ocean. They thought she would wash out to sea, leaving Grimaldi on the hook for her disappearance."

"I don't understand. What happened that buggered up their plans?"

Doris' tone changed suddenly. "You did, Doherty. You had to take on Richie Grimaldi as a client; you couldn't just leave things alone, could you? First the girl's dead body washed up. That was something they never figured would happen. Then you went and visited with Eddie. Afterwards he was spooked. He called me to say he was thinking about going to the police in hopes of saving his own hide. The way he looked at it they might go easy on him since he didn't actually kill the girl, only helped in disposing of her body. He thought he could help himself if he gave the cops Willis and Finnegan. He was worried that after the girl was discovered those two would see him as a problem. But I knew if he went to the police he would take everyone down with him including me. I told him to keep his trap shut until he saw how things played out. That's why I thought the poor fool shot himself. Now I realize from what you've told me, Fats and Brian must've killed Eddie and tried to make it look like a suicide."

"Are you willing to tell this story to the police? If you go in of your own accord I'm sure some kind of deal can be worked out. You'll have to give them the Willis brothers and Finnegan in return. And you'll have to tell them about your ex-husband's role in the girl's murder. "

"I don't know, Doherty, I'm scared. It sounds like Brian Willis is a homicidal maniac who hates women. Are you going to protect me from him?"

"The least I can do is try."

259

Doris was much too drunk to drive to her apartment in North Providence so Doherty agreed to take her home. She stayed conscious long enough to give him directions, but was half-asleep by the time they reached her building. It was all he could do to escort her up the three flights of stairs to her digs. Looking around he realized he barely remembered the place from the first time he'd been there. He turned on a table lamp inside the living room and eased Doris down onto her couch. Hoping to feed her a cup of coffee he went into the kitchen looking to get some going in a percolator.

When he returned she was out cold, snoring loudly. He took off her coat and shoes, put her legs up and added a pillow under her head. Now the coffee would only be for him. While drinking a cup he sat in an armchair across from her in the small living room while watching her sleep. His concern was what her frame of mind would be when she sobered up. Would she be willing to tell her story to the police or would she stonewall them as Willis and Finnegan had suggested? At this point Doris was the only one besides those two and Willis' bartender brother who knew the nasty details of Adrian Colardo's abduction and subsequent murder. Even though she hadn't known until he told her that Eddie's death wasn't a suicide, he hoped the murder of her ex-husband would touch her conscience enough that she'd spill what she knew to the cops.

When it looked as if Doris was out for the night, Doherty took a blanket off the bed in her other room and covered her drunken body. Then, rather than return to West Warwick he decided to sack out on her bed. He thought it would be a good idea to keep Doris company until morning when she would have her wits about her. Maybe then he'd be able to talk some sense into her.

He was out cold when he was awakened a loud knock on the apartment door. Apparently Doris was still sound asleep in the other room. Before Doherty could arouse himself he heard the door fly open. Brian Willis burst into the living room in an angry fury. Doris awoke at the sudden noise. Doherty hung back behind the bedroom door waiting to hear what Willis had to say. Meanwhile he instinctively reached into his jacket pocket before remembering he'd left his .38 locked in the glove box of his car.

Willis apparently had seen them leaving the Biltmore together and demanded to know what she was doing with "that two-bit private eye."

Not to be intimidated she told him that Doherty had informed her that Eddie hadn't committed suicide after all; he'd been murdered. Hearing this Doherty edged a little closer to the doorway, preparing to spring into the other room if things took a bad turn between her and Willis.

"I wouldn't believe anything that crumb is feeding you. He's trying to use you to keep that scumbag Grimaldi out of trouble with the law."

Doris raised her voice. "I know you bastards killed Eddie. He called me when you were down in Narragansett and told me what you'd done to that poor girl. You were only supposed to throw a scare into Grimaldi. No one was supposed to get hurt!"

Willis laughed as if two murders were somehow a cause for humor. "Your ex-husband was acting like a little scaredy cat. I knew he'd squeal on us to save his own neck first chance he got. I told Fats not to send him down there with me; that me and my brother would take care of the girl. But Fats wanted Eddie to help me as a way of working off his debts. Fats got a big kick out of humiliating your ex. I told him I could handle things without Eddie."

"Handle things, huh? Yeah, you handled things just fine. You beat up, raped and killed some innocent girl!"

"Why don't you shut your face, you sleazy gash, before I shut it for you!" Willis shouted. He then slapped Doris hard enough that she let out a high-pitched shriek. "I oughta…"

"Oughta do what?" Doherty said as he stepped out of the bedroom. "Kill her like you did Adrian Colardo and Eddie Donahue?"

For a moment Brian Willis was caught off-guard, having no inkling that anyone else was in the apartment. Willis pointed at Doherty and shouted, "What the hell is he doing here? Were you screwing him before I showed up?"

"No, I was just keeping an eye on Doris in case some creep like you came by to threaten her."

Willis pulled a leather-handled sap out of his back pocket and strode across the room in Doherty's direction. The first swing caught Doherty in the upper part of his left arm; he felt the shock of it from his wrist to his shoulder. The second swing hit him in the neck and he would've fallen to the floor if he hadn't hit the armchair on his way down. This gave Doris the opportunity to snatch up the table lamp and smash it against the back of Willis' head. When he turned on her a smile creased his face. Apparently Willis liked hitting women because the smile remained there as he switched the sap to his left hand before punching her in the face with his right. Blood immediately began pouring out of her nose and down onto her ruffled front blouse.

By turning his attention to Doris, Willis gave Doherty a chance to recover. Although his left arm still felt useless he powered into Willis with a block from behind that caught the killer in his kidney area. Willis let out a loud "oof" sound as he landed on the sofa where Doris'd been sleeping just minutes before. Doherty grabbed the blanket and quickly twisted part of it around his injured left arm. Using it to block Willis' next swing with the sap, he hit him with a strong right to the jaw and then another to the mid-section. Although Willis was a big man, outweighing Doherty by a good twenty pounds, it was his experience that big men were often soft in the middle where they carried much of their weight.

Willis doubled over from the gut punch but recovered more quickly than Doherty expected. He came at him with the sap once more. This time Doherty hit him hard enough on the side of his head to spin the big man around. Before Willis could respond, Doris emerged from the kitchen brandishing a large carving knife. Willis didn't see the knife, as he was too busy rubbing his rapidly swelling jaw. She strode toward him and plunged the blade straight into his chest. The big man stood up to his full height looking at the woman then over his shoulder at Doherty. He seemed stunned by this turn of events. Slowly he turned in Doherty's direction, blood now forming in a circle around where the knife was protruding from his chest. He dropped the sap and looked down at the knife as if wondering how it had gotten where it was. He grasped the handle before slowly sinking to his knees and then awkwardly onto his back.

Doherty immediately knelt down and began searching for a pulse at the bleeding man's neck. It was there but faint. He pressed his ear close to Willis' mouth to listen for any breathing. It too was thin. Doris stood looking at the body lying on her living room floor without saying a word.

"Call the police, tell them we need an ambulance!" Doherty shouted at her. Doris remained where she was. When she didn't move he quickly stood and asked where her phone was. She muttered that it was on the wall in the kitchen. He called the police emergency number. When the dispatcher requested the address he told him to hold on and asked Doris for the number of her apartment building.

"Is he still alive?" she asked in a stony voice.

"Doris, what the hell is the address here?" She didn't respond for a full ten seconds. Meanwhile he could hear the dispatcher squawking on the other end of the line. When she eventually gave up the address, he passed it onto the station. The voice on the other end asked for Doherty's name. He gave it to him before hanging up.

Knowing this was going to be a long night Doherty immediately put in a call to Sgt. DeSimone at his home number. After several rings there was a murmured response, indicating the EP cop had been sleeping. Doherty gave him an abridged version of what had transpired at Doris Donahue's apartment along with her address. He suggested that DeSimone might want to get Squillante to come along with him.

Once the phone calls had been made, Doherty turned his attention back to Doris Donahue. She was still staring at Willis' body as her victim bled out all over her carpet. From his wartime experiences Doherty knew there was nothing they could do to save Brian Willis. He would be dead within minutes. From the position the knife had entered his chest he could see that it was a mortal wound.

"We've got to get our stories straight before the cops get here," he said to Doris. She was now holding her head, trying as best she could to understand what had transpired in the last quarter hour.

"God, I think I'm still drunk from those martinis."

Doherty grabbed her by the shoulders and shook her. "Well you better sober up - and I mean fast. What're are we going to tell the police when they get here?"

"I dunno. You tell me."

"Okay, here's what we're going to say: We came back here after drinking in the lounge at the Biltmore. You had too much to drink so I drove you home in my car. When we got here you fell asleep on the couch and I went into your bedroom to sack out. You got that so far?" Doris nodded her head, but he wasn't sure she was following things. For his part Doherty was trying to compose their story on the fly.

"You'd been drinking and were asleep when Willis came knocking on your door. You didn't let him in. He came in either because we left the door unlocked or he picked it. Maybe they'll find some lock picking tools on him. As far as you knew I'd gone home. You didn't know I was still here, sleeping in your bedroom. Got that?" She nodded again, still trying to clear her gin-soaked head.

"You got into an argument with Willis. You told him you knew that your ex-husband hadn't killed himself, he'd been murdered. You can tell the police you got that info from me. Hearing this, Willis understood you could cause him a lot of trouble. So he came at you with his sap. Now here comes the hard part: I'm going to have to hit you with his club so you'll have something to show the cops besides your bloody nose to indicate you feared for your life."

"Why do you have to do that?" she asked, not sure she was up for any more physical punishment.

"Because you just stabbed a man to death. You've got to make the police believe you feared for your life so you stabbed Brian Willis in self-defense. If you tell them about his role in the deaths of Adrian Colardo and your ex-husband, they'll understand why you were afraid you'd be his next victim. It's vital that you convince them that Willis was out to hurt you badly or kill you. That's why you stuck him with your kitchen knife."

Doherty took out his handkerchief and carefully picked up the small club lying by Willis' dead body.

"I'm going to hit you in your upper left arm, where your flesh is thickest. I'll try not to hurt you too much, but I need to hit you hard enough to raise a good welt."

As Doris was contemplating this turn of events, Doherty quickly smashed the sap against her left bicep.

"Mary, mother of God! Did you have to hit me that hard?"

"Yes I did," he answered as Doris rubbed the pain in her upper arm.

"Now for the rest of the story: once I heard the commotion in here I came out of the bedroom. By then you'd already stuck the knife into Willis' chest. As long as they don't examine me too closely for injuries, I think I can convince them I didn't come onto the scene until you'd already stabbed Willis in self-defense. Can you follow that?"

Doris waggled her head. "I guess so. Why can't I just say I came to your rescue like I did?"

"Because then it won't look like you had to stab him. Don't get me wrong I appreciate your trying to prevent him from hurting me any worse than he already had. But that won't be enough to stand up in court. At best they'll have to charge you with something even if you eventually get off. By following my plan the cops will see this as an obvious case of self-defense. You being a woman and the potential victim will make it easier for them to close this out. Especially since Willis has a record of beating up women."

They could hear sirens in the distance. "Now, let's go over it one more time to make sure we're on the same page."

Chapter Thirty

O ver the next half hour Doris Donahue's tiny apartment filled up with
more cops than the place could hold. In addition to three uniforms
who initially showed up, two plainclothes North Providence police
officers arrived on the scene shortly thereafter along with two ambulance
attendants. It didn't take long for them to establish that Brian Willis was
dead. Two of the uniform cops had taken preliminary statements from Doris
and Doherty while a third kept an eye on Willis' body.

Once the plainclothes guys got there they told two of the uniform cops
to go down to the street to keep the crowd at bay. They ordered the third to
stand in front of the door outside of the apartment building to insure that no
one entered the premises unless they were tenants. During this lull in the action Doherty took a peek through the blinds at the scene outside. Even
though it was long after midnight the two cop cars with their gumball lights
spinning on top had attracted a sizeable crowd.

Before the detectives had an opportunity to question Doherty and Doris
at length, DeSimone arrived with Squillante in tow. One of the North Providence detectives huddled with his out-of-town cohorts in the hallway while
the other one kept a close eye on the two witnesses. Doherty couldn't hear
what they were discussing; he assumed it had to do with jurisdictional issues
and how Willis' death related to two other murders. When they returned one

of the NP cops asked Doris to accompany him and Squillante into the bedroom for a little chat. The other plainclothes officer sat with Doherty and DeSimone in the living room. In due course a gurney was wheeled in and the ambulance guys covered Willis' body with the knife in his chest sticking up under the sheet. With some effort they placed the heavy body on the gurney and lugged it down the three flights of stairs.

Doherty repeated the story he had concocted for the two uniformed cops, all the while stealing glances at DeSimone to see if it was holding water with him. He could tell from the outset that the EP detective was the smarter of his two questioners. After twenty minutes of this routine the other plainclothes NP cop came out of the bedroom and asked to speak in private with his colleague who'd been questioning Doherty. They exited the apartment and Doherty could hear them descending the stairs.

When he was alone with DeSimone, the East Providence lieutenant leaned in and said in a soft voice, "I thought you'd like to know that we took some hair and clothing fibers from the trunk of the impounded Pontiac. It looks like they match those of Adrian Colardo. We brought her parents in and they recognized a piece of cloth that got caught on the jack handle in the trunk as matching a nightgown belonging to their daughter. For the time being we're still working on the prints. If the Donahue woman backs up your story, it looks like the guy she stabbed may be directly implicated in the Colardo girl's death."

"What about the brother, the one who works as a bartender at the Greene Inn down in Narragansett?"

"He lawyered up right from the jump, but the state police have been all over him ever since we alerted them. With his brother and Eddie Donahue both dead that more or less leaves him holding the bag. They feel it won't be long before he agrees to a deal that will corroborate most of what you've told us."

"And Fats Finnegan?"

For the first time DeSimone smiled. "They've decided to let your buddy Sgt. Squillante have a go at Michael Finnegan. I'm not sure what they'll be able to charge him with; at worst it could be conspiracy to commit a kidnapping. That would still set him up for some serious jail time, which won't be very pleasant for someone as corpulent as he is."

The North Providence cops returned and now everything took on an awkward pitch. For the next five minutes they stood in the doorway of the kitchen smoking cigarettes and casting knowing glances in Doherty direction. Even DeSimone seemed uncomfortable with the tone of their conversation. When they came back into the living room the one named Duncan resumed his position on the couch next to DeSimone.

"Seems like we've got a bit of a discrepancy in your stories, Mr. Doherty."

Doherty bit his lip, automatically assuming Doris Donahue had folded under the police interrogation.

"How so?"

Duncan was somewhere in his thirties, pudgy cheeked with a pink faced complexion. He leaned forward with his elbows resting on his knees. He gave Doherty his best policeman's hard stare. Must be something he picked it up from watching Jack Webb on *Dragnet*.

"The woman in the other room says she didn't know anything about the girl's abduction and murder until he ex-husband called her crying about it over the phone."

"I don't follow."

"A while ago you told us she was the one who made the call that convinced this Donahue fella to go along with the plan to kidnap the Colardo girl. You said their purpose was to throw a scare into your client, Richard Grimaldi."

"That's what she told me."

"Well it's not what she's saying now. She said she didn't know anything about any such plan and only found out about it after her ex-husband told her how things went sideways down in South County. Thanks to the Willis guy they just wheeled out of here."

Ah, so Doris was not going to be so honest after all. Once sobered up she realized with both Willis and Eddie dead there was no one who could tie her to the kidnapping plot. Finnegan maybe, though only if he knew Willis used Doris to rope Eddie into their scheme. With Willis now dead, Finnegan could deny ever having asked Doris to contact Eddie. If she told the same story as the fat man then it would be Doherty's word against hers. And as Willis' latest victim, she'd be the more sympathetic witness. They would assume Doherty's interest in this whole business was only in getting his client, Grimaldi, off the hook. From what DeSimone told him about the traces of the dead girl found in the Pontiac, he'd most likely succeeded in that respect. What he hadn't bargained on was Doris Donahue's sense of personal survival. If the police swallowed her story, the odds were she'd get off scot-free. The killing of Brian Willis would be seen as an open-and-shut case of self-defense, mostly because of how Doherty coached her with her explanation. Doris would bear no responsibility for her ex-husband's death.

Since it was already quite late it was agreed by all parties that Doherty and Doris Donahue would come into the North Providence police station in the morning to fill out written statements as to what had transpired in her apartment that night. The NP detectives requested that they come separately and make their statements as such. The fact that they weren't being taken to the station house and interrogated through the night was a good sign. It meant that for the time being the cops were buying Doris' self-defense claim. Apparently they saw Doherty as nothing more than a less than innocent bystander, and a non-participant in Willis' death.

He would have stayed around to see what Doris was up to, but a couple of the cops remained with her so there was no chance he'd get to talk with her privately. Perhaps it was just as well. A woman who'd kill a man like Willis with no sense of remorse was not someone he wanted to be alone with right now.

All the way back to West Warwick Doherty was trying to dope out how the night's events would play in the news. He knew they'd emphasize the salacious aspects of the killing. Doherty figured they would characterize him as Doris' current bedmate caught in a love nest with a woman who killed a jealous former lover after he'd broken into her apartment in a fit of rage. No doubt they would question why Doherty hadn't come to the beleaguered woman's rescue.

It would take another day or two before Willis' role in the abduction and killing of Adrian Colardo's would be added to the story. Soon after, he hoped, the East Providence cops would let it be known that Eddie Donahue's suicide was no longer being considered a suicide but rather a related murder. Three associated murders in a state where most killings were either mob hits or crimes of passion would fill the papers and newscasts in Rhode Island for a month.

Two years ago Doherty was tagged as the guy who'd killed an ex-Nazi in self-defense. That death had made him something of a folk hero in many parts of the state. It was also a boon to his formerly subsistence investigations operation. Now he'd be seen as the guy who failed to protect the woman he was sleeping with - a woman who ultimately was brave enough to defend herself against a deadly killer.

Maybe it was better if Doris escaped complicity in the Colardo murder. At least then she wouldn't be tied to the kidnappers; instead she'd be seen as someone who had mercifully killed a ruthless murderer. There were so many factors that Doherty had to consider once this tale played out in public, not the least of which was how Nina Vitale would take to the notion that her boyfriend was in another woman's bedroom when that woman was attacked by a hardened killer. Nina's folks weren't too hot on their relationship to begin with. When the events of that night went public, his role in it could be the proverbial straw that broke the camel's back of their relationship. He hoped he'd have a chance to explain things to her. If she decided to bail because of the kind of work he did and the people he consorted with, then so be it. He just didn't want Nina to think he was sleeping with some other woman when he'd promised fidelity to her.

Finally he had to consider his role in getting Richie Grimaldi out from under for Adrian's murder. In the beginning a part of him had wished Grimaldi *was* responsible for the girl's death. That would have given his client some well-deserved payback for all the women he'd used and then cast aside. But he'd agreed to work on Grimaldi's behalf. His job was to see that the truth came out no matter where the chips might fall. He'd worked the case the only way he knew how, by sniffing out who the real killers were. It was just that everything which had occurred over the past few weeks left a sour taste in his mouth.

Grimaldi was still a low-rent gigolo; Doris Donahue a conniver who had manipulated her poor fool of an ex-husband into participating in a hare-brained scheme that went south because an angry woman hater like Brian Willis couldn't keep his hands off an innocent girl. What offended him most of all was that the plot was hatched at a VFW post where war veterans were supposed to be able to commiserate with their former brothers in arms. The only innocent in this whole business was Adrian Colardo, and even she was foolish enough to think a guy like Grimaldi cared about her and her unhappiness with her loveless marriage. In the end all Doherty could say was that the whole think stunk.

Chapter Thirty-One

Agnes was already behind her desk by the time Doherty staggered up the stairs just shy of the noon hour. He'd spent a long and restless night trying to put together all the pieces that connected the three deaths to each other. His secretary gave him an uncomfortable look as soon as he came through the door at Doherty and Associates.

"We've had a dozen calls so far. Several were from newspapers, radio stations and television. They all wanted a comment from you about last night's stabbin'. The rest were crank calls sayin' demeanin' things about you. I won't bother to repeat those. A couple were filled with curse words. And finally there was a call from Gus. He left you the name of the person whose phone number you were askin' about."

Doherty sat down in the chair across from Agnes. He made a motion toward the coffee machine that sat on a shelf behind her desk. She poured him a cup and waited patiently for an explanation of what had happened at Doris Donahue's apartment. It took nearly forty-five minutes for him to detail the events of the previous day. Along the way he did his best to explain to her how the murders of Adrian Colardo, Eddie Donahue and Brian Willis were all connected. Agnes shook her head in disbelief at various points along the way.

"And this Donahue woman refuses to fess up about her role in gettin' her ex-husband killed?"

"So far, yeah. We each have to go into the North Providence police station sometime today to give them a written statement about what we witnessed last night. I have no idea what she's going to say. I'll bet even money she doesn't admit to anything that'll put herself inside the kidnapping plot."

"Then how will she explain why this Willis fellow wanted to hurt her?"

"Well, for one she can say that her ex-husband spilled the beans to her about what happened with the Colardo girl at the brother's house in Narragansett. She'll try to convince the police that Willis came for her because he couldn't trust her to keep her mouth shut, especially after she learned that her ex-husband's death was a murder and not the result of suicide. That plus the fact Willis has a history of beating up women will make her look like the bravest and most sympathetic person in the state."

"You look troubled. What else is bothering you?"

Doherty took his time considering what he needed to get off his chest. He lit a Camel and took a healthy swig of coffee, wishing it had a shot of booze in it.

"I have a hunch Doris Donahue was sleeping with Willis. That leads me to believe she was involved in this thing deeper than she's admitting even to herself."

"What do you mean by deeper?"

"I hate saying this, but I have a nagging suspicion she knew right from the start that Willis was liable to hurt that girl in some way - rape her and maybe even kill her. I'm thinking she wanted to do more than just throw a scare into Grimaldi; she wanted to frame him for whatever bad things happened to Adrian Colardo. She harbored a deep anger in her toward our client that needed to be satisfied."

"That's a mighty big accusation, boss."

"I know. And the worst part is I have no way of proving it. She's certainly not going to admit anything along those lines to the North Providence police. With Donahue and Willis both dead there's nobody to prevent Doris from skating on the crimes connected to the girl's abduction let alone her murder. I guess I didn't take her to be as devious a person as she apparently is."

"Where does that leave you?"

Doherty had to laugh at his own predicament. "It leaves me as the guy in the bedroom who didn't come out to protect a poor damsel in distress. The worst part is she may've played me the whole time after she found out I was working for Grimaldi."

"Some damsel. You helped her by makin' the stabbin' of Willis look more like self-defense than it really was. And this is how she thanks you?"

"Right now any further description I give the police about Doris' involvement in this business will be nothing more than my word against hers. Finnegan is the only one who can add any coals to that fire. And I'm not banking on him to toss her over the side. He'll be too concerned with saving his own fat ass to connect himself to Doris in any way. I don't think the cops will be inclined to believe either Finnegan or me over Doris given her role in bringing down Willis."

"So what are you going to say when you go up to North Providence?"

"I'll tell them what I know. I'm sure they'll see me as a guy who's trying to bend his story to protect himself and his client. I can't delve into any suspicions I harbor about what was going on between Doris and Brian Willis because I have no proof. It's merely a gut feeling. They'll only be able to get that out of her if they put her on the grill. Based on the way they were treating her last night I don't see that happening."

"When are you headin' up that way?"

"As soon as I finish a second cup of your coffee."

"What should I tell anyone else who calls?"

"Don't answer the phone. Just let it go to the machine unless it's someone we know."

"Do you want the message from Gus?"

"Don't tell me; the number Donahue wrote in the book belonged to his ex-wife."

"Bingo."

A light snow was falling as Doherty made his way to North Providence. Apart from a vague idea of how to get to Doris' apartment he was pretty much unfamiliar with that town. Once in Providence he took Smith Street to

Fruit Hill Avenue and headed north. He passed by the turnoff for the street where Grimaldi's cousin had his palatial home. He wondered if his client was still hiding out or was back at the restaurant now that he was exonerated for the Colardo murder.

Once over the line into North Providence Fruit Hill Ave turned into Ridge Street. A sign in the center of town directed him to the police station. It was a low slung, one story brick building set back from the street by grassy lot partially covered with snow. He parked out front and trudged through the accumulating slush to the station house. At the front desk he identified himself and asked for Sgt. Duncan. A call was made and in due time Doherty was escorted back to a series of cubicles.

Duncan was not in but his cohort, who along with Squillante had questioned Doris last night, was. He introduced himself as Sgt. Copobianco and ushered Doherty into a small conference room. The sergeant was tall with a thatch of curly hair and a dark complexion common among Italians of Sicilian extraction. Doherty didn't see any signs of Doris Donahue and thought it best not to ask about her. Copobianco filled out some info on a police interrogation form, asked Doherty a few perfunctory questions and then slid the form in his direction.

"Before you put anything in writing, I'd like you to repeat to me what you told Officer Duncan and that East Providence detective last night."

Doherty complied with the request, omitting Doris' role in the kidnapping scheme while emphasizing her fear that Brian Willis had showed up at her apartment to cause her harm. He didn't want to muddy the waters with any accusations he wouldn't be able to substantiate.

"Why didn't you do more to help Mrs. Donahue protect herself from her assailant?"

"I did," Doherty said, taking off his jacket and rolling up his sleeve to show the Copobianco the large welt on his left bicep. "The bastard hit me with his sap, once here and once on my neck," he added, pulling his shirt collar aside to reveal the purple mark near his collarbone. "After he knocked me down he turned on Mrs. Donahue."

"Why didn't you say that last night?"

Doherty shrugged. "Nobody asked me. All they wanted to know was where I was when Willis barged into the apartment. I told them I was in the bedroom fast asleep, which was the truth. I only woke up when I heard the commotion in the other room between him and Mrs. Donahue."

"Why did she let this Willis fellow in if she feared for her safety? We saw no signs of a forced entry."

"You'll have to ask her that. According to her Willis had a knack for picking locks. Maybe that's how he got in - unless in our inebriated states we accidentally left the door unlocked. We were both pretty drunk when we got to her place."

He could've mentioned that this was also how Willis had gotten into Room Six at the Anchor Inn and abducted Adrian Colardo, but wasn't about to make Copobianco's job any more complicated than it already was. Doherty didn't have much confidence that this small town detective would be able to grasp the nuances of this case and its connection to the other two murders.

"All I know is that after I came out of the bedroom this Willis goon attacked me with his little club. He accused me of sleeping with Mrs. Donahue. Then he turned on her and started smacking her around. It was when he came back to deal with me that she shoved the knife into him."

Copobianco looked a little skeptical with this explanation. He nervously fiddled with the blank forms on the table between them. After nearly a minute of staring at Doherty and consulting his notes from the night before, he said,

"Something doesn't seem right here. Based on what you're saying this guy hit you twice with his sap, turned on the girl and smacked her around and then turned back to deal with you when you came at him a second time. So how does this Donahue girl come up from behind him and thrust a knife into his chest? Seems to me it's more likely she would've stabbed him in the back."

Doherty shook his head. "I don't know, it all happened so fast. Maybe it was when she smashed the lamp over his head. He must've turned back in her direction and that's when she stabbed him."

"So you're saying she smashed him with a lamp and also had a knife in her hand ready to stab him? Sounds like a lot of things for her to be manipulating with just two hands. What were you doing when she stabbed him?"

"Me? Nothing. I was just standing there."

Copobianco leaned in closer to Doherty. "When we examined Willis' body we found some serious bruising on the dead man's face. The kind of bruises usually caused by hard punches. They weren't bruises this Donahue woman could've administered by hitting him with a porcelain lamp. Did you at any time sock Willis in the jaw?"

"Maybe I did. I can't remember. I guess in the heat of the action I must've hit him while trying to protect myself. I was pretty sore at what he'd done to me with his sap."

"Could be you hit him hard enough to spin him around so the girl could push a knife into his chest." This last remark came out sounding more like a suggestion than a question.

"Yeah, it could've happened that way. I don't really remember. All I know is that Doris Donahue feared for her life, and probably for mine too. Willis was a violent man so there wasn't much room for discussion."

"We were just wondering if there was some other reason Mrs. Donahue wanted this Willis fellow dead?"

"Once again you'll have to ask her about that."

Copobianco turned the statement form in Doherty's direction. "Write out what you just told me. I wouldn't worry too much if it doesn't match up with what you told the uniforms or Sgt. Duncan last night. Nobody's gonna miss Brian Willis, especially if he's also responsible for the death of that girl down in Narragansett. You two might've done the world a big favor."

"Gee thanks, Sergeant. Do you think you could tell that to the press? They're not painting a very pretty picture of me and my actions last night."

"Sorry, bud. That's not our problem."

Chapter Thirty-Two

Doherty laid low for a few days waiting for the newsboys to turn their attention to Brian Willis' role in the rape and murder of Adrian Colardo. The nasty details of that crime quickly pushed him off the front pages and stories in the newscasts. On the other hand, Doris Donahue remained a person of great interest to the public, though gradually as a less sympathetic one. Her role in these events became murkier when it was revealed that her ex-husband, Eddie, had been involved in the kidnapping plot before being murdered by Brian Willis. Doherty would've felt sorry for the negative press Doris was now getting if she hadn't brought it on herself.

A week after the stabbing, Doherty pulled his Chevy out of Belanger's garage and headed north toward Providence. It was time to tie up a few loose ends. The snow that had been falling a few days earlier hadn't amounted to much. Most of it had melted or hardened into ice packs. His first stop was downtown to see if Doris had reappeared in the women's lingerie department at Cherry & Webb. As with his earlier visits he was still the only man roaming around among the nightgowns and women's undergarments. There was no sign of Doris, but her work friend, Ellen, caught his eye before he was able to duck out.

"Hi there, big fella," she said with a smile on her face. "Can I help you find something for that special woman in your life?" She was a nice looking girl if somewhat on the plump side. She wore her blond hair in a flip at the neck and had on pink lipstick, a color that seemed out of place on her pretty face.

"I was hoping to have a word with Doris Donahue. I don't see her around."

Ellen gave him a sly smile. "The store had to let her go because of all the publicity around that murder at her apartment."

This news didn't seem to bother Ellen very much. With Doris gone she could now be the girl who flirted with the odd man who ventured into the women's lingerie department.

"I'm sorry to hear that. Have you spoken to her since she left?"

"Not really. We weren't exactly friends. Just work mates you might say."

"So you don't know if she's working somewhere else?"

Ellen shrugged indifferently. "I don't know who would hire her. I mean she stabbed some jealous guy to death in her apartment," she said as if she were personally offended by Doris' actions. Apparently Ellen didn't know Doherty was the other man who'd been on the scene.

"If it's any consolation the man she killed had already murdered two other people. You might say he deserved to die, although it would've been better if the police were able to arrest him first."

"Yeah, whatever. Are you sure I can't help you with something?" the girl asked, edging her ample body a little closer to him.

"No, I just came by to see how Doris was doing."

His next stop was Fortunato's Italian Cuisine. Big Tony greeted him when he came through the door.

"If you're lookin' for Richie, he's back in the kitchen. He don't wanna be out front till all those news guys stop lookin' for him."

"How has all the publicity been for business?"

Tony smiled and shook his big head. "Was great for a while when everybody thought Richie was a killer. Me and Freddie couldn't move customers in and out fast enough. One day we almost ran outta tomato sauce. My fadder couldn't been happier. Then after Richie got cleared people stopped comin' in to get a look at the murderer. It's better this way. Now we're back to our reg'lar customers."

"You'll have to excuse me, Tony. I need to step into the back to have a few words with my client."

Richie was stocking shelves and moving things around in the kitchen. It looked like he'd invented some busy work just to keep himself out of the public eye. He wiped his paws on his sauce-splattered apron and shook Doherty's hand.

"I guess I should thank you for what you did for me."

"Yes, you should, especially since I almost got killed by that rat bastard Brian Willis in the process."

"He was one of those guys we rousted down at the VFW, right?"

"Yeah, he was the big guy who sucker punched you."

"Doris killed the prick, huh? From what Friedman told me it was him along with Doris' ex-husband who snatched Adrian and later strangled her."

"That's about the size of it."

"That Doris is some kind of dame. I guess I shouldn't have let her get away."

"You didn't let her *get away*, Richie, you dumped her. If you remember correctly, you betrayed her by banging her best friend. You want to know the truth, I think Doris was in on the planning with Willis and her ex-husband to snatch Adrian so you'd get blamed for her disappearance. She wanted you to go to jail for what you did to her."

"No shit!" Richie said, as if he was proud that he'd hurt a woman so badly she'd want to frame him for kidnapping if not murder.

"By the way, here's your bill," Doherty said handing Grimaldi the item-ized list Agnes had typed up of his expenses.

"What's this for? What about the hundred I gave you that first day?"

"That was my retainer. This is for my expenses. You should've read the fine print on the contract you signed."

Grimaldi gave the list some close scrutiny. "I'll pay this when I get a chance. That Jew Friedman has bled me dry for whatever the hell it was he did for me."

Doherty stepped forward and grabbed Grimaldi by the throat. He pushed him hard up against a wall. He leaned in just a few inches from his client's face and said, "Listen to me you cheap low-rent hustler: I got your ass out of a murder rap and almost got myself killed in the process. Two other people died because you like to go around banging other men's wives. You'll pay me every cent you owe me or I'll smash your teeth in. I'm tired of being jerked around by a piece of shit like you."

Grimaldi was stunned by the ferocity of Doherty's attack. He held up his hands in surrender. "All right, all right. I'll write you a check. You don't have to get all steamed up about things."

"Actually I do. This case has left me feeling so grimy not even your money will help me wash it off. After you write the check, I'll be on my way and out of your life."

Grimaldi slowly walked over to a small office off the kitchen. A bunch of envelopes and invoices with ringed coffee stains and cigarette ash on them littered the desktop. He sat down and pulled a large checkbook out of a drawer. Reluctantly he wrote a check on the restaurant's account for the full amount he owed to Doherty and Associates. Doherty scratched 'paid in full' across the itemized receipt and handed it to Grimaldi.

"One other thing, Richie. In the future if I were you I'd try to keep my pecker in my pants."

"No can do, Mr. PI."

"Suit yourself. But if you ever need an investigator again, don't call me. You can contact your lawyer friend Friedman instead."

On the way out Doherty slapped Tony Fortunato on the back and said, "Be seein' ya, big fella."

"Yeah, you too, Doherty."

He knew if he could help it he'd never grace Fortunato's Italian Cuisine again. And if his luck held, he'd never have to look at Grimaldi's self-satisfied face either.

After leaving the restaurant Doherty headed north up Fruit Hill Avenue to North Providence. He wasn't entirely sure how to get to Doris Donahue's

281

apartment building, but after a few wrong turns he eventually located the place. It was a cold dreary day and there were no TV trucks or other news hounds staking out the building anymore. The scene of Willis' stabbing death was already yesterday's news now that the press and TV had moved onto covering Adrian Colardo's murder in South County.

The front door to the building was unlocked so Doherty mounted the stairs to Doris' third floor apartment. When he got there he was surprised to find her door partially ajar. He stuck his head in and called her name. There was no answer. The police notice that had been posted on her door indicating the apartment was a crime scene had been torn off and lay crumpled on the hallway floor. He slipped inside and called for Doris a second time. There was still no answer.

All of the furniture was in place including pieces from the shattered lamp, which lay on the living room rug. The only reminder of that night was a now fading chalk circle drawn by the police where Willis' body had been. Inside the circle were some brown stains from the blood that had seeped out of his chest.

Most of the kitchen utensils were where they'd been except for the large carving knife Doris had imbedded in Brian Willis' body. Doherty checked the bedroom. The covers were pulled off the bed and its sheets were gone. He slid open the drawers to Doris' dresser. They were empty except for some dust balls caught in the corner crevices. Save for the few empty hangers that clung to its crossbar, her closet was likewise barren of clothes. Although most of the furniture was still in the apartment there were no visible signs that Doris Donahue, or her ex-husband Eddie, had ever lived here. There were no notes pinned to the refrigerator and no female odors to indicate a woman had recently applied some perfume or other ointment to herself in this space.

He gave the apartment a second going over, even opening the doors below the vanity in her bathroom to see if Doris had left any old cosmetics or other containers behind. Nothing. There were no traces that this apartment had ever been rented by a woman who had wantonly stabbed to death her lover and conspirator in a kidnapping here.

He left the apartment door partially opened as he'd found it and descended to the landing. There was a small sign that said 'Superintendent' in a jagged hand-written script by the bank of mailboxes in foyer. It pointed down a flight of stairs in the rear of the entryway. Doherty walked down a set of creaky steps to a darkened basement. He could hear an old furnace rattling away somewhere nearby. The smell of its fumes hit him even before he reached the bottom. A low wattage naked light bulb illuminated a more official looking "Superintendent' sign mounted above a plain wooden door. He knocked and waited patiently. Finally it opened a crack and a grizzly face featuring a serious five o'clock shadow answered it. A wary expression passed across the man's mug.

"Yeah," he said in a voice filtered through a few thousand cigarettes.

"Are you the super here?"

The man, who had a black moustache that was only slightly longer than the rest of the hair sprouting on his unshaven face answered, "That's what it says on the sign, don't it? You lookin' for an apartment?"

"No, I came to see the woman from 3B; her name is Donahue."

"Are you from the papers or the TV?"

"No. I'm a friend of Mrs. Donahue," Doherty said almost as an apology.

"She don't live here no more. Moved out the beginnin' of the week."

Doherty looked over the man's shoulder and saw a small TV with big rabbit ears sitting on a box facing a beat up old chair. The super's apartment smelled of cigar smoke, which probably helped him cover the unpleasant odor coming off the nearby furnace.

"Do you know where she went? Did she leave a forwarding address?"

The super looked Doherty up and down for the first time. "Said she was goin' to live with a relative in Ohio. That's all I know. If you want the address you'll have to contact the company that owns the buildin'. I only take care of the maintenance."

"How come she left all her furniture behind?"

The super shook his head. "They weren't hers. The apartment comes furnished. You sure you're not lookin' for a place?"

"No, only the woman who lived in 3B. If she comes back or gets in touch, could you call me or at least give her one of my cards." Doherty handed the super two of his business cards.

The man read one of the cards, his lips moving slowly as he did. "Private Investigations? What does that mean?"

"I'm a private detective. The woman upstairs was one of my clients," he lied.

"A private eye, huh? Like on TV?"

"Yeah, exactly like the guys on the TV shows," he said before leaving.

He thought about checking with the real estate agency that handled the building. Their sign was plastered on the outside wall beside the front door with its name below the advertisement for 'Luxury Apartments'. As he drove back to West Warwick he wondered if they'd have a hard time renting an apartment where someone had been stabbed to death. On second thought, in Rhode Island that might make apartment 3B all the more attractive.

Chapter Thirty-Three

E ddie Donahue's funeral was held on a cold overcast day. Doherty had seen the obituary in the *Providence Journal* a couple of days before and decided to pay his last respects to the fellow vet. The deceased had been waked at a funeral home in Cumberland, but the burial was being held at the Swan Point Cemetery on the East Side of Providence. Doherty was surprised since he knew Swan Point was where some of Rhode Island's more famous politicians and other luminaries were interred. Further on in the obituary it mentioned that Ed Donahue Jr. was the son of one of Providence's most prominent tax attorneys, the late Edward Donahue Sr. Given Eddie's propensity for running up large gambling debts, it was evident that the father's skills in handling money hadn't rubbed off on his son.

Most of the obituary focused on Eddie's meritorious service in the army during World War Two. It also listed him as a former employee of Brown and Sharpe and American Screw. As far as Doherty could tell, both of those were pipe dreams, no doubt drummed up by his sister, Meg Garrett, to make it sound like her brother was a solid citizen rather than the sad sack loser he was. There was no mention in the article of Eddie's ex-wife, his membership at the Kevin O'Donnell VFW Post #365 or his being the victim of a murder. Once again, those omissions were probably the work of his overprotective sister.

Doherty arrived at the gravesite just as the casket was being unloaded from the funeral home's hearse. There were only a few mourners by the grave. He recognized a couple of guys he'd seen during his two trips to the VFW post; there was no sign of Fats Finnegan. Standing in front of the small group were Meg Garrett, her husband Neil, and an elderly woman holding Meg's hand that he assumed was Eddie's mother. A mid-sized backhoe rested not far from the gravesite. Apparently the ground was frozen so solid that heavy machinery was required to dig the six-foot hole.

As Doherty edged closer to the site he noticed that an accompanying plot held the grave of Edward Donahue Sr., deceased in June of 1948. Ample space was set aside beside the dead father for his wife when her time came. Nearby were gravestones for other Donahue ancestors from previous generations.

Eddie's casket, draped with an American flag, was carried to the gravesite by a military honor guard. Three other soldiers stood by with rifles poised to give him a three-shot salute. Another stood at attention holding a bugle to his chest. Doherty'd been to enough funerals of fellow soldiers and vets to know the protocol for such burials. Before the casket was lowered into the ground a priest in full regalia gave a benediction and sprinkled some holy water on Eddie's coffin. If his death had been ruled a suicide rather than murder, the church would not have allowed such a ritual to be performed.

The flag was removed from the wooden coffin and folded into triangular segments, as was the custom for handling one. The folded flag was then presented to Meg Garrett on the mistaken belief that she was the dead man's wife not his sister. The soldier accompanied this presentation with a snappy salute. Meg seemed a little flustered and quickly handed the flag to Eddie's mother. The older woman took the folded cloth and held it awkwardly against her chest.

Before the casket was lowered into the ground the three-shot salute was fired. In the dead winter air the sound of gunfire felt unusually loud. Then the soldier with the bugle played Taps as Eddie Donahue was lowered to his final resting place. Soon the few of Eddie's pals who'd come began to move away from the gravesite. No doubt they were on their way back to the O'Donnell to drink toasts to Eddie's swift ascension to heaven, or wherever the poor bastard was headed.

Meg and Eddie's mother each tossed some dirt onto the coffin. Meg's husband Neil elected not to join them. At this point Doherty stepped forward and tossed a handful of dirt into the hole as well. It was the least he could do for a fellow vet. After all, he was a missing man Doherty failed to locate before he was killed. He turned and walked slowly in the direction of his car. Before he could exit the cemetery he was caught up by Eddie's sister.

"Mr. Doherty. I want to thank you so much for coming to my brother's funeral. I'm disappointed more of his friends didn't show up to see him off."

Doherty wondered if Eddie Donahue had any real friends besides the two guys from the post that came. And they were probably nothing more than drinking buddies at the O'Donnell. For his part Fats Finnegan was conspicuous by his absence.

"It's kind of a cold day. Perhaps some more of his pals will toast him later at the O'Donnell post," Doherty said in a weak attempt to cheer up Mrs. Garrett about the poor attendance at her brother's funeral.

"That place was the undoing of my Eddie," she spit out.

"Yeah, well," was all Doherty could think to say.

"I noticed that *she* couldn't find it in her heart to make it to her husband's funeral."

He didn't have to ask whom Meg was referring to. "I went by the apartment a few days ago and was told Doris was already gone. The super said she moved to Ohio to stay with relatives."

"Eddie's life was never the same after he hooked up with that woman. If I'd had my way…" Meg Garrett didn't finish saying what she would've done with her way.

"I'm going to take off now. I'm sorry about your brother. From his obit it sounded like he was a good soldier. I'm glad the honor guard came to send him off in military fashion."

Meg began to weep. Doherty knew he should have hugged her or offered some other form of comfort for her grief. He just didn't have any comforting left in him. He would leave that to her husband Neil, the bowling champ.

Acknowledgements

First and foremost I would like to thank my wife and best friend Jeanne Berkman for doing yeoman (woman) service reading and editing this book. Her suggestions at times were invaluable. I would also like to recognize our good friend Tempe Goodhue who lent some editing help early on in the writing process. I thank Donna Rodgers for giving me important information about the Greene Inn and for setting me straight that no matter what others may say, it was always spelled Greene ending with an *e*. In addition the Narragansett Historical Society was instrumental in giving me information as to what the layout of the beach town of Narragansett was like in the early 1960s. Paula Rabbitt, of the Hilton Hotel in Providence, sent me several drawings and photographs of what the Sheraton Hilton, as it was so named at the time the book is set, looked like in the 1950s and 60s. Especially useful were photos of the Falstaff Room, where I set a number of meetings between characters in the book. She was not sure if the Falstaff was a tavern room, but I made it one for purposes of the narrative. My brother Don Kafrissen set me straight on which Pontiacs were common in 1958 and what they looked like. He is always my go-to guy whenever I need advice on old cars and memories of Rhode Island back in the day. I would also like to recognize my old, long-lost childhood friend from West Warwick days, John Barba, who helped me recall what the old town was like back when we were kids. It is through the Doherty books and his friend Paul Kenyon that John and I recently became reacquainted after so many lost years. He likewise expressed his undying appreciation for the tidbits I remember from our time as youngsters growing up in West Warwick in the 1950s. Our discussions brought back many fond memories for both of us.

www.ingramcontent.com/pod-product-compliance
Lightning Source LLC
Chambersburg PA
CBHW071449170626
46811CB00007B/2515